# IN THE SHADOW OF THE THRONE

WORDS BY: **KATE SHERIDAN**

ART BY: **GAIA CARDINALI**

LETTERS BY: **MICAH MYERS**

EDITS BY: **MICHAEL MOCCIO**

AUTHENTICITY READER: **CATHERINE SOLAS GRAY**

LOGO DESIGN: **DIANA BERMÚDEZ**

BOOK DESIGN: **MIGUEL A. ZAPATA**

MAVERICK

**Laura Chacón**
Founder

**Mark London**
CEO and Chief
Creative Officer

**Mark Irwin**
VP of Business
Development

**Chris Fernandez**
Publisher

**Cecilia Medina**
Chief Financial
Officer

**Allison Pond**
Marketing Director

**Giovanna T. Orozco**
Production Manager

**Miguel A. Zapata**
Design Director

**Lauren Hitzhusen**
Senior Editor

**Chas! Pangburn**
Senior Editor

**Maya Lopez**
Marketing Manager

**Brian Hawkins**
Editor

**Diana Bermúdez**
Graphic Designer

**David Reyes**
Graphic Designer

**Adriana T. Orozco**
Interactive Media
Designer

**Nicolás Zea Arias**
Audiovisual Production

**Frank Silva**
Executive Assistant

**Pedro Herrera**
Retail Associate

**Stephanie Hidalgo**
Office Manager

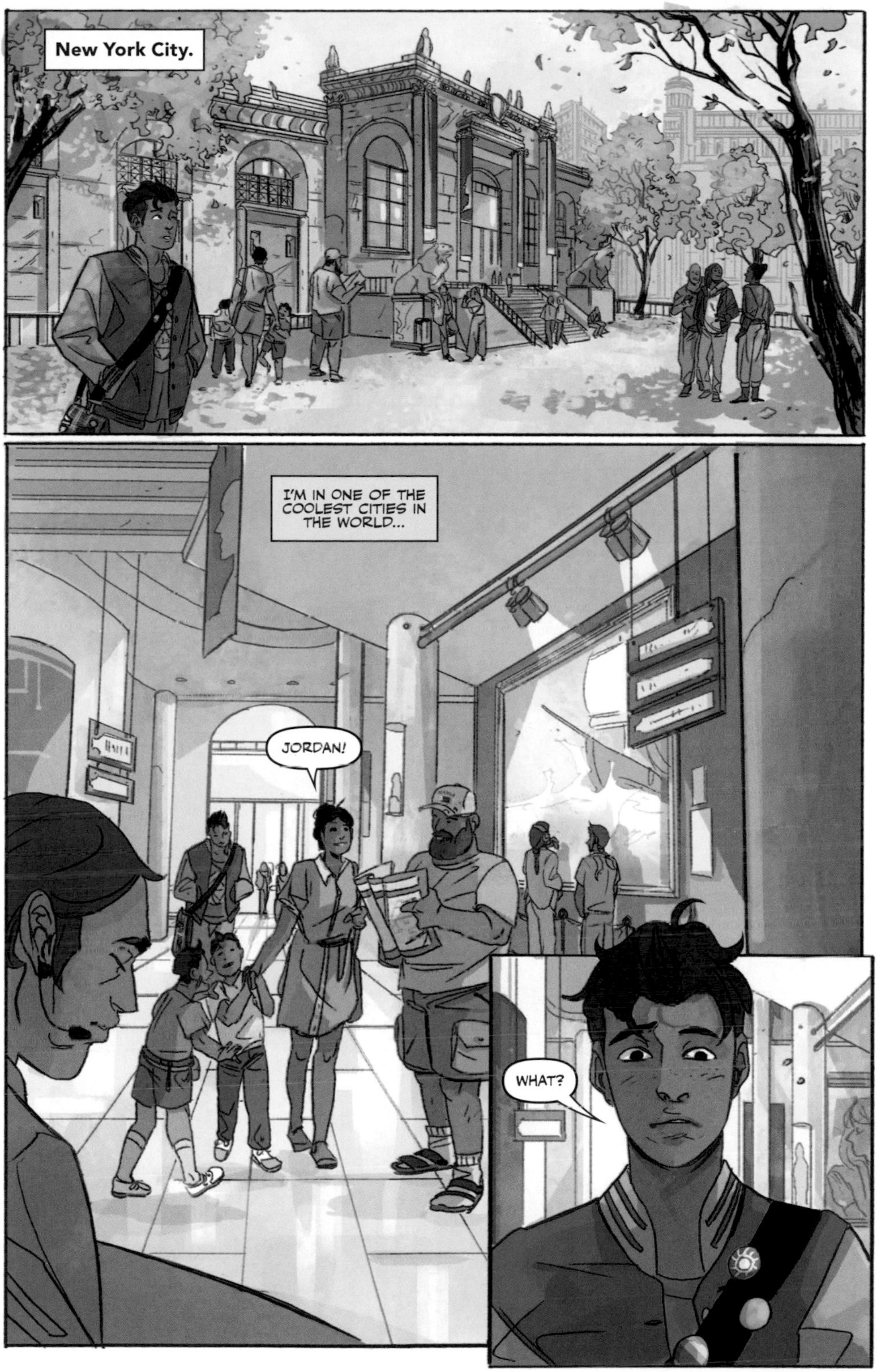
New York City.
I'M IN ONE OF THE COOLEST CITIES IN THE WORLD...
JORDAN!
WHAT?

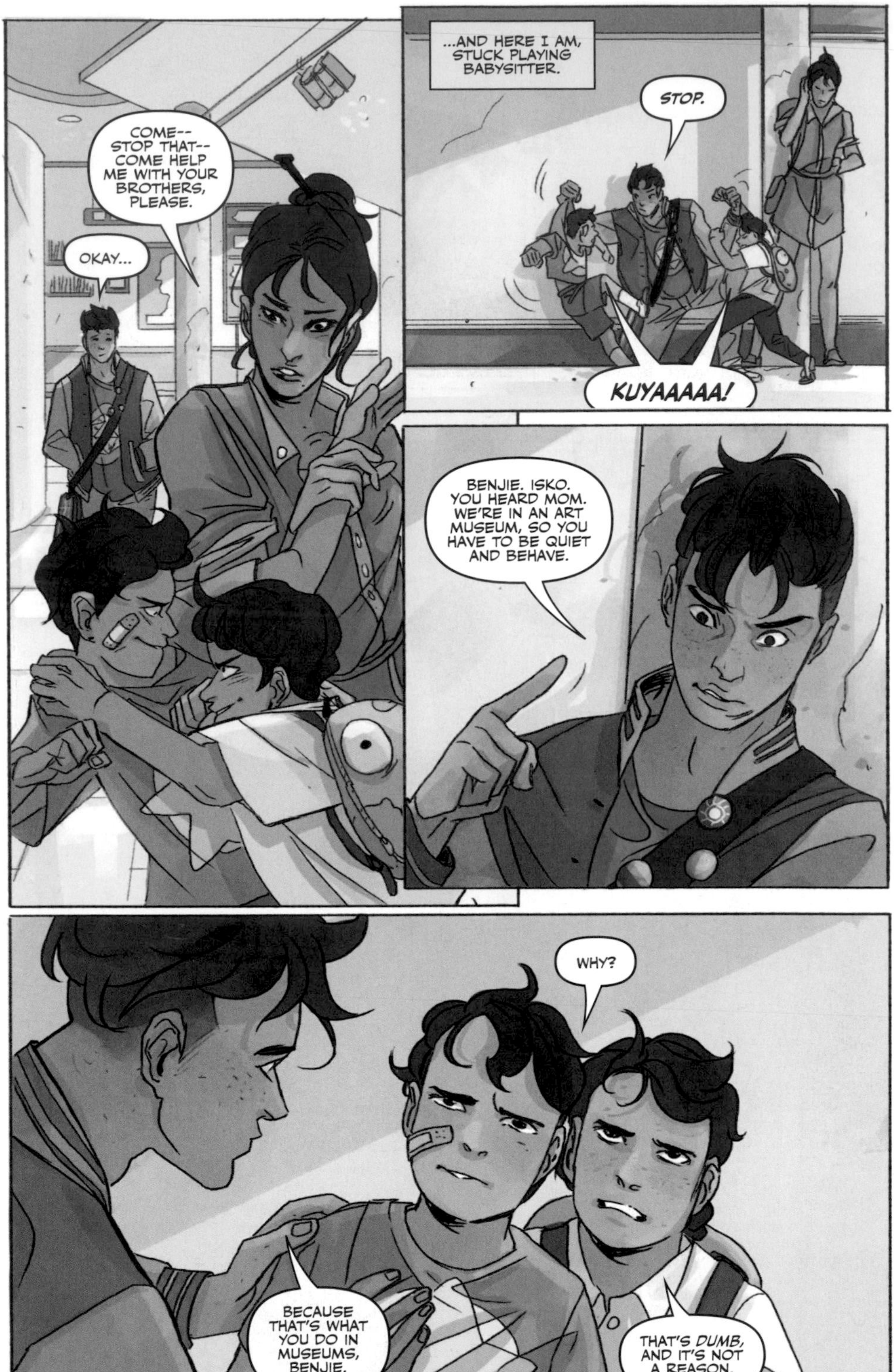

COME-- STOP THAT-- COME HELP ME WITH YOUR BROTHERS, PLEASE.
OKAY...
...AND HERE I AM, STUCK PLAYING BABYSITTER.
STOP.
KUYAAAAA!
BENJIE. ISKO. YOU HEARD MOM. WE'RE IN AN ART MUSEUM, SO YOU HAVE TO BE QUIET AND BEHAVE.
WHY?
BECAUSE THAT'S WHAT YOU DO IN MUSEUMS, BENJIE.
THAT'S *DUMB*, AND IT'S NOT A REASON.

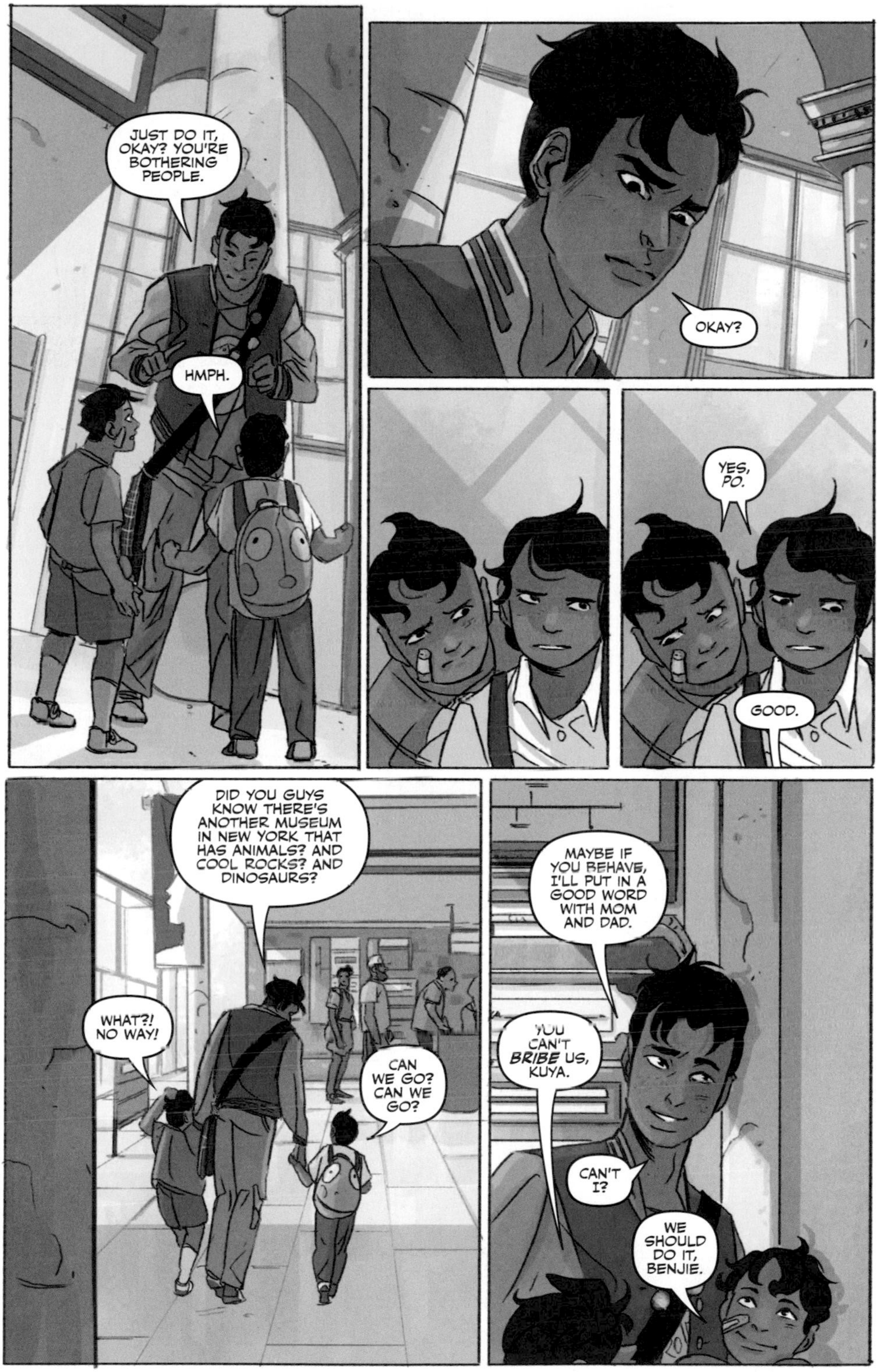
JUST DO IT, OKAY? YOU'RE BOTHERING PEOPLE.
HMPH.
OKAY?
YES, PO.
GOOD.
DID YOU GUYS KNOW THERE'S ANOTHER MUSEUM IN NEW YORK THAT HAS ANIMALS? AND COOL ROCKS? AND DINOSAURS?
WHAT?! NO WAY!
CAN WE GO? CAN WE GO?
MAYBE IF YOU BEHAVE, I'LL PUT IN A GOOD WORD WITH MOM AND DAD.
YOU CAN'T *BRIBE* US, KUYA.
CAN'T I?
WE SHOULD DO IT, BENJIE.

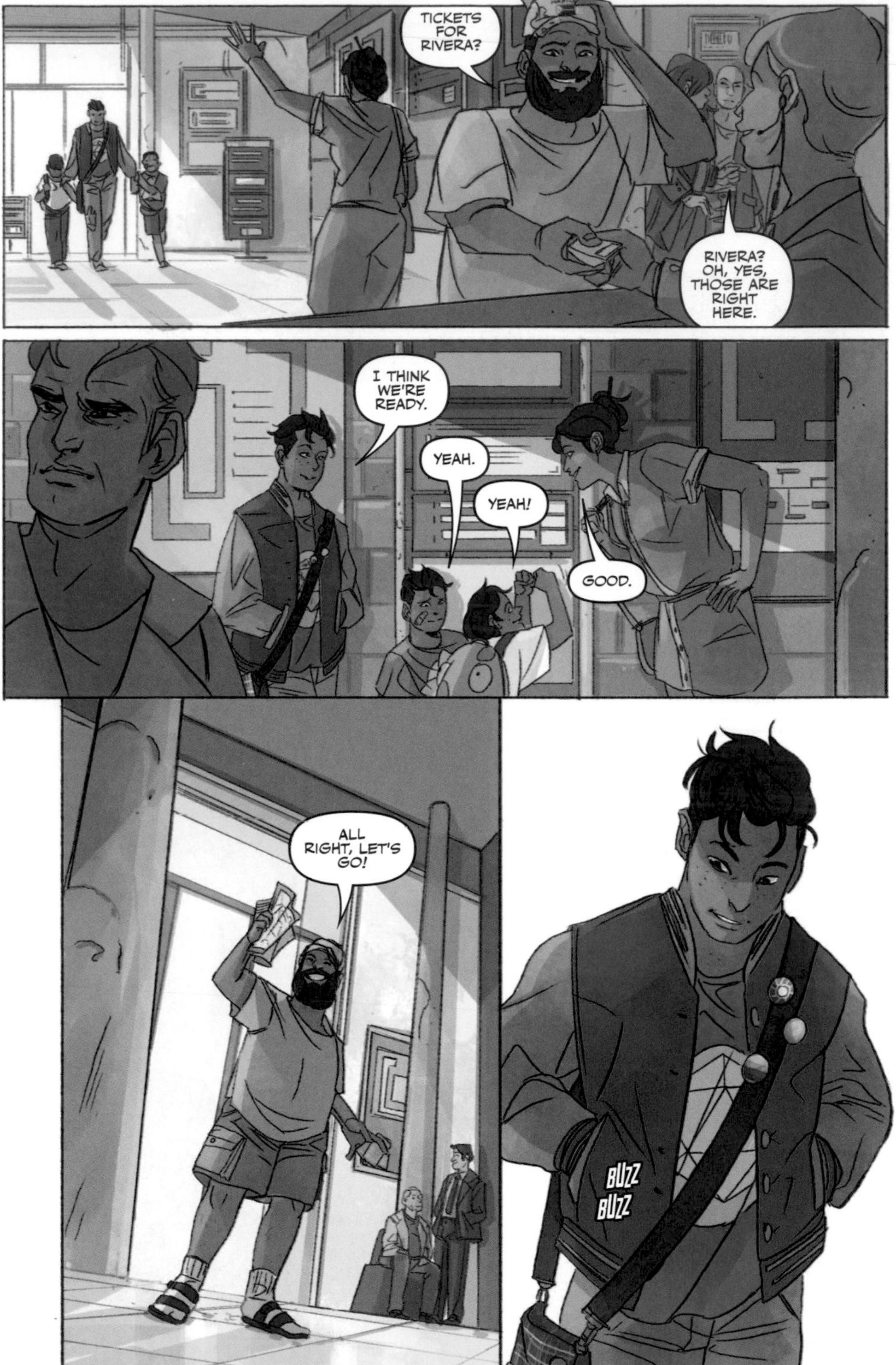
TICKETS FOR RIVERA?
RIVERA? OH, YES, THOSE ARE RIGHT HERE.
I THINK WE'RE READY.
YEAH.
YEAH!
GOOD.
ALL RIGHT, LET'S GO!
BUZZ
BUZZ

soooo hows nyc?? 👀

don't ask lol

that bad huh?

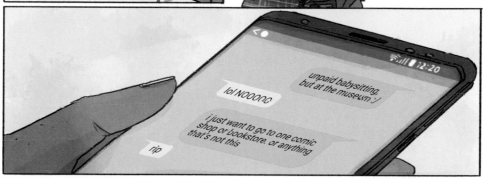

unpaid babysitting, but at the museum :/

lol NOOOOG

I just want to go to one comic shop or bookstore, or anything that's not this

rip

PHONE AWAY.

DAD!

YOU KNOW THE VACATION RULES. NO PHONE--

NO PHONE UNTIL WE'RE BACK AT THE HOTEL. *I KNOW.* I'M JUST CHECKING IN WITH MY FRIENDS.

CHECK IN WHEN WE GET BACK. IT'S FAMILY TIME. WE REALLY APPRECIATE YOU KEEPING AN EYE ON THE BOYS FOR A BIT.

...YES, PO.

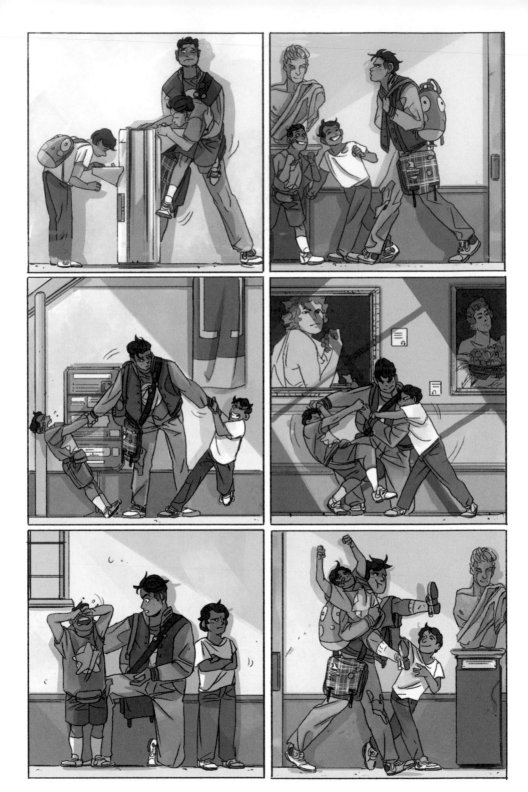

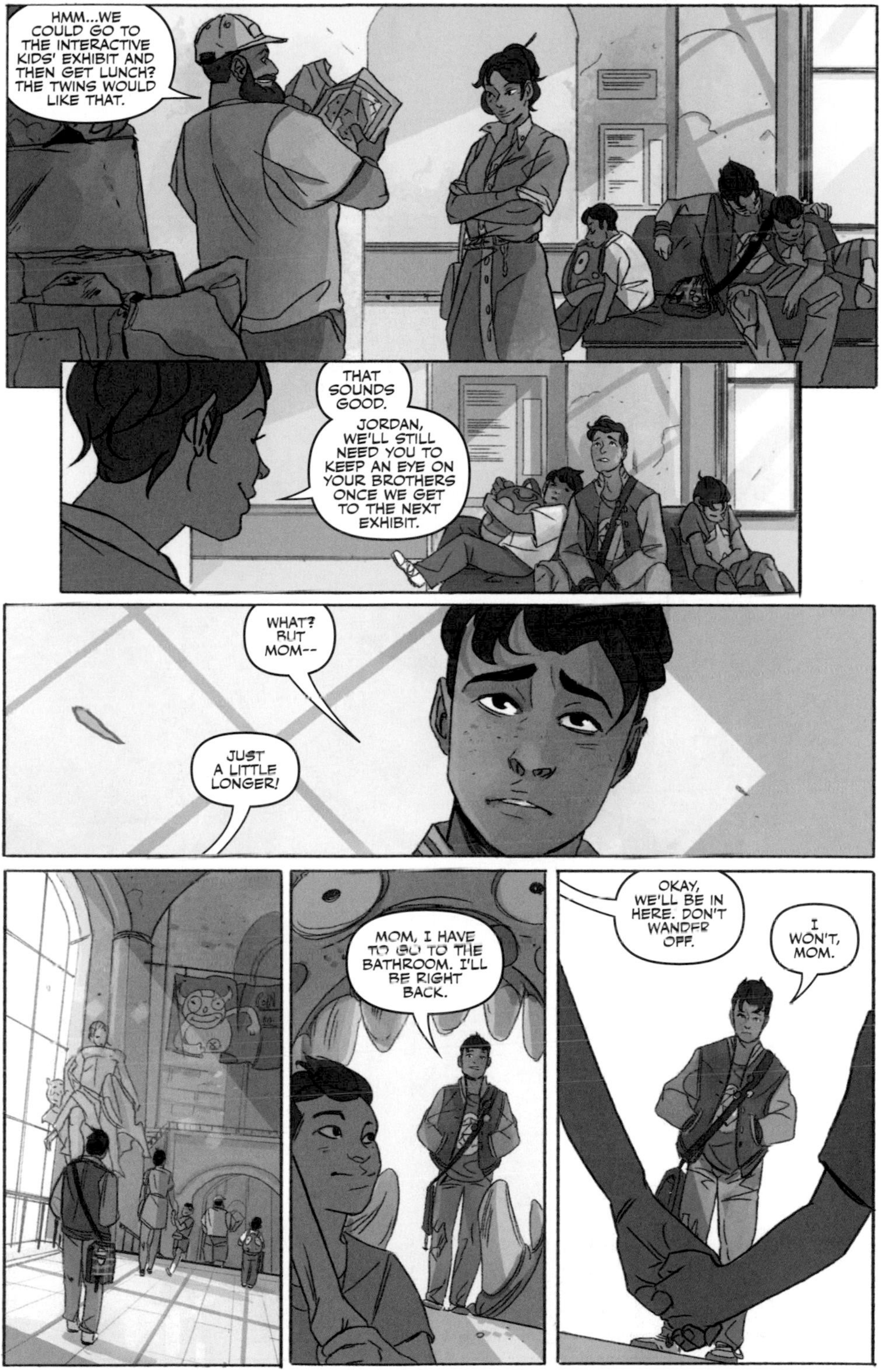
HMM...WE COULD GO TO THE INTERACTIVE KIDS' EXHIBIT AND THEN GET LUNCH? THE TWINS WOULD LIKE THAT.
THAT SOUNDS GOOD.
JORDAN, WE'LL STILL NEED YOU TO KEEP AN EYE ON YOUR BROTHERS ONCE WE GET TO THE NEXT EXHIBIT.
WHAT? BUT MOM--
JUST A LITTLE LONGER!
MOM, I HAVE TO GO TO THE BATHROOM. I'LL BE RIGHT BACK.
OKAY, WE'LL BE IN HERE. DON'T WANDER OFF.
I WON'T, MOM.

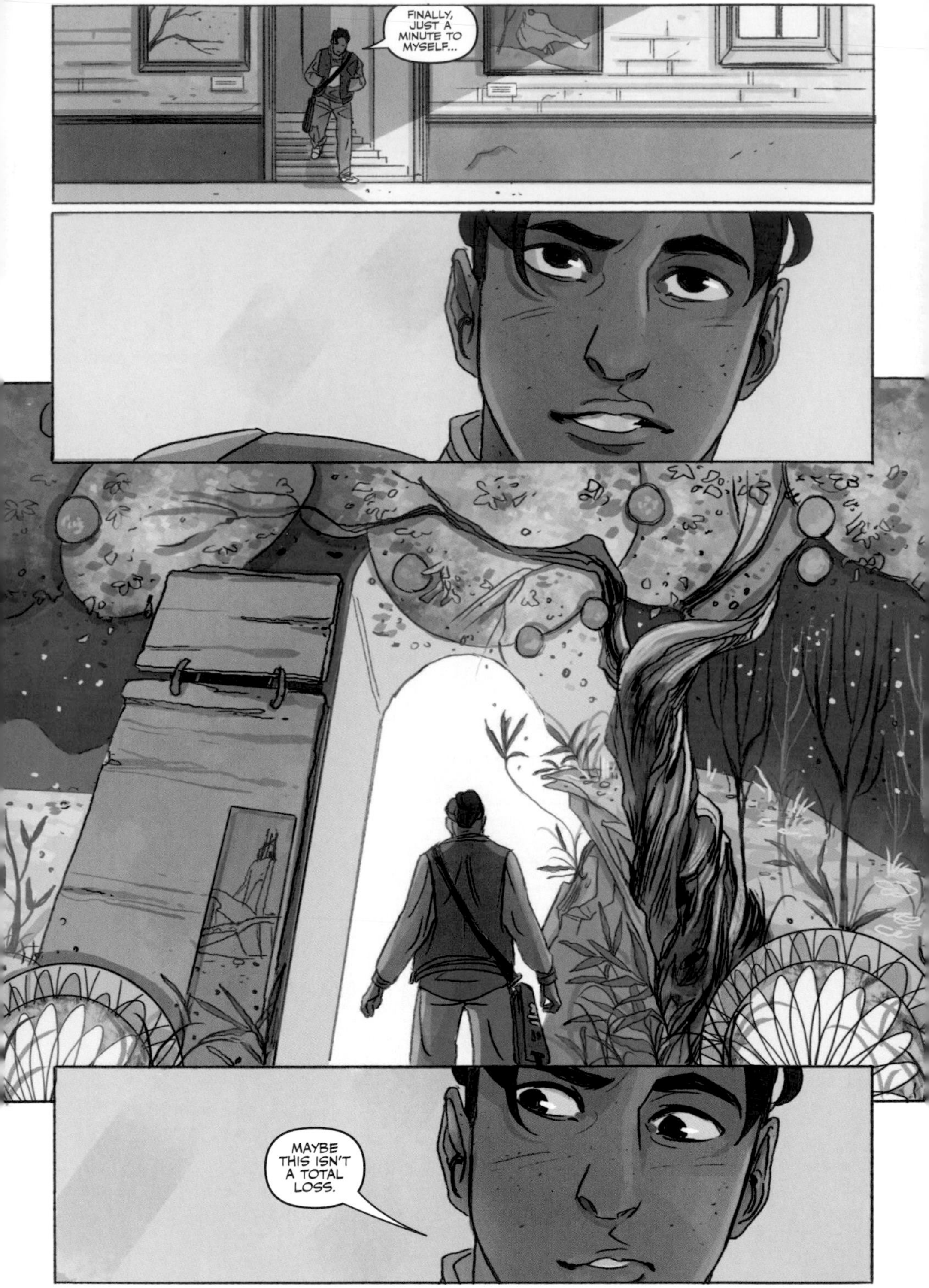
FINALLY, JUST A MINUTE TO MYSELF...
MAYBE THIS ISN'T A TOTAL LOSS.

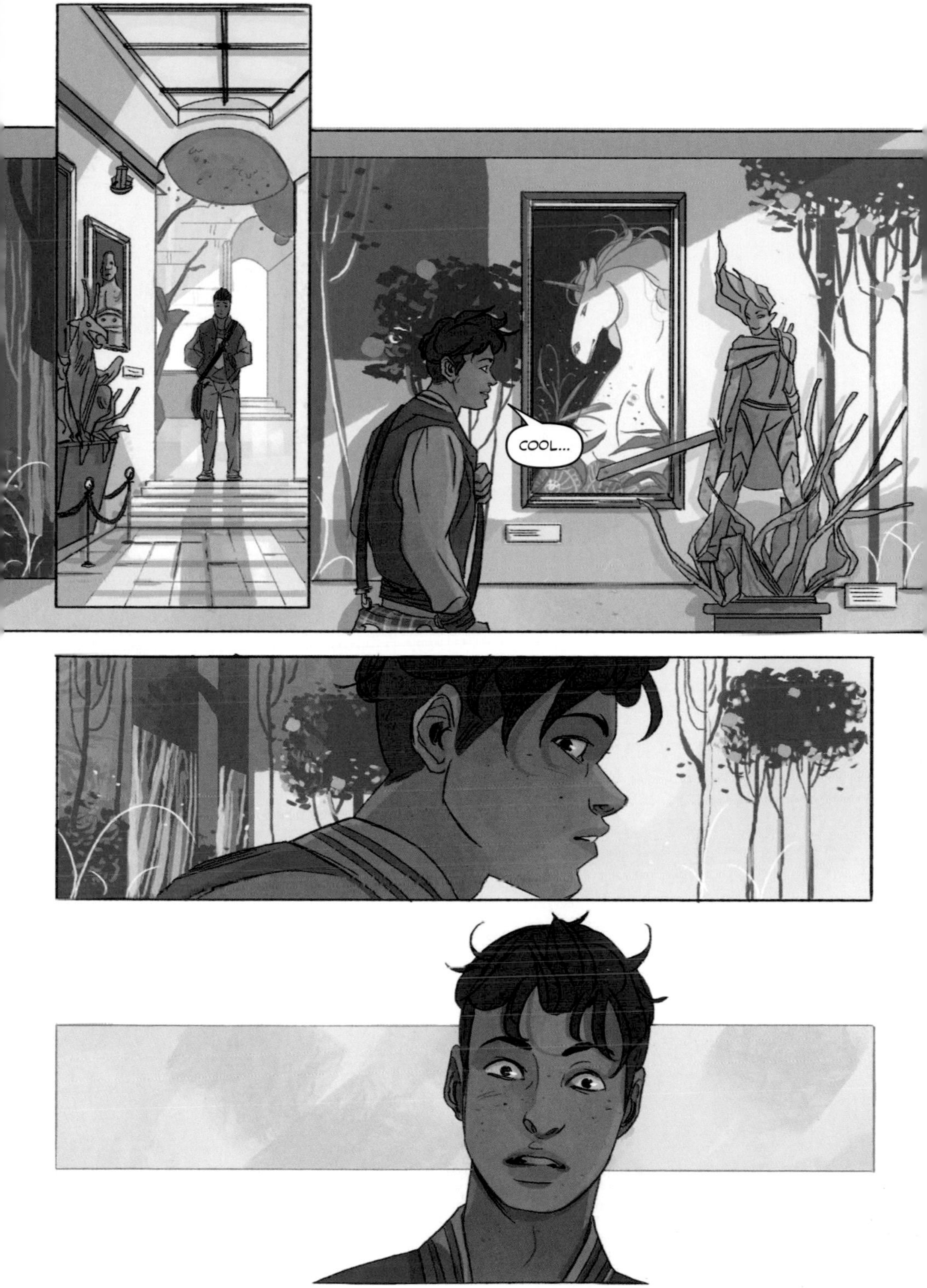
COOL...

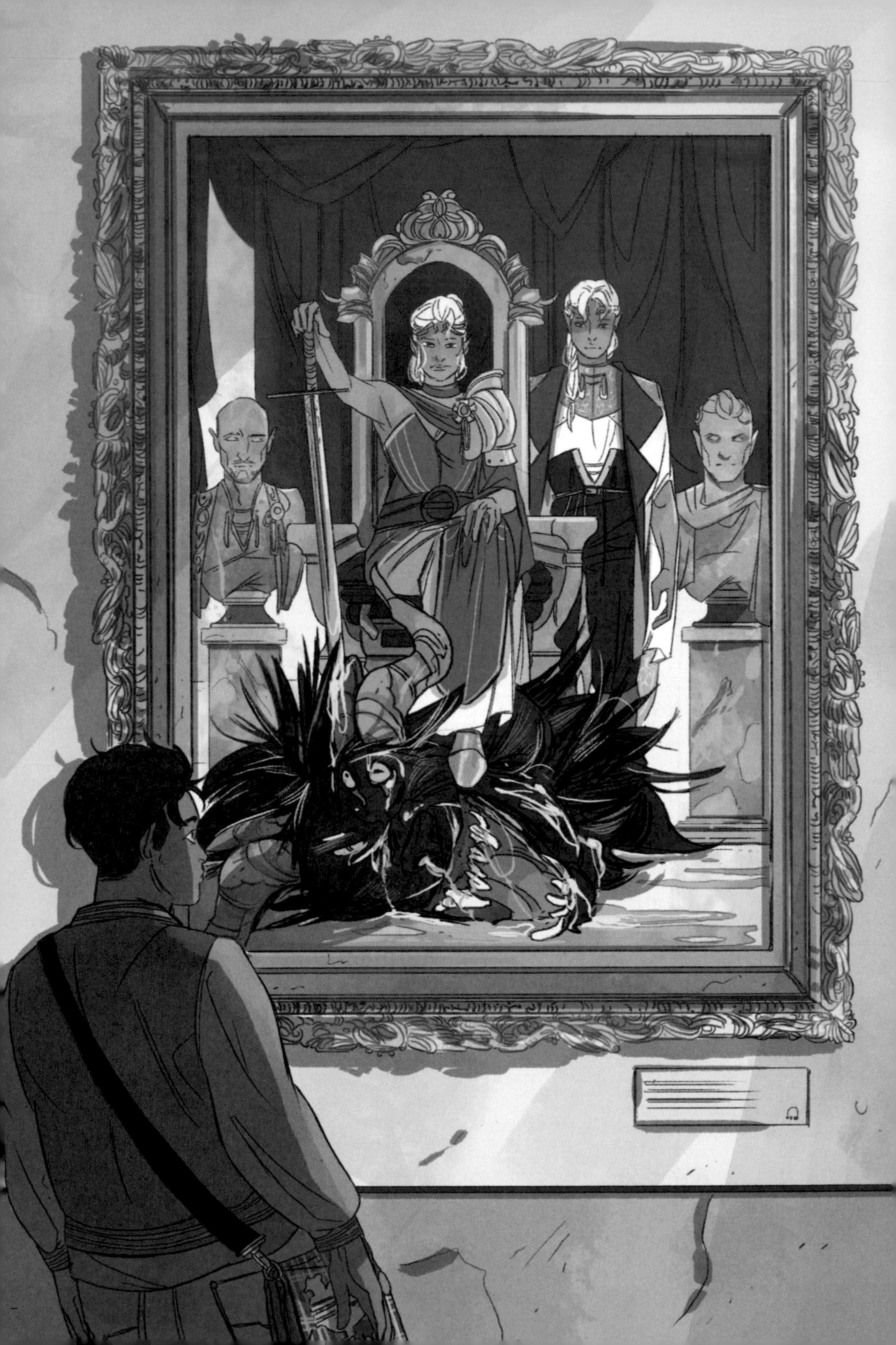

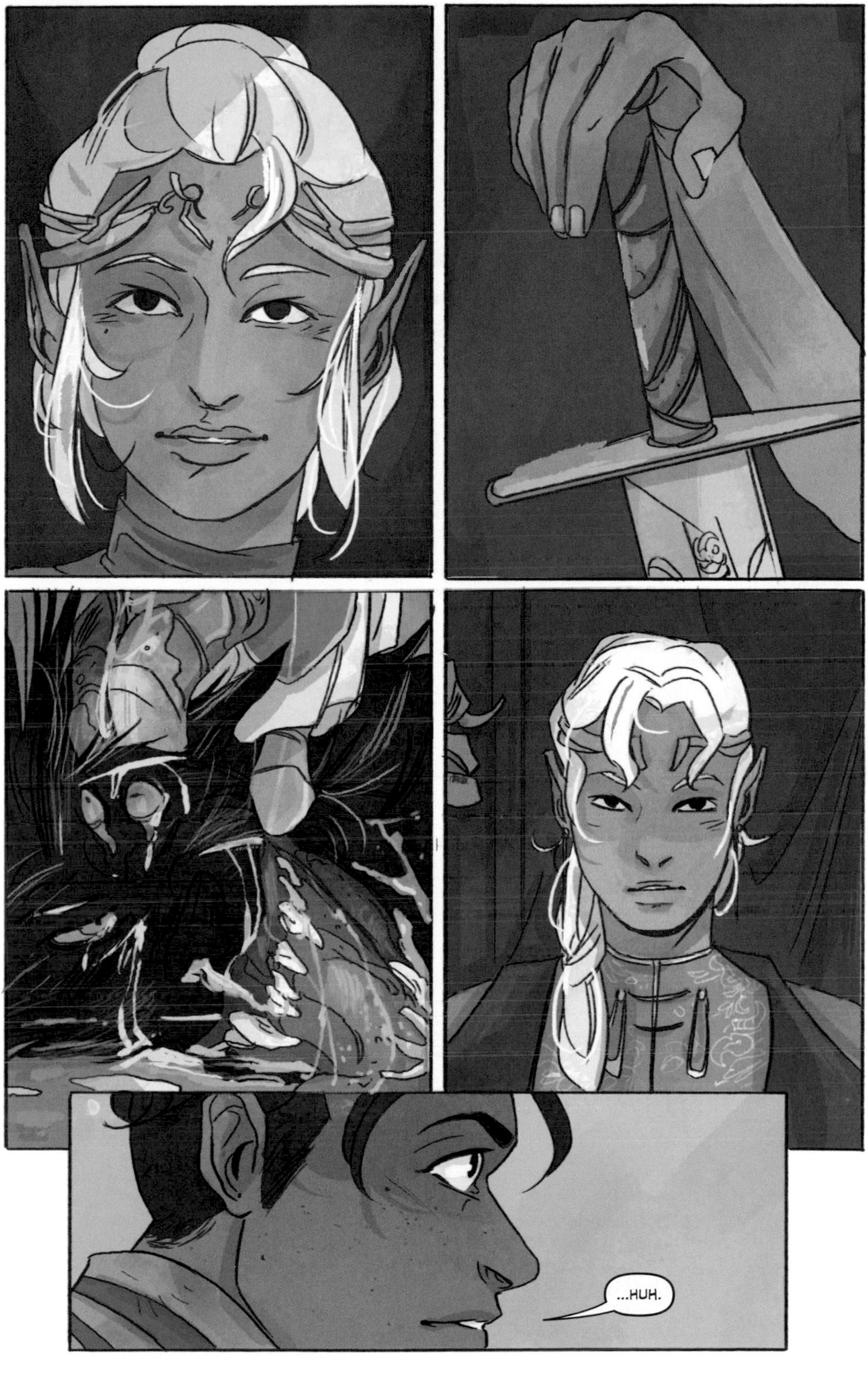
...HUH.

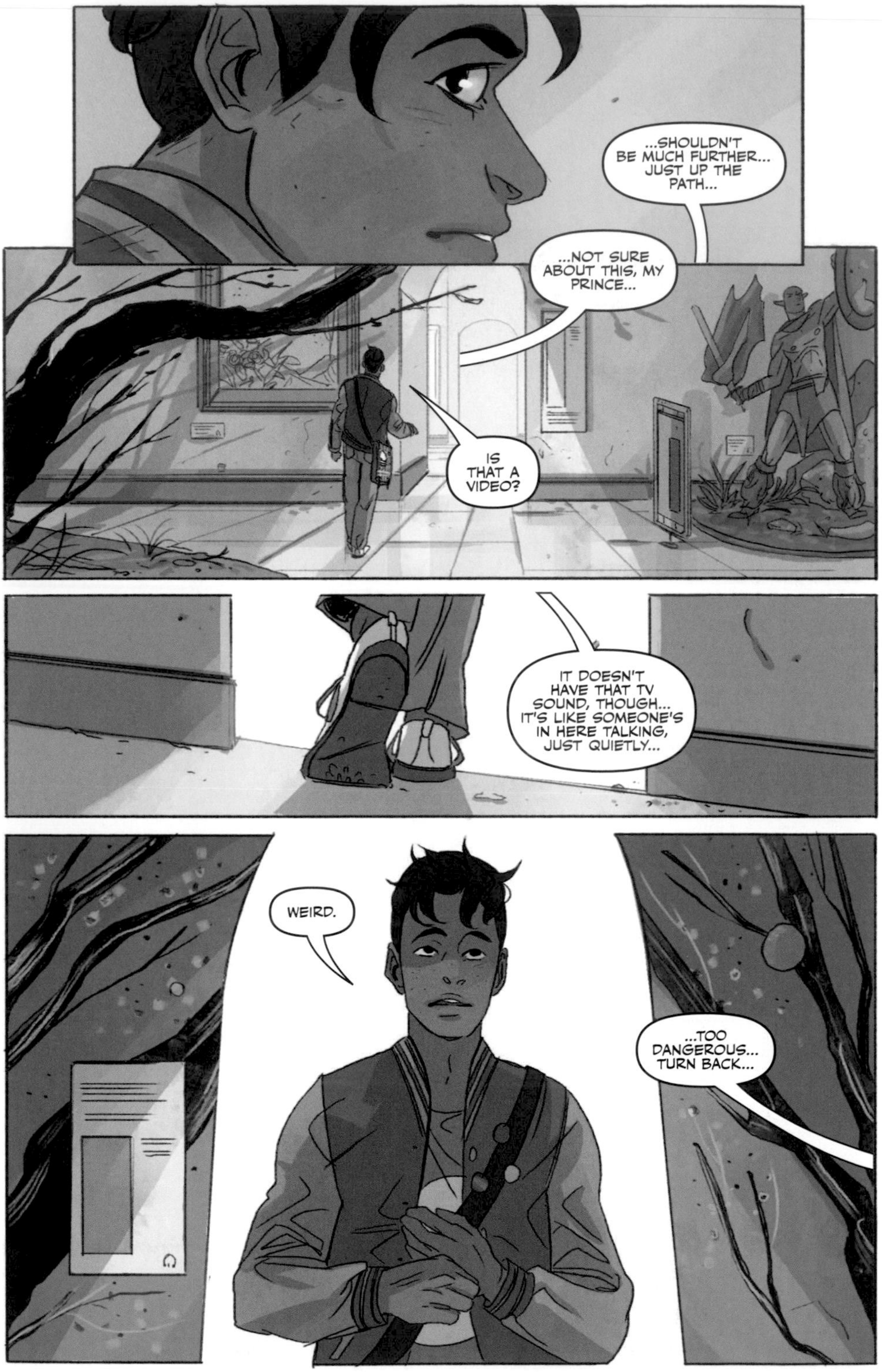
...SHOULDN'T BE MUCH FURTHER... JUST UP THE PATH...
...NOT SURE ABOUT THIS, MY PRINCE...
IS THAT A VIDEO?
IT DOESN'T HAVE THAT TV SOUND, THOUGH... IT'S LIKE SOMEONE'S IN HERE TALKING, JUST QUIETLY...
WEIRD.
...TOO DANGEROUS... TURN BACK...

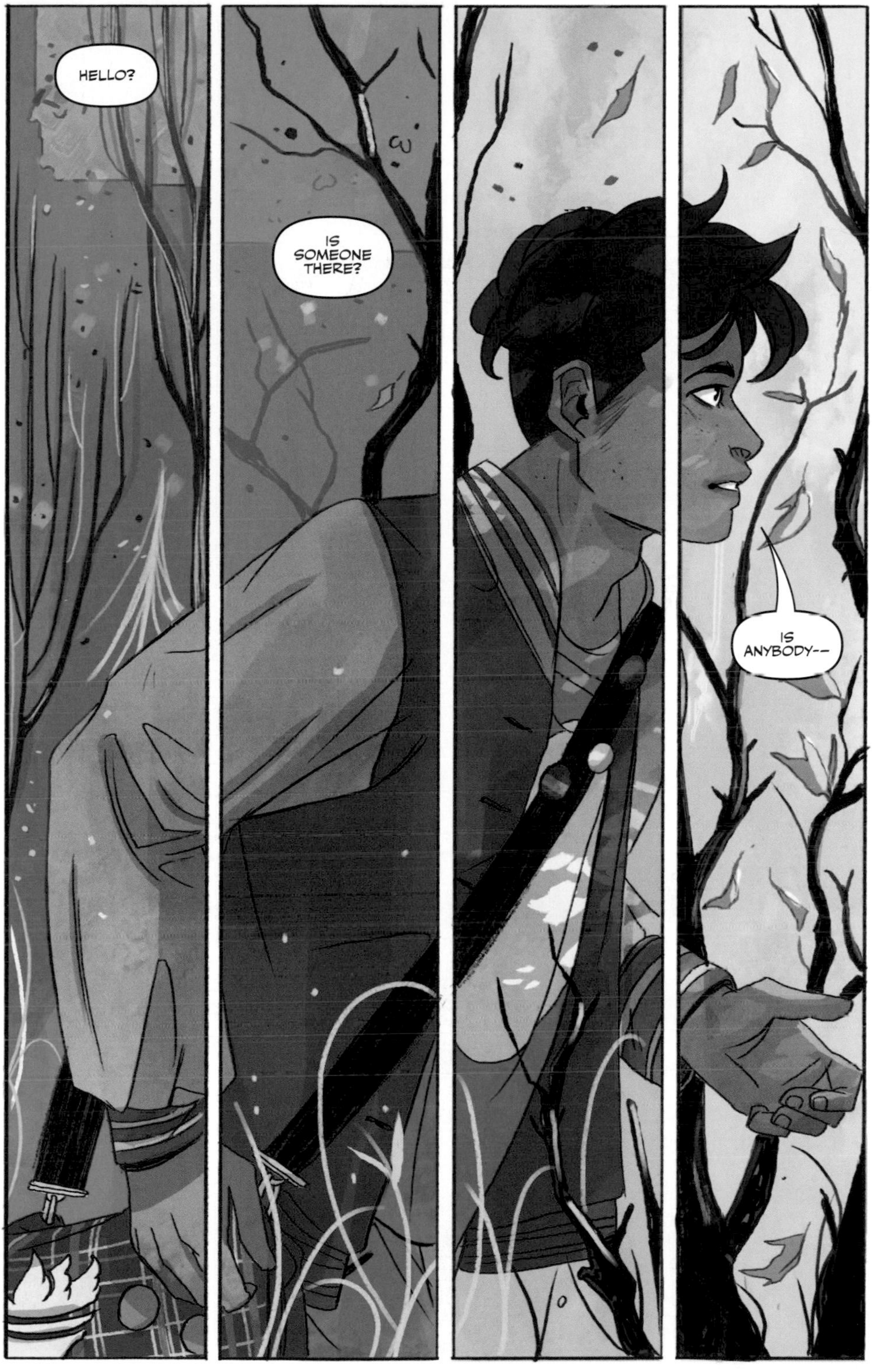
HELLO?
IS SOMEONE THERE?
IS ANYBODY--

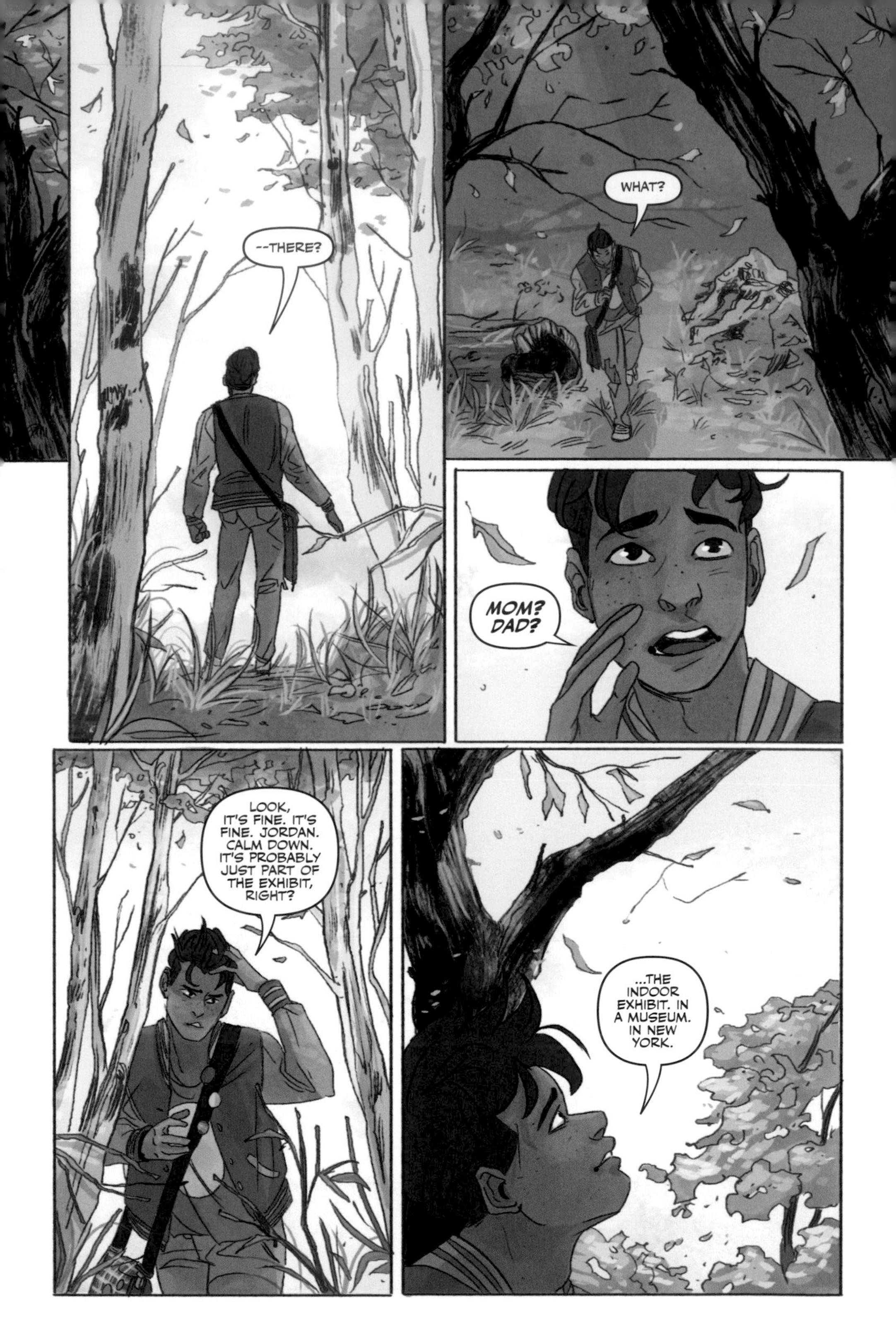
--THERE?
WHAT?
MOM? DAD?
LOOK, IT'S FINE. IT'S FINE. JORDAN. CALM DOWN. IT'S PROBABLY JUST PART OF THE EXHIBIT, RIGHT?
...THE INDOOR EXHIBIT. IN A MUSEUM. IN NEW YORK.

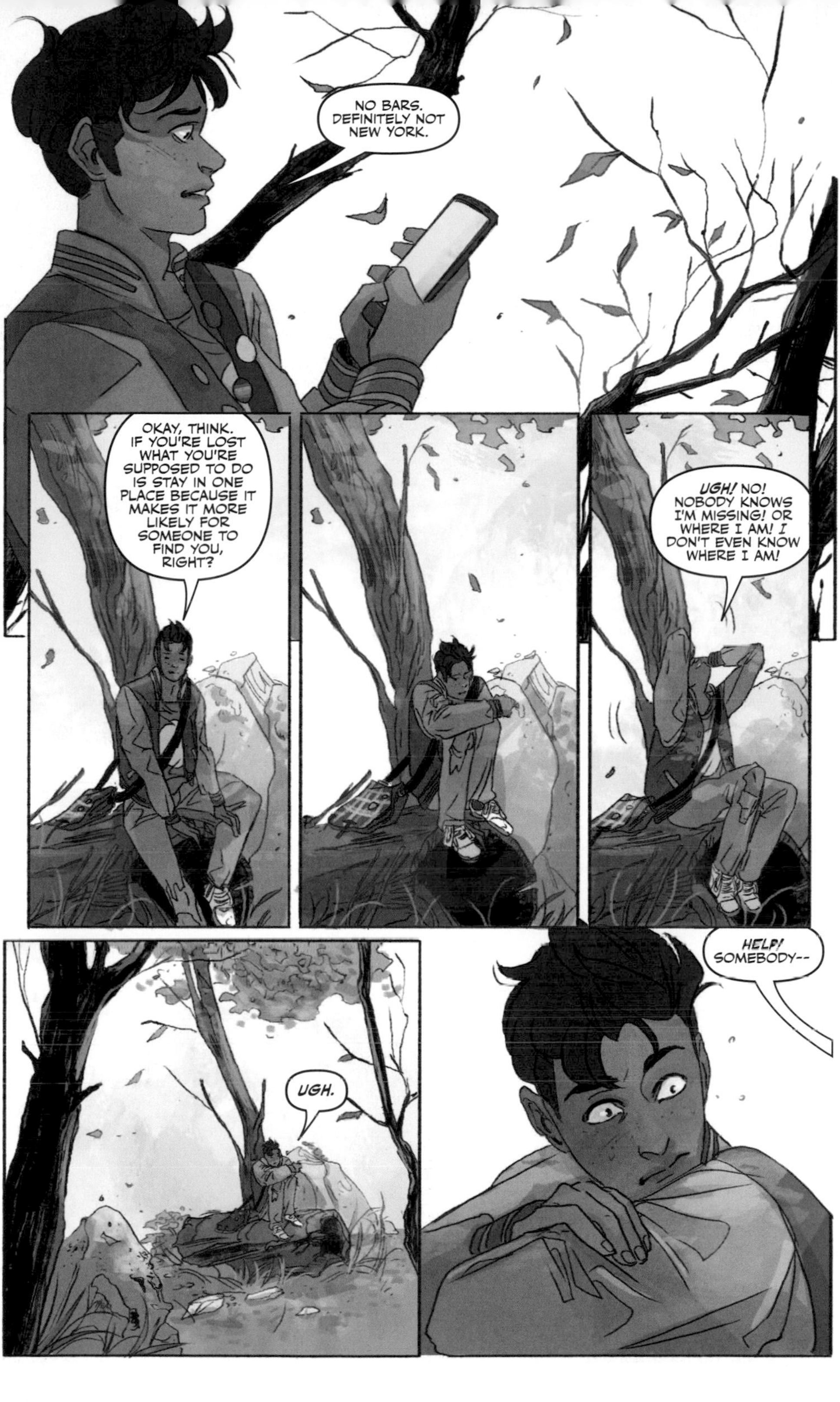
NO BARS. DEFINITELY NOT NEW YORK.
OKAY, THINK. IF YOU'RE LOST WHAT YOU'RE SUPPOSED TO DO IS STAY IN ONE PLACE BECAUSE IT MAKES IT MORE LIKELY FOR SOMEONE TO FIND YOU, RIGHT?
UGH! NO! NOBODY KNOWS I'M MISSING! OR WHERE I AM! I DON'T EVEN KNOW WHERE I AM!
UGH.
HELP! SOMEBODY--

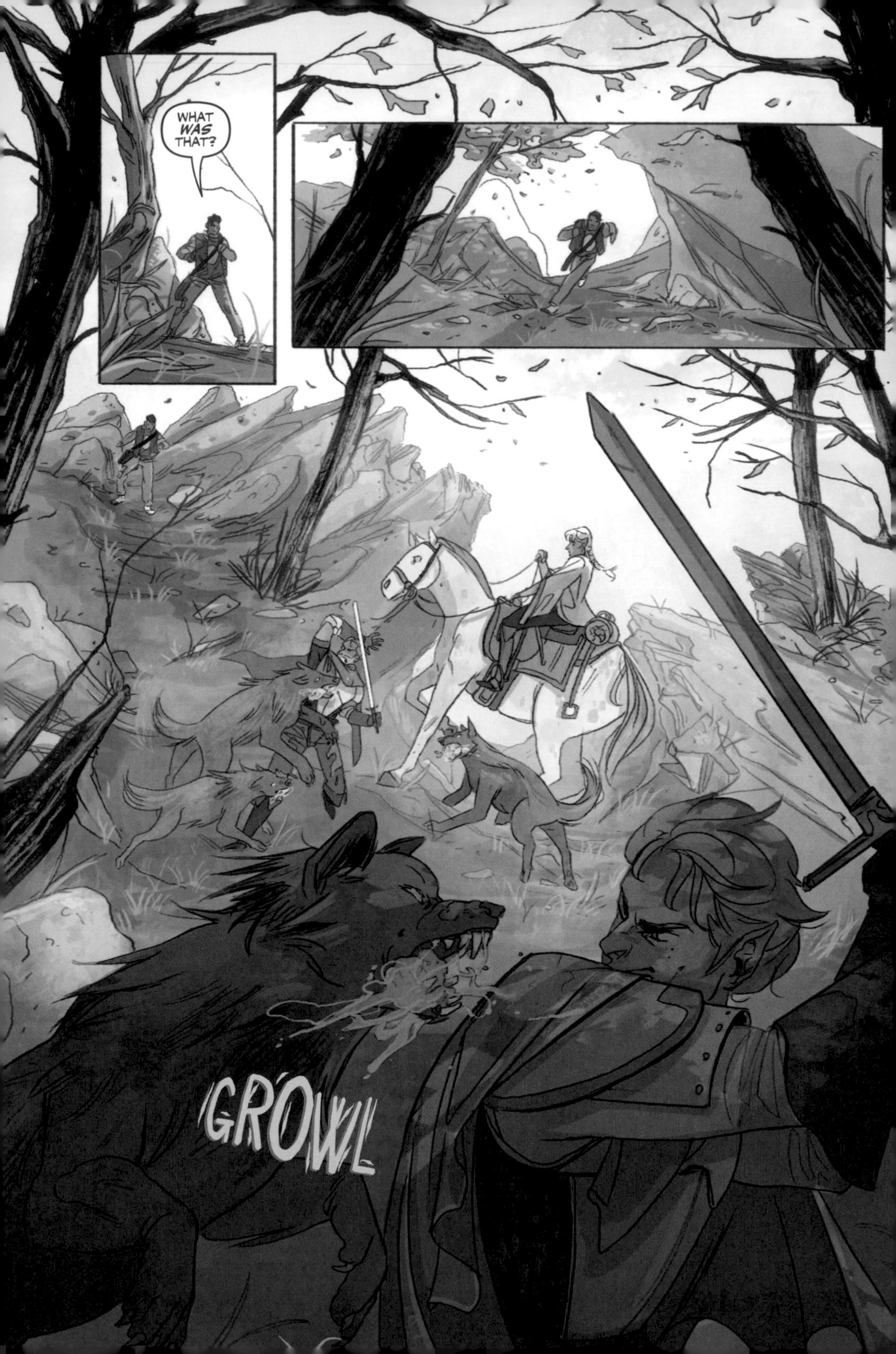
WHAT WAS THAT?
GROWL

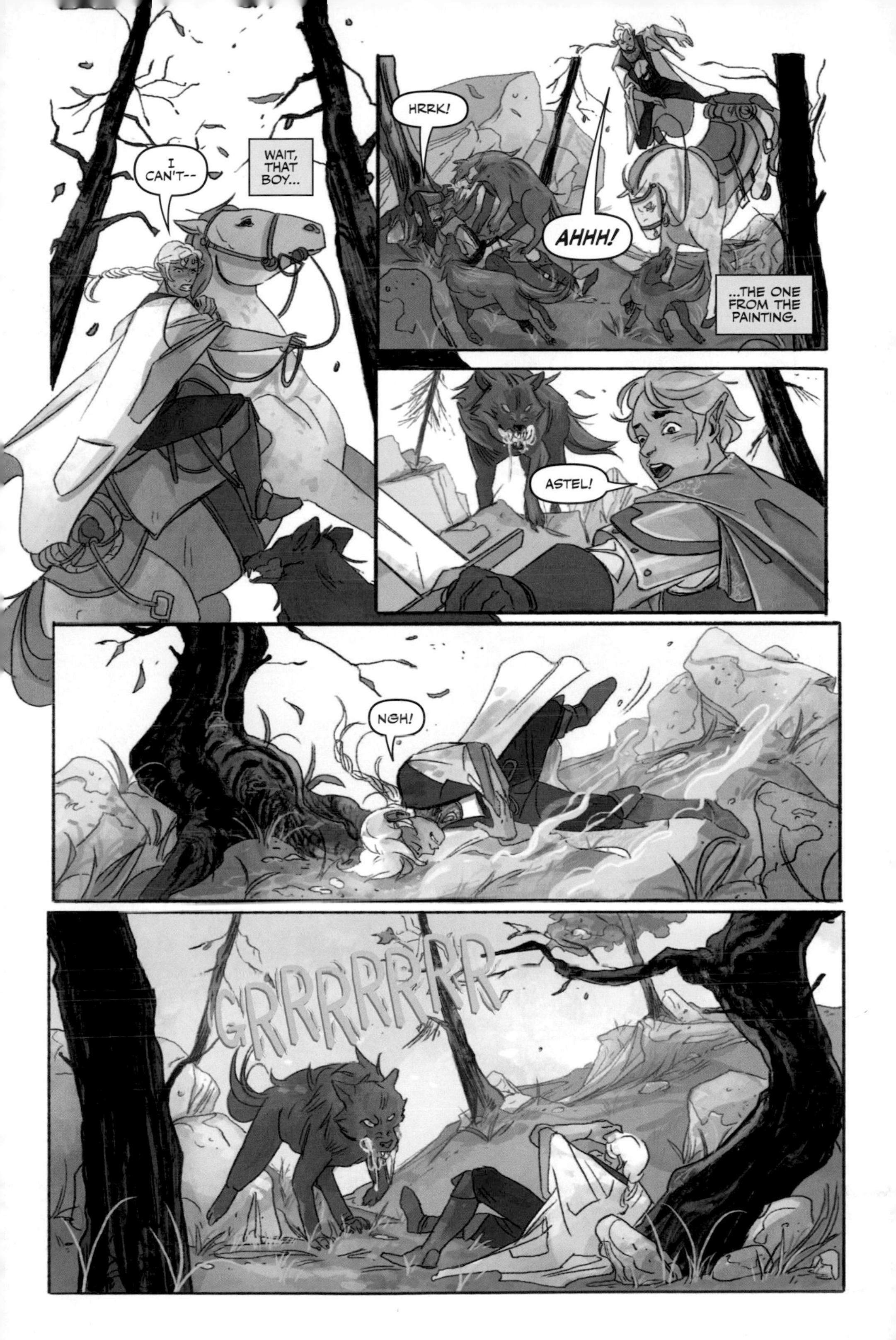
I CAN'T--
WAIT, THAT BOY...
HRRK!
AHHH!
...THE ONE FROM THE PAINTING.
ASTEL!
NGH!
GRRRRRRR

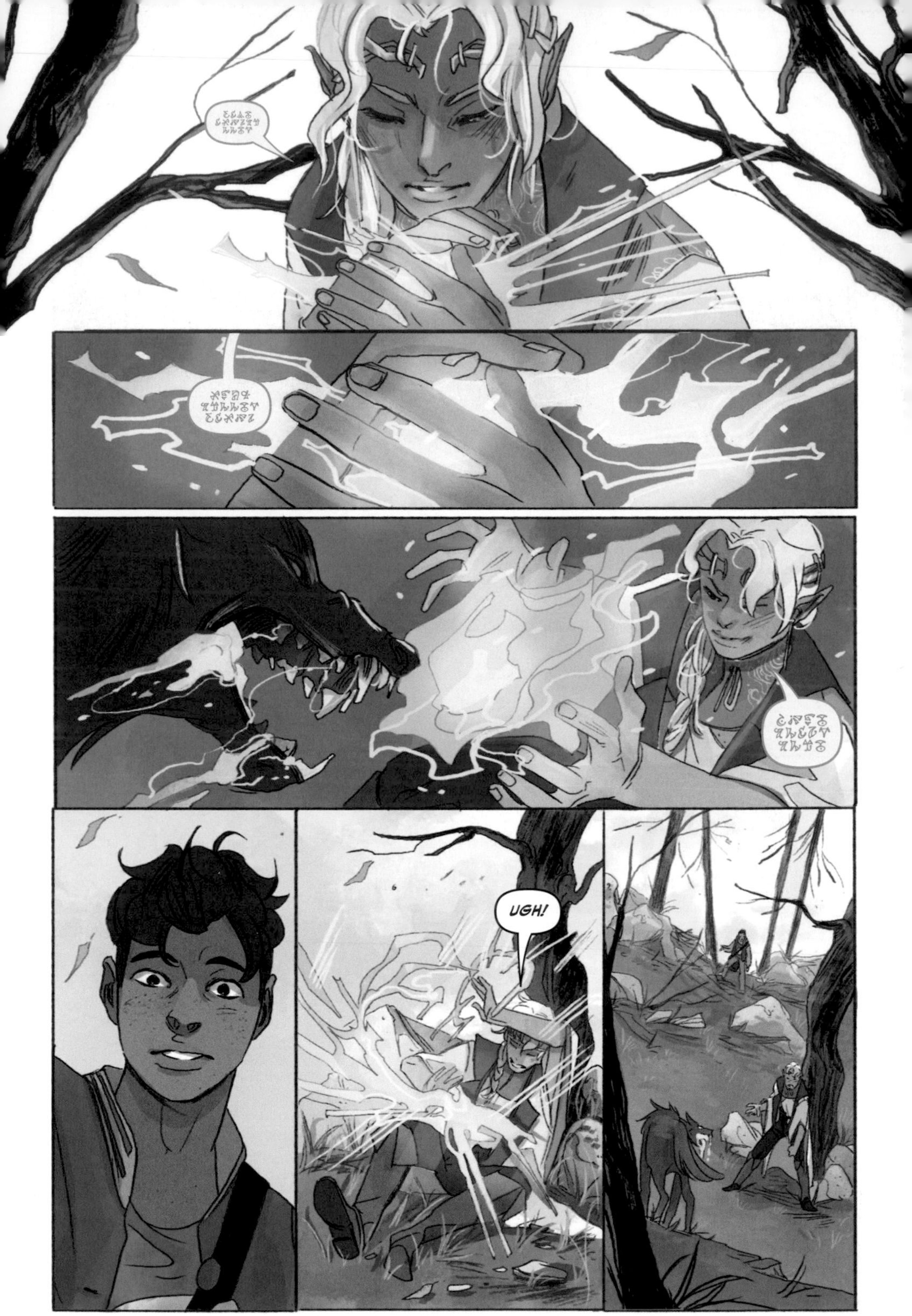
UGH!

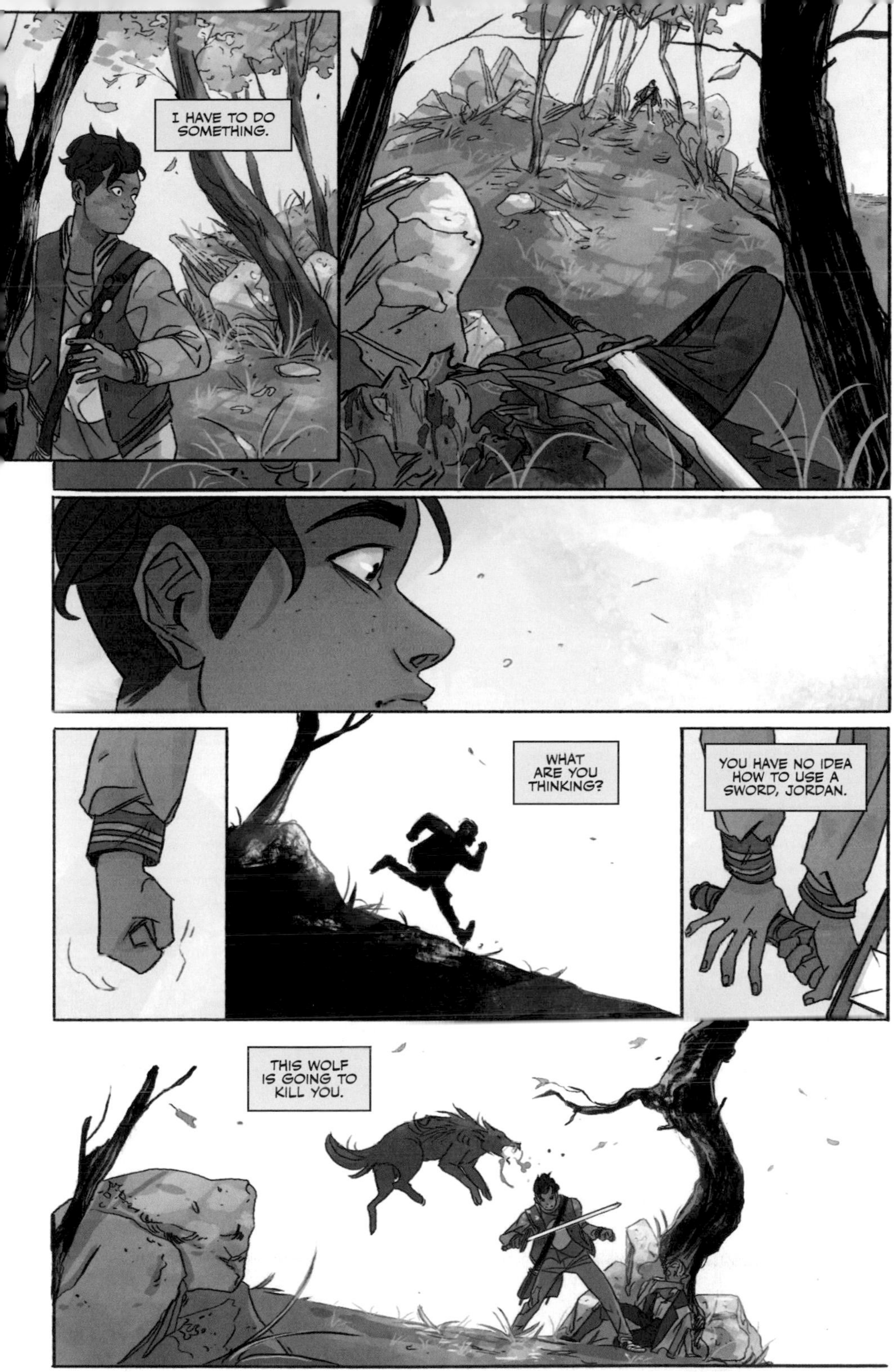
I HAVE TO DO SOMETHING.
WHAT ARE YOU THINKING?
YOU HAVE NO IDEA HOW TO USE A SWORD, JORDAN.
THIS WOLF IS GOING TO KILL YOU.

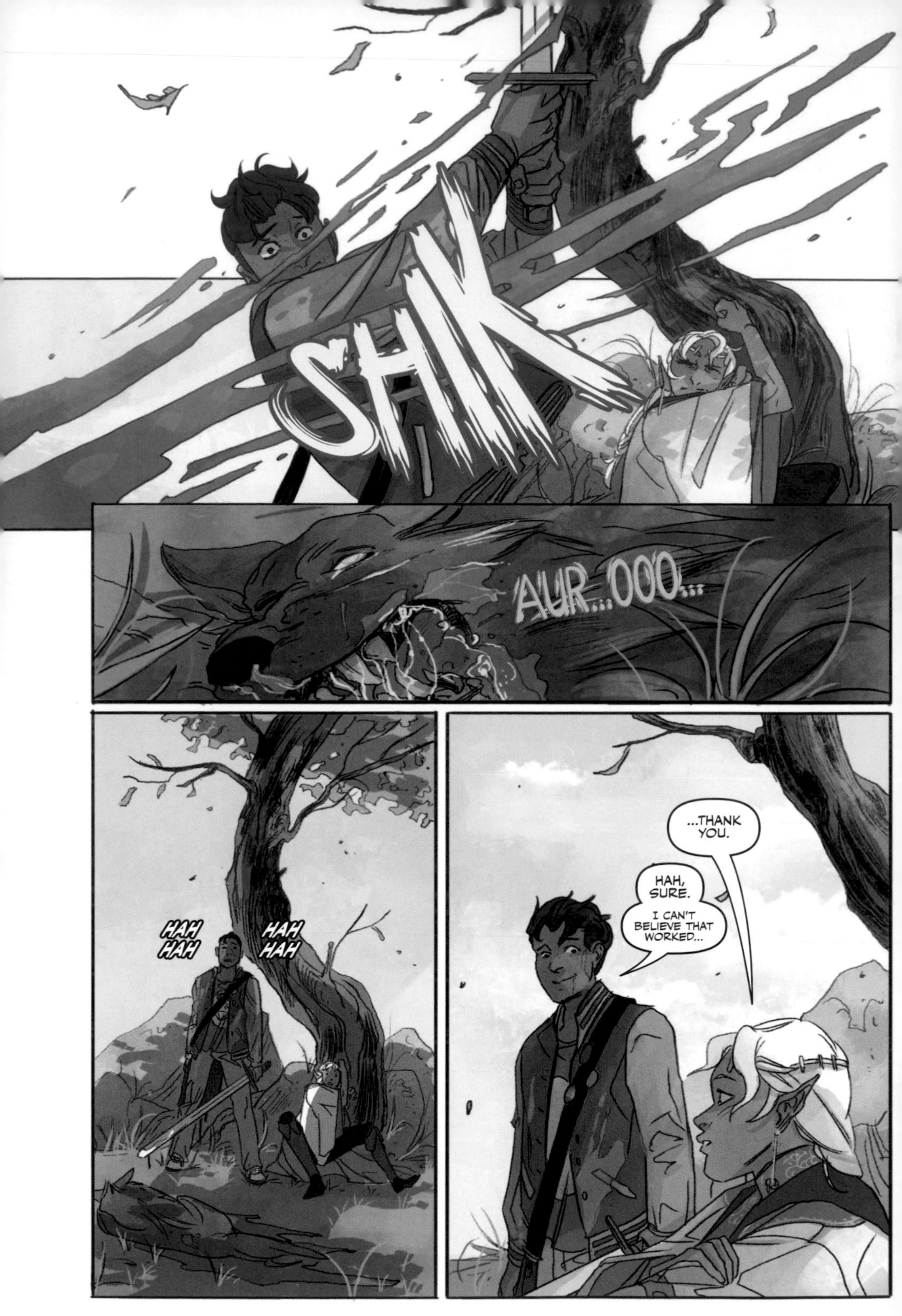
SHIK
AUR...OOO...
HAH HAH
HAH HAH
...THANK YOU.
HAH, SURE.
I CAN'T BELIEVE THAT WORKED...

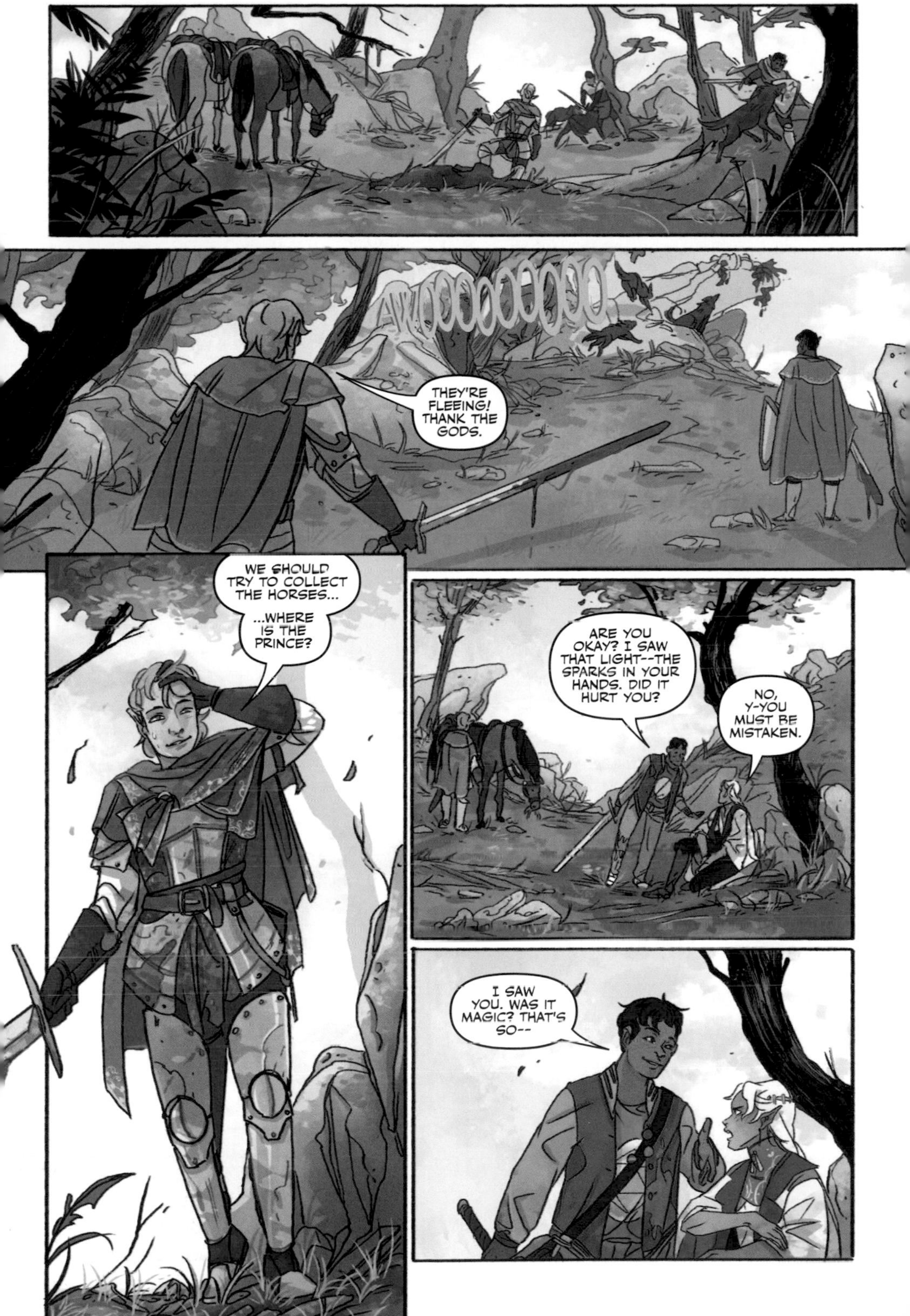
AWOOOOOOOOOO
THEY'RE FLEEING! THANK THE GODS.
WE SHOULD TRY TO COLLECT THE HORSES...
...WHERE IS THE PRINCE?
ARE YOU OKAY? I SAW THAT LIGHT--THE SPARKS IN YOUR HANDS. DID IT HURT YOU?
NO, Y-YOU MUST BE MISTAKEN.
I SAW YOU. WAS IT MAGIC? THAT'S SO--

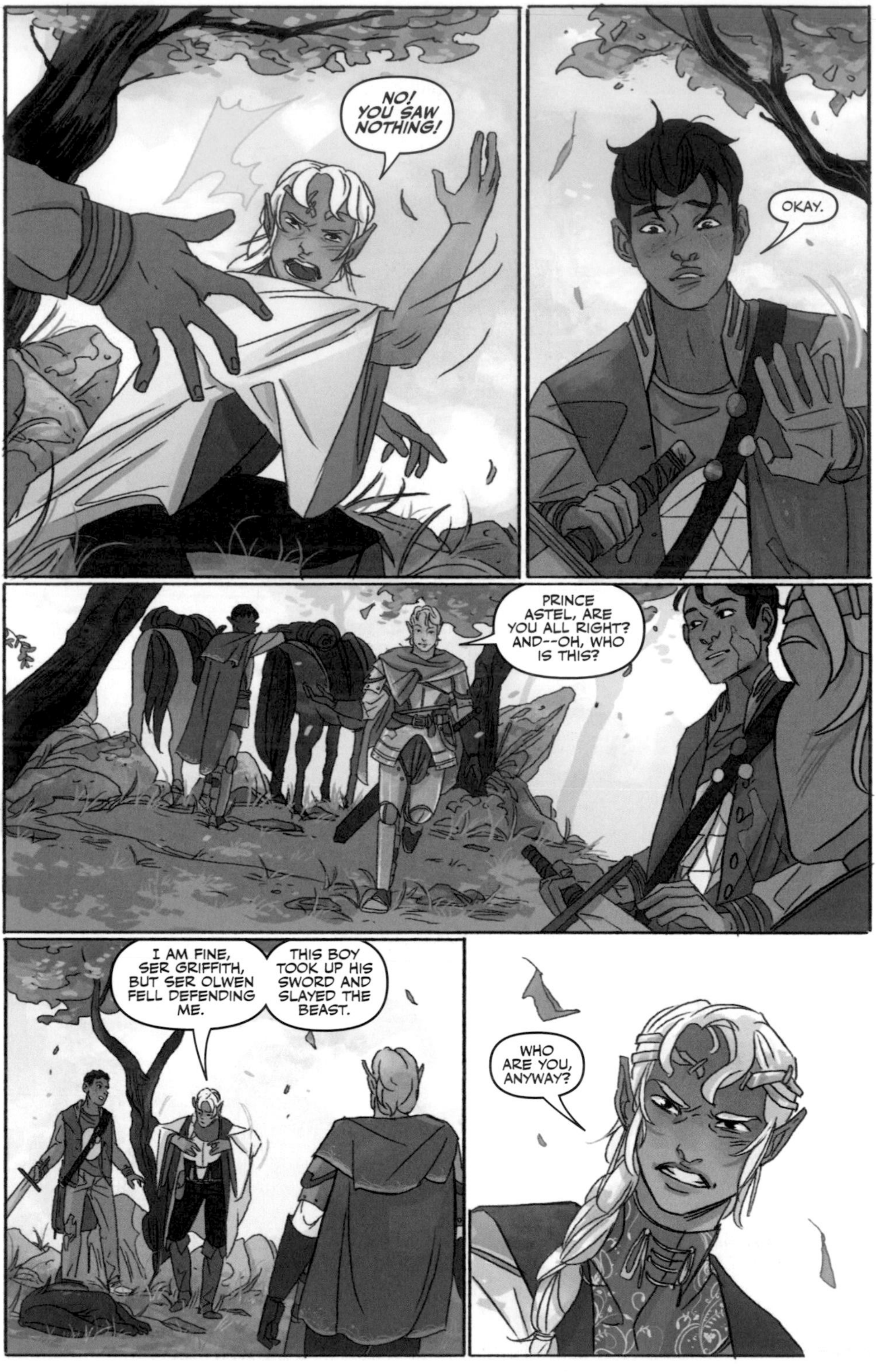
NO! YOU SAW NOTHING!
OKAY.
PRINCE ASTEL, ARE YOU ALL RIGHT? AND--OH, WHO IS THIS?
I AM FINE, SER GRIFFITH, BUT SER OLWEN FELL DEFENDING ME.
THIS BOY TOOK UP HIS SWORD AND SLAYED THE BEAST.
WHO ARE YOU, ANYWAY?

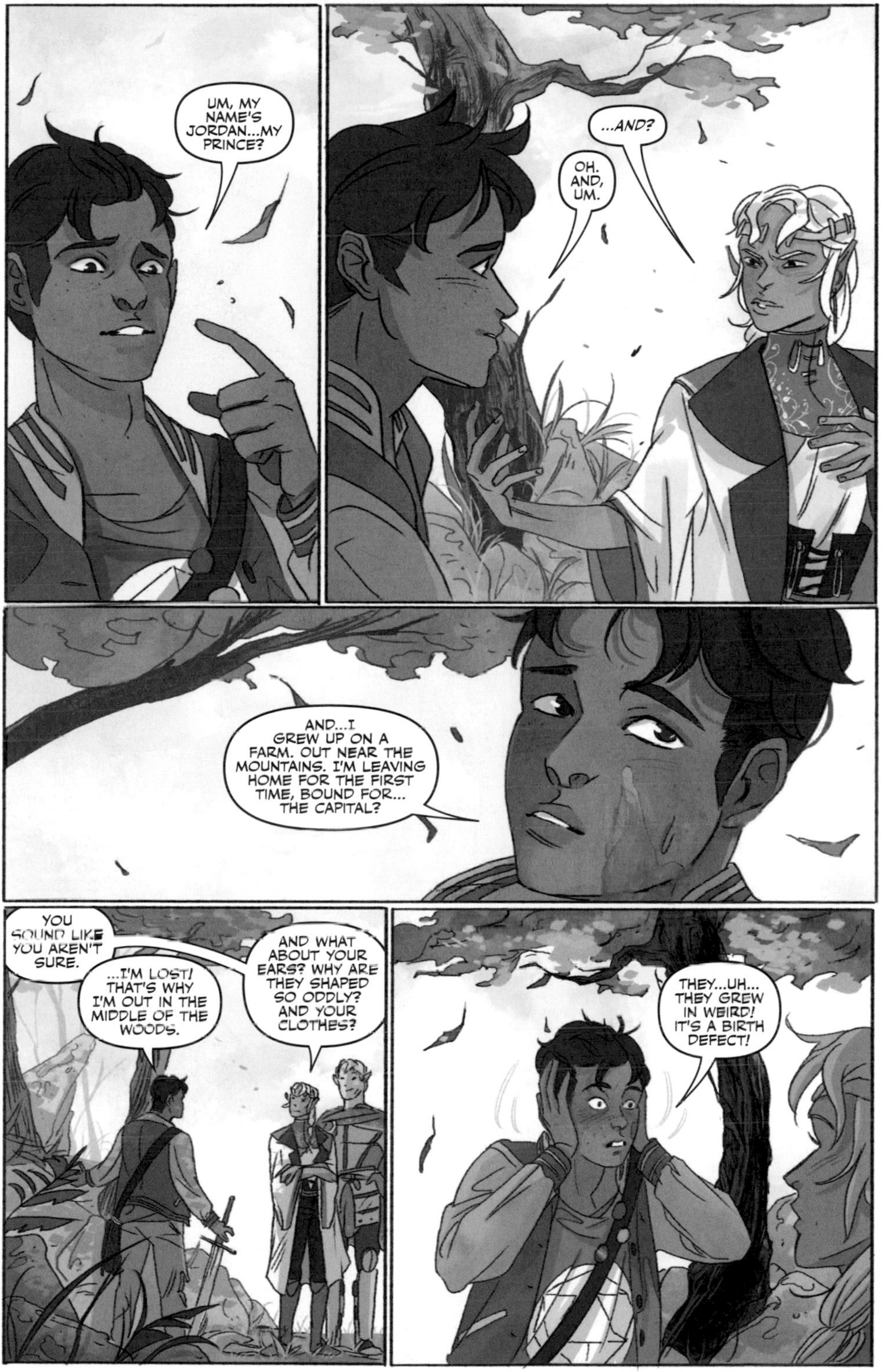
UM, MY NAME'S JORDAN...MY PRINCE?
...AND?
OH. AND, UM.
AND...I GREW UP ON A FARM. OUT NEAR THE MOUNTAINS. I'M LEAVING HOME FOR THE FIRST TIME, BOUND FOR... THE CAPITAL?
YOU SOUND LIKE YOU AREN'T SURE.
...I'M LOST! THAT'S WHY I'M OUT IN THE MIDDLE OF THE WOODS.
AND WHAT ABOUT YOUR EARS? WHY ARE THEY SHAPED SO ODDLY? AND YOUR CLOTHES?
THEY...UH... THEY GREW IN WEIRD! IT'S A BIRTH DEFECT!

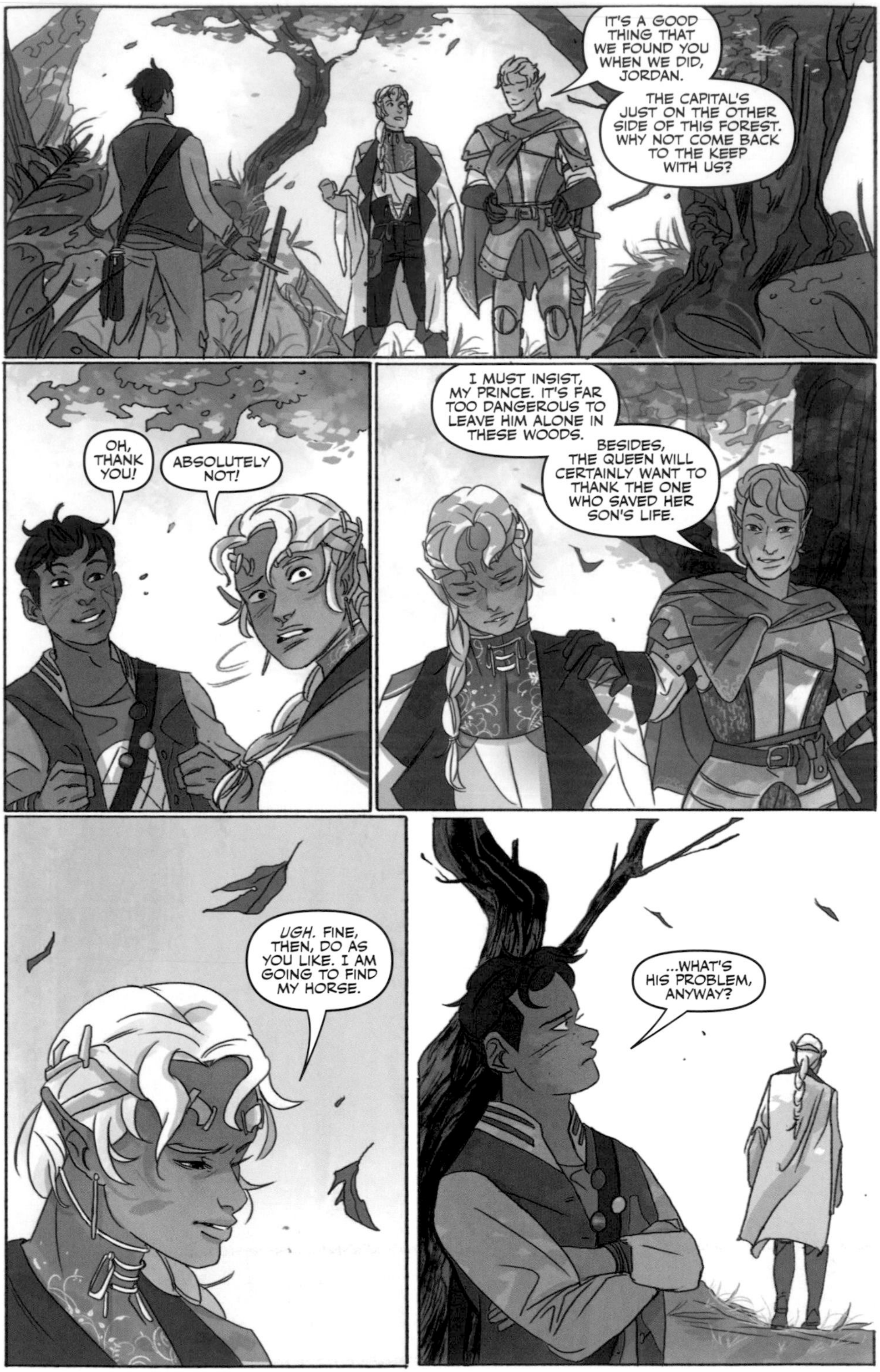
IT'S A GOOD THING THAT WE FOUND YOU WHEN WE DID, JORDAN.
THE CAPITAL'S JUST ON THE OTHER SIDE OF THIS FOREST. WHY NOT COME BACK TO THE KEEP WITH US?
OH, THANK YOU!
ABSOLUTELY NOT!
I MUST INSIST, MY PRINCE. IT'S FAR TOO DANGEROUS TO LEAVE HIM ALONE IN THESE WOODS.
BESIDES, THE QUEEN WILL CERTAINLY WANT TO THANK THE ONE WHO SAVED HER SON'S LIFE.
*UGH.* FINE, THEN, DO AS YOU LIKE. I AM GOING TO FIND MY HORSE.
...WHAT'S HIS PROBLEM, ANYWAY?

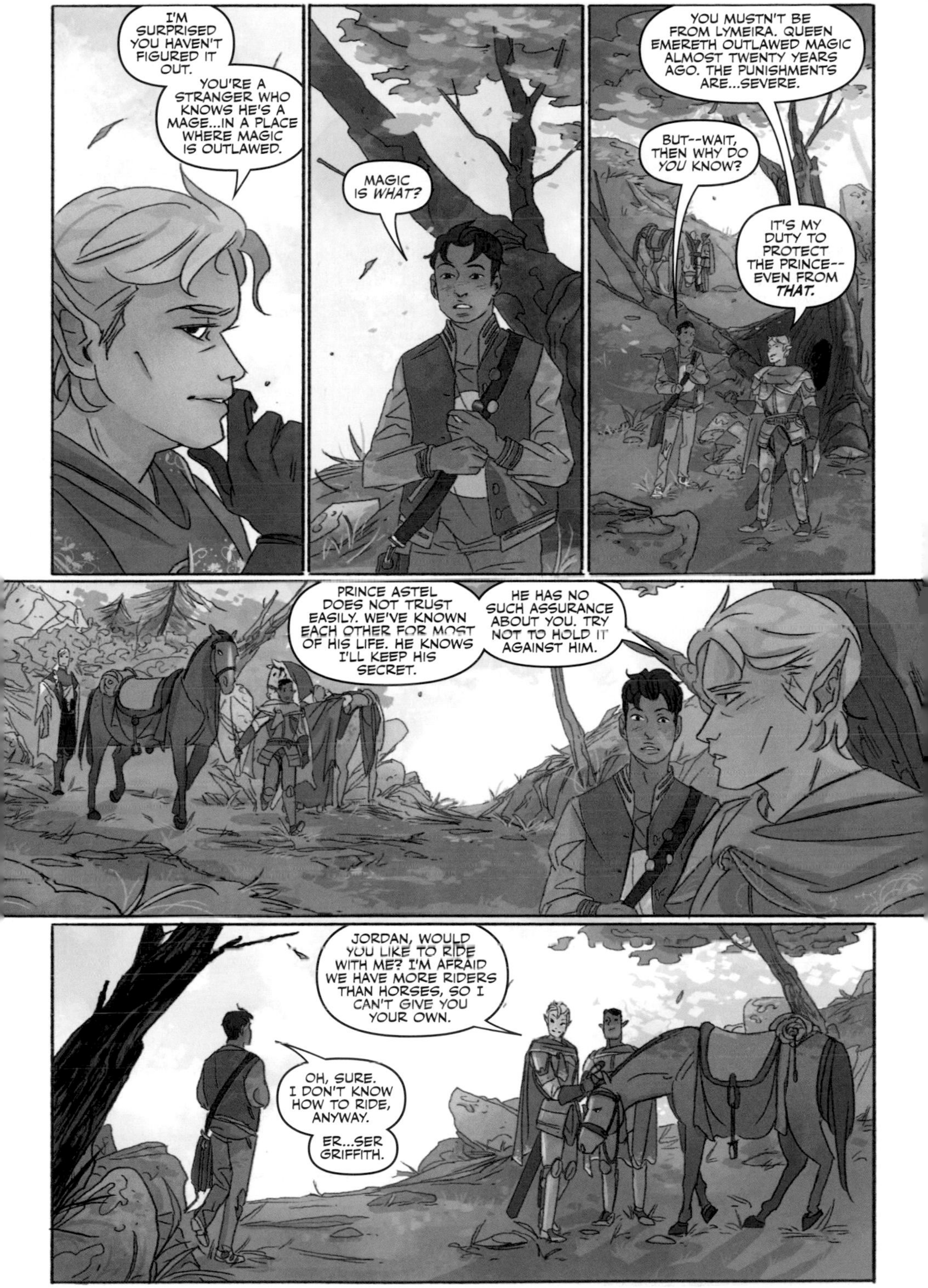
I'M SURPRISED YOU HAVEN'T FIGURED IT OUT.
YOU'RE A STRANGER WHO KNOWS HE'S A MAGE...IN A PLACE WHERE MAGIC IS OUTLAWED.
MAGIC IS *WHAT*?
YOU MUSTN'T BE FROM LYMEIRA. QUEEN EMERETH OUTLAWED MAGIC ALMOST TWENTY YEARS AGO. THE PUNISHMENTS ARE...SEVERE.
BUT--WAIT, THEN WHY DO *YOU* KNOW?
IT'S MY DUTY TO PROTECT THE PRINCE--EVEN FROM ***THAT.***
PRINCE ASTEL DOES NOT TRUST EASILY. WE'VE KNOWN EACH OTHER FOR MOST OF HIS LIFE. HE KNOWS I'LL KEEP HIS SECRET.
HE HAS NO SUCH ASSURANCE ABOUT YOU. TRY NOT TO HOLD IT AGAINST HIM.
JORDAN, WOULD YOU LIKE TO RIDE WITH ME? I'M AFRAID WE HAVE MORE RIDERS THAN HORSES, SO I CAN'T GIVE YOU YOUR OWN.
OH, SURE. I DON'T KNOW HOW TO RIDE, ANYWAY.
ER...SER GRIFFITH.

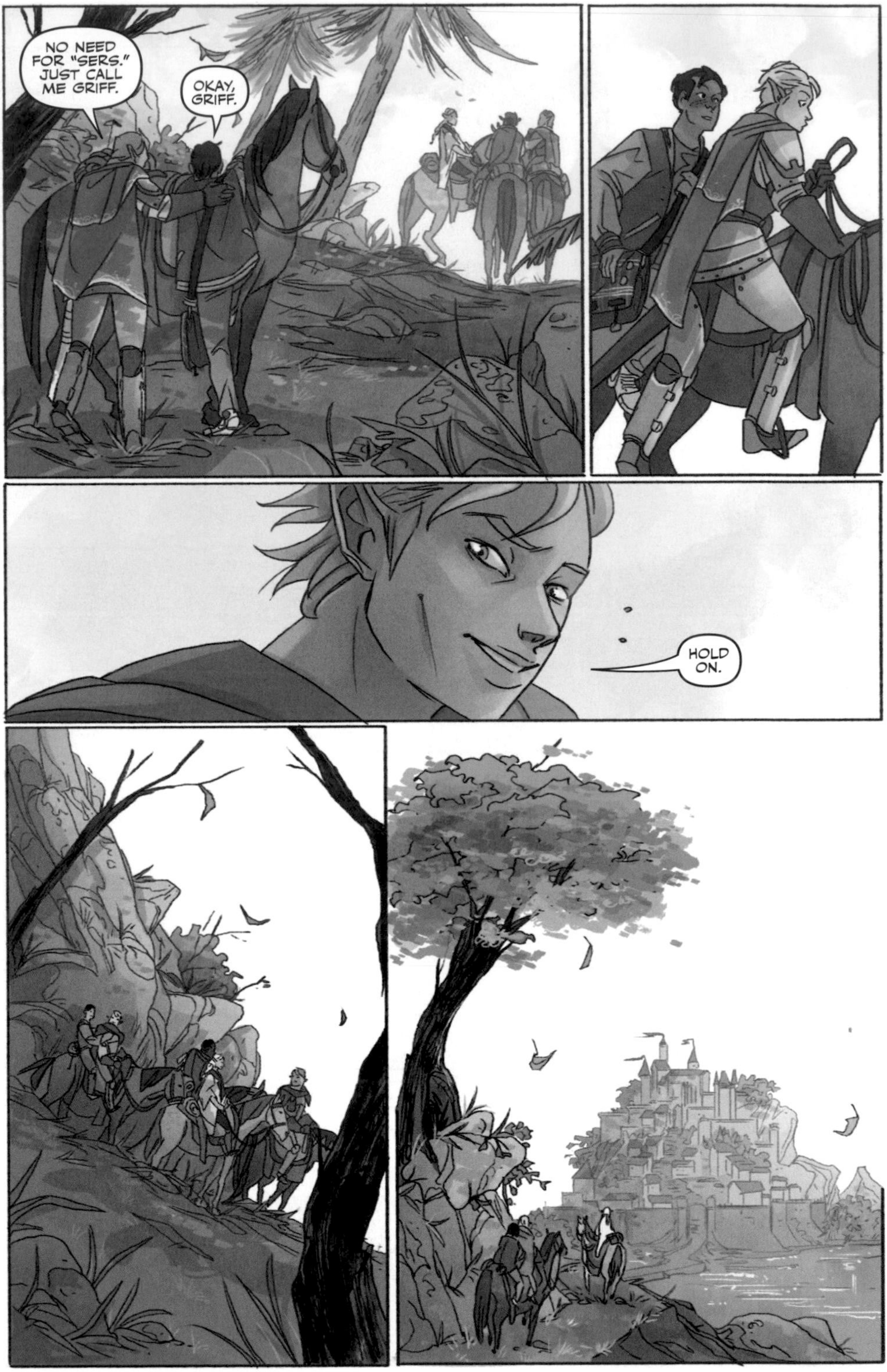
NO NEED FOR "SERS." JUST CALL ME GRIFF.
OKAY, GRIFF.
HOLD ON.

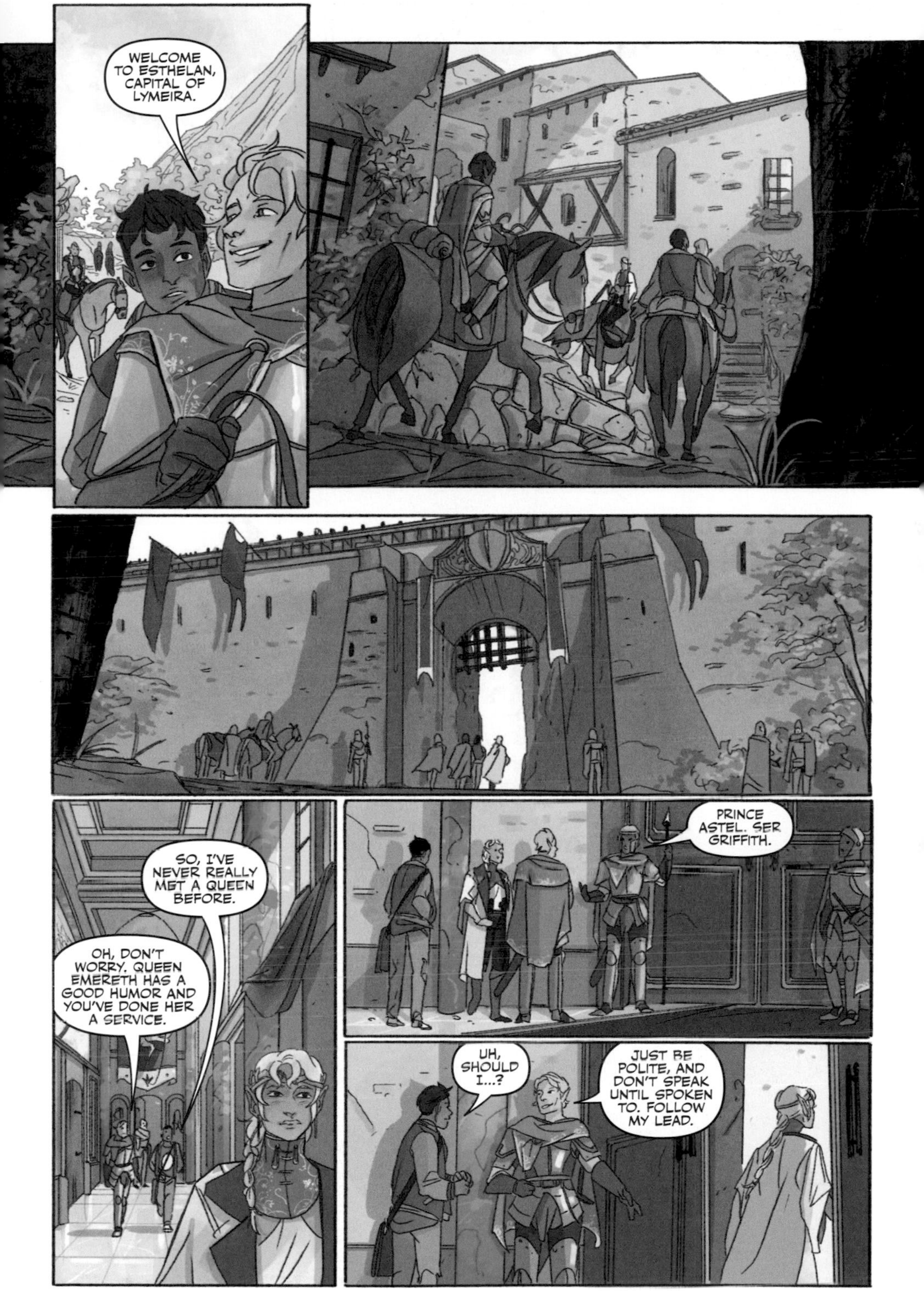
WELCOME TO ESTHELAN, CAPITAL OF LYMEIRA.
SO, I'VE NEVER REALLY MET A QUEEN BEFORE.
OH, DON'T WORRY. QUEEN EMERETH HAS A GOOD HUMOR AND YOU'VE DONE HER A SERVICE.
PRINCE ASTEL. SER GRIFFITH.
UH, SHOULD I...?
JUST BE POLITE, AND DON'T SPEAK UNTIL SPOKEN TO. FOLLOW MY LEAD.

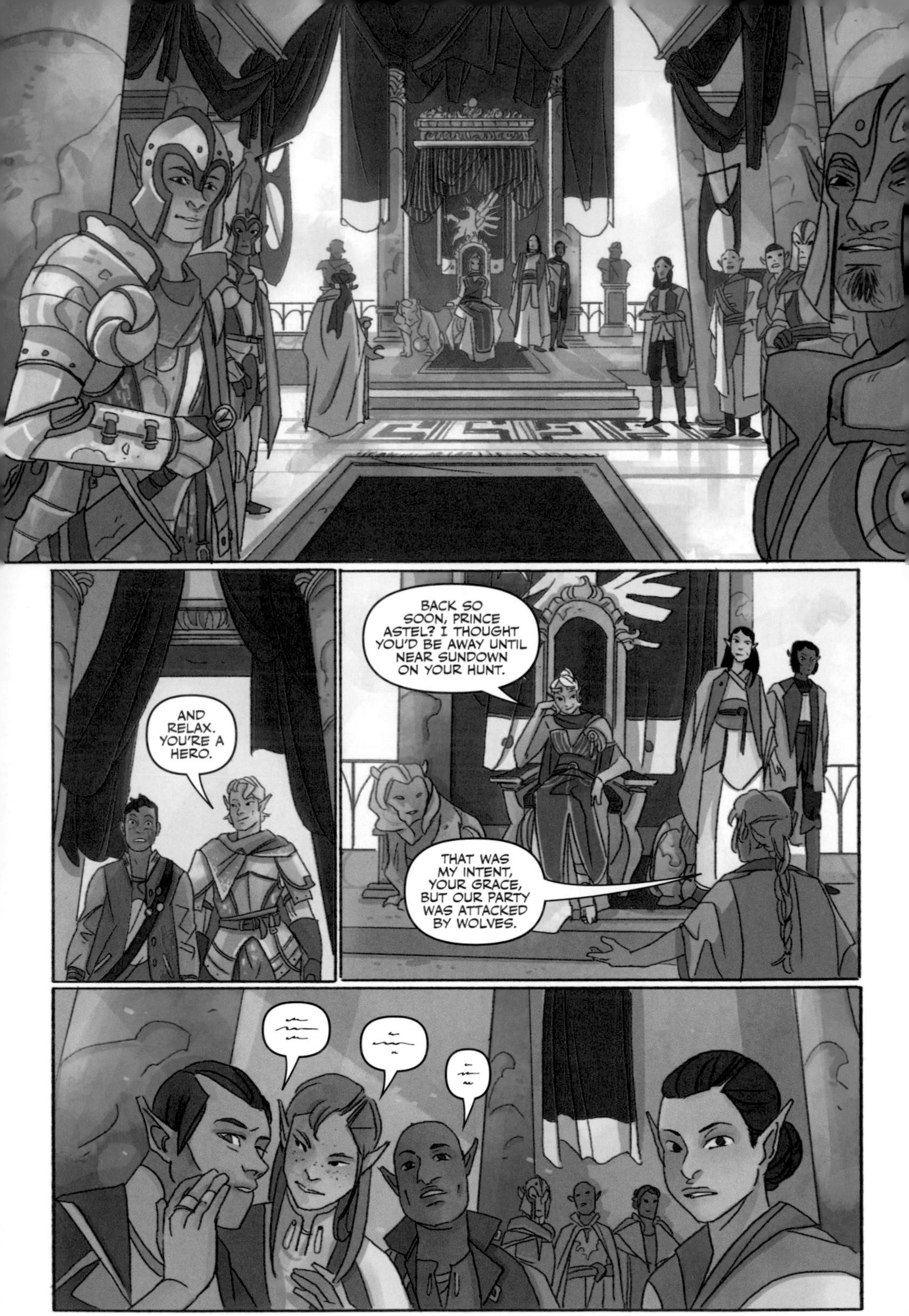
AND RELAX. YOU'RE A HERO.
BACK SO SOON, PRINCE ASTEL? I THOUGHT YOU'D BE AWAY UNTIL NEAR SUNDOWN ON YOUR HUNT.
THAT WAS MY INTENT, YOUR GRACE, BUT OUR PARTY WAS ATTACKED BY WOLVES.

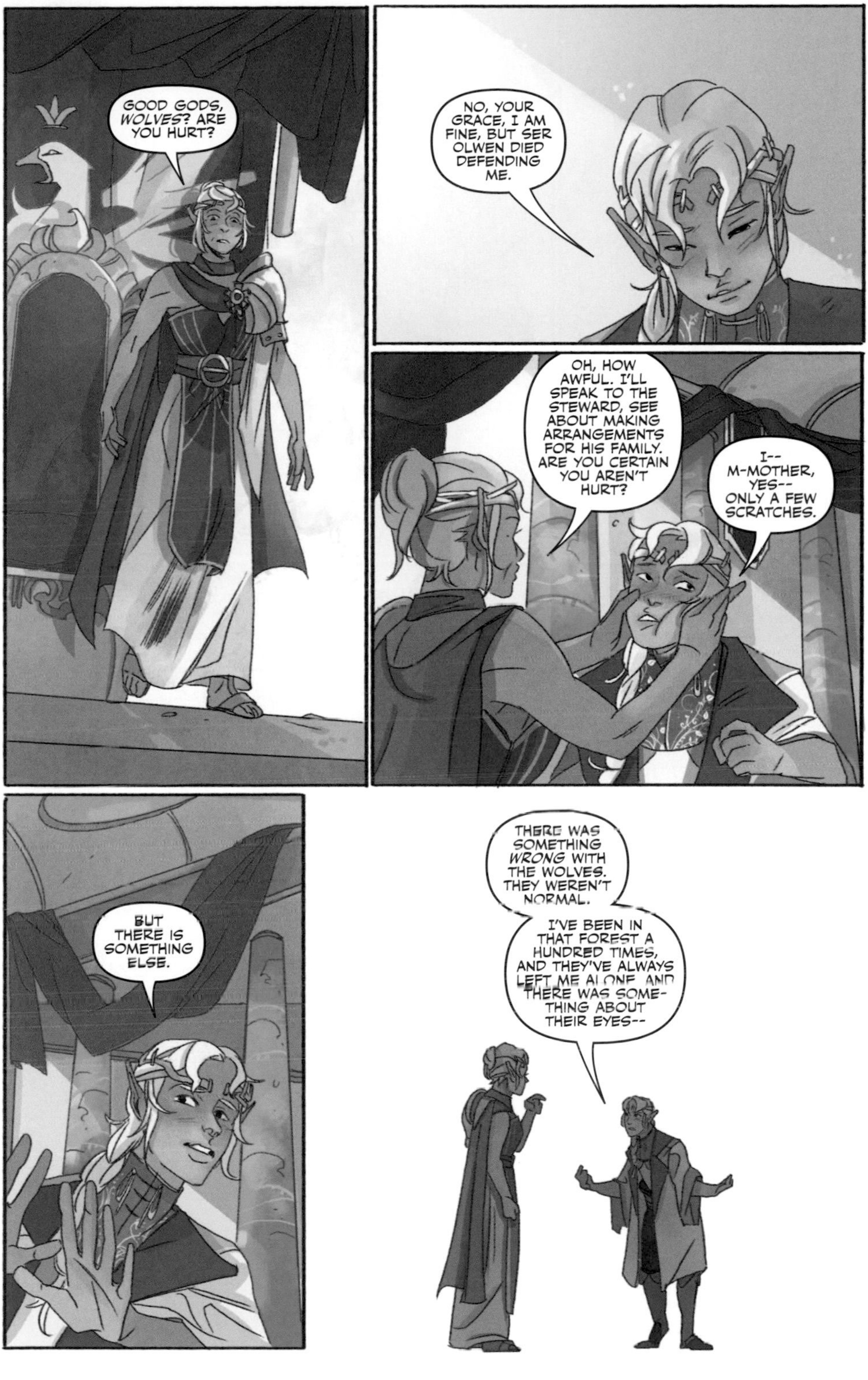
GOOD GODS, *WOLVES*? ARE YOU HURT?
NO, YOUR GRACE, I AM FINE, BUT SER OLWEN DIED DEFENDING ME.
OH, HOW AWFUL. I'LL SPEAK TO THE STEWARD, SEE ABOUT MAKING ARRANGEMENTS FOR HIS FAMILY. ARE YOU CERTAIN YOU AREN'T HURT?
I-- M-MOTHER, YES-- ONLY A FEW SCRATCHES.
BUT THERE IS SOMETHING ELSE.
THERE WAS SOMETHING *WRONG* WITH THE WOLVES. THEY WEREN'T NORMAL.
I'VE BEEN IN THAT FOREST A HUNDRED TIMES, AND THEY'VE ALWAYS LEFT ME ALONE, AND THERE WAS SOMETHING ABOUT THEIR EYES--

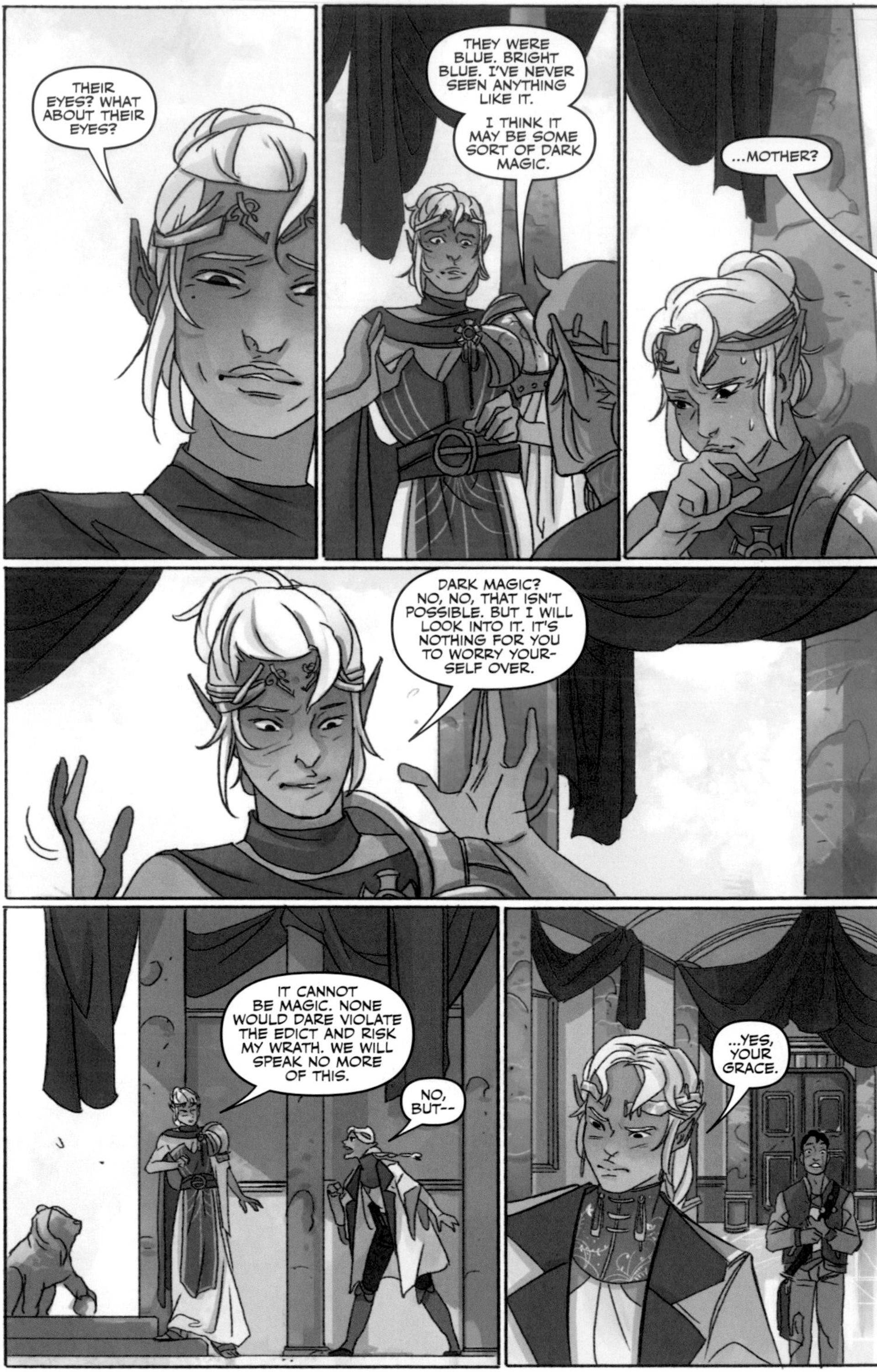
THEIR EYES? WHAT ABOUT THEIR EYES?
THEY WERE BLUE. BRIGHT BLUE. I'VE NEVER SEEN ANYTHING LIKE IT.
I THINK IT MAY BE SOME SORT OF DARK MAGIC.
...MOTHER?
DARK MAGIC? NO, NO, THAT ISN'T POSSIBLE. BUT I WILL LOOK INTO IT. IT'S NOTHING FOR YOU TO WORRY YOUR-SELF OVER.
IT CANNOT BE MAGIC. NONE WOULD DARE VIOLATE THE EDICT AND RISK MY WRATH. WE WILL SPEAK NO MORE OF THIS.
NO, BUT--
...YES, YOUR GRACE.

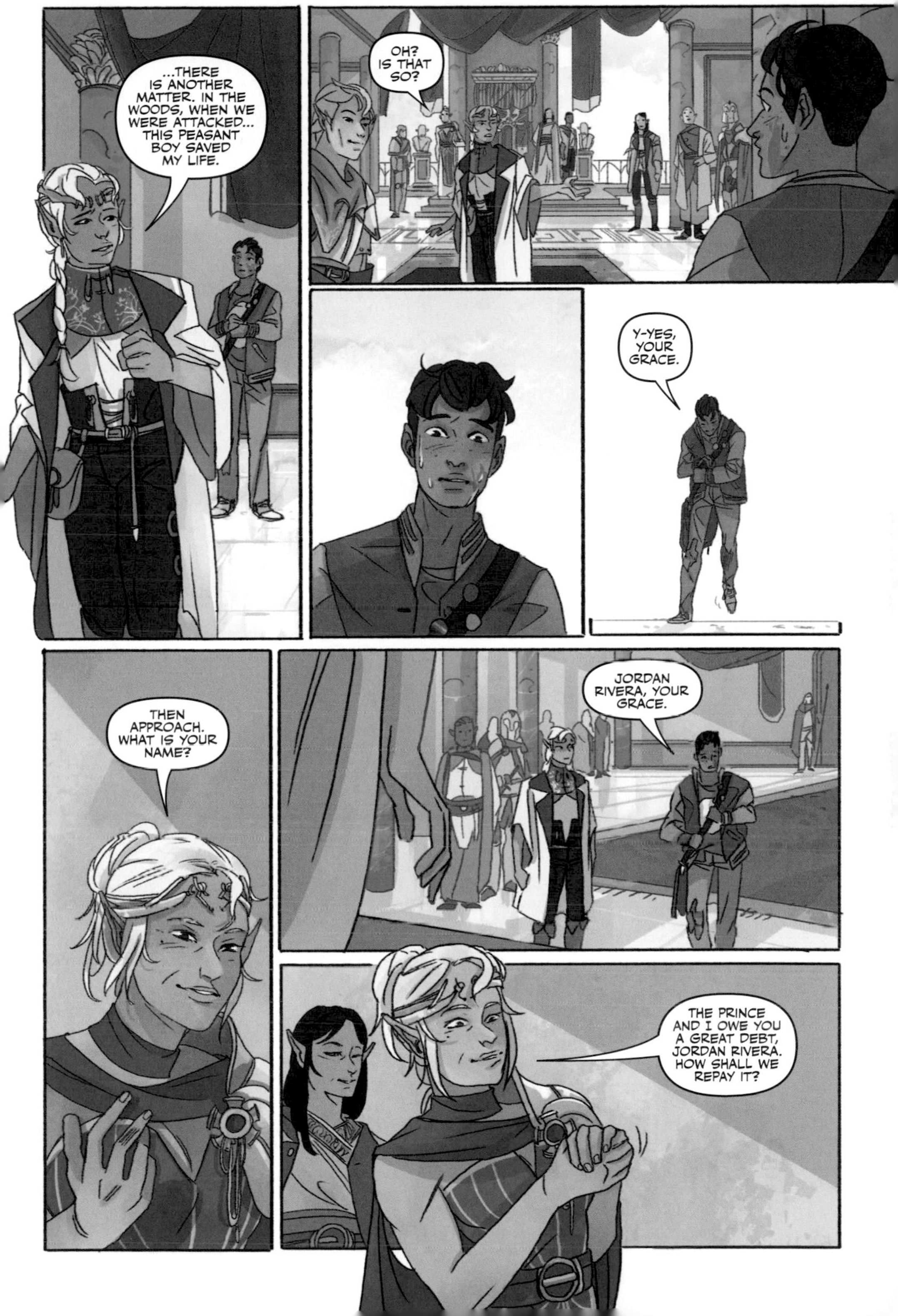
...THERE IS ANOTHER MATTER. IN THE WOODS, WHEN WE WERE ATTACKED... THIS PEASANT BOY SAVED MY LIFE.
OH? IS THAT SO?
Y-YES, YOUR GRACE.
THEN APPROACH. WHAT IS YOUR NAME?
JORDAN RIVERA, YOUR GRACE.
THE PRINCE AND I OWE YOU A GREAT DEBT, JORDAN RIVERA. HOW SHALL WE REPAY IT?

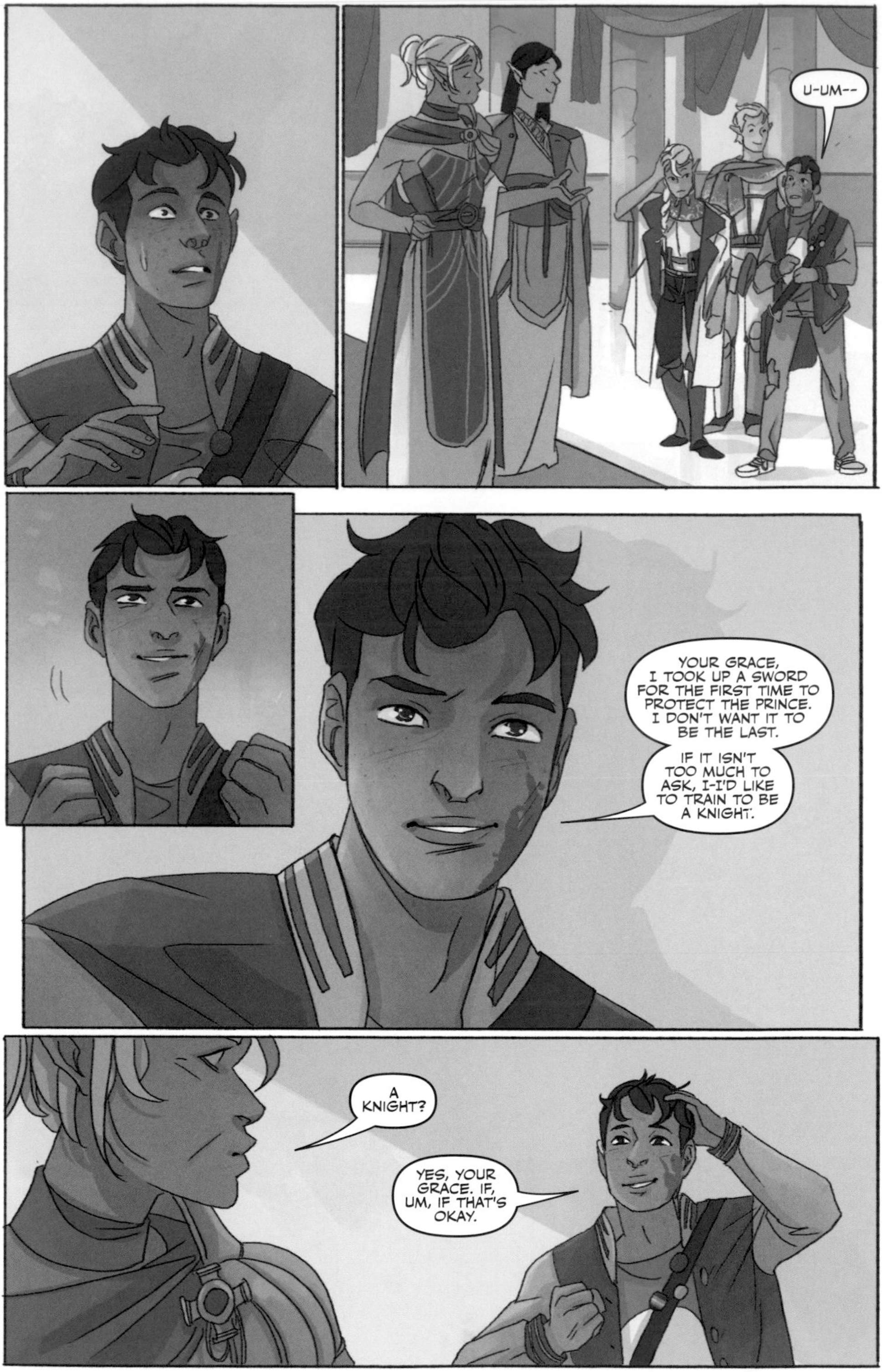
U-UM--
YOUR GRACE, I TOOK UP A SWORD FOR THE FIRST TIME TO PROTECT THE PRINCE. I DON'T WANT IT TO BE THE LAST.
IF IT ISN'T TOO MUCH TO ASK, I-I'D LIKE TO TRAIN TO BE A KNIGHT.
A KNIGHT?
YES, YOUR GRACE. IF, UM, IF THAT'S OKAY.

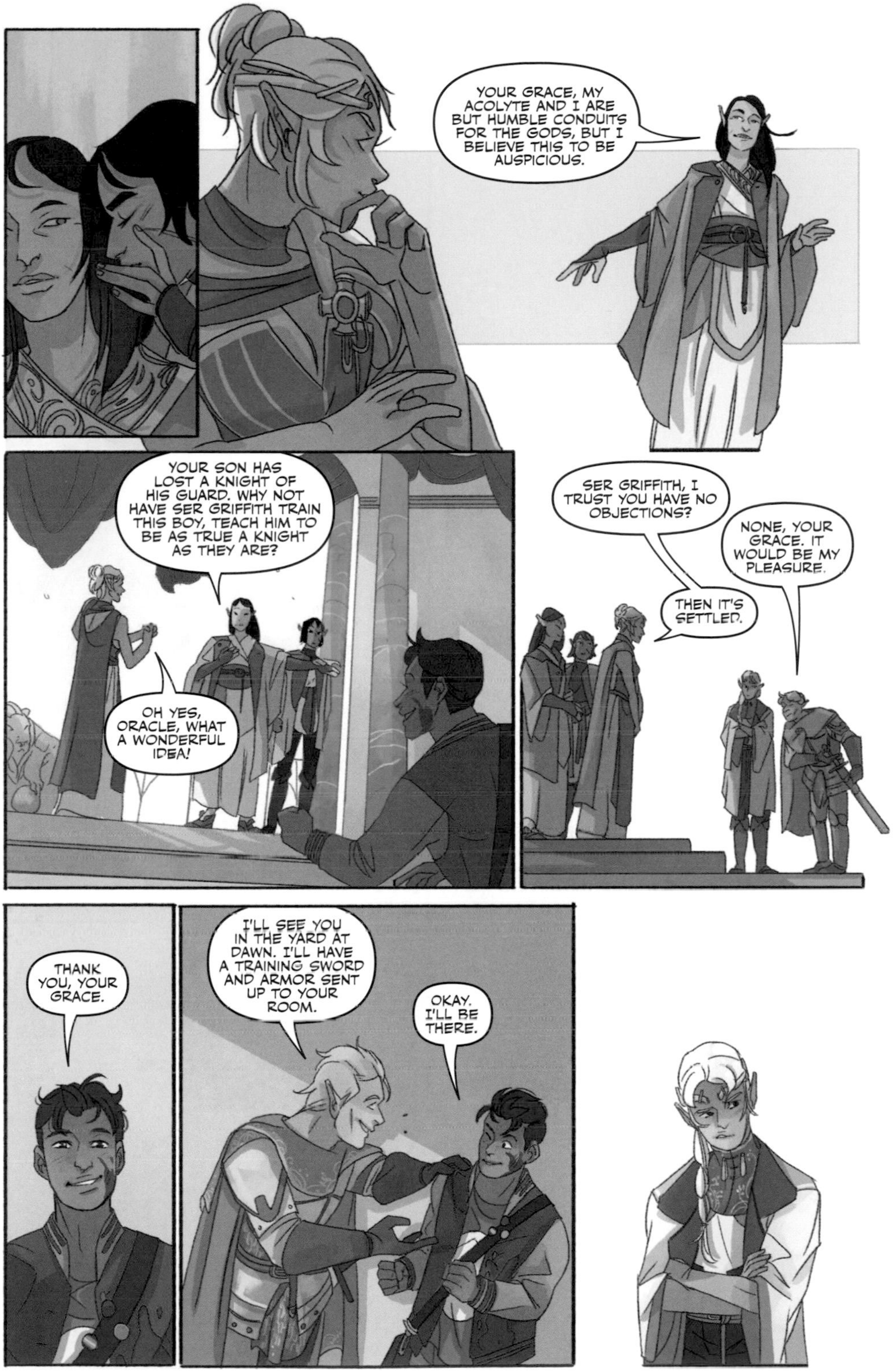

YOUR GRACE, MY ACOLYTE AND I ARE BUT HUMBLE CONDUITS FOR THE GODS, BUT I BELIEVE THIS TO BE AUSPICIOUS.
YOUR SON HAS LOST A KNIGHT OF HIS GUARD. WHY NOT HAVE SER GRIFFITH TRAIN THIS BOY, TEACH HIM TO BE AS TRUE A KNIGHT AS THEY ARE?
OH YES, ORACLE, WHAT A WONDERFUL IDEA!
SER GRIFFITH, I TRUST YOU HAVE NO OBJECTIONS?
NONE, YOUR GRACE. IT WOULD BE MY PLEASURE.
THEN IT'S SETTLED.
THANK YOU, YOUR GRACE.
I'LL SEE YOU IN THE YARD AT DAWN. I'LL HAVE A TRAINING SWORD AND ARMOR SENT UP TO YOUR ROOM.
OKAY. I'LL BE THERE.

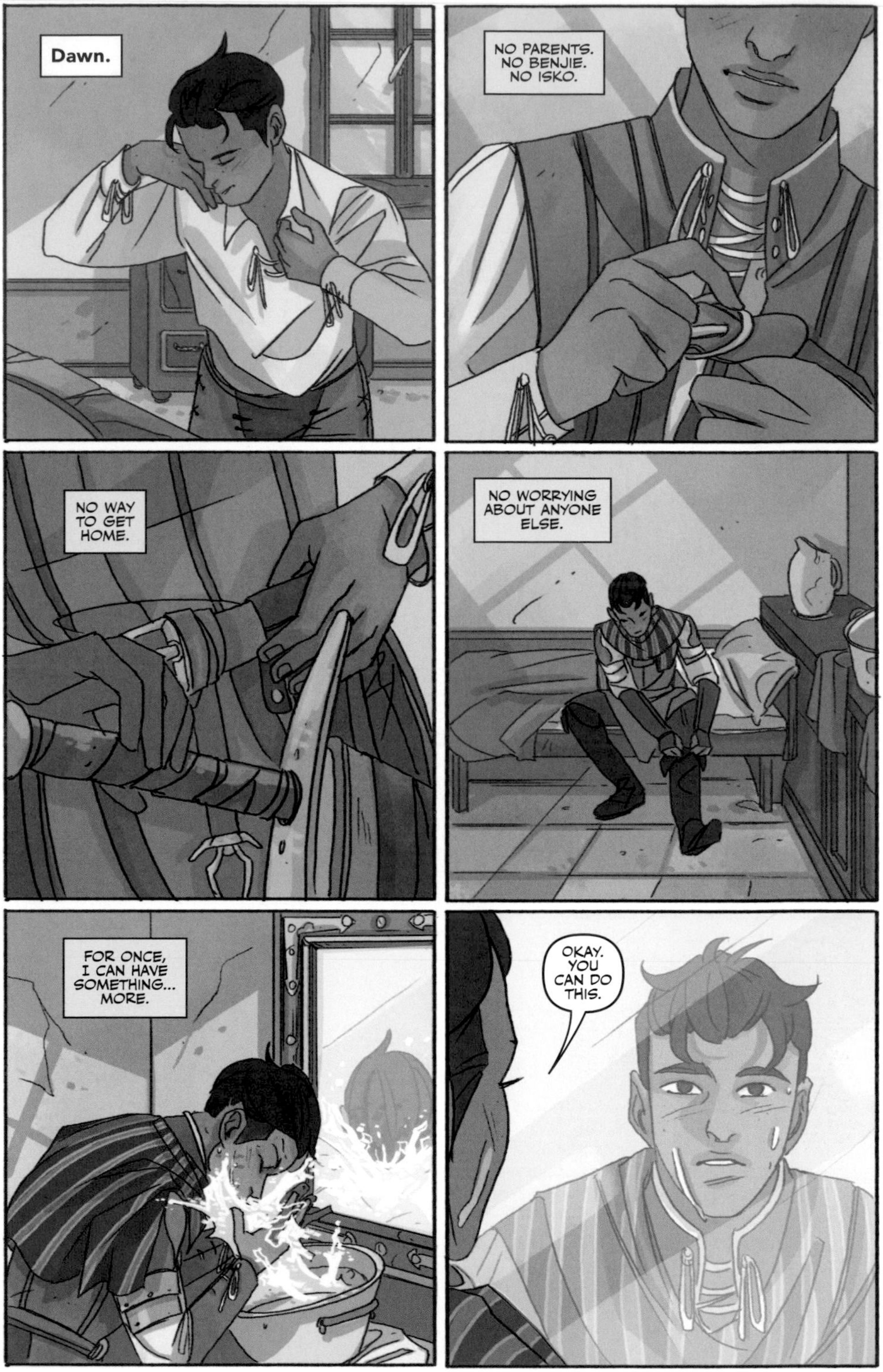
Dawn.
NO PARENTS. NO BENJIE. NO ISKO.
NO WAY TO GET HOME.
NO WORRYING ABOUT ANYONE ELSE.
FOR ONCE, I CAN HAVE SOMETHING... MORE.
OKAY. YOU CAN DO THIS.

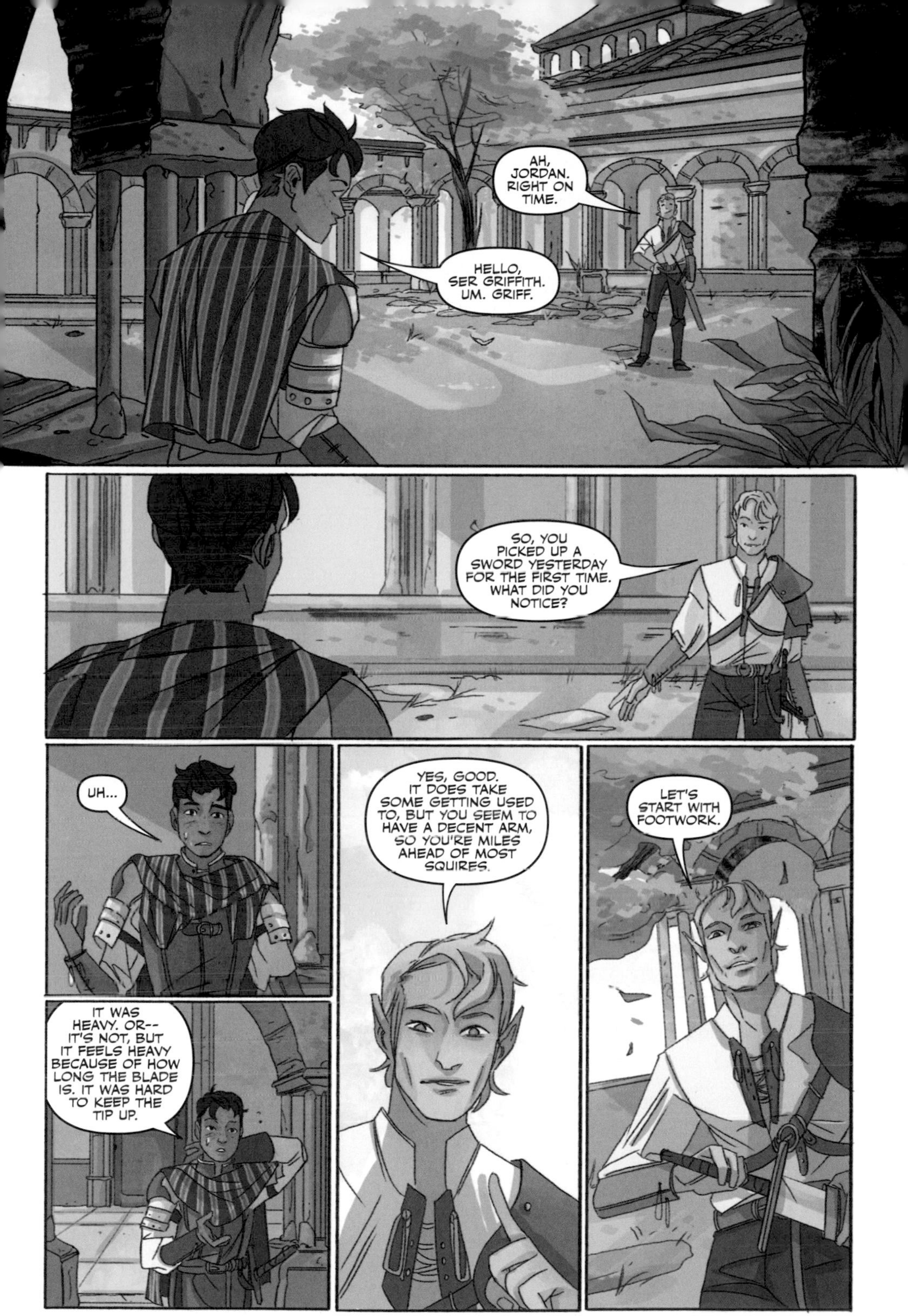
AH, JORDAN. RIGHT ON TIME.
HELLO, SER GRIFFITH. UM. GRIFF.
SO, YOU PICKED UP A SWORD YESTERDAY FOR THE FIRST TIME. WHAT DID YOU NOTICE?
UH...
IT WAS HEAVY. OR-- IT'S NOT, BUT IT FEELS HEAVY BECAUSE OF HOW LONG THE BLADE IS. IT WAS HARD TO KEEP THE TIP UP.
YES, GOOD. IT DOES TAKE SOME GETTING USED TO, BUT YOU SEEM TO HAVE A DECENT ARM, SO YOU'RE MILES AHEAD OF MOST SQUIRES.
LET'S START WITH FOOTWORK.

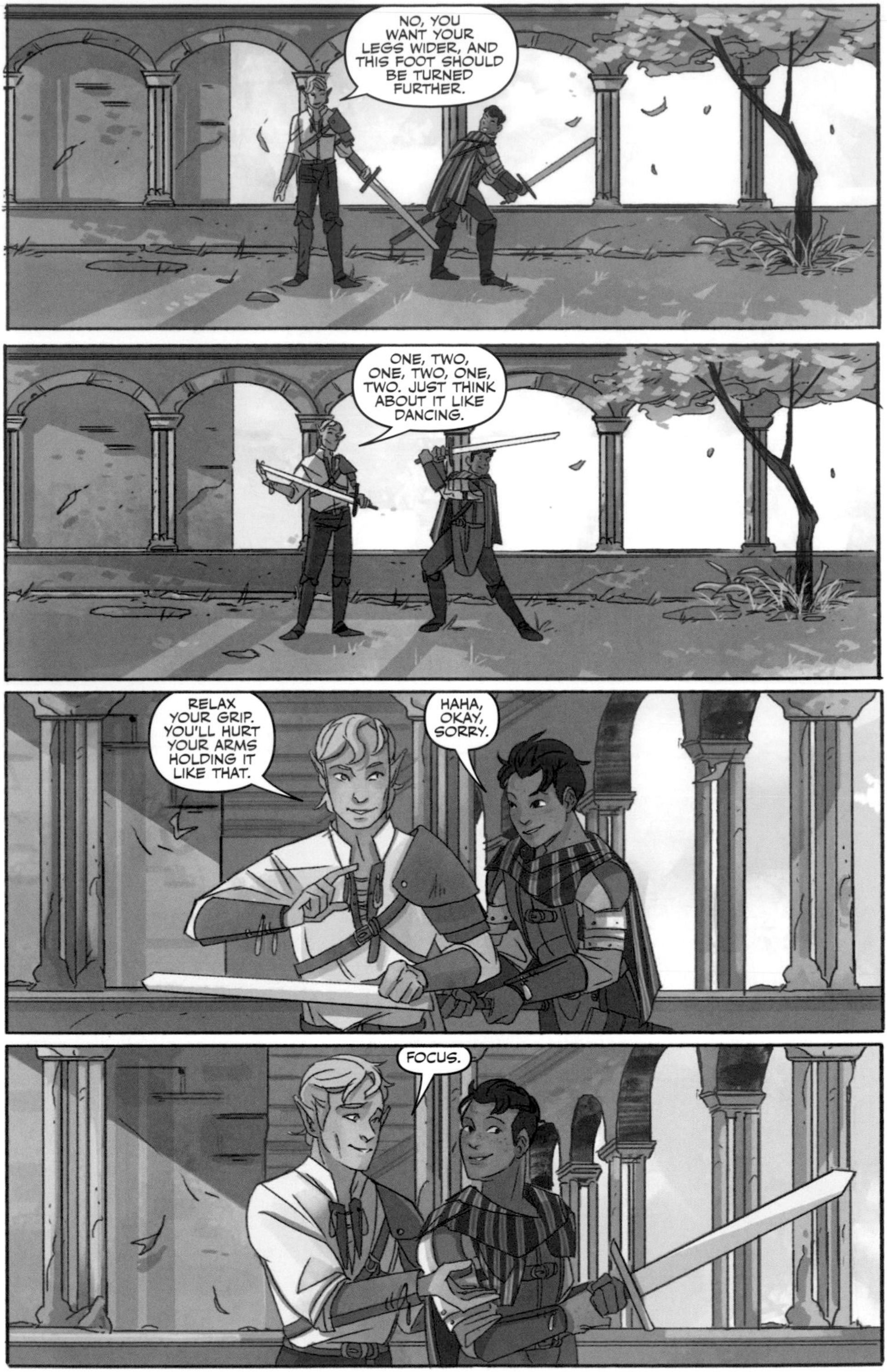
NO, YOU WANT YOUR LEGS WIDER, AND THIS FOOT SHOULD BE TURNED FURTHER.
ONE, TWO, ONE, TWO, ONE, TWO. JUST THINK ABOUT IT LIKE DANCING.
RELAX YOUR GRIP. YOU'LL HURT YOUR ARMS HOLDING IT LIKE THAT.
HAHA, OKAY, SORRY.
FOCUS.

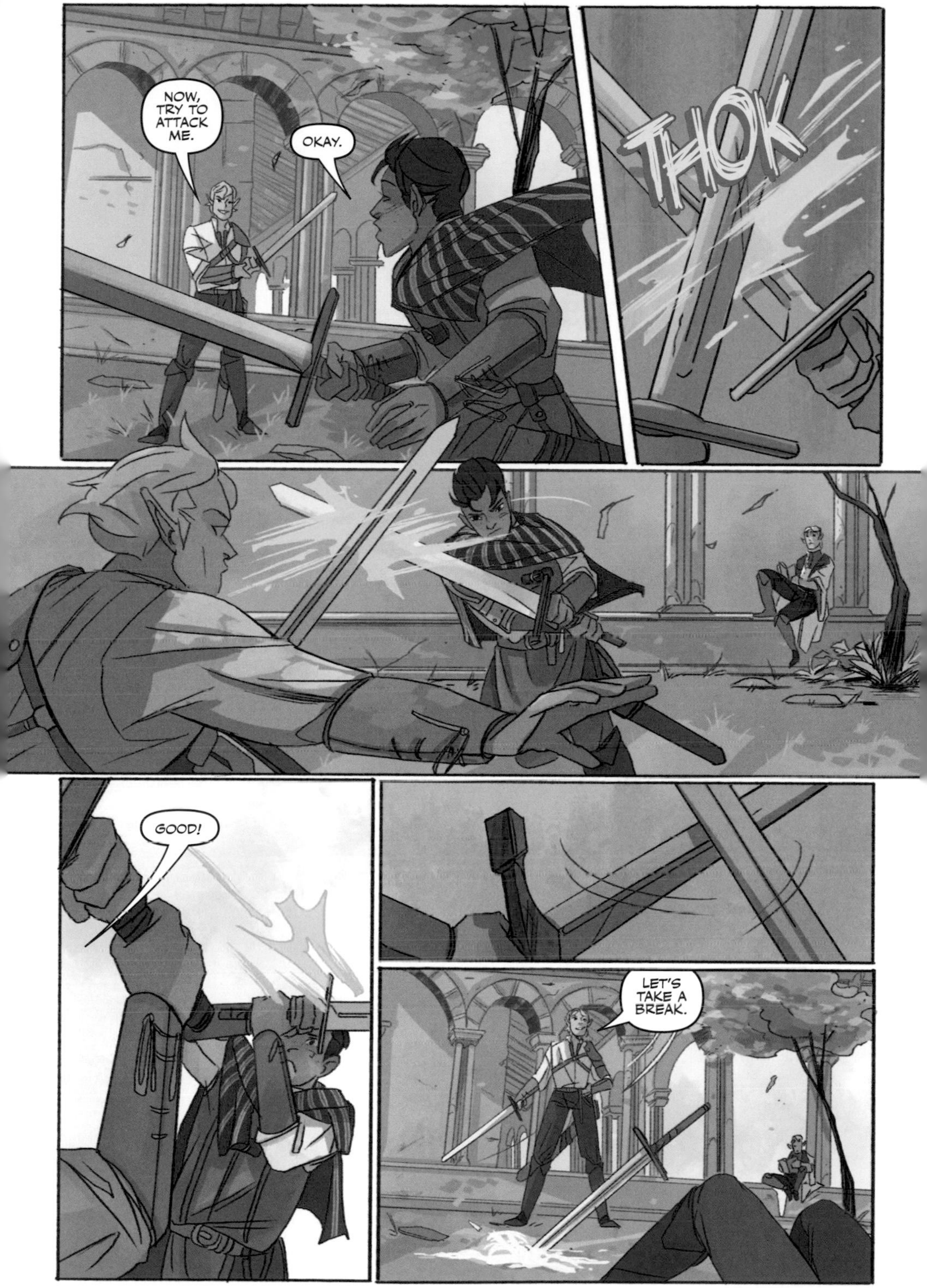
NOW, TRY TO ATTACK ME.
OKAY.
THOK
GOOD!
LET'S TAKE A BREAK.

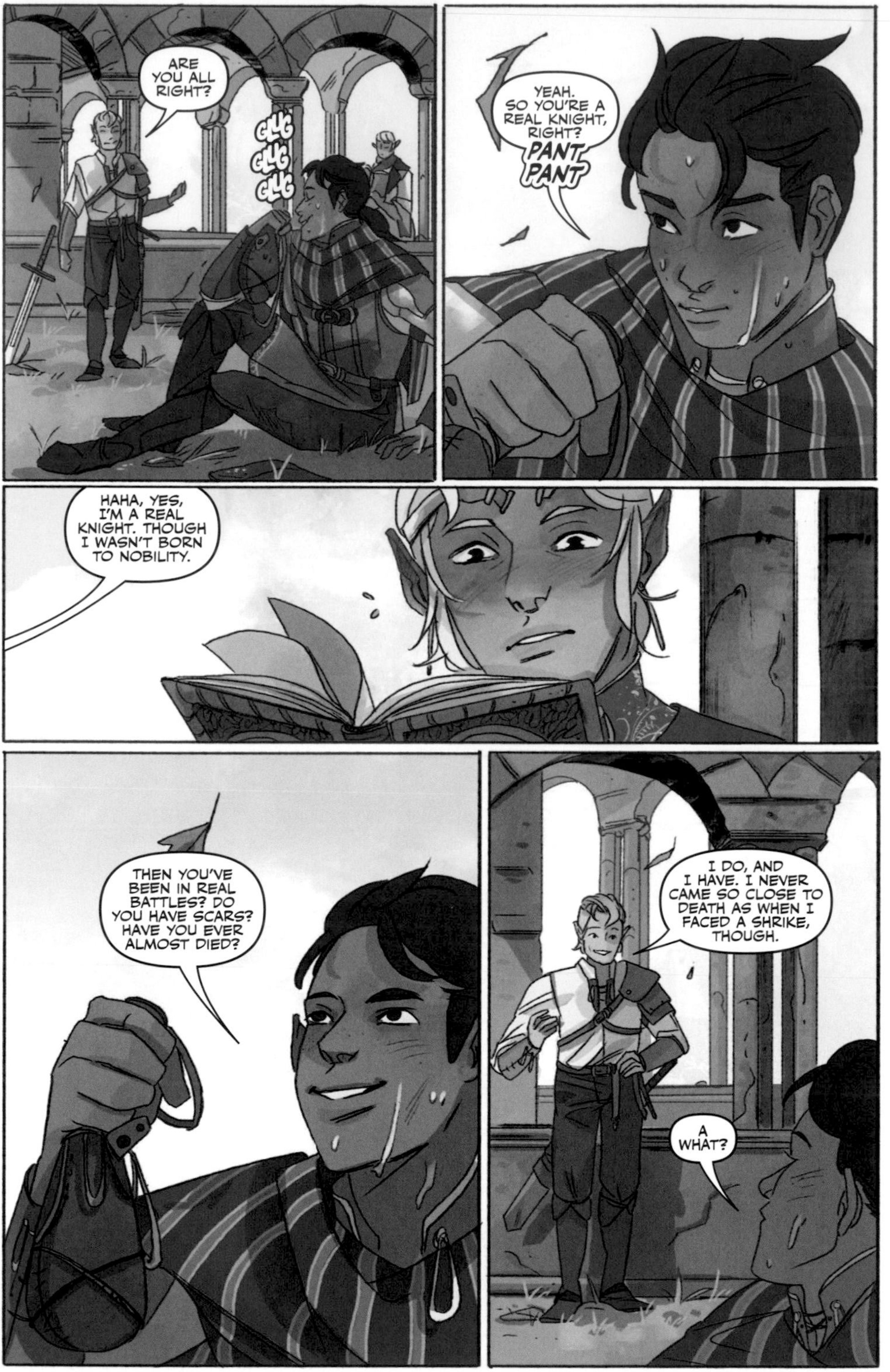
ARE YOU ALL RIGHT?
GLUG GLUG GLUG
YEAH. SO YOU'RE A REAL KNIGHT, RIGHT?
PANT PANT
HAHA, YES, I'M A REAL KNIGHT. THOUGH I WASN'T BORN TO NOBILITY.
THEN YOU'VE BEEN IN REAL BATTLES? DO YOU HAVE SCARS? HAVE YOU EVER ALMOST DIED?
I DO, AND I HAVE. I NEVER CAME SO CLOSE TO DEATH AS WHEN I FACED A SHRIKE, THOUGH.
A WHAT?

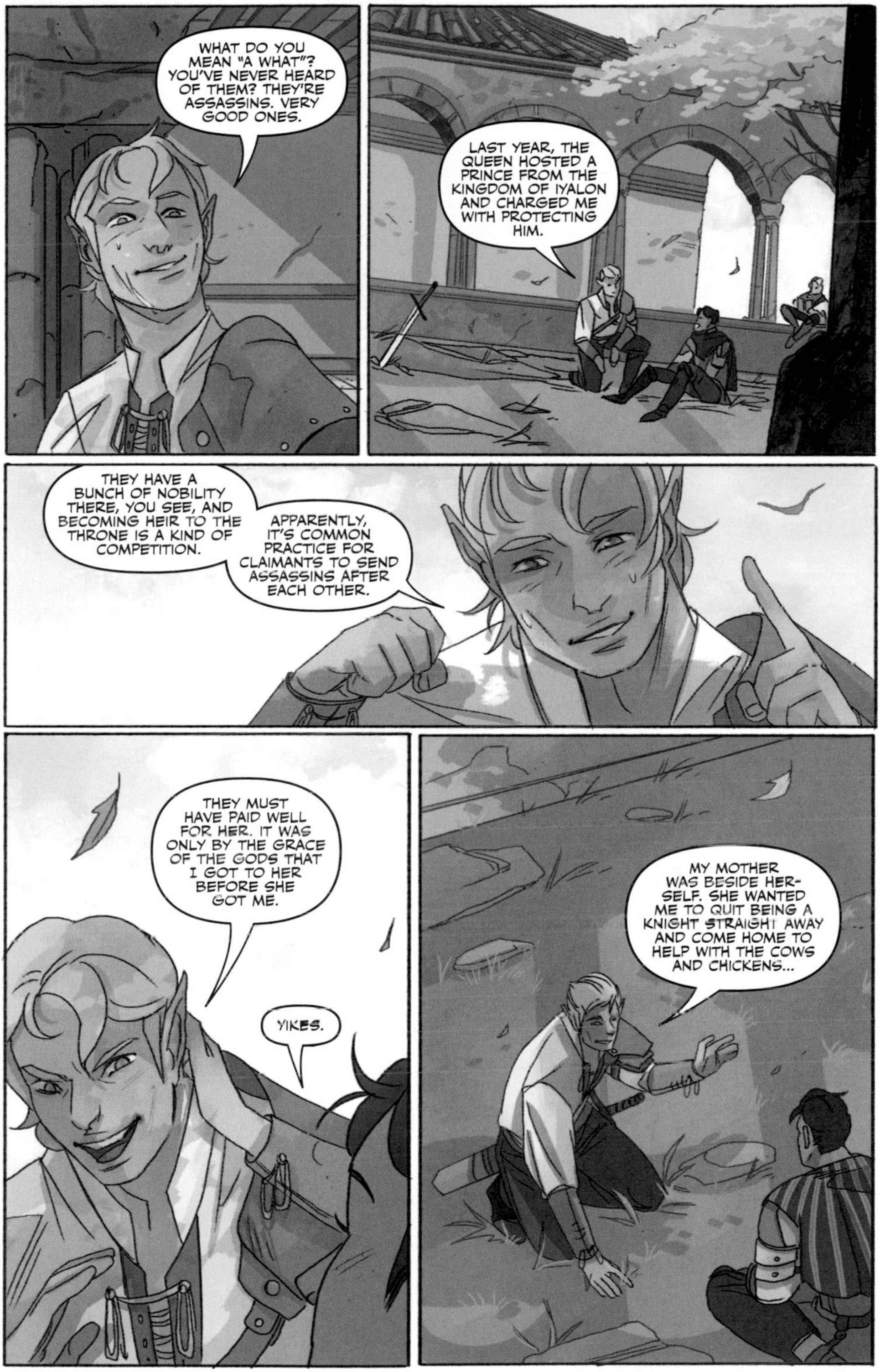
WHAT DO YOU MEAN "A WHAT"? YOU'VE NEVER HEARD OF THEM? THEY'RE ASSASSINS. VERY GOOD ONES.
LAST YEAR, THE QUEEN HOSTED A PRINCE FROM THE KINGDOM OF IYALON AND CHARGED ME WITH PROTECTING HIM.
THEY HAVE A BUNCH OF NOBILITY THERE, YOU SEE, AND BECOMING HEIR TO THE THRONE IS A KIND OF COMPETITION.
APPARENTLY, IT'S COMMON PRACTICE FOR CLAIMANTS TO SEND ASSASSINS AFTER EACH OTHER.
THEY MUST HAVE PAID WELL FOR HER. IT WAS ONLY BY THE GRACE OF THE GODS THAT I GOT TO HER BEFORE SHE GOT ME.
YIKES.
MY MOTHER WAS BESIDE HER-SELF. SHE WANTED ME TO QUIT BEING A KNIGHT STRAIGHT AWAY AND COME HOME TO HELP WITH THE COWS AND CHICKENS...

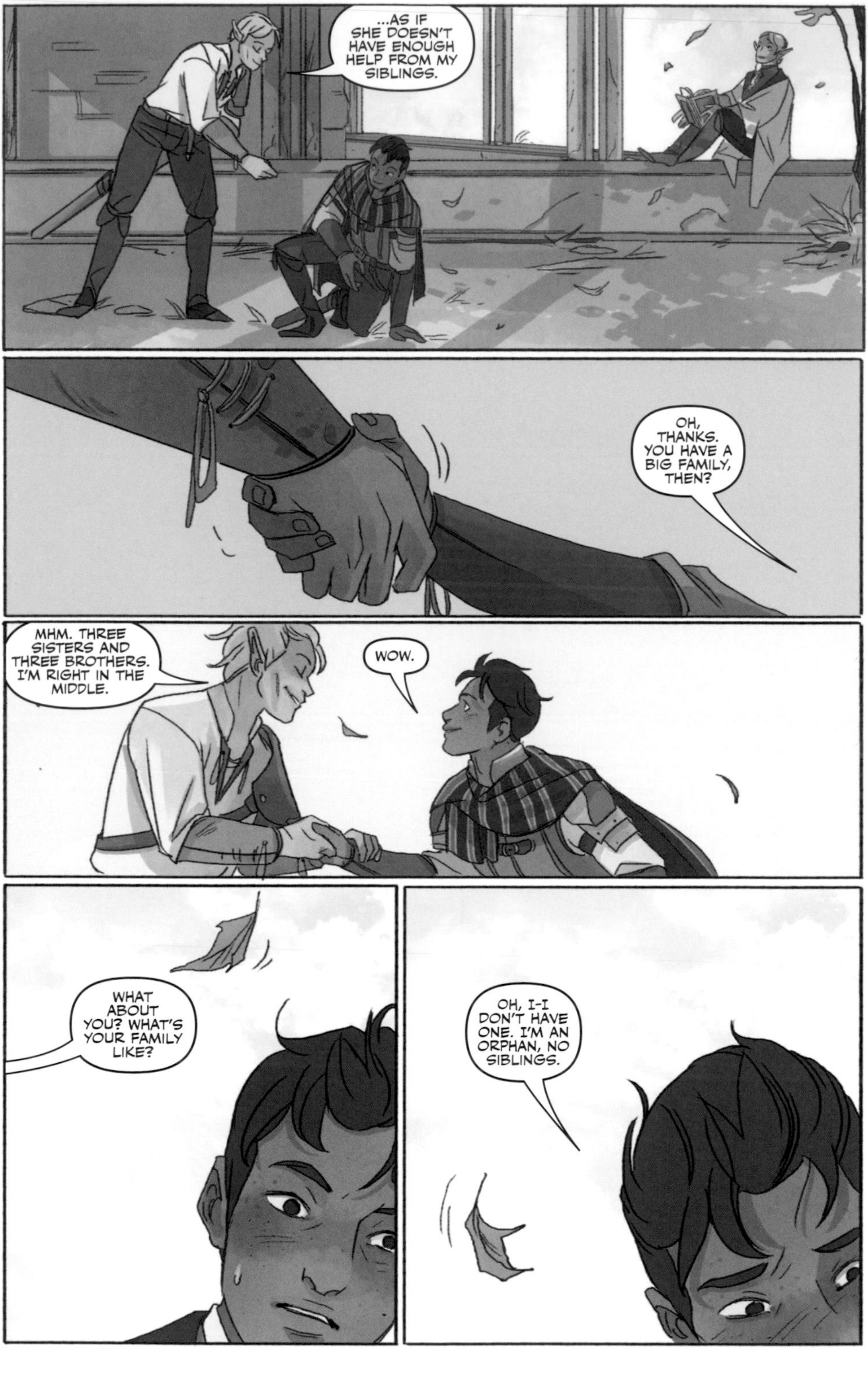
...AS IF SHE DOESN'T HAVE ENOUGH HELP FROM MY SIBLINGS.
OH, THANKS. YOU HAVE A BIG FAMILY, THEN?
MHM. THREE SISTERS AND THREE BROTHERS. I'M RIGHT IN THE MIDDLE.
WOW.
WHAT ABOUT YOU? WHAT'S YOUR FAMILY LIKE?
OH, I-I DON'T HAVE ONE. I'M AN ORPHAN, NO SIBLINGS.

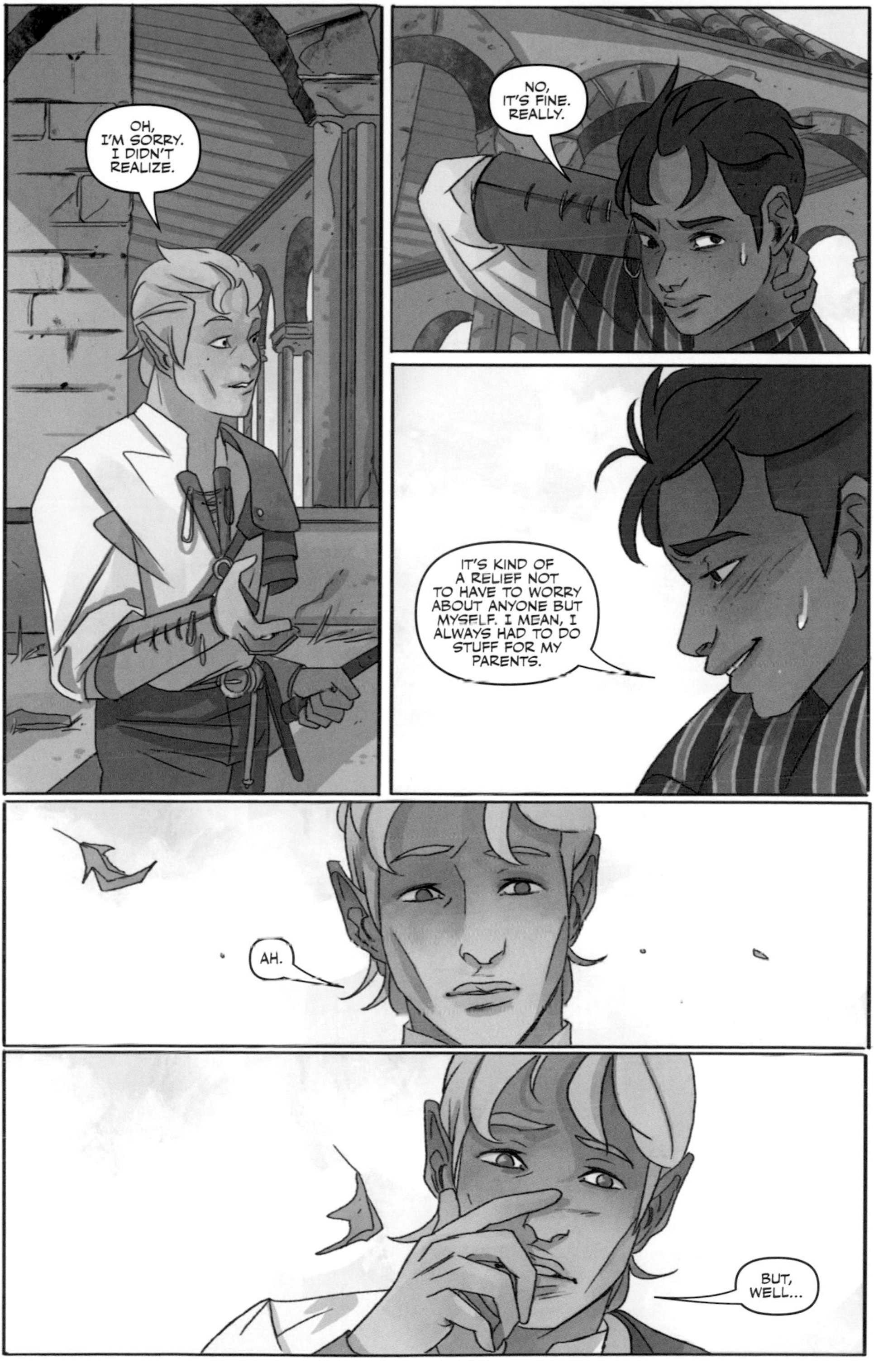
OH, I'M SORRY. I DIDN'T REALIZE.
NO, IT'S FINE. REALLY.
IT'S KIND OF A RELIEF NOT TO HAVE TO WORRY ABOUT ANYONE BUT MYSELF. I MEAN, I ALWAYS HAD TO DO STUFF FOR MY PARENTS.
AH.
BUT, WELL...

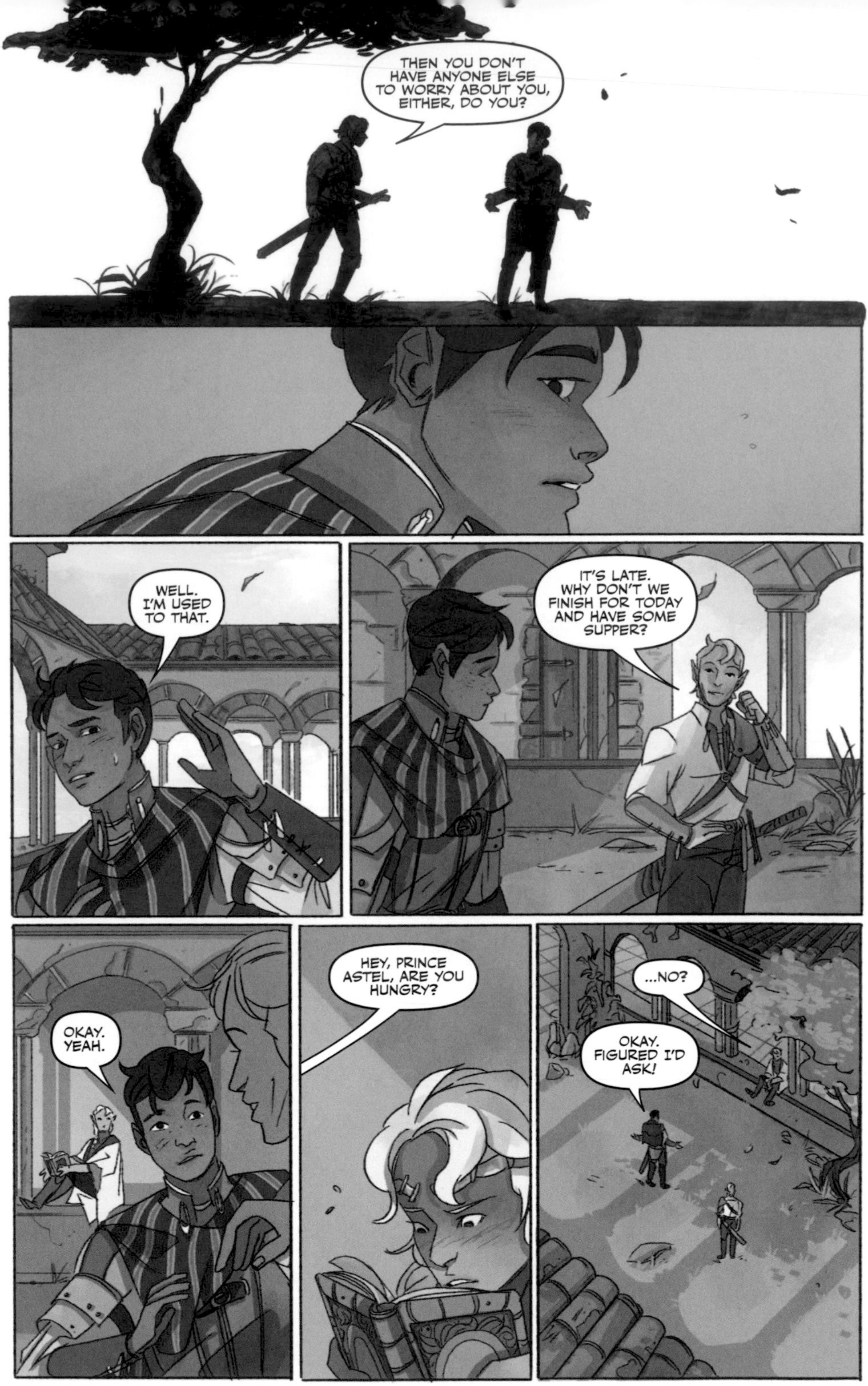
THEN YOU DON'T HAVE ANYONE ELSE TO WORRY ABOUT YOU, EITHER, DO YOU?
WELL. I'M USED TO THAT.
IT'S LATE. WHY DON'T WE FINISH FOR TODAY AND HAVE SOME SUPPER?
OKAY. YEAH.
HEY, PRINCE ASTEL, ARE YOU HUNGRY?
...NO?
OKAY. FIGURED I'D ASK!

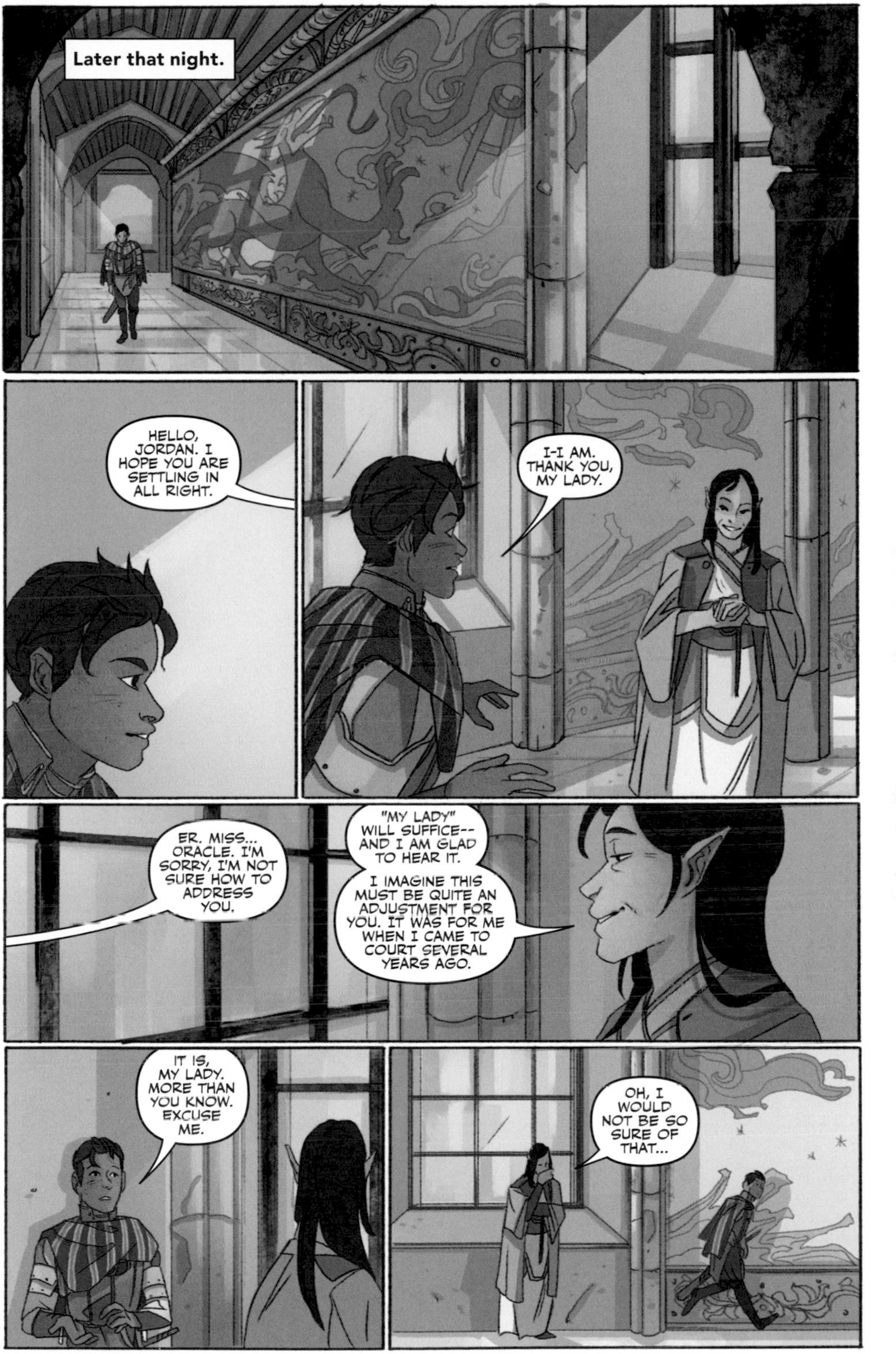
Later that night.
HELLO, JORDAN. I HOPE YOU ARE SETTLING IN ALL RIGHT.
I-I AM. THANK YOU, MY LADY.
ER. MISS... ORACLE. I'M SORRY, I'M NOT SURE HOW TO ADDRESS YOU.
"MY LADY" WILL SUFFICE-- AND I AM GLAD TO HEAR IT.
I IMAGINE THIS MUST BE QUITE AN ADJUSTMENT FOR YOU. IT WAS FOR ME WHEN I CAME TO COURT SEVERAL YEARS AGO.
IT IS, MY LADY. MORE THAN YOU KNOW. EXCUSE ME.
OH, I WOULD NOT BE SO SURE OF THAT...

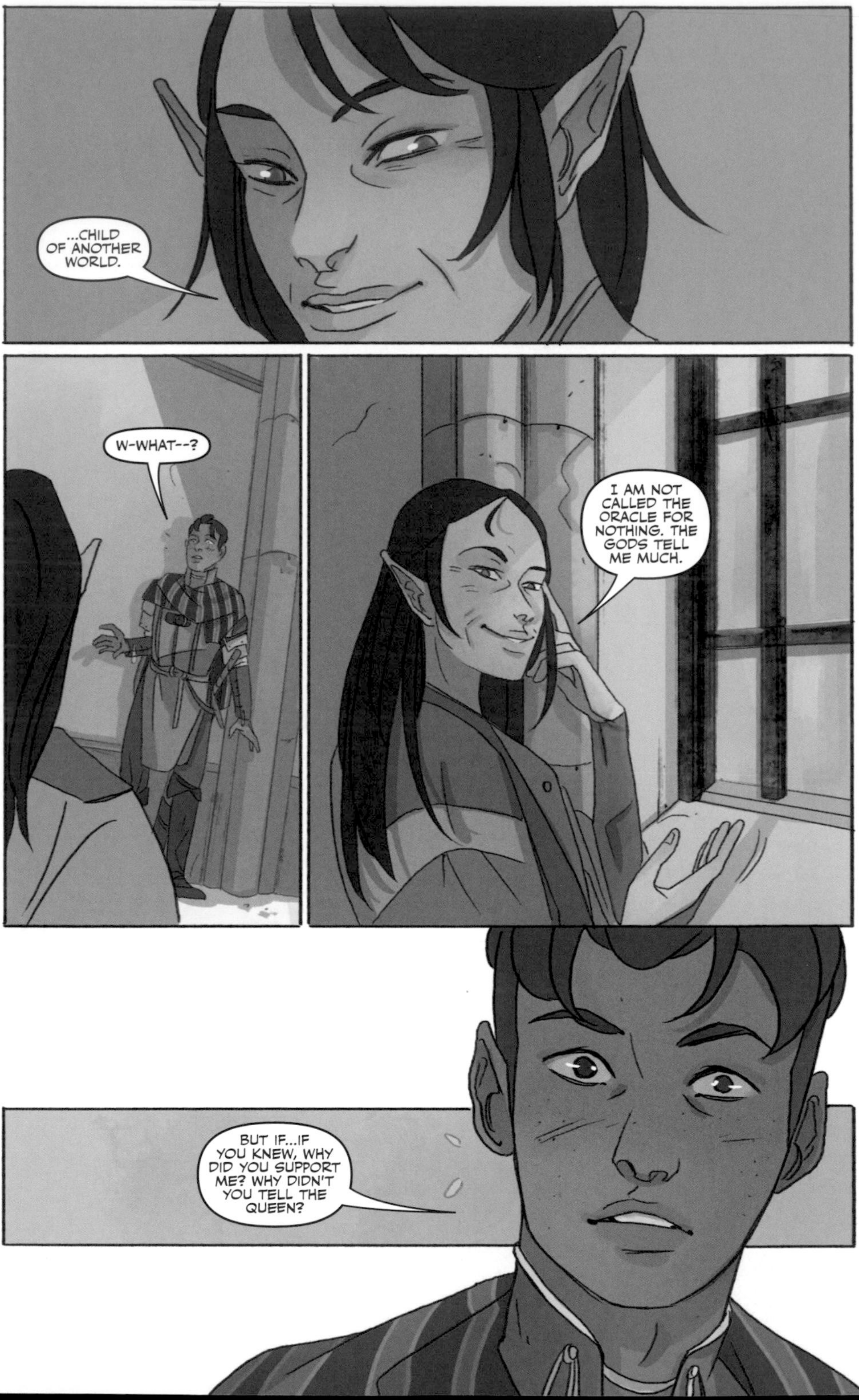
...CHILD OF ANOTHER WORLD.
W-WHAT--?
I AM NOT CALLED THE ORACLE FOR NOTHING. THE GODS TELL ME MUCH.
BUT IF...IF YOU KNEW, WHY DID YOU SUPPORT ME? WHY DIDN'T YOU TELL THE QUEEN?

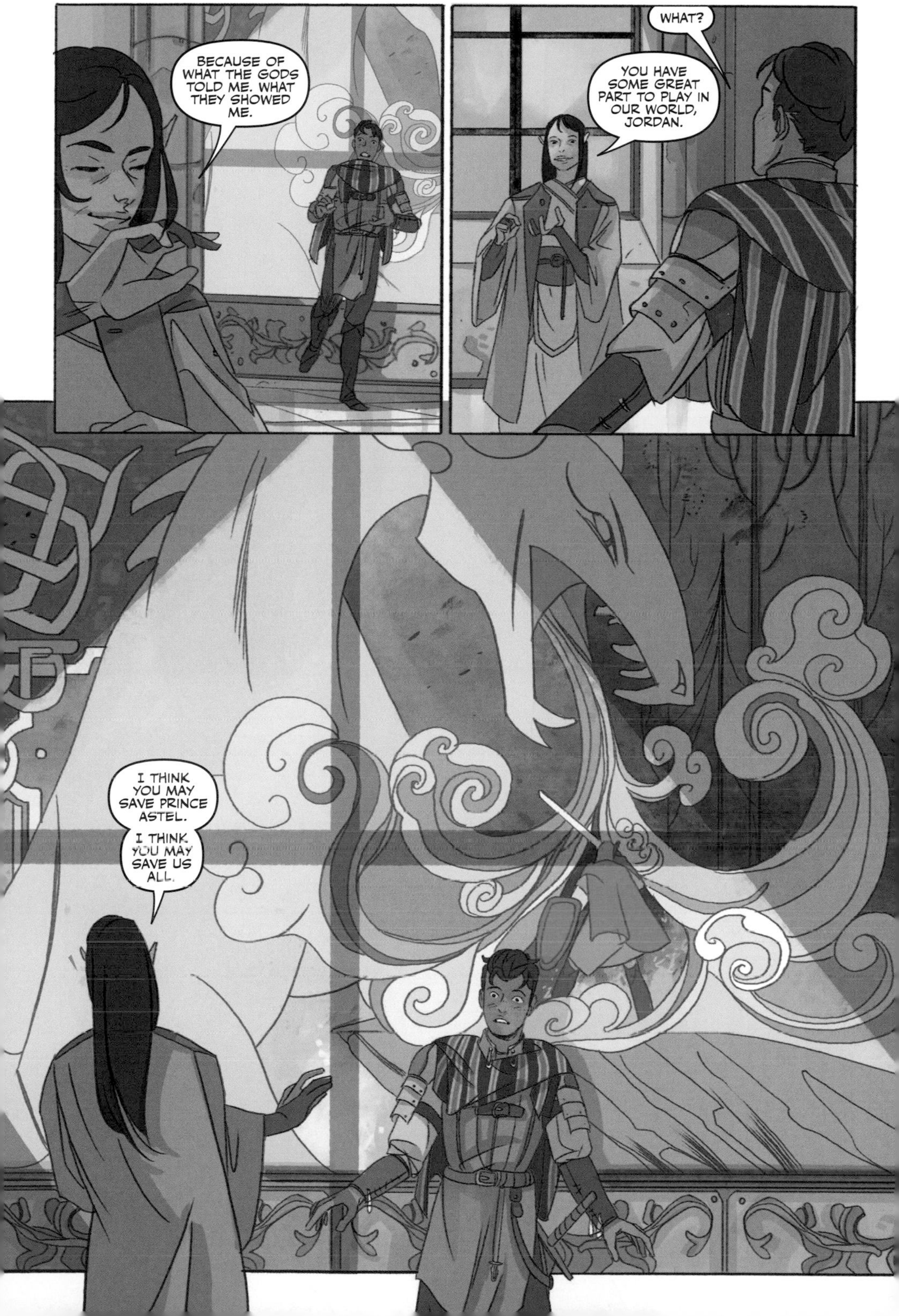
BECAUSE OF WHAT THE GODS TOLD ME. WHAT THEY SHOWED ME.
WHAT?
YOU HAVE SOME GREAT PART TO PLAY IN OUR WORLD, JORDAN.
I THINK YOU MAY SAVE PRINCE ASTEL.
I THINK YOU MAY SAVE US ALL.

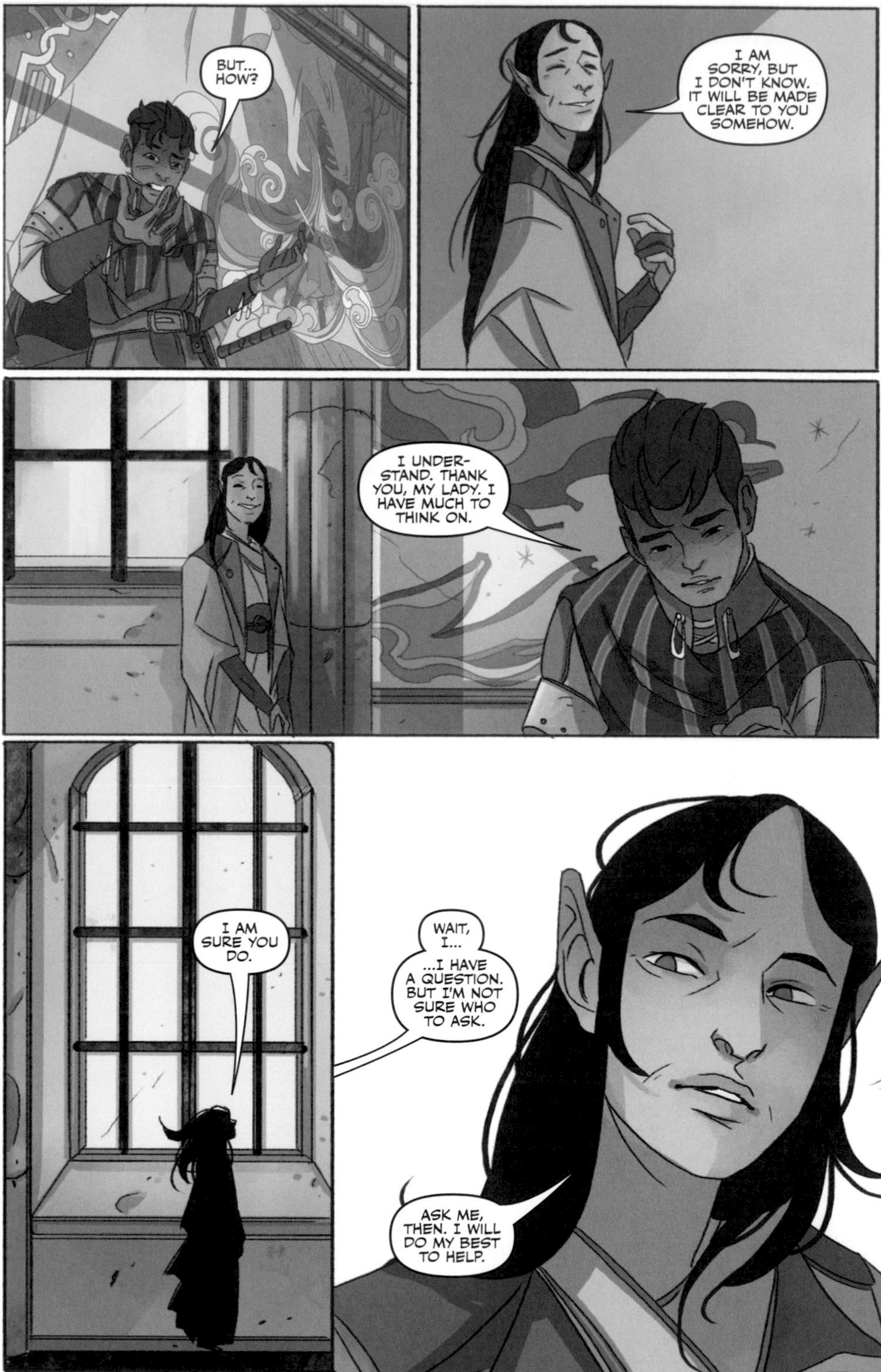
BUT... HOW?
I AM SORRY, BUT I DON'T KNOW. IT WILL BE MADE CLEAR TO YOU SOMEHOW.
I UNDER-STAND. THANK YOU, MY LADY. I HAVE MUCH TO THINK ON.
I AM SURE YOU DO.
WAIT, I...
...I HAVE A QUESTION. BUT I'M NOT SURE WHO TO ASK.
ASK ME, THEN. I WILL DO MY BEST TO HELP.

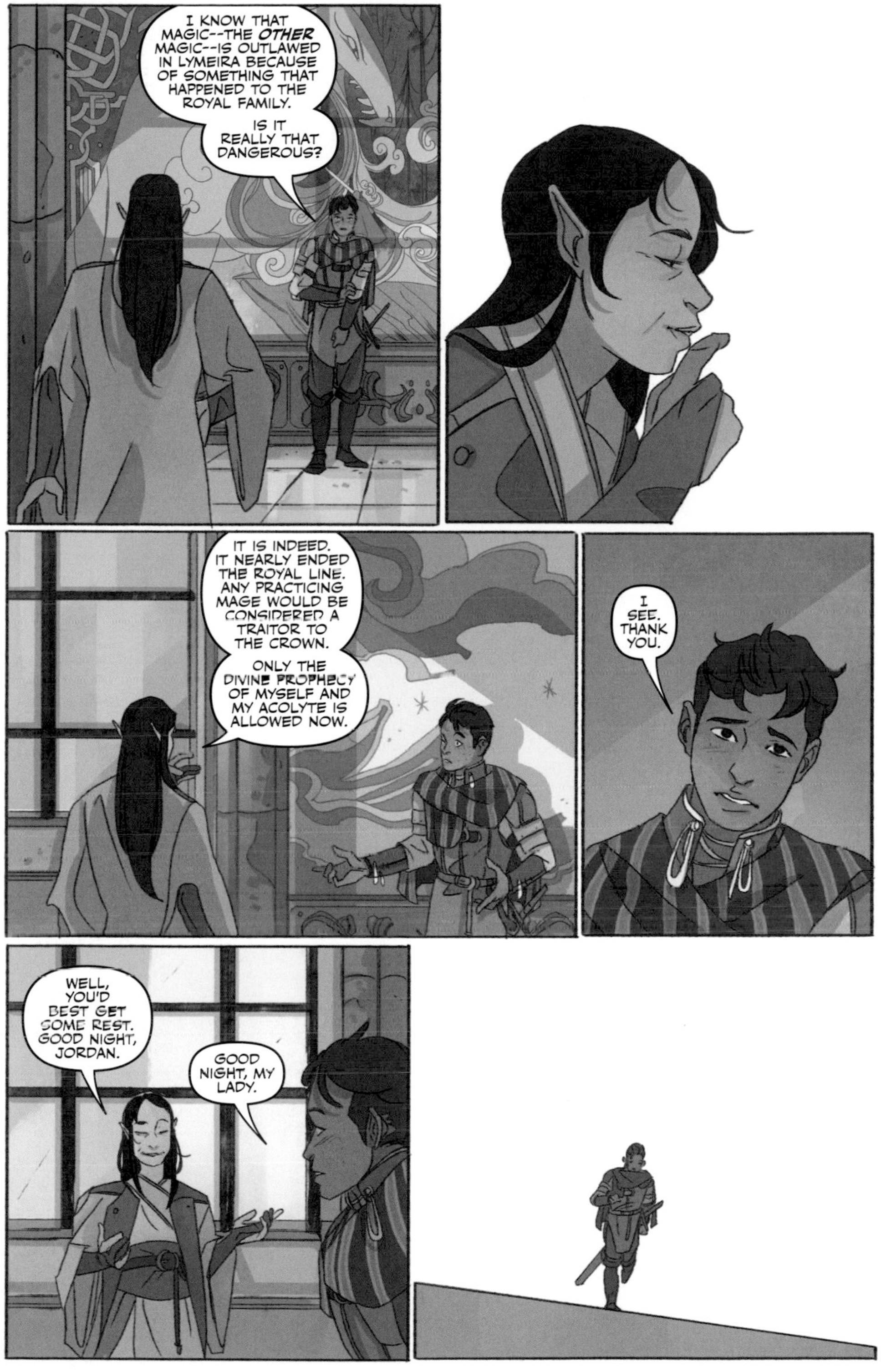
I KNOW THAT MAGIC--THE OTHER MAGIC--IS OUTLAWED IN LYMEIRA BECAUSE OF SOMETHING THAT HAPPENED TO THE ROYAL FAMILY.
IS IT REALLY THAT DANGEROUS?
IT IS INDEED. IT NEARLY ENDED THE ROYAL LINE. ANY PRACTICING MAGE WOULD BE CONSIDERED A TRAITOR TO THE CROWN.
ONLY THE DIVINE PROPHECY OF MYSELF AND MY ACOLYTE IS ALLOWED NOW.
I SEE. THANK YOU.
WELL, YOU'D BEST GET SOME REST. GOOD NIGHT, JORDAN.
GOOD NIGHT, MY LADY.

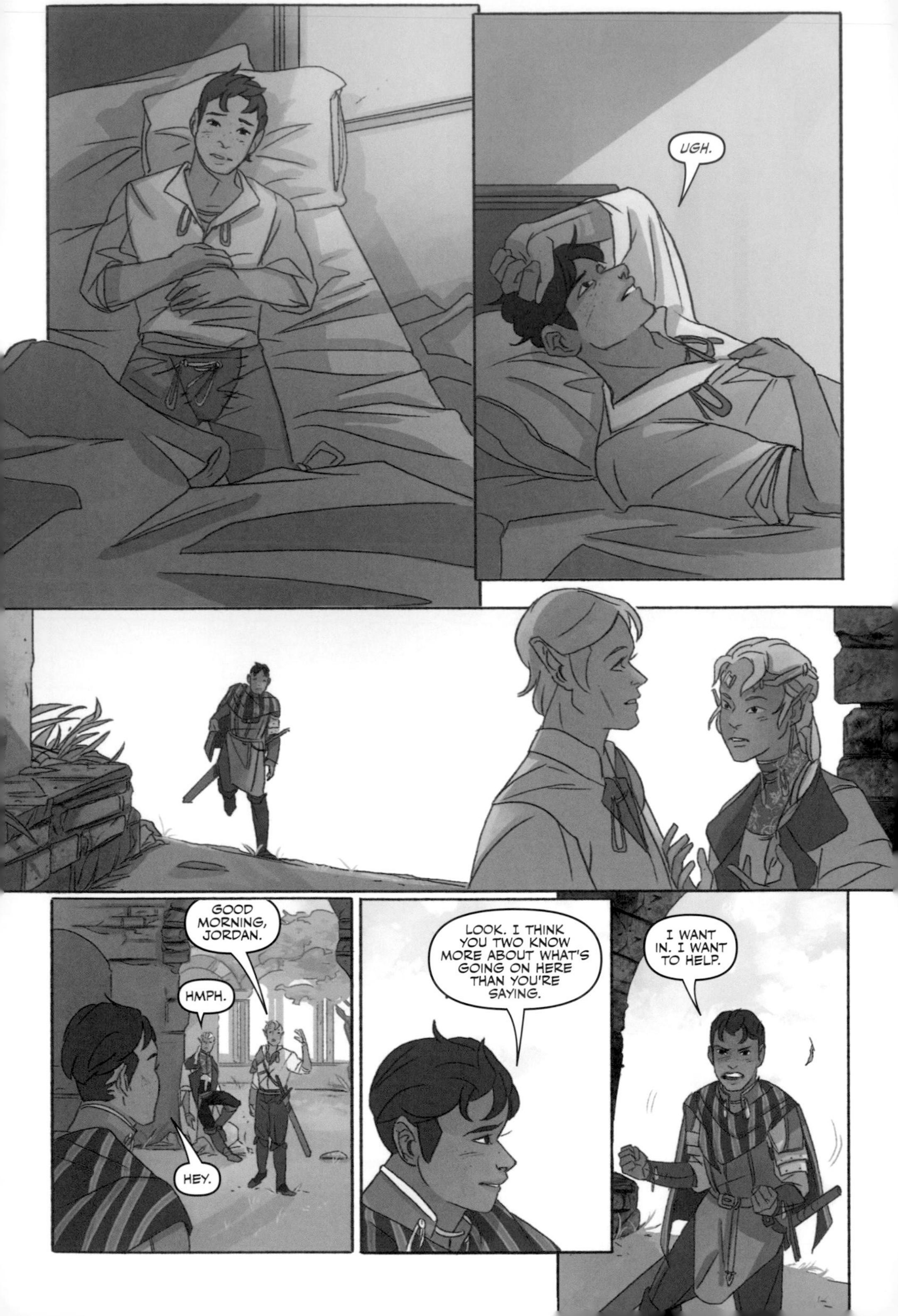
UGH.
GOOD MORNING, JORDAN.
HMPH.
HEY.
LOOK. I THINK YOU TWO KNOW MORE ABOUT WHAT'S GOING ON HERE THAN YOU'RE SAYING.
I WANT IN. I WANT TO HELP.

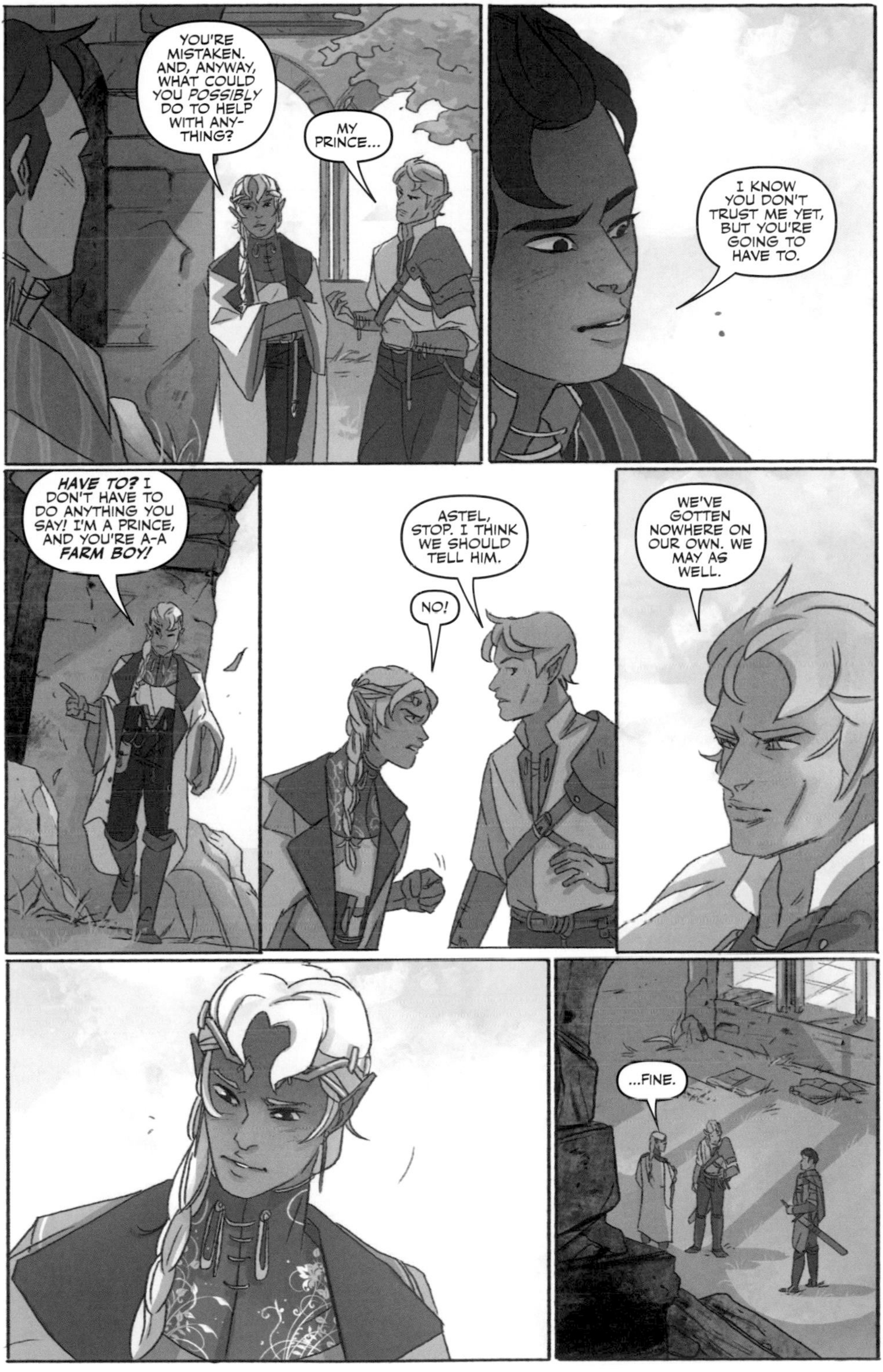
YOU'RE MISTAKEN. AND, ANYWAY, WHAT COULD YOU *POSSIBLY* DO TO HELP WITH ANY-THING?
MY PRINCE...
I KNOW YOU DON'T TRUST ME YET, BUT YOU'RE GOING TO HAVE TO.
***HAVE TO?*** I DON'T HAVE TO DO ANYTHING YOU SAY! I'M A PRINCE, AND YOU'RE A-A ***FARM BOY!***
ASTEL, STOP. I THINK WE SHOULD TELL HIM.
NO!
WE'VE GOTTEN NOWHERE ON OUR OWN. WE MAY AS WELL.
...FINE.

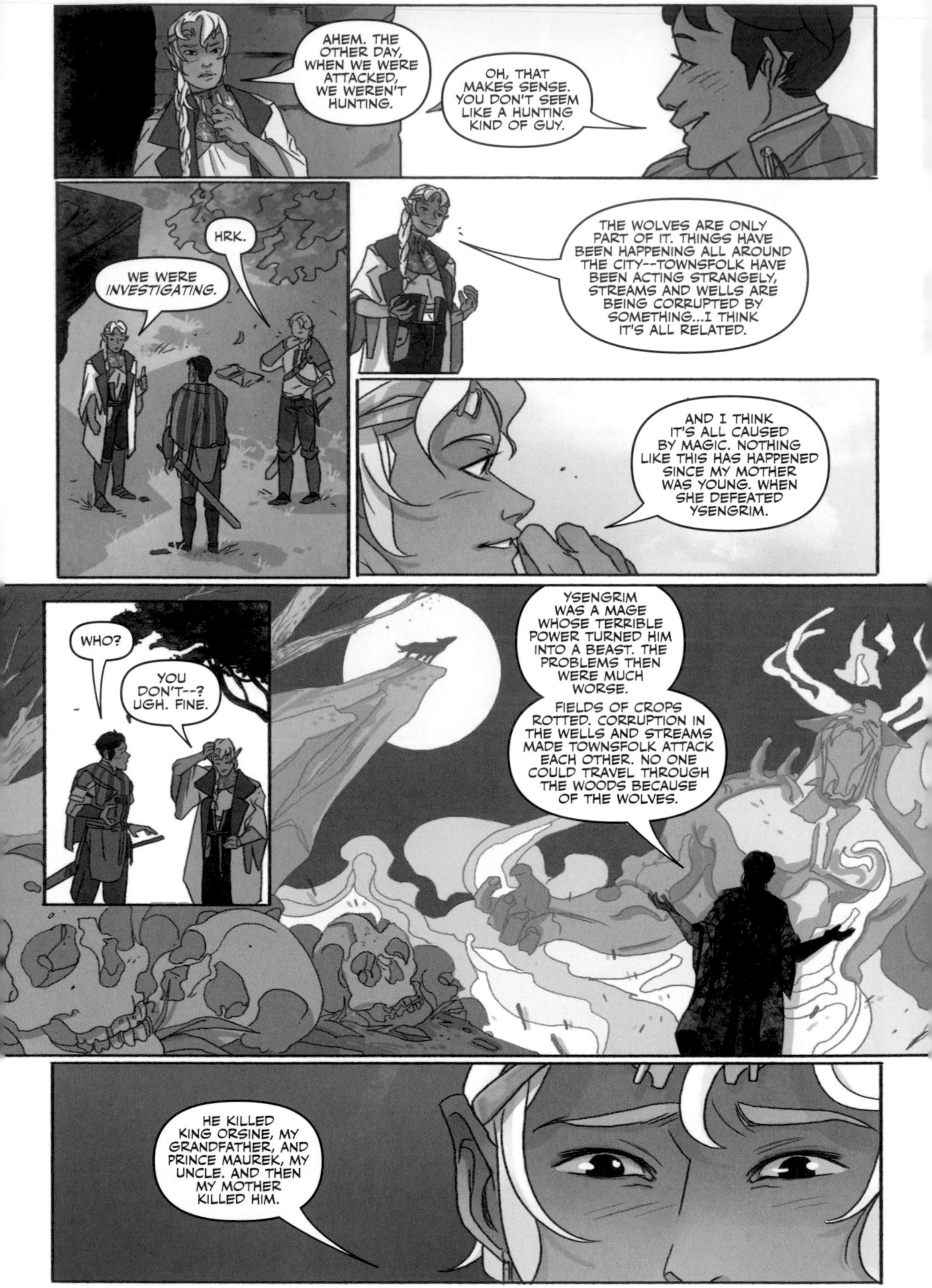
AHEM. THE OTHER DAY, WHEN WE WERE ATTACKED, WE WEREN'T HUNTING.
OH, THAT MAKES SENSE. YOU DON'T SEEM LIKE A HUNTING KIND OF GUY.
WE WERE *INVESTIGATING.*
HRK.
THE WOLVES ARE ONLY PART OF IT. THINGS HAVE BEEN HAPPENING ALL AROUND THE CITY--TOWNSFOLK HAVE BEEN ACTING STRANGELY, STREAMS AND WELLS ARE BEING CORRUPTED BY SOMETHING...I THINK IT'S ALL RELATED.
AND I THINK IT'S ALL CAUSED BY MAGIC. NOTHING LIKE THIS HAS HAPPENED SINCE MY MOTHER WAS YOUNG. WHEN SHE DEFEATED YSENGRIM.
WHO?
YOU DON'T--? UGH. FINE.
YSENGRIM WAS A MAGE WHOSE TERRIBLE POWER TURNED HIM INTO A BEAST. THE PROBLEMS THEN WERE MUCH WORSE.
FIELDS OF CROPS ROTTED. CORRUPTION IN THE WELLS AND STREAMS MADE TOWNSFOLK ATTACK EACH OTHER. NO ONE COULD TRAVEL THROUGH THE WOODS BECAUSE OF THE WOLVES.
HE KILLED KING ORSINE, MY GRANDFATHER, AND PRINCE MAUREK, MY UNCLE. AND THEN MY MOTHER KILLED HIM.

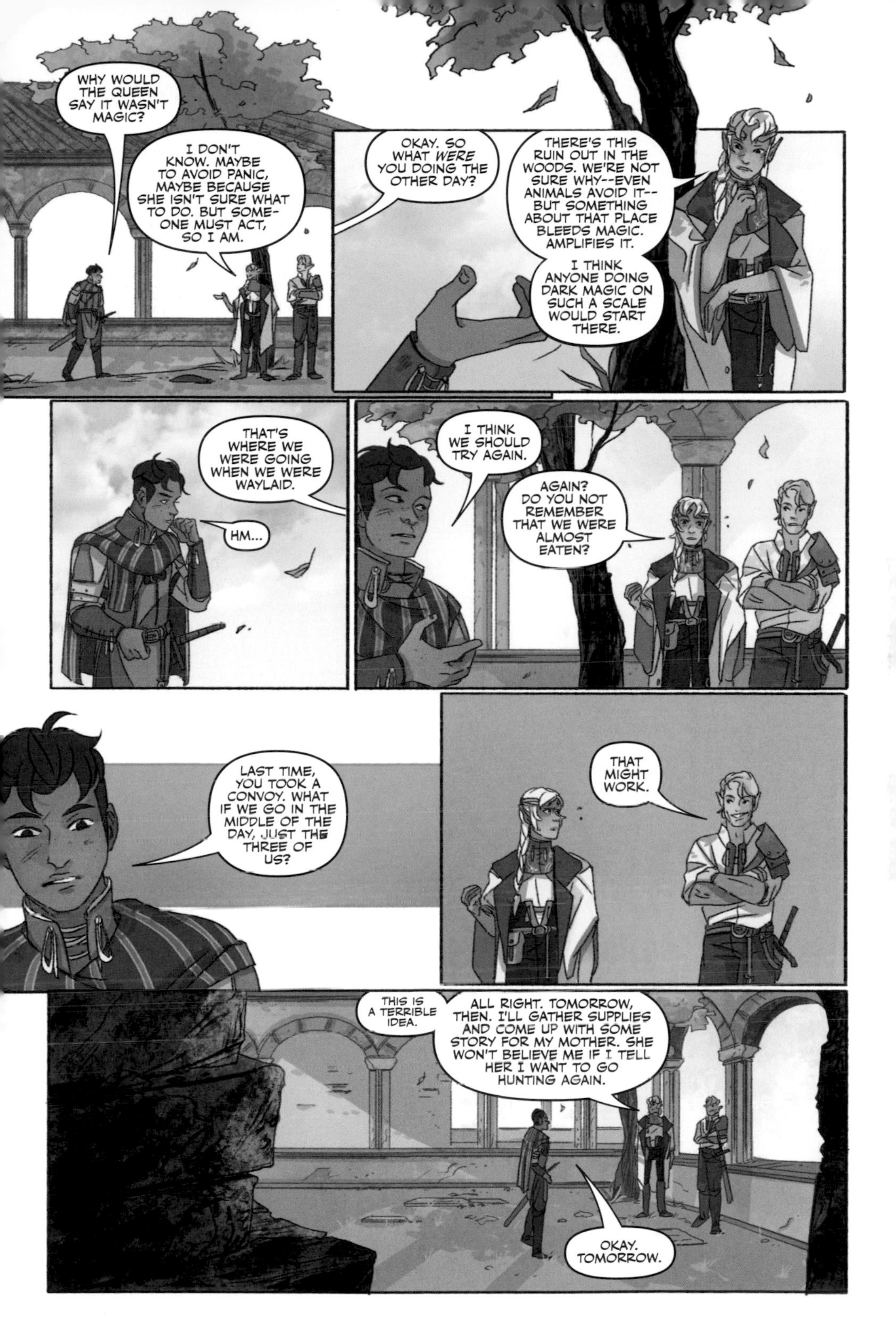
WHY WOULD THE QUEEN SAY IT WASN'T MAGIC?
I DON'T KNOW. MAYBE TO AVOID PANIC, MAYBE BECAUSE SHE ISN'T SURE WHAT TO DO. BUT SOME-ONE MUST ACT, SO I AM.
OKAY. SO WHAT *WERE* YOU DOING THE OTHER DAY?
THERE'S THIS RUIN OUT IN THE WOODS. WE'RE NOT SURE WHY--EVEN ANIMALS AVOID IT--BUT SOMETHING ABOUT THAT PLACE BLEEDS MAGIC. AMPLIFIES IT.
I THINK ANYONE DOING DARK MAGIC ON SUCH A SCALE WOULD START THERE.
THAT'S WHERE WE WERE GOING WHEN WE WERE WAYLAID.
HM...
I THINK WE SHOULD TRY AGAIN.
AGAIN? DO YOU NOT REMEMBER THAT WE WERE ALMOST EATEN?
LAST TIME, YOU TOOK A CONVOY. WHAT IF WE GO IN THE MIDDLE OF THE DAY, JUST THE THREE OF US?
THAT MIGHT WORK.
THIS IS A TERRIBLE IDEA.
ALL RIGHT. TOMORROW, THEN. I'LL GATHER SUPPLIES AND COME UP WITH SOME STORY FOR MY MOTHER. SHE WON'T BELIEVE ME IF I TELL HER I WANT TO GO HUNTING AGAIN.
OKAY. TOMORROW.

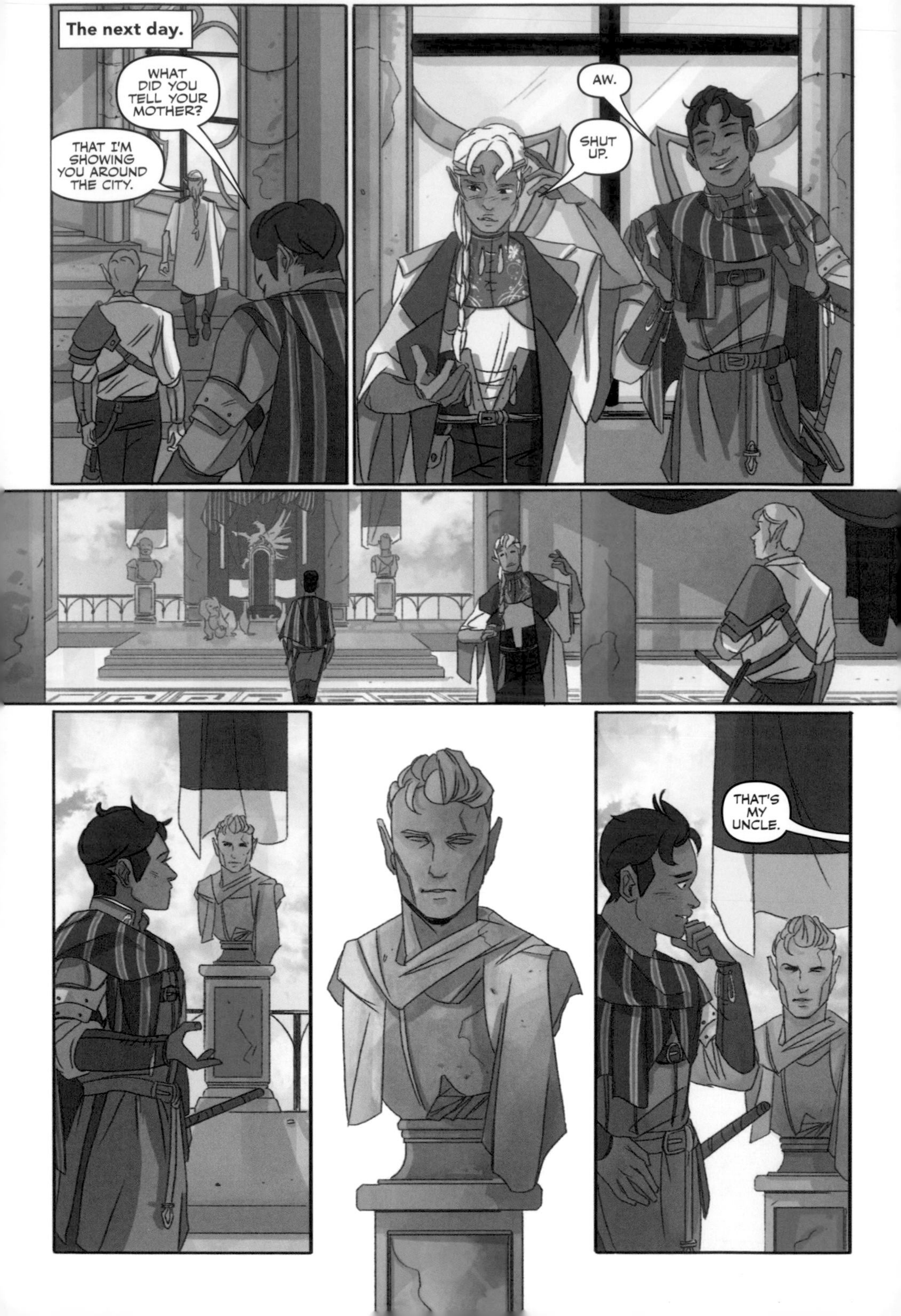
The next day.
WHAT DID YOU TELL YOUR MOTHER?
THAT I'M SHOWING YOU AROUND THE CITY.
AW.
SHUT UP.
THAT'S MY UNCLE.

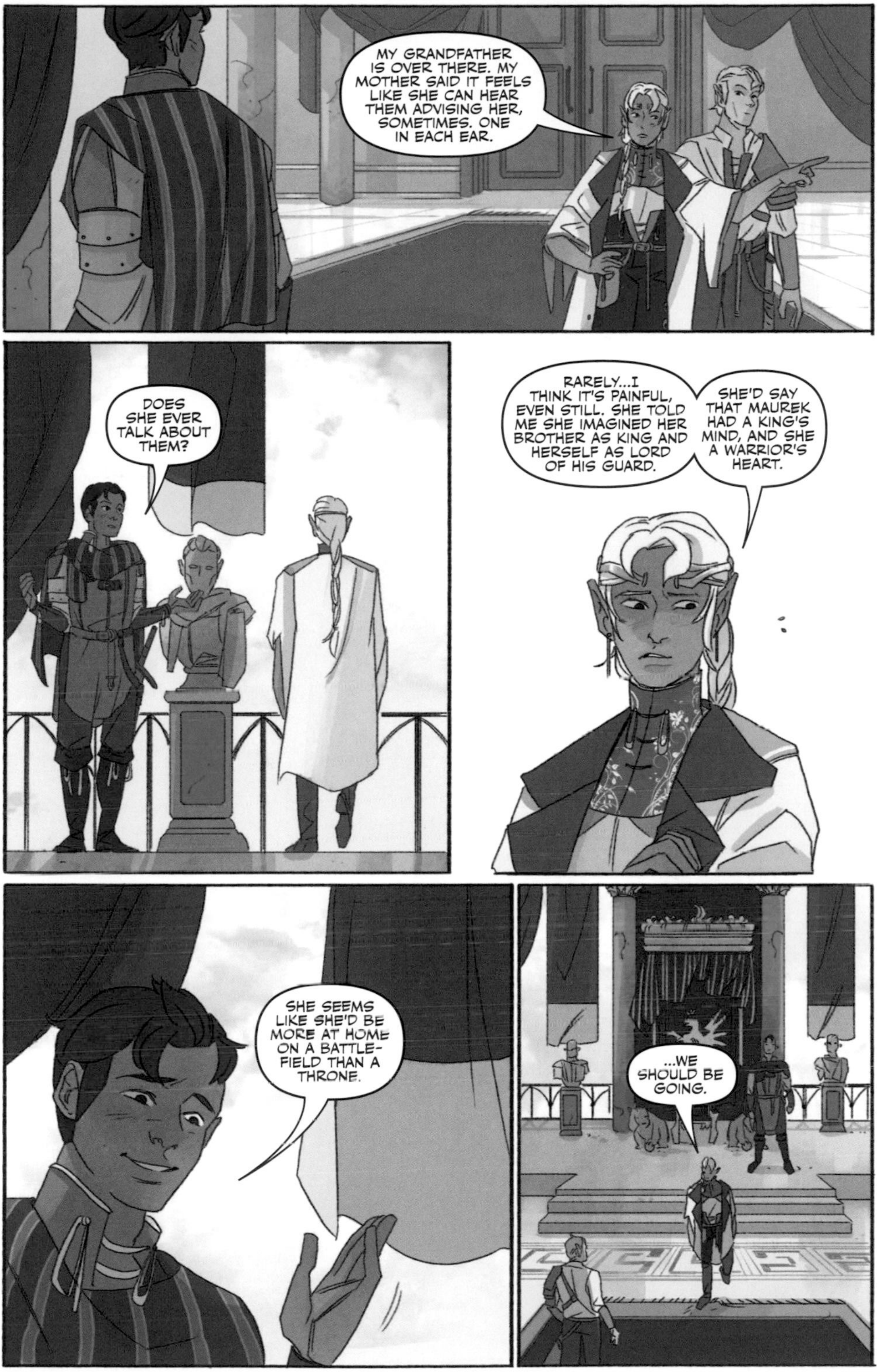
MY GRANDFATHER IS OVER THERE. MY MOTHER SAID IT FEELS LIKE SHE CAN HEAR THEM ADVISING HER, SOMETIMES. ONE IN EACH EAR.
DOES SHE EVER TALK ABOUT THEM?
RARELY...I THINK IT'S PAINFUL, EVEN STILL. SHE TOLD ME SHE IMAGINED HER BROTHER AS KING AND HERSELF AS LORD OF HIS GUARD.
SHE'D SAY THAT MAUREK HAD A KING'S MIND, AND SHE A WARRIOR'S HEART.
SHE SEEMS LIKE SHE'D BE MORE AT HOME ON A BATTLE-FIELD THAN A THRONE.
...WE SHOULD BE GOING.

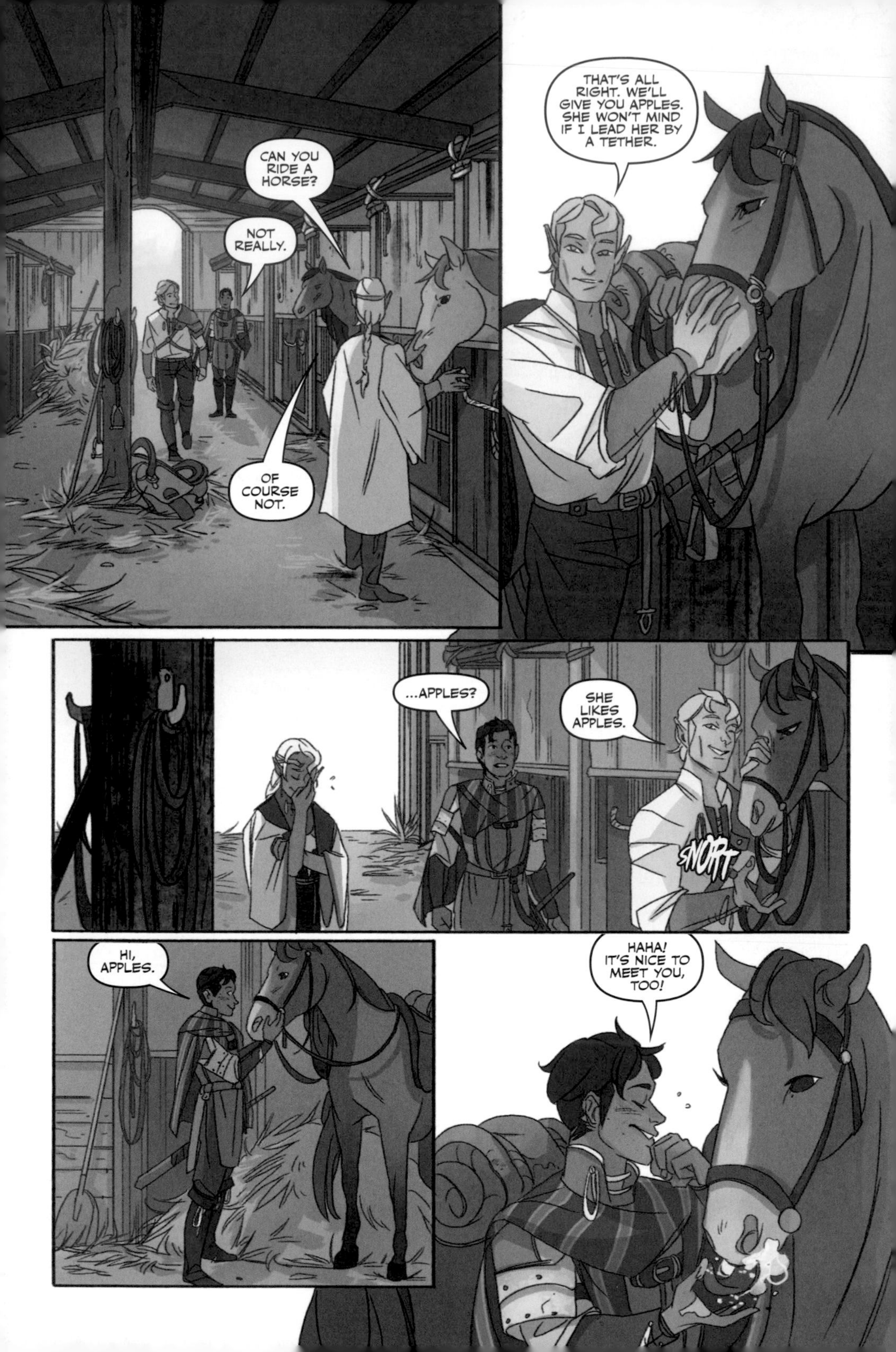
CAN YOU RIDE A HORSE?
NOT REALLY.
OF COURSE NOT.
THAT'S ALL RIGHT. WE'LL GIVE YOU APPLES. SHE WON'T MIND IF I LEAD HER BY A TETHER.
...APPLES?
SHE LIKES APPLES.
SNORT
HI, APPLES.
HAHA! IT'S NICE TO MEET YOU, TOO!

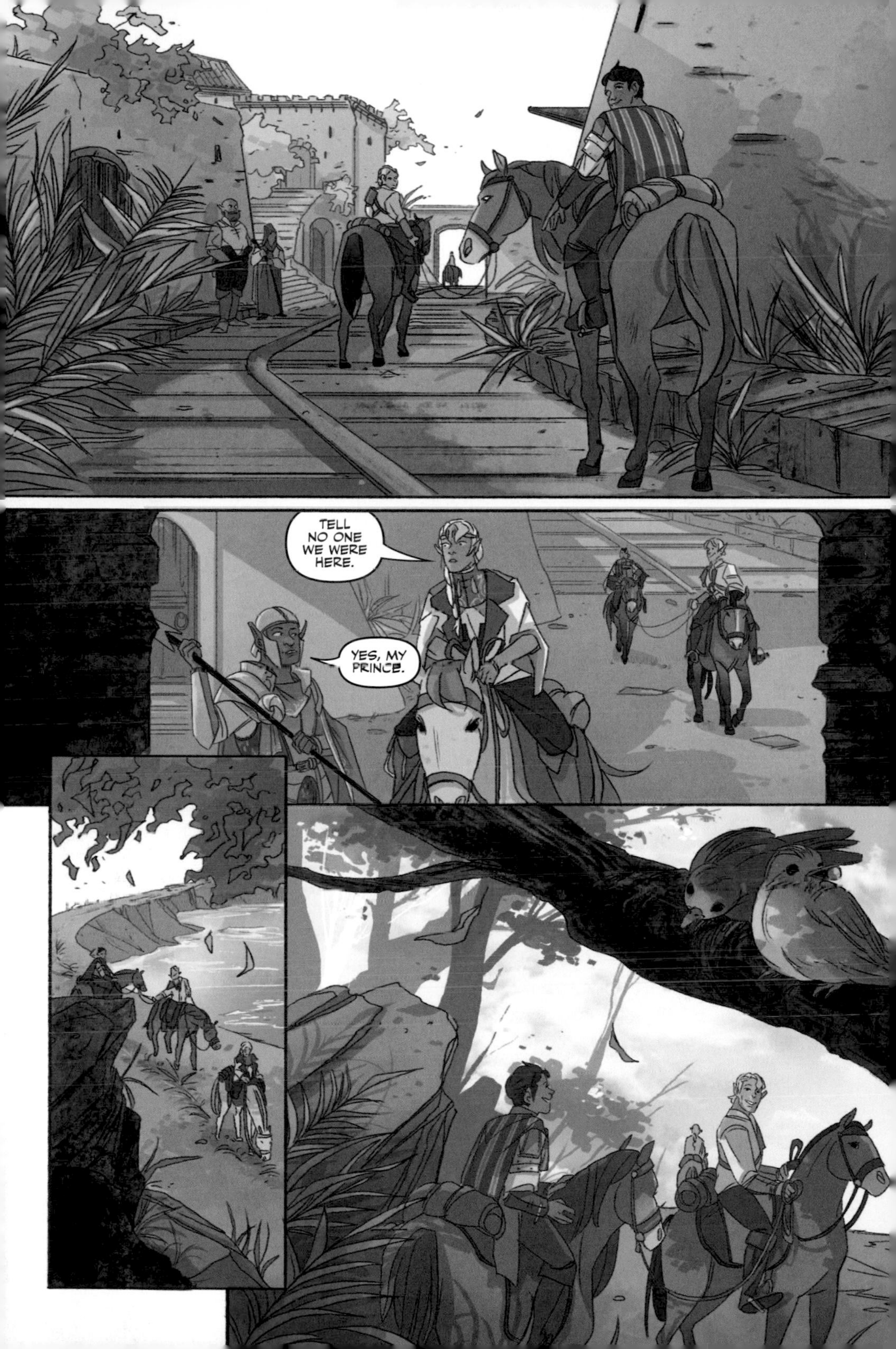
TELL NO ONE WE WERE HERE.
YES, MY PRINCE.

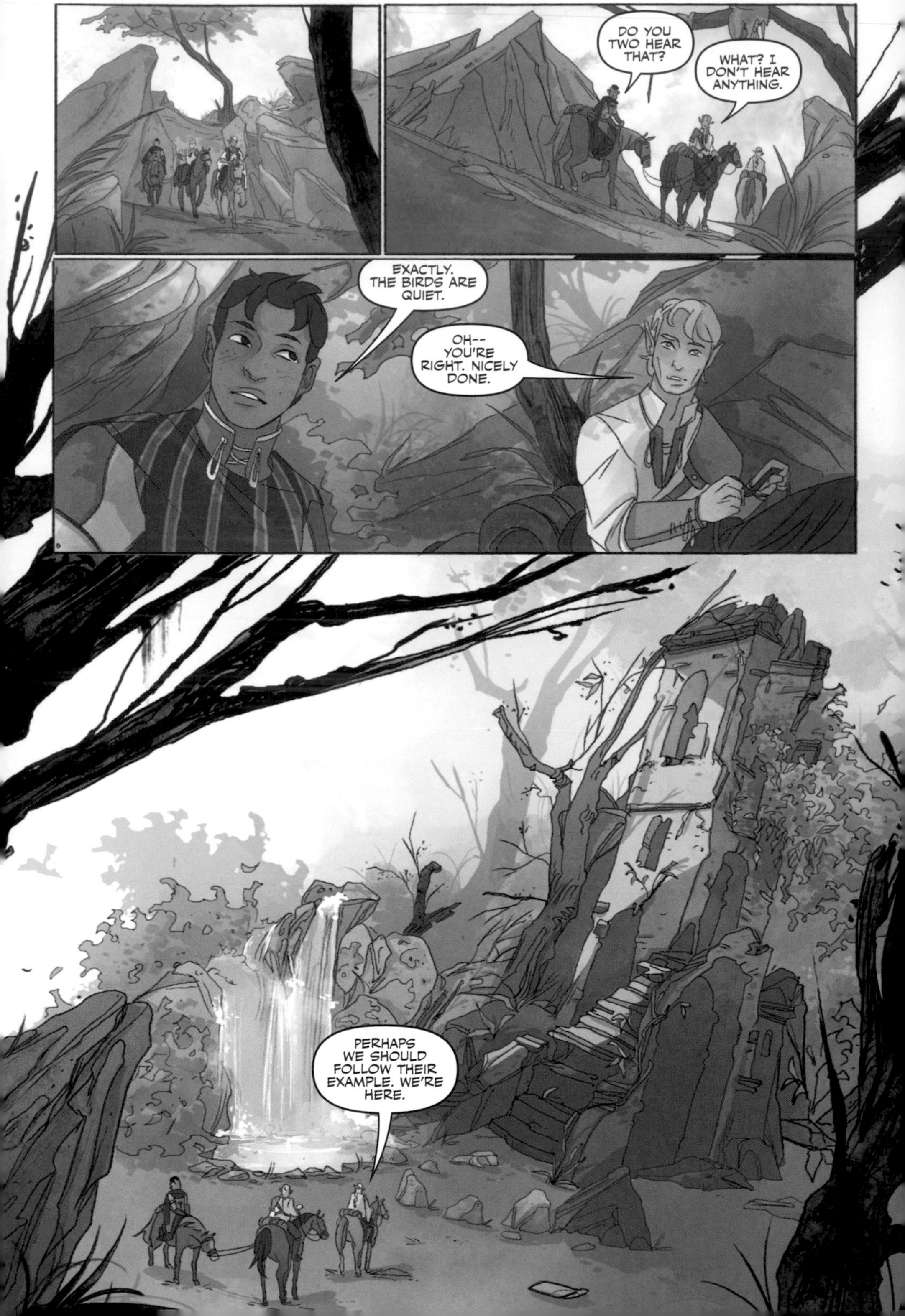
DO YOU TWO HEAR THAT?
WHAT? I DON'T HEAR ANYTHING.
EXACTLY. THE BIRDS ARE QUIET.
OH-- YOU'RE RIGHT. NICELY DONE.
PERHAPS WE SHOULD FOLLOW THEIR EXAMPLE. WE'RE HERE.

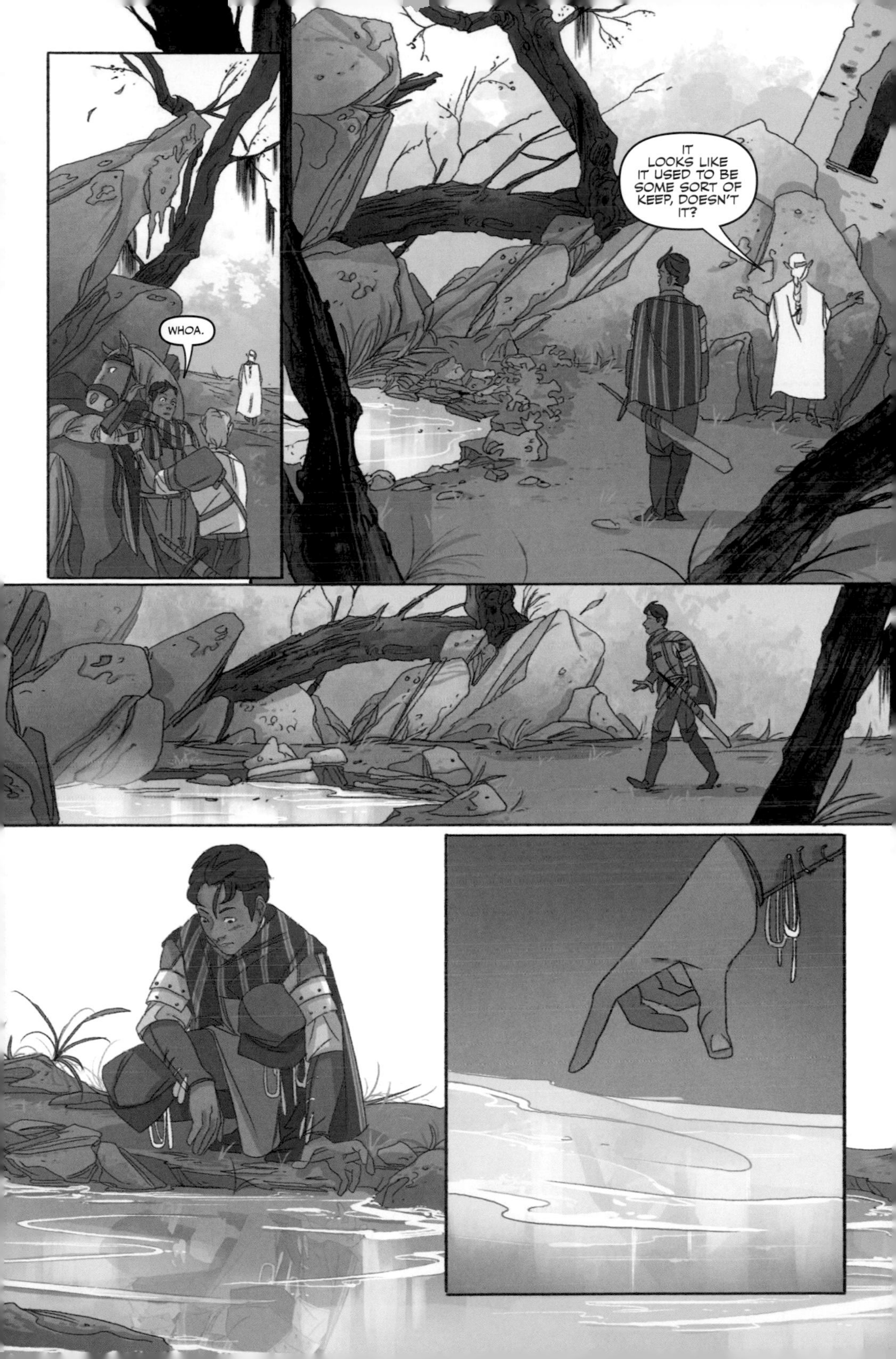
WHOA.
IT LOOKS LIKE IT USED TO BE SOME SORT OF KEEP, DOESN'T IT?

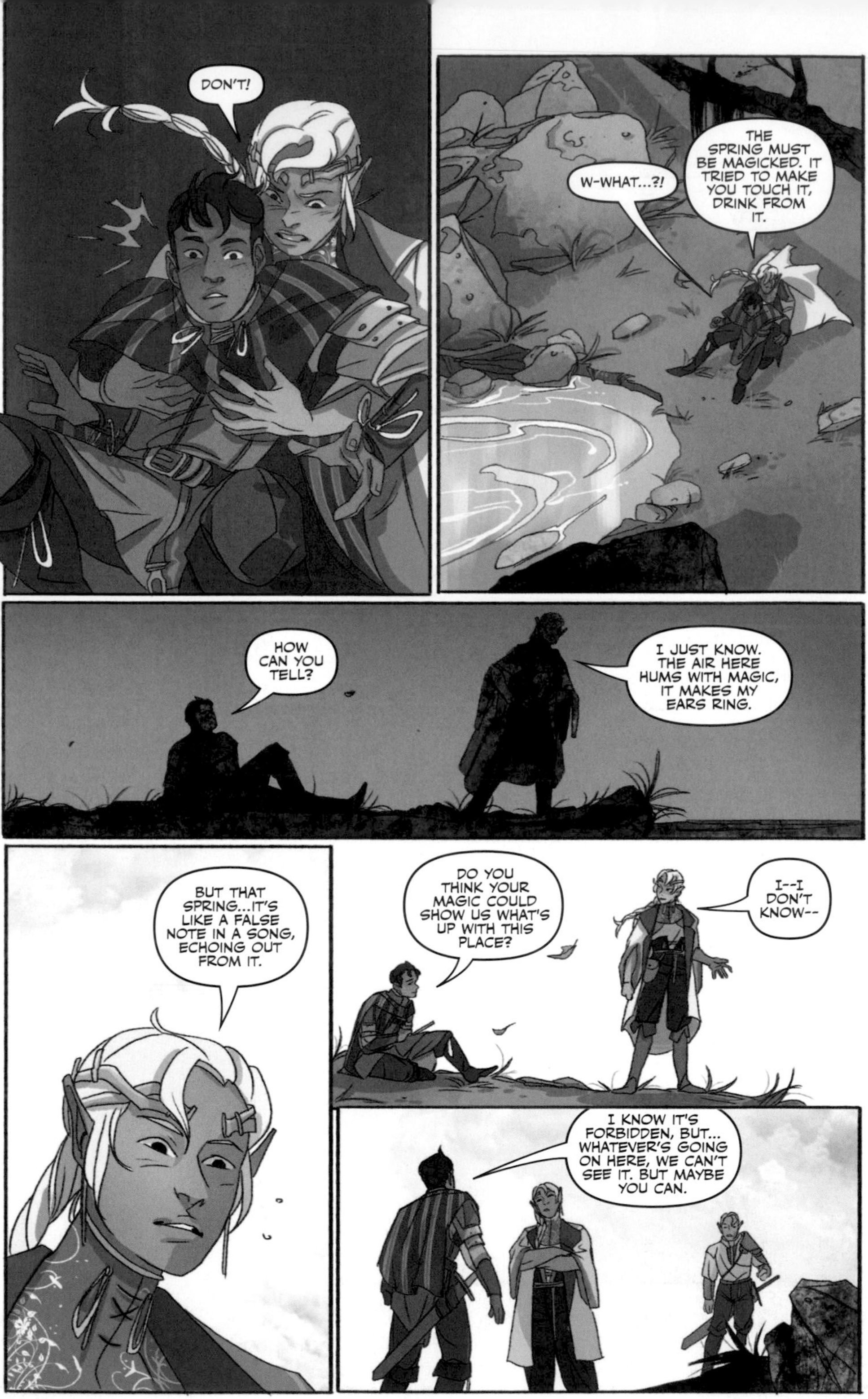
DON'T!
W-WHAT...?!
THE SPRING MUST BE MAGICKED. IT TRIED TO MAKE YOU TOUCH IT, DRINK FROM IT.
HOW CAN YOU TELL?
I JUST KNOW. THE AIR HERE HUMS WITH MAGIC, IT MAKES MY EARS RING.
BUT THAT SPRING...IT'S LIKE A FALSE NOTE IN A SONG, ECHOING OUT FROM IT.
DO YOU THINK YOUR MAGIC COULD SHOW US WHAT'S UP WITH THIS PLACE?
I--I DON'T KNOW--
I KNOW IT'S FORBIDDEN, BUT... WHATEVER'S GOING ON HERE, WE CAN'T SEE IT. BUT MAYBE YOU CAN.

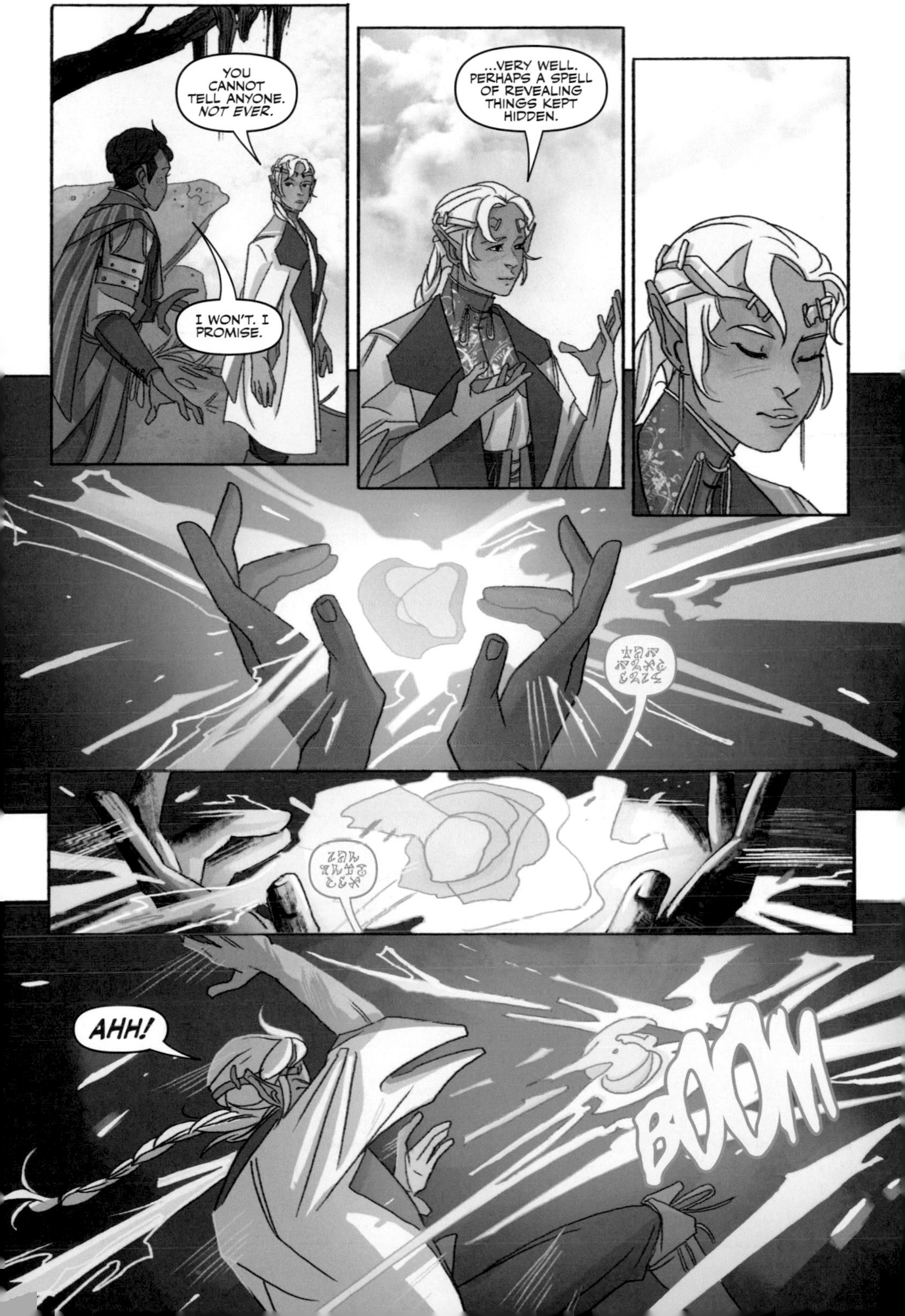
YOU CANNOT TELL ANYONE. NOT EVER.
I WON'T. I PROMISE.
...VERY WELL. PERHAPS A SPELL OF REVEALING THINGS KEPT HIDDEN.
AHH!
BOOM

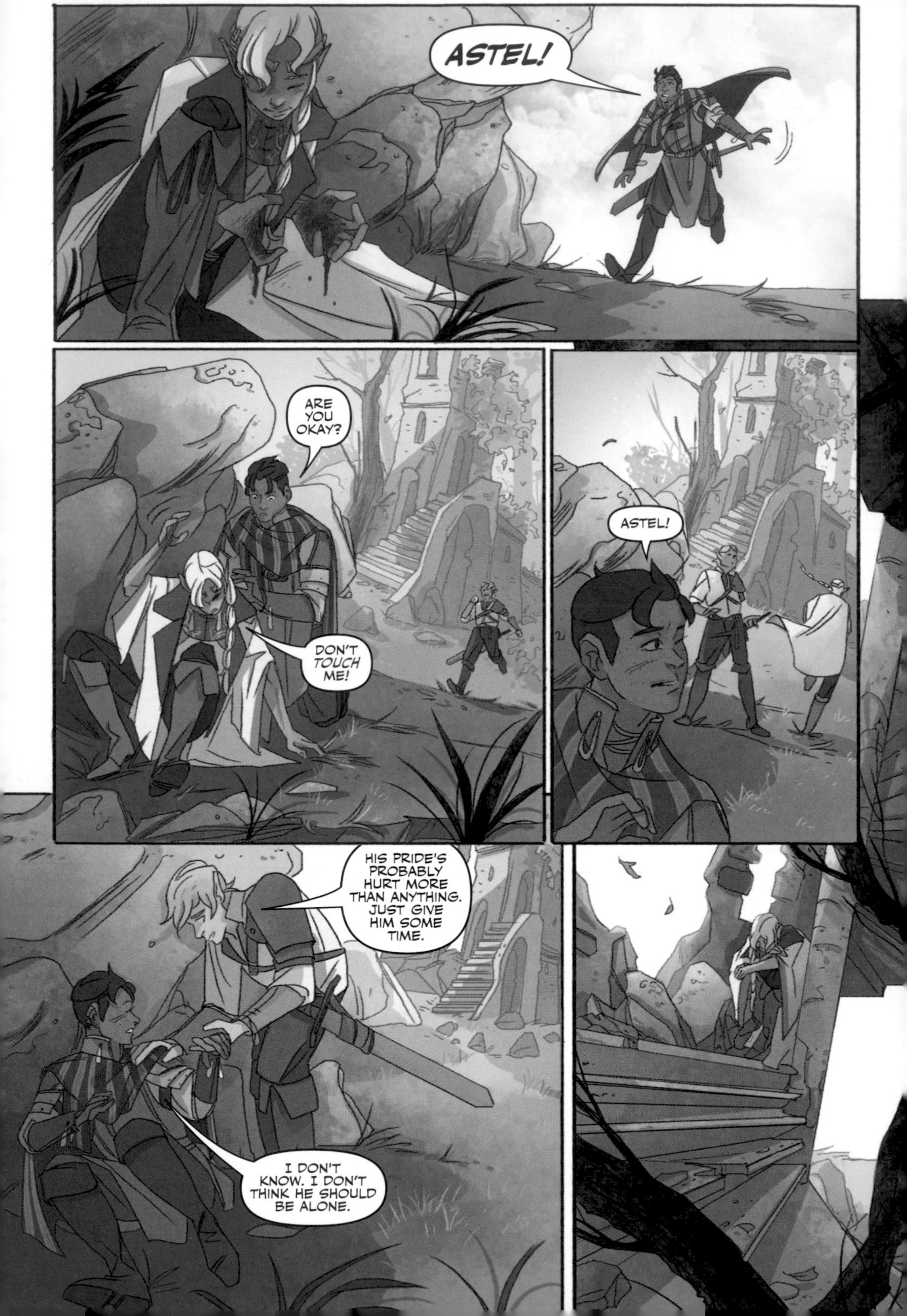
ASTEL!
ARE YOU OKAY?
DON'T *TOUCH* ME!
ASTEL!
HIS PRIDE'S PROBABLY HURT MORE THAN ANYTHING. JUST GIVE HIM SOME TIME.
I DON'T KNOW. I DON'T THINK HE SHOULD BE ALONE.

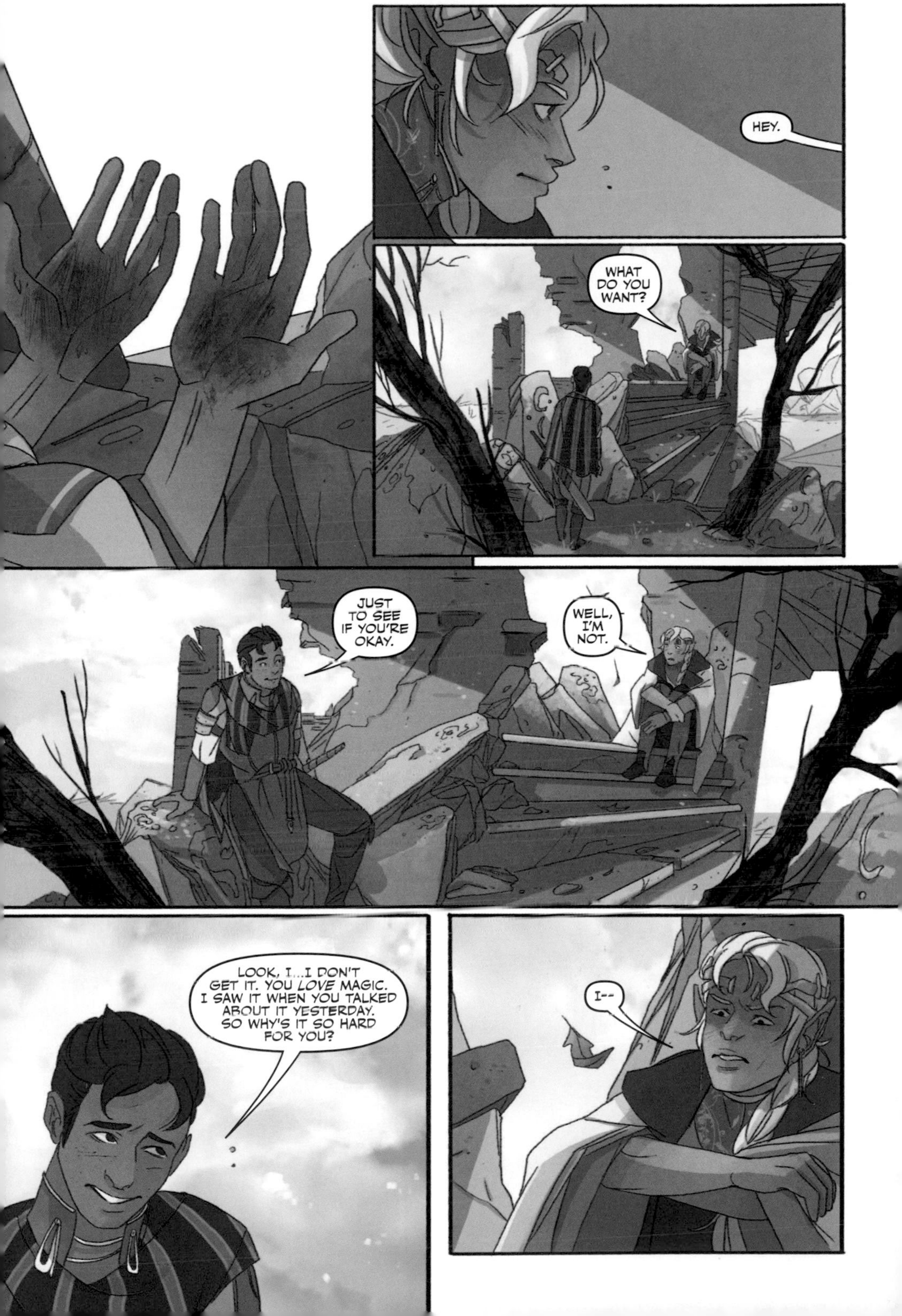
HEY.
WHAT DO YOU WANT?
JUST TO SEE IF YOU'RE OKAY.
WELL, I'M NOT.
LOOK, I...I DON'T GET IT. YOU *LOVE* MAGIC. I SAW IT WHEN YOU TALKED ABOUT IT YESTERDAY. SO WHY'S IT SO HARD FOR YOU?
I--

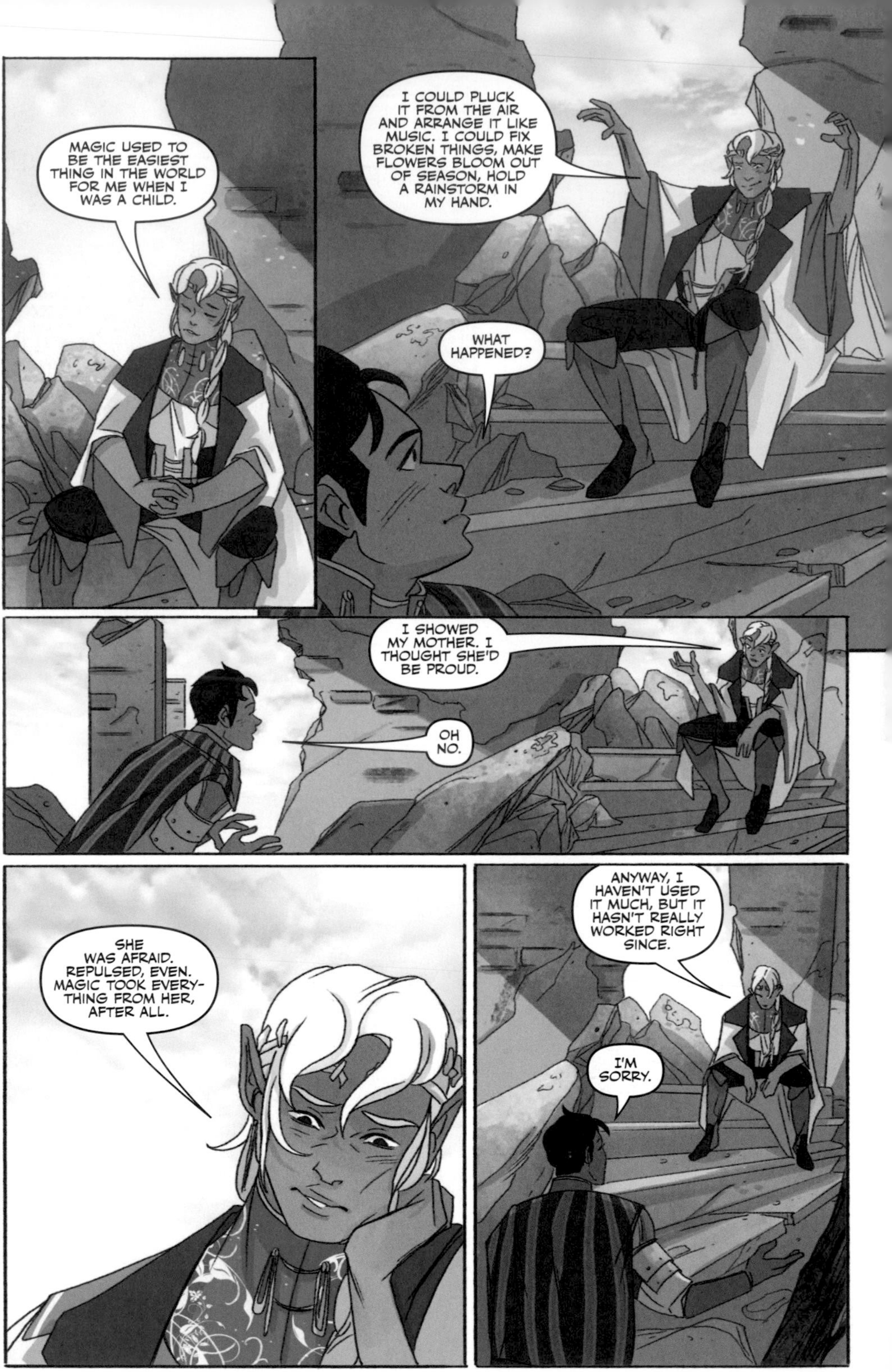
MAGIC USED TO BE THE EASIEST THING IN THE WORLD FOR ME WHEN I WAS A CHILD.
I COULD PLUCK IT FROM THE AIR AND ARRANGE IT LIKE MUSIC. I COULD FIX BROKEN THINGS, MAKE FLOWERS BLOOM OUT OF SEASON, HOLD A RAINSTORM IN MY HAND.
WHAT HAPPENED?
I SHOWED MY MOTHER. I THOUGHT SHE'D BE PROUD.
OH NO.
SHE WAS AFRAID. REPULSED, EVEN. MAGIC TOOK EVERY-THING FROM HER, AFTER ALL.
ANYWAY, I HAVEN'T USED IT MUCH, BUT IT HASN'T REALLY WORKED RIGHT SINCE.
I'M SORRY.

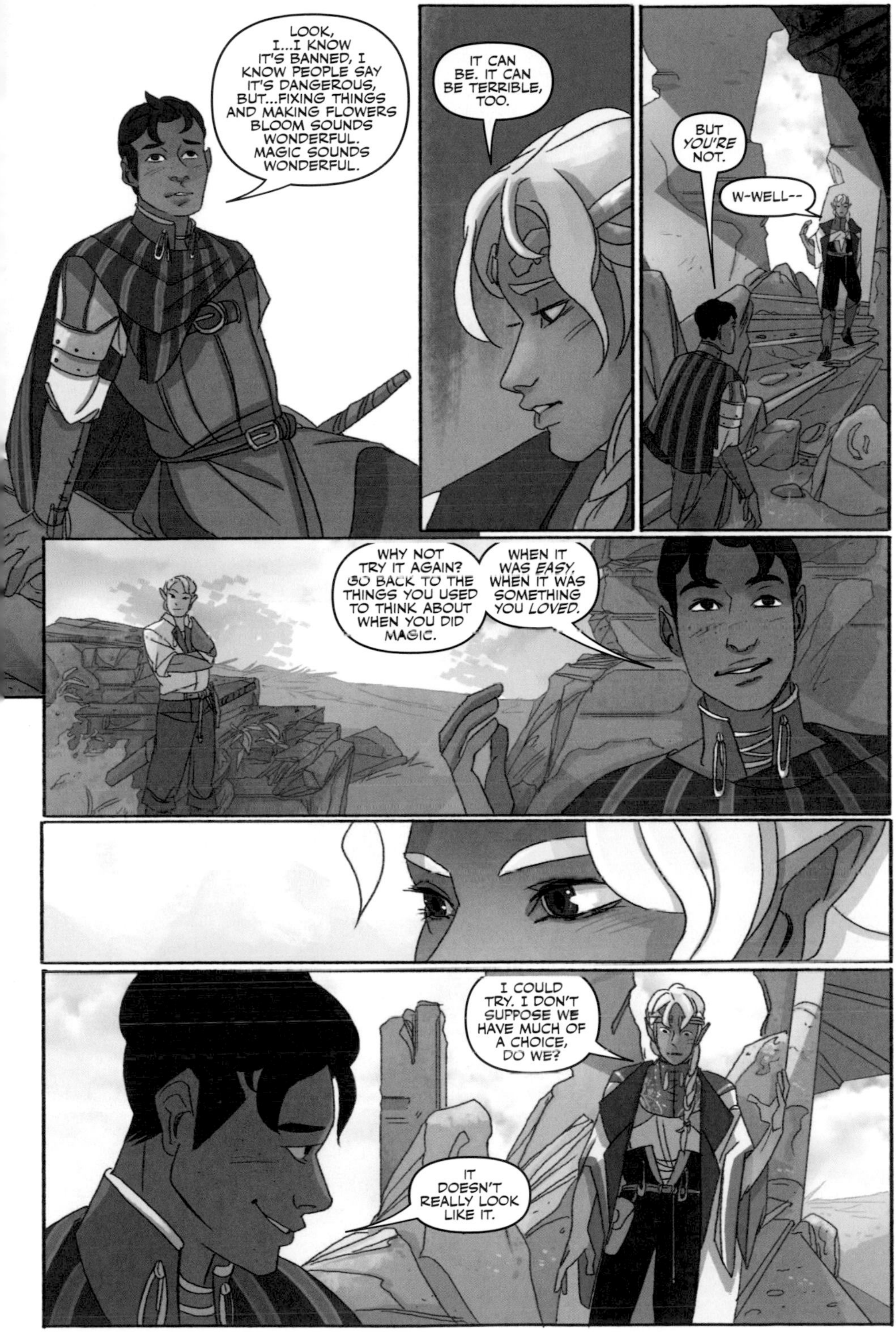
LOOK, I...I KNOW IT'S BANNED, I KNOW PEOPLE SAY IT'S DANGEROUS, BUT...FIXING THINGS AND MAKING FLOWERS BLOOM SOUNDS WONDERFUL. MAGIC SOUNDS WONDERFUL.
IT CAN BE. IT CAN BE TERRIBLE, TOO.
BUT *YOU'RE* NOT.
W-WELL--
WHY NOT TRY IT AGAIN? GO BACK TO THE THINGS YOU USED TO THINK ABOUT WHEN YOU DID MAGIC.
WHEN IT WAS *EASY*. WHEN IT WAS SOMETHING YOU *LOVED*.
I COULD TRY. I DON'T SUPPOSE WE HAVE MUCH OF A CHOICE, DO WE?
IT DOESN'T REALLY LOOK LIKE IT.

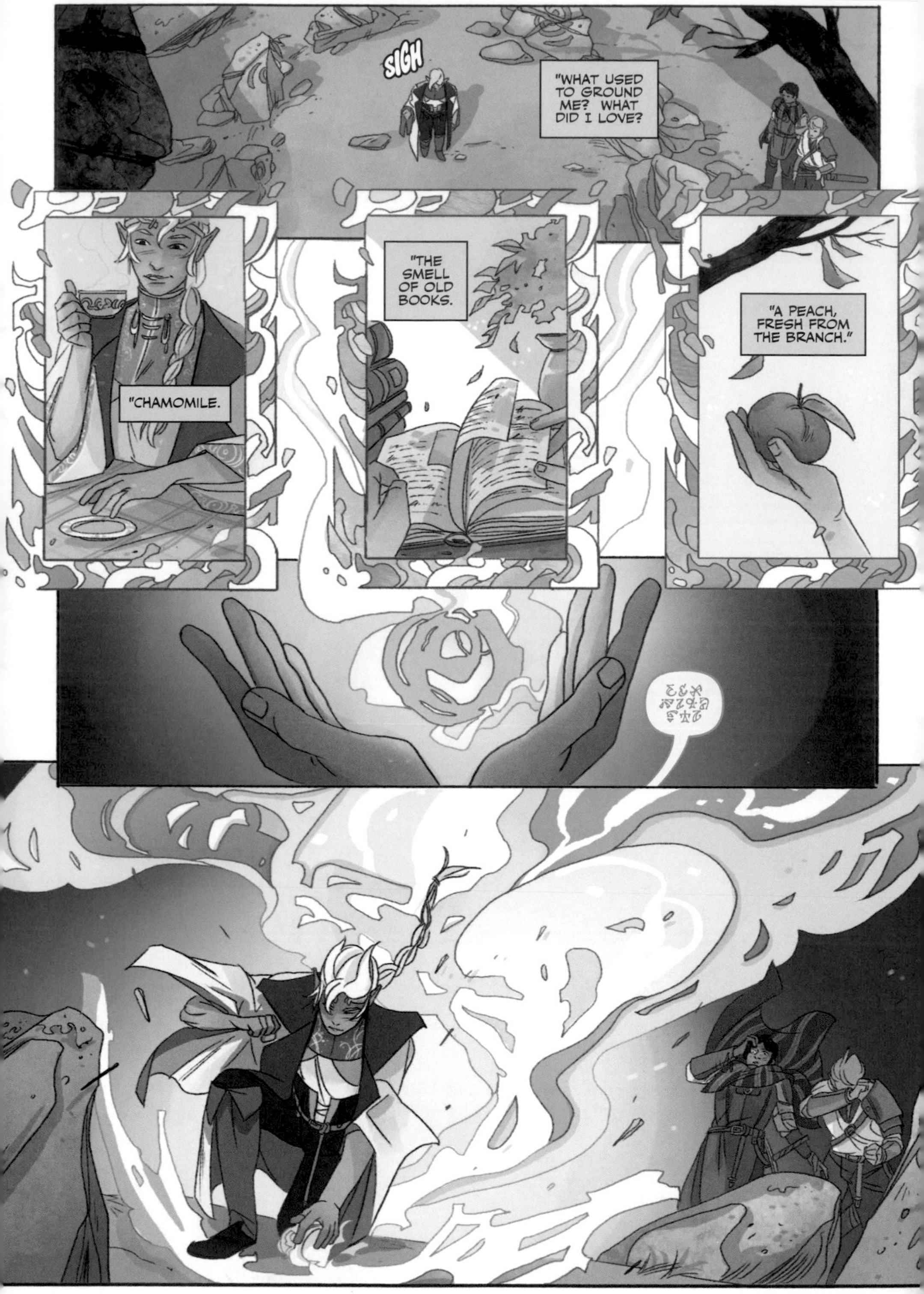
SIGH
"WHAT USED TO GROUND ME? WHAT DID I LOVE?
"CHAMOMILE.
"THE SMELL OF OLD BOOKS.
"A PEACH, FRESH FROM THE BRANCH."

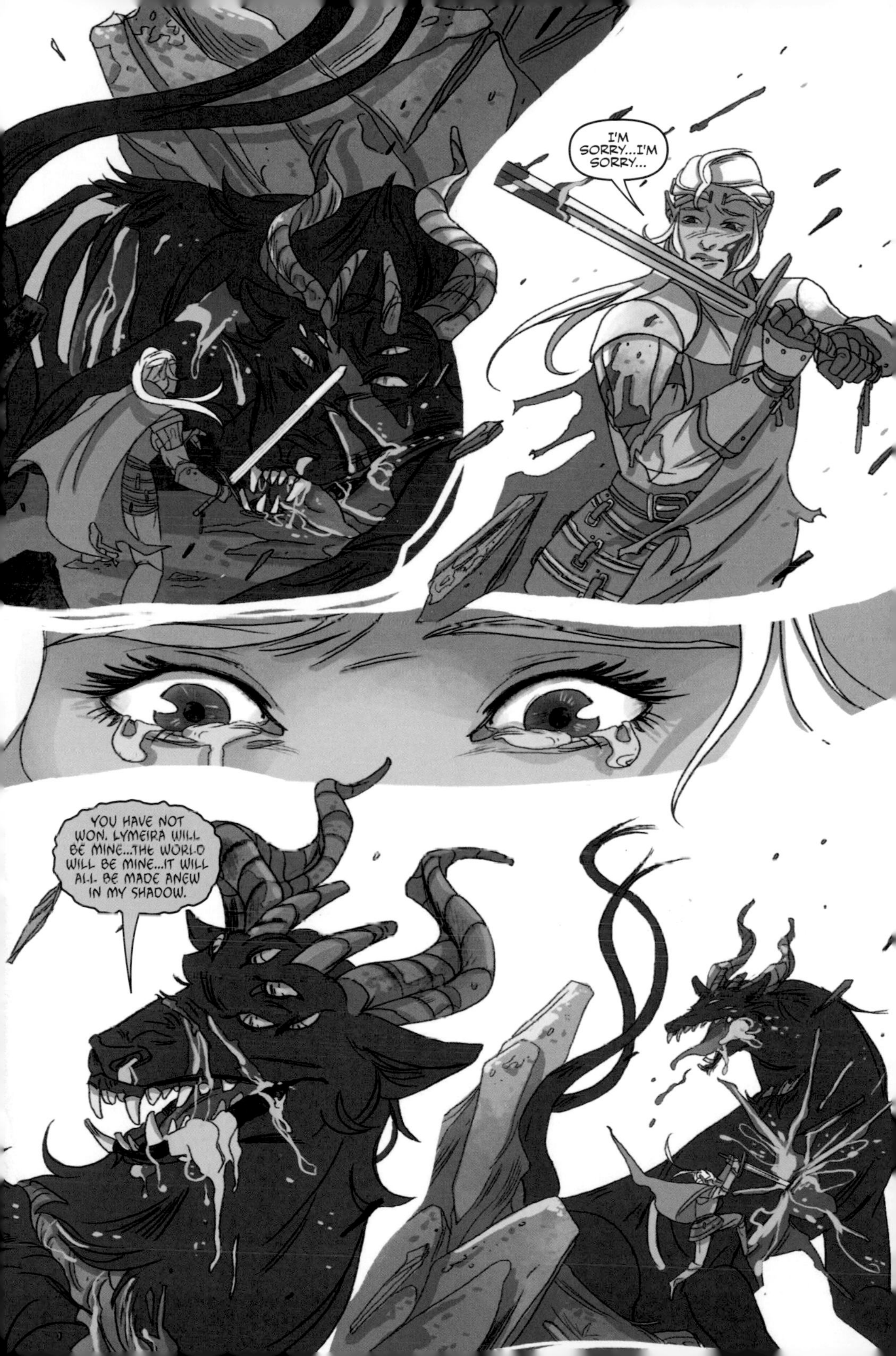
I'M SORRY...I'M SORRY...
YOU HAVE NOT WON. LYMEIRA WILL BE MINE...THE WORLD WILL BE MINE...IT WILL ALL BE MADE ANEW IN MY SHADOW.

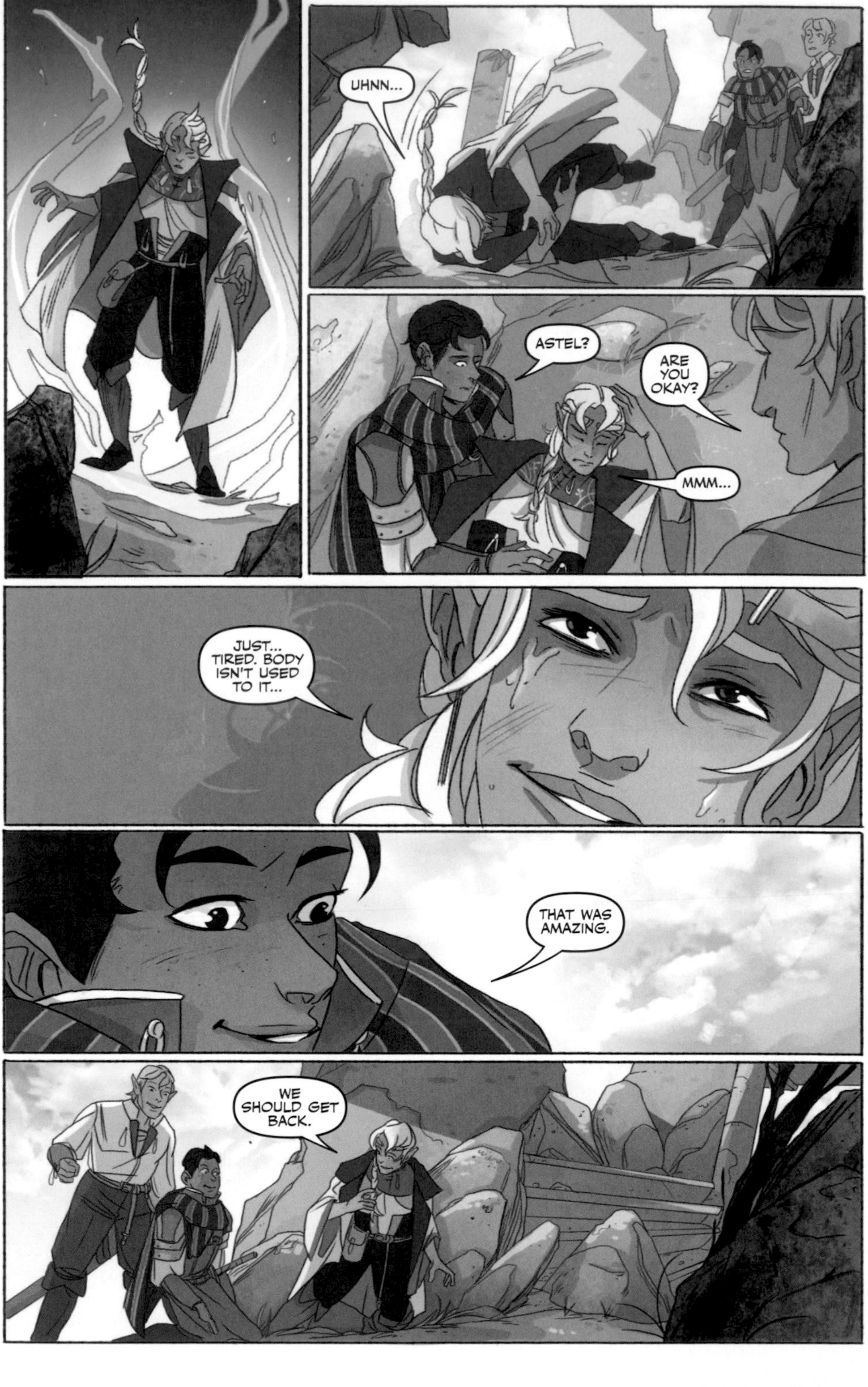
UHNN...
ASTEL?
ARE YOU OKAY?
MMM...
JUST... TIRED. BODY ISN'T USED TO IT...
THAT WAS AMAZING.
WE SHOULD GET BACK.

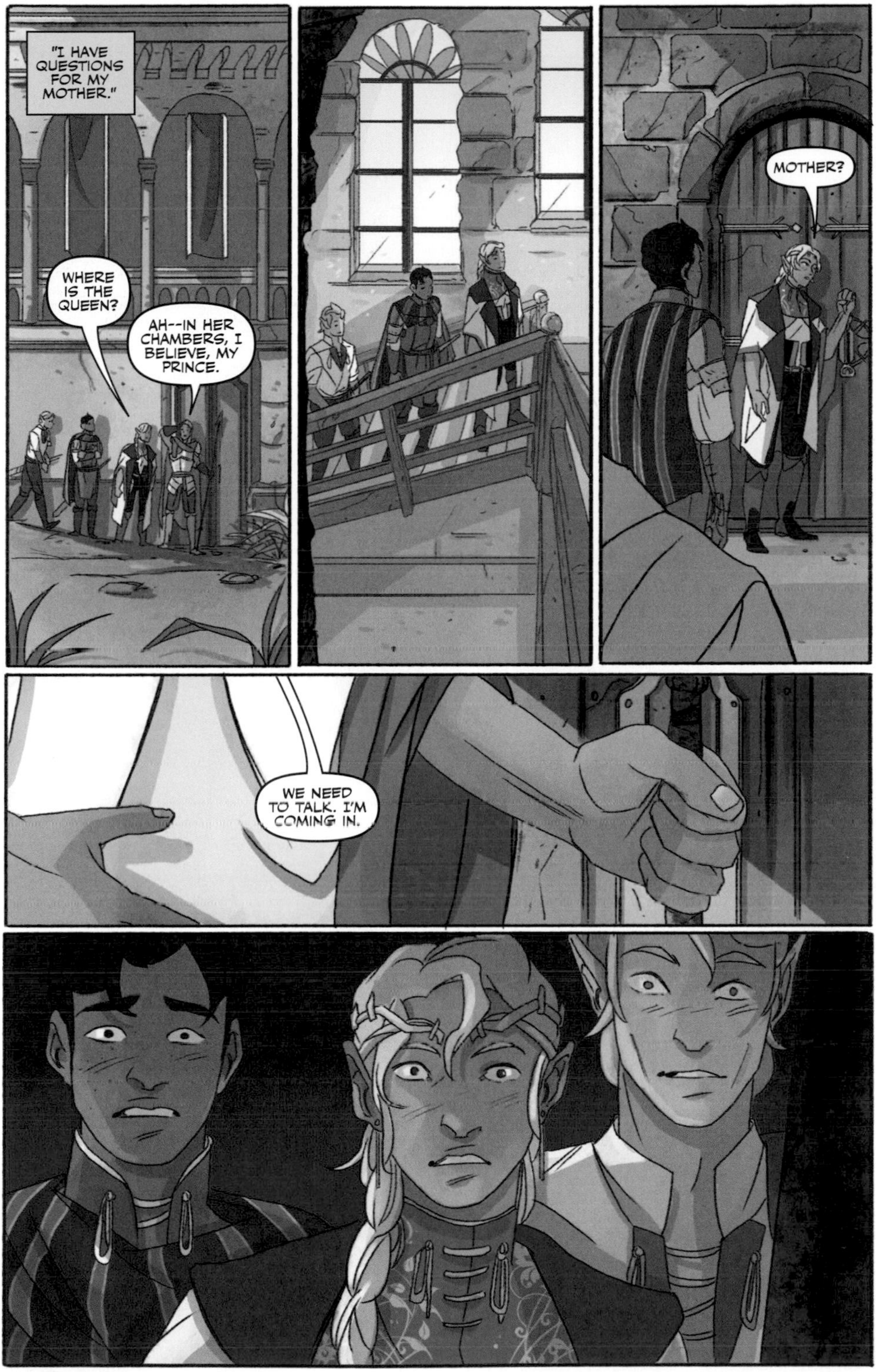
"I HAVE QUESTIONS FOR MY MOTHER."
WHERE IS THE QUEEN?
AH--IN HER CHAMBERS, I BELIEVE, MY PRINCE.
MOTHER?
WE NEED TO TALK. I'M COMING IN.

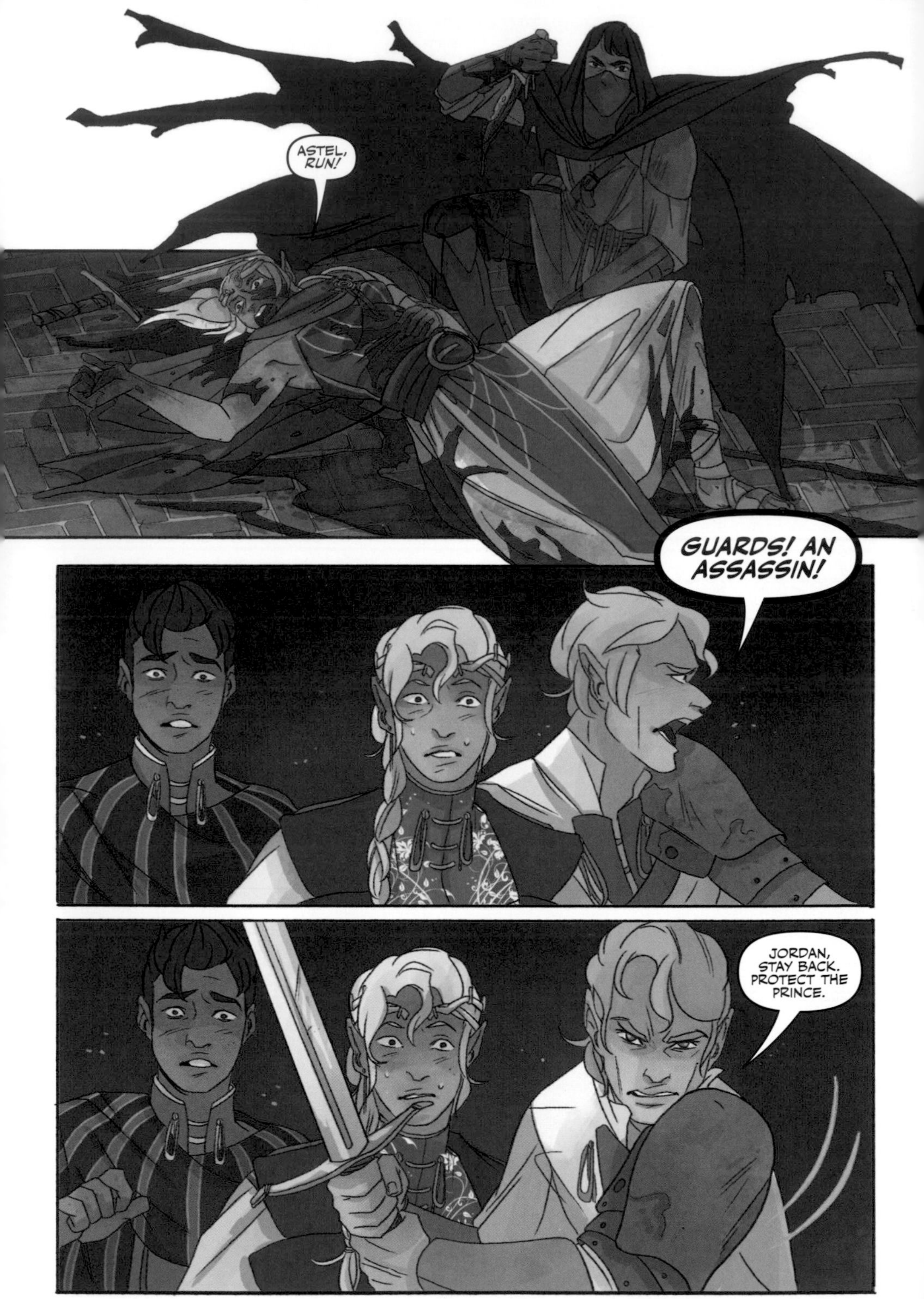
ASTEL, RUN!
GUARDS! AN ASSASSIN!
JORDAN, STAY BACK. PROTECT THE PRINCE.

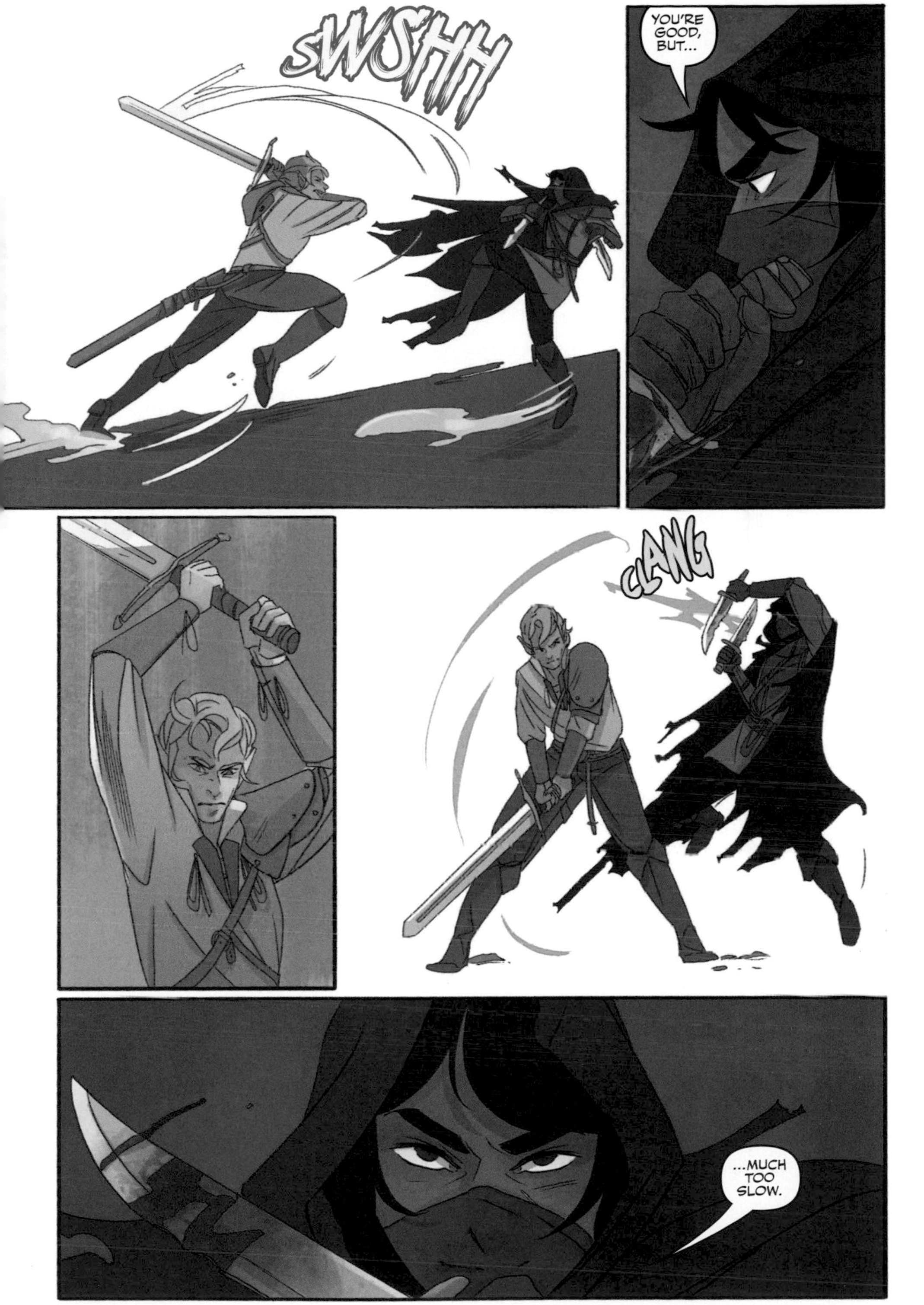
SWSHH
YOU'RE GOOD, BUT...
CLANG
...MUCH TOO SLOW.

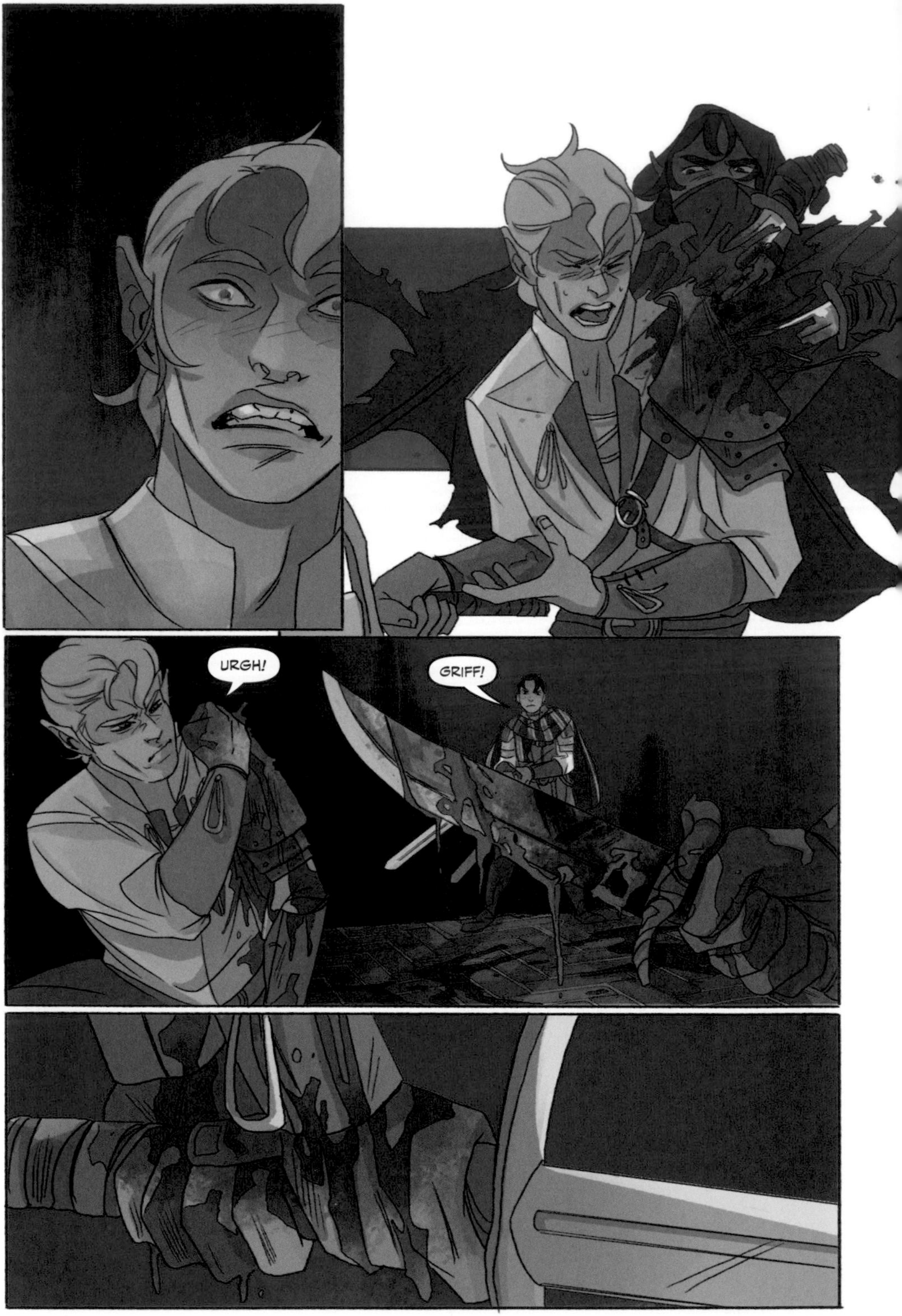
URGH!
GRIFF!

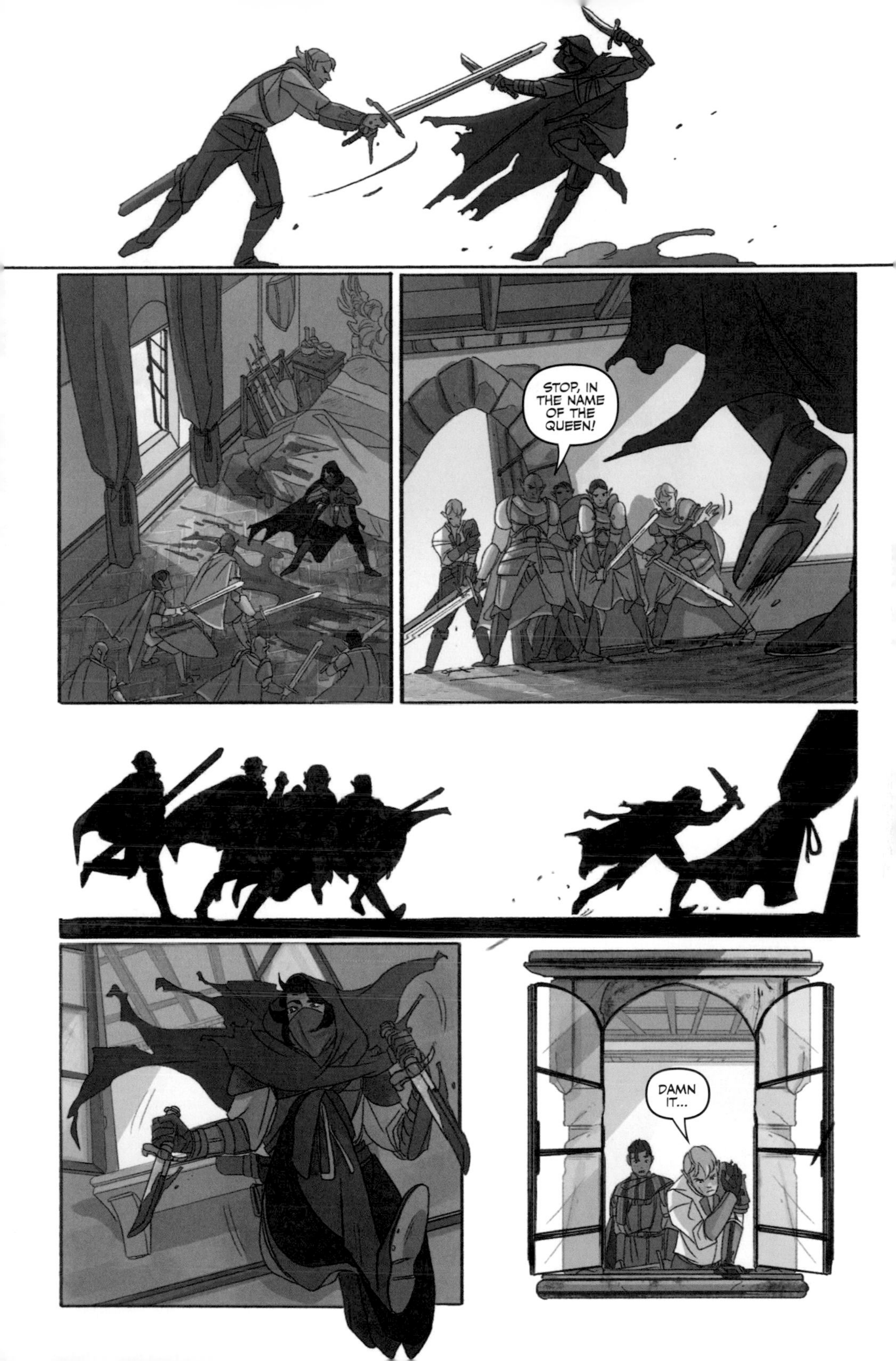
STOP, IN THE NAME OF THE QUEEN!
DAMN IT...

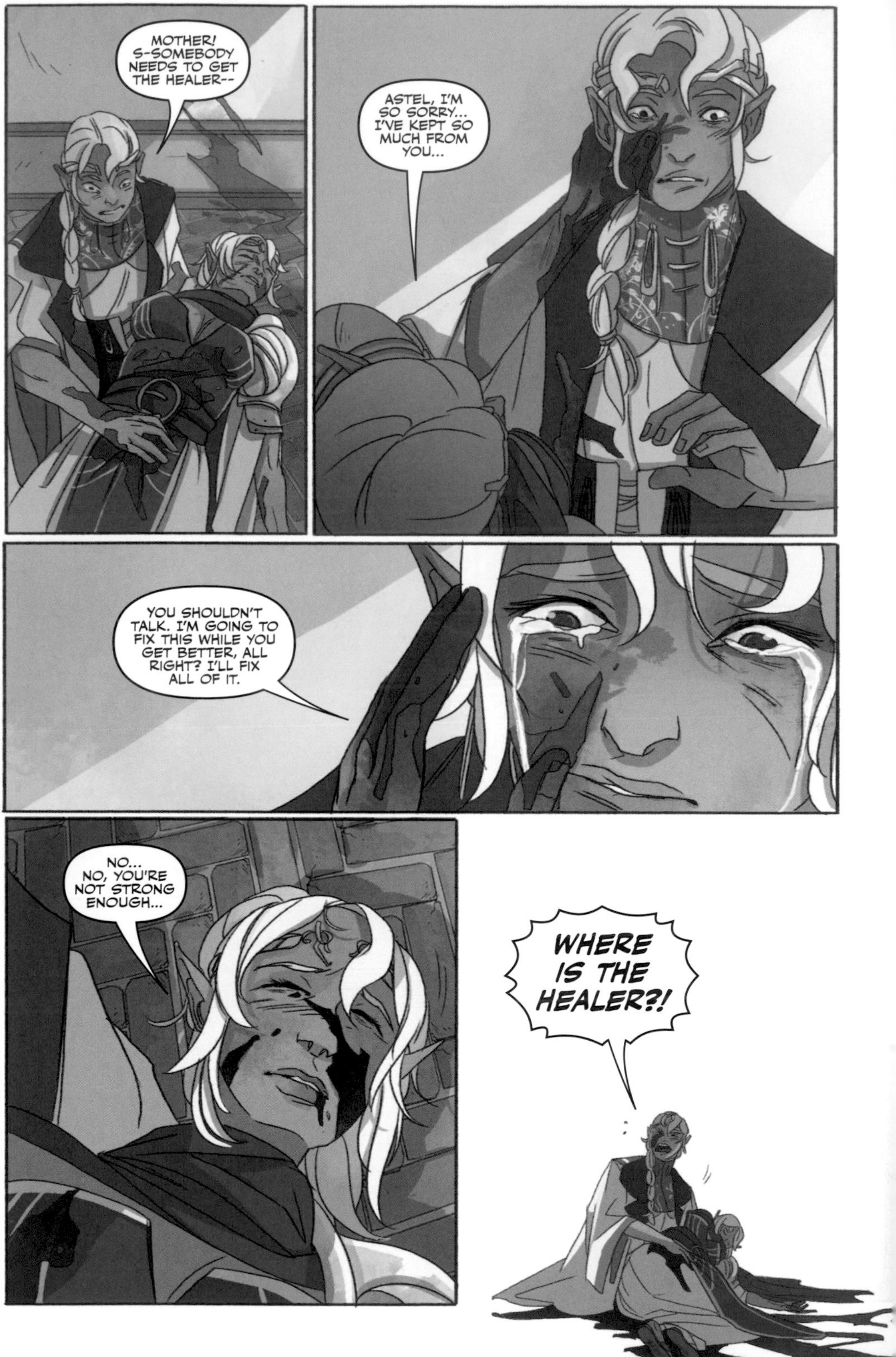
MOTHER! S-SOMEBODY NEEDS TO GET THE HEALER--
ASTEL, I'M SO SORRY... I'VE KEPT SO MUCH FROM YOU...
YOU SHOULDN'T TALK. I'M GOING TO FIX THIS WHILE YOU GET BETTER, ALL RIGHT? I'LL FIX ALL OF IT.
NO... NO, YOU'RE NOT STRONG ENOUGH...
WHERE IS THE HEALER?!

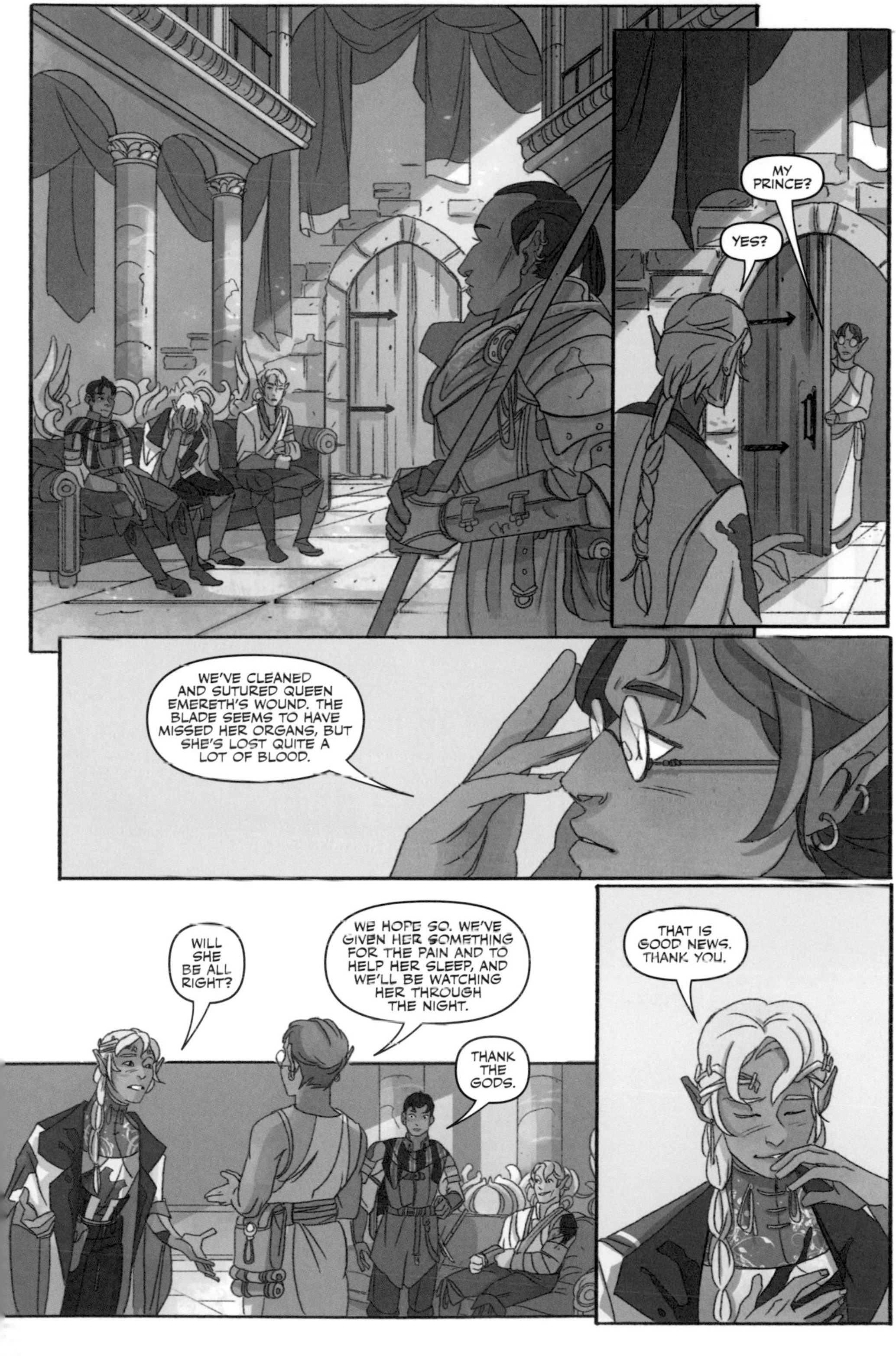
MY PRINCE?
YES?
WE'VE CLEANED AND SUTURED QUEEN EMERETH'S WOUND. THE BLADE SEEMS TO HAVE MISSED HER ORGANS, BUT SHE'S LOST QUITE A LOT OF BLOOD.
WILL SHE BE ALL RIGHT?
WE HOPE SO. WE'VE GIVEN HER SOMETHING FOR THE PAIN AND TO HELP HER SLEEP, AND WE'LL BE WATCHING HER THROUGH THE NIGHT.
THANK THE GODS.
THAT IS GOOD NEWS. THANK YOU.

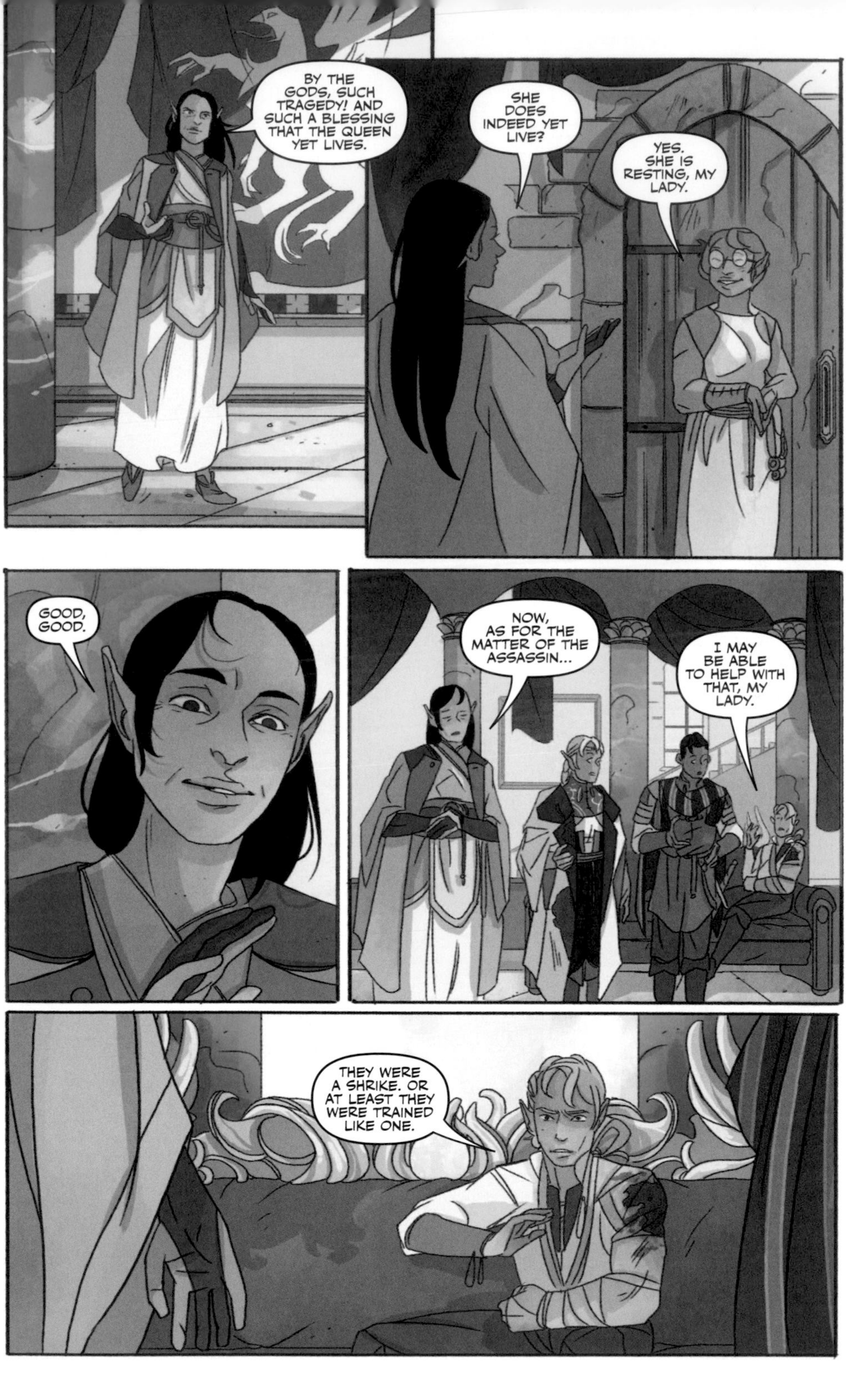
BY THE GODS, SUCH TRAGEDY! AND SUCH A BLESSING THAT THE QUEEN YET LIVES.
SHE DOES INDEED YET LIVE?
YES. SHE IS RESTING, MY LADY.
GOOD, GOOD.
NOW, AS FOR THE MATTER OF THE ASSASSIN...
I MAY BE ABLE TO HELP WITH THAT, MY LADY.
THEY WERE A SHRIKE. OR AT LEAST THEY WERE TRAINED LIKE ONE.

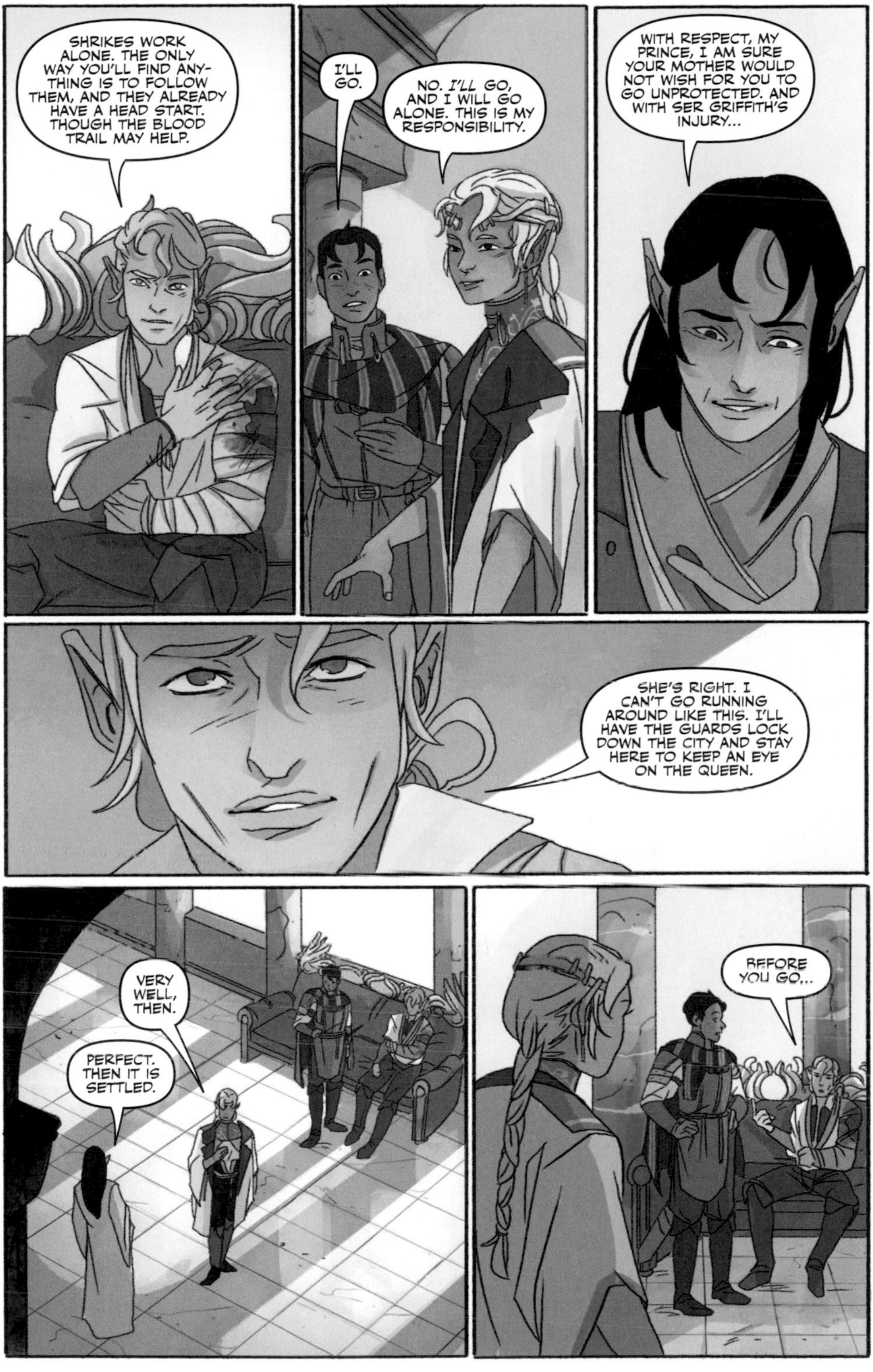
SHRIKES WORK ALONE. THE ONLY WAY YOU'LL FIND ANY-THING IS TO FOLLOW THEM, AND THEY ALREADY HAVE A HEAD START. THOUGH THE BLOOD TRAIL MAY HELP.
I'LL GO.
NO. *I'LL* GO, AND I WILL GO ALONE. THIS IS MY RESPONSIBILITY.
WITH RESPECT, MY PRINCE, I AM SURE YOUR MOTHER WOULD NOT WISH FOR YOU TO GO UNPROTECTED. AND WITH SER GRIFFITH'S INJURY...
SHE'S RIGHT. I CAN'T GO RUNNING AROUND LIKE THIS. I'LL HAVE THE GUARDS LOCK DOWN THE CITY AND STAY HERE TO KEEP AN EYE ON THE QUEEN.
VERY WELL, THEN.
PERFECT. THEN IT IS SETTLED.
BEFORE YOU GO...

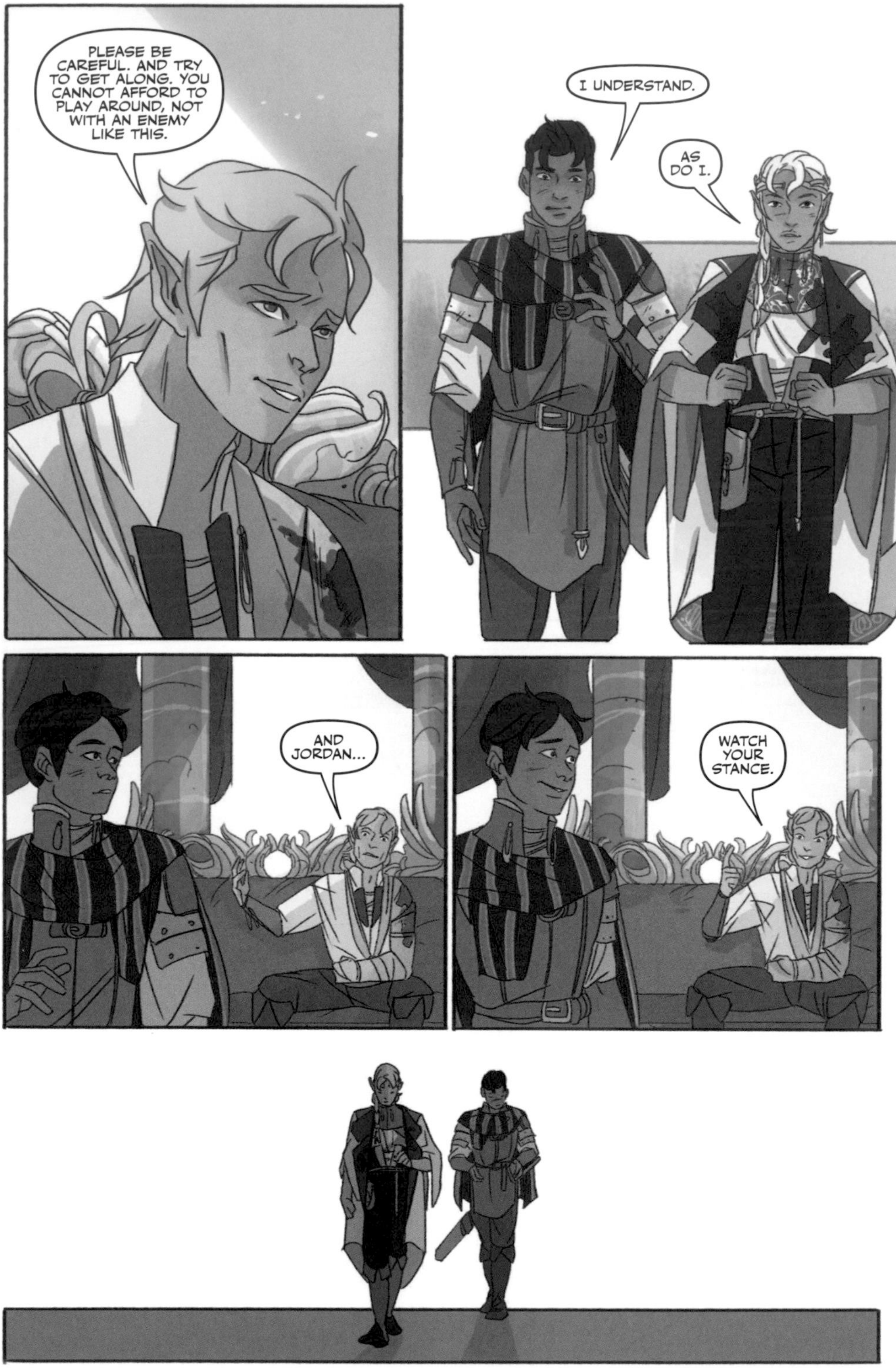
PLEASE BE CAREFUL. AND TRY TO GET ALONG. YOU CANNOT AFFORD TO PLAY AROUND, NOT WITH AN ENEMY LIKE THIS.
I UNDERSTAND.
AS DO I.
AND JORDAN...
WATCH YOUR STANCE.

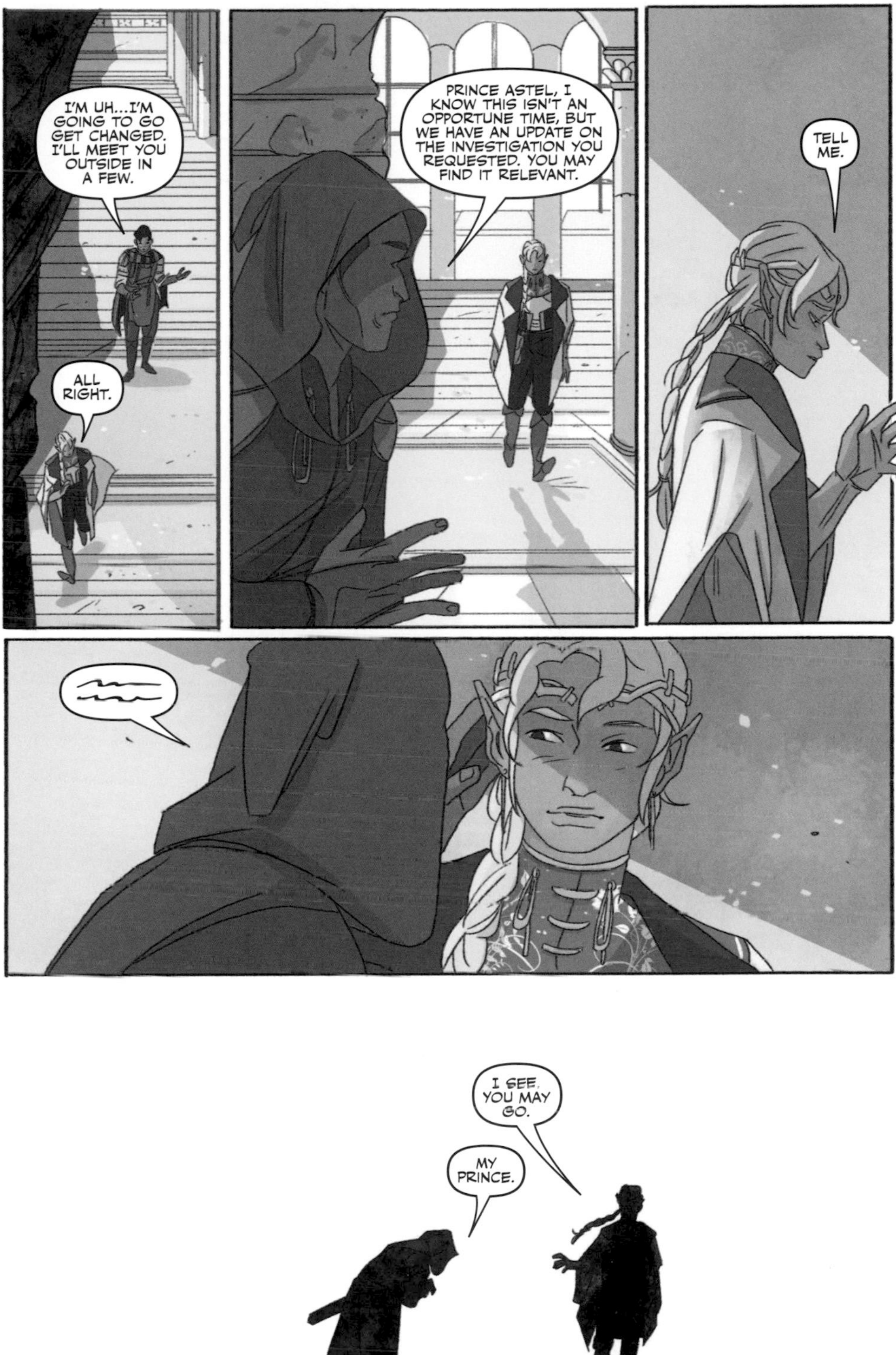
I'M UH...I'M GOING TO GO GET CHANGED. I'LL MEET YOU OUTSIDE IN A FEW.
ALL RIGHT.
PRINCE ASTEL, I KNOW THIS ISN'T AN OPPORTUNE TIME, BUT WE HAVE AN UPDATE ON THE INVESTIGATION YOU REQUESTED. YOU MAY FIND IT RELEVANT.
TELL ME.
I SEE. YOU MAY GO.
MY PRINCE.

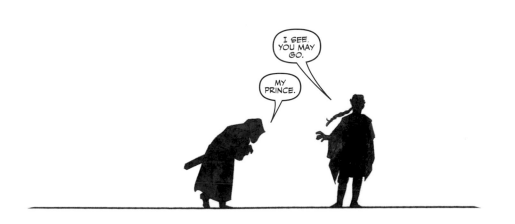

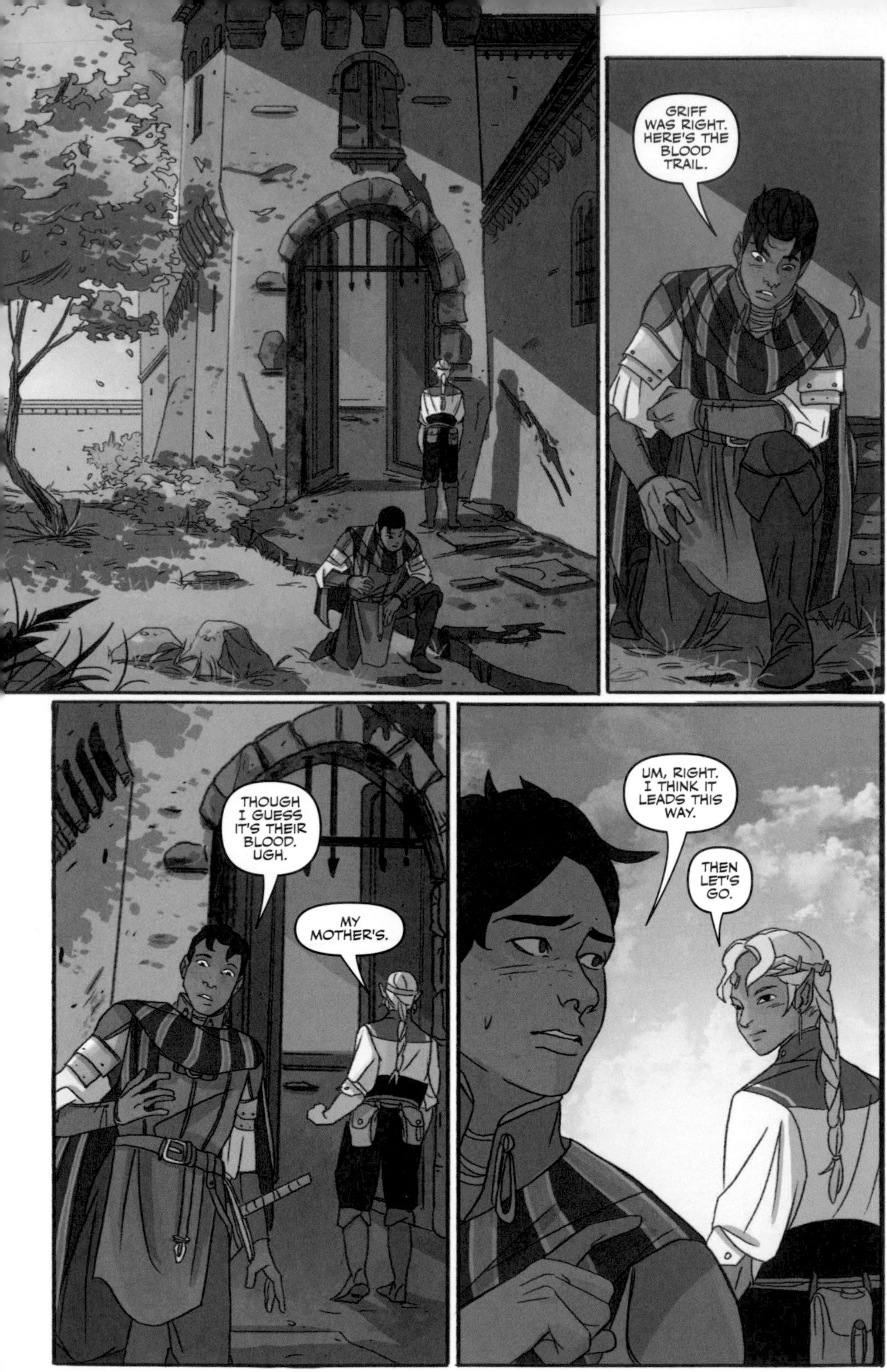
GRIFF WAS RIGHT. HERE'S THE BLOOD TRAIL.
THOUGH I GUESS IT'S THEIR BLOOD. UGH.
MY MOTHER'S.
UM, RIGHT. I THINK IT LEADS THIS WAY.
THEN LET'S GO.

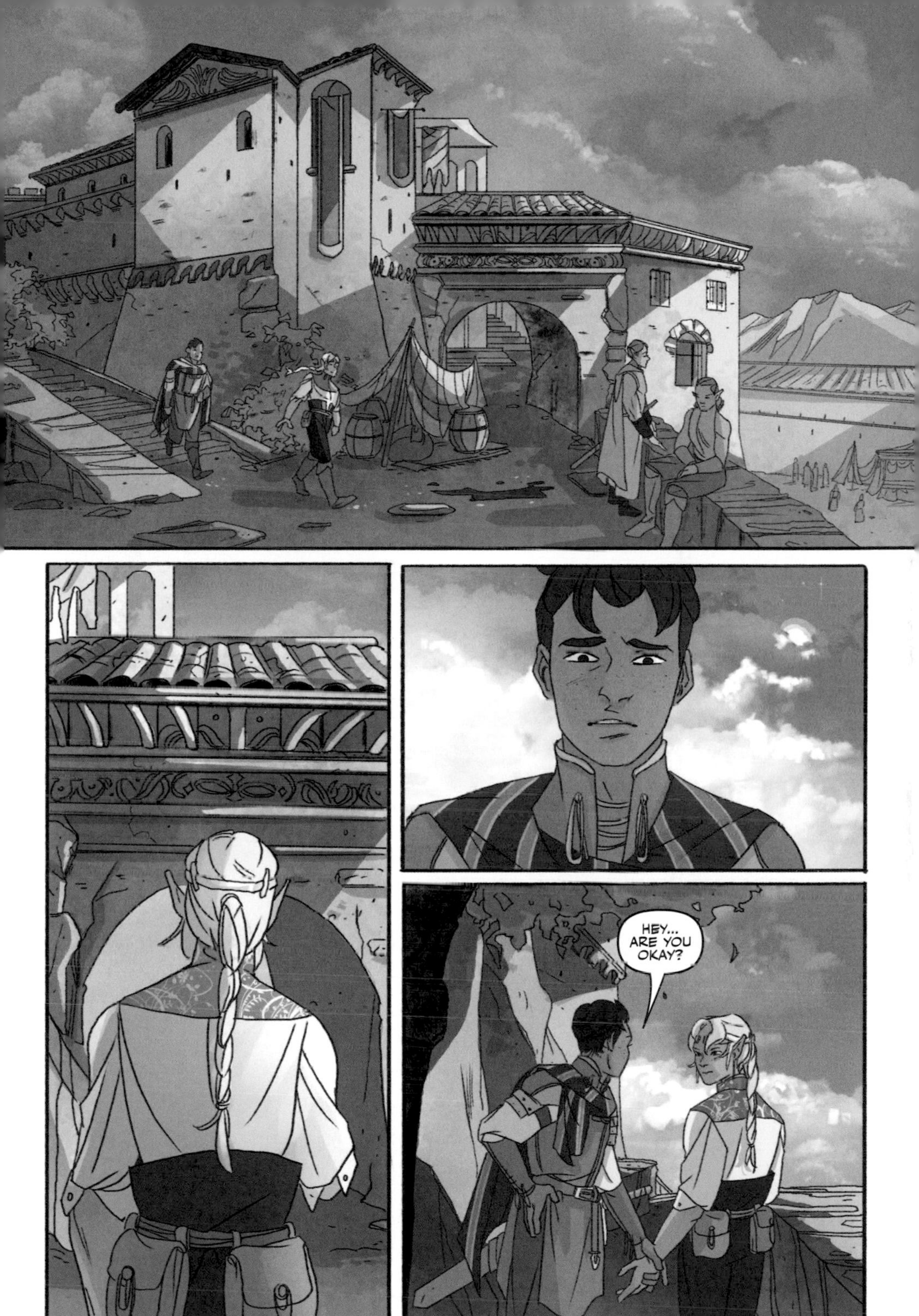
HEY... ARE YOU OKAY?

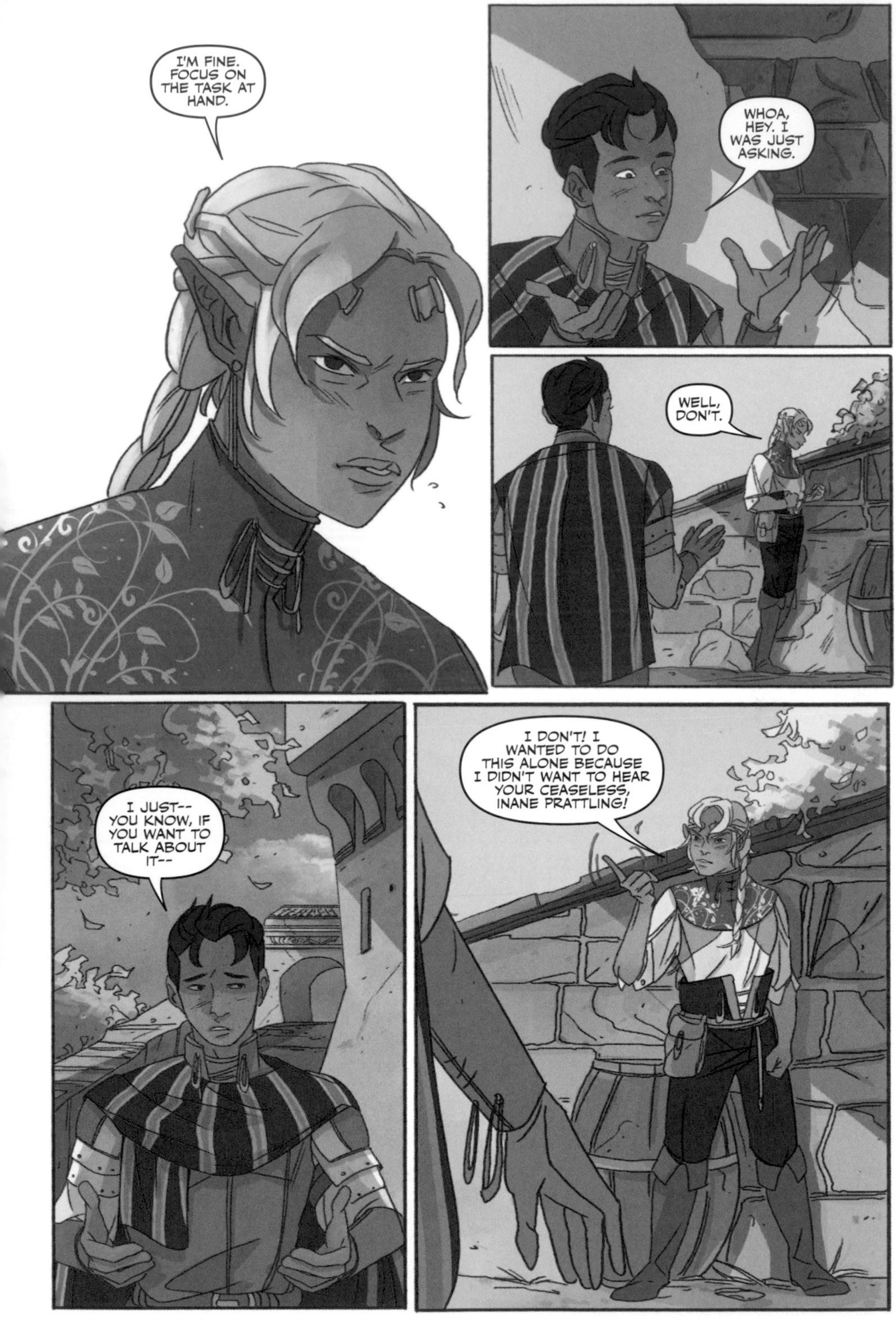
I'M FINE. FOCUS ON THE TASK AT HAND.
WHOA, HEY. I WAS JUST ASKING.
WELL, DON'T.
I JUST-- YOU KNOW, IF YOU WANT TO TALK ABOUT IT--
I DON'T! I WANTED TO DO THIS ALONE BECAUSE I DIDN'T WANT TO HEAR YOUR CEASELESS, INANE PRATTLING!

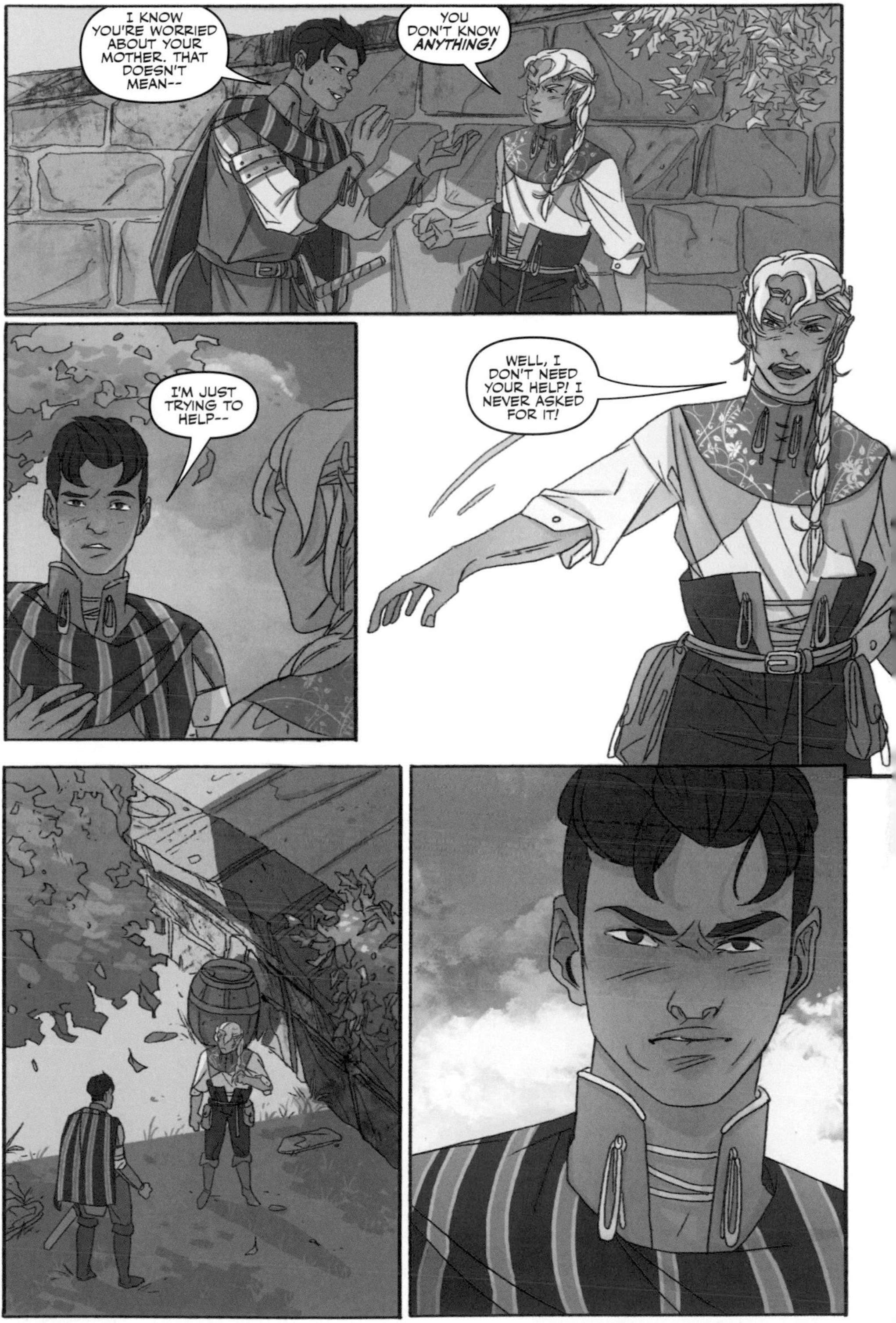

I KNOW YOU'RE WORRIED ABOUT YOUR MOTHER. THAT DOESN'T MEAN--
YOU DON'T KNOW *ANYTHING!*
I'M JUST TRYING TO HELP--
WELL, I DON'T NEED YOUR HELP! I NEVER ASKED FOR IT!

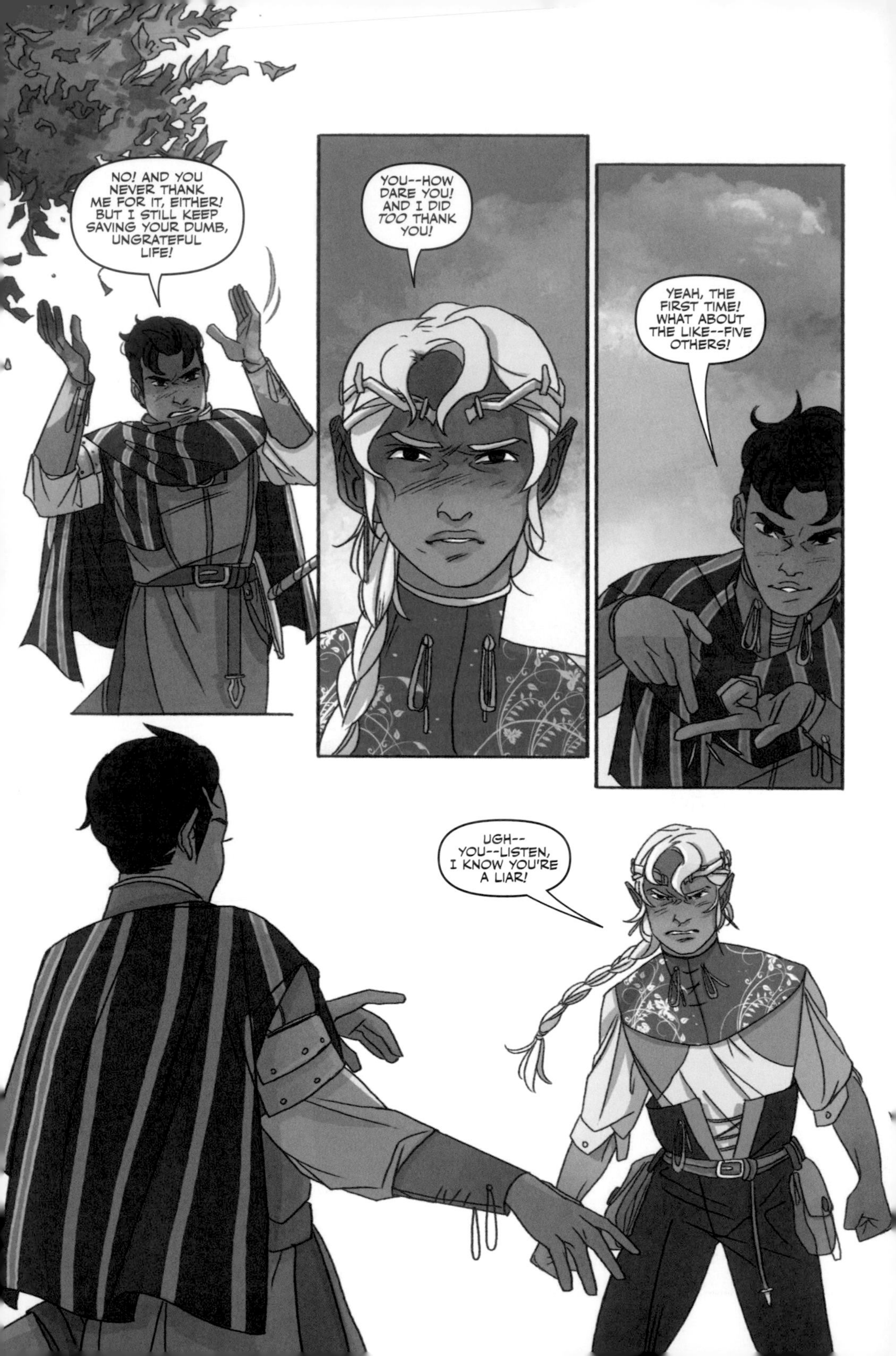
NO! AND YOU NEVER THANK ME FOR IT, EITHER! BUT I STILL KEEP SAVING YOUR DUMB, UNGRATEFUL LIFE!
YOU--HOW DARE YOU! AND I DID *TOO* THANK YOU!
YEAH, THE FIRST TIME! WHAT ABOUT THE LIKE--FIVE OTHERS!
UGH-- YOU--LISTEN, I KNOW YOU'RE A LIAR!

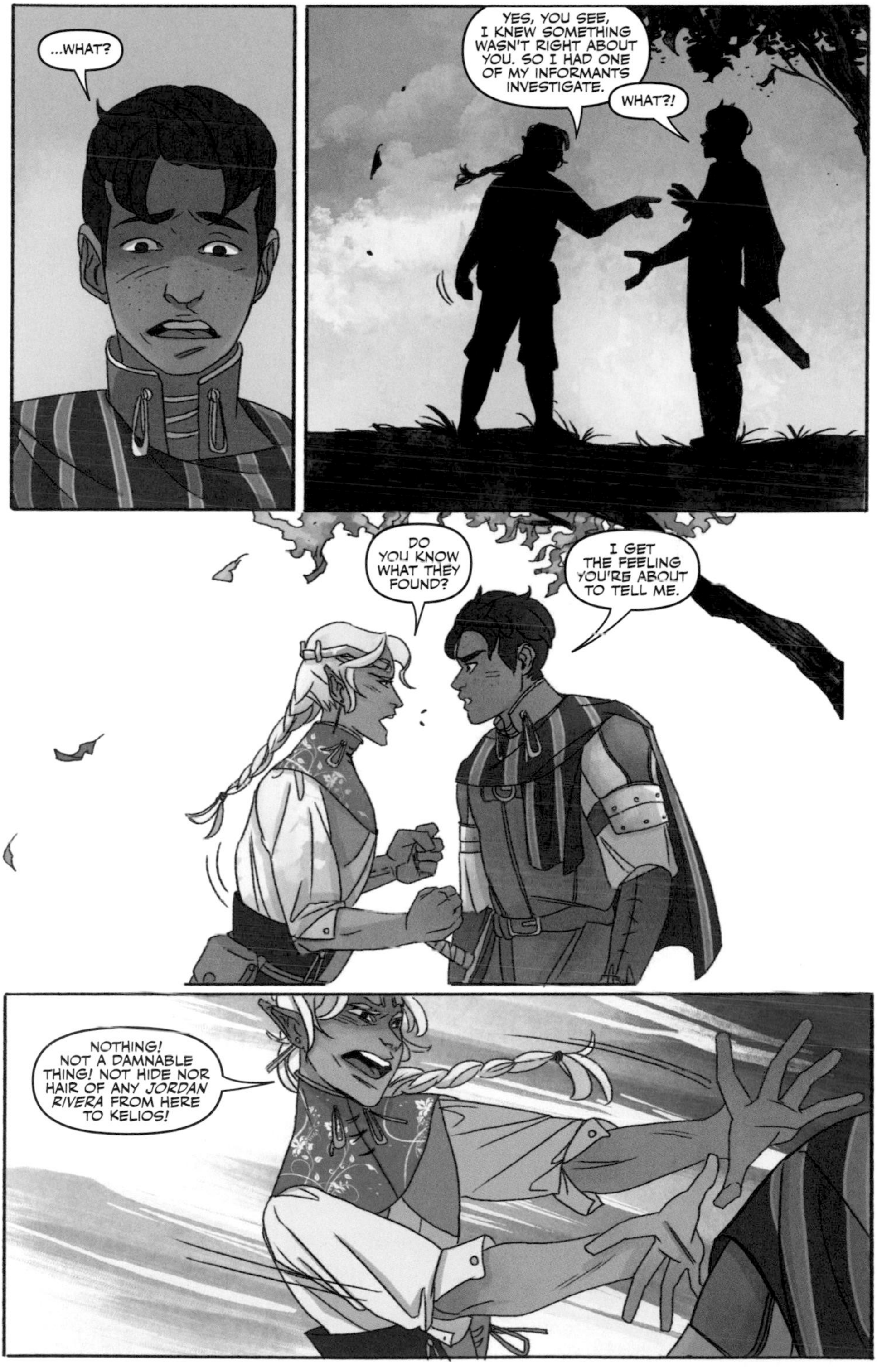
...WHAT?
YES, YOU SEE, I KNEW SOMETHING WASN'T RIGHT ABOUT YOU. SO I HAD ONE OF MY INFORMANTS INVESTIGATE.
WHAT?!
DO YOU KNOW WHAT THEY FOUND?
I GET THE FEELING YOU'RE ABOUT TO TELL ME.
NOTHING! NOT A *DAMNABLE* THING! NOT HIDE NOR HAIR OF ANY *JORDAN RIVERA* FROM HERE TO KELIOS!

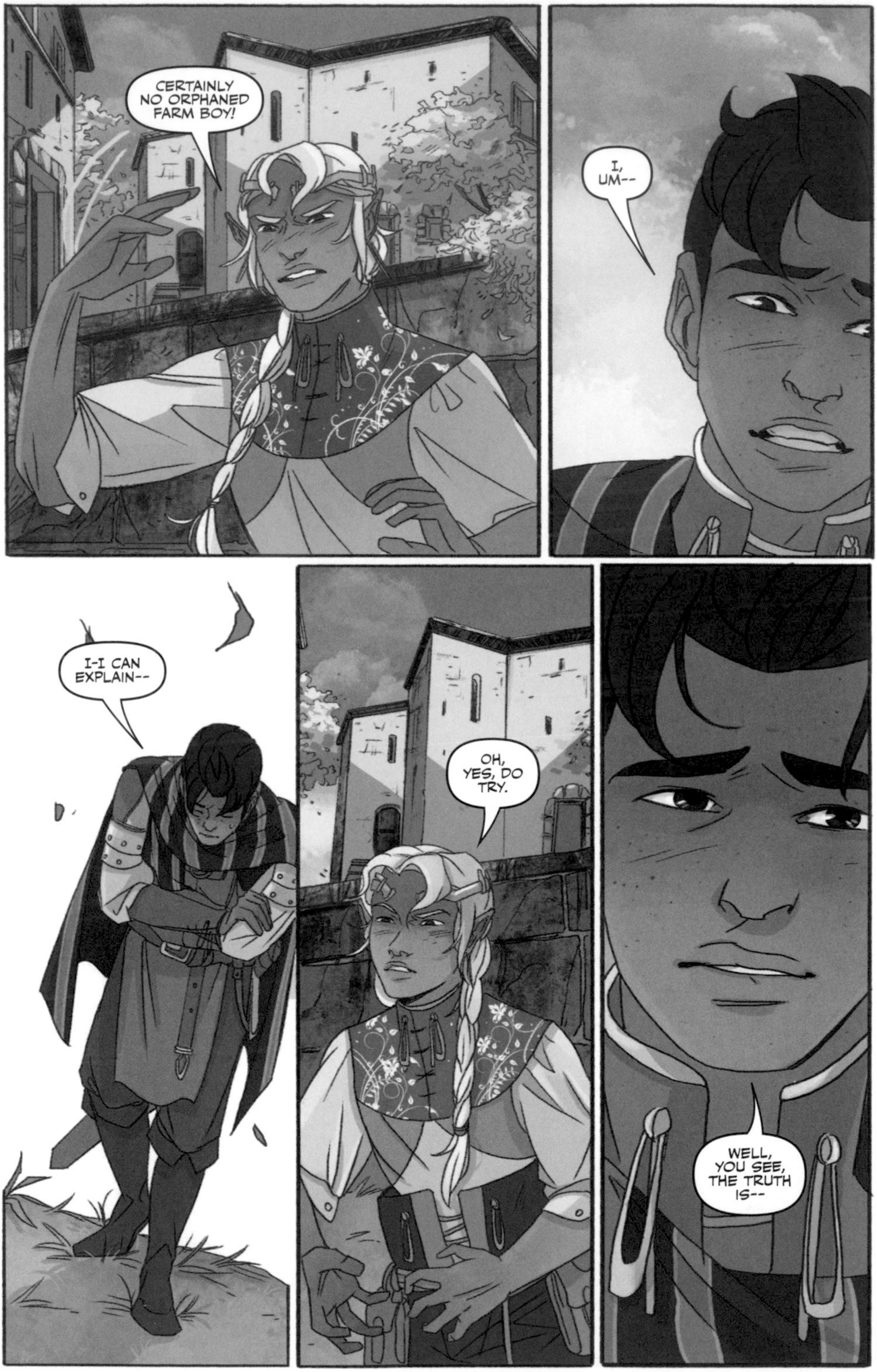
CERTAINLY NO ORPHANED FARM BOY!
I, UM--
I-I CAN EXPLAIN--
OH, YES, DO TRY.
WELL, YOU SEE, THE TRUTH IS--

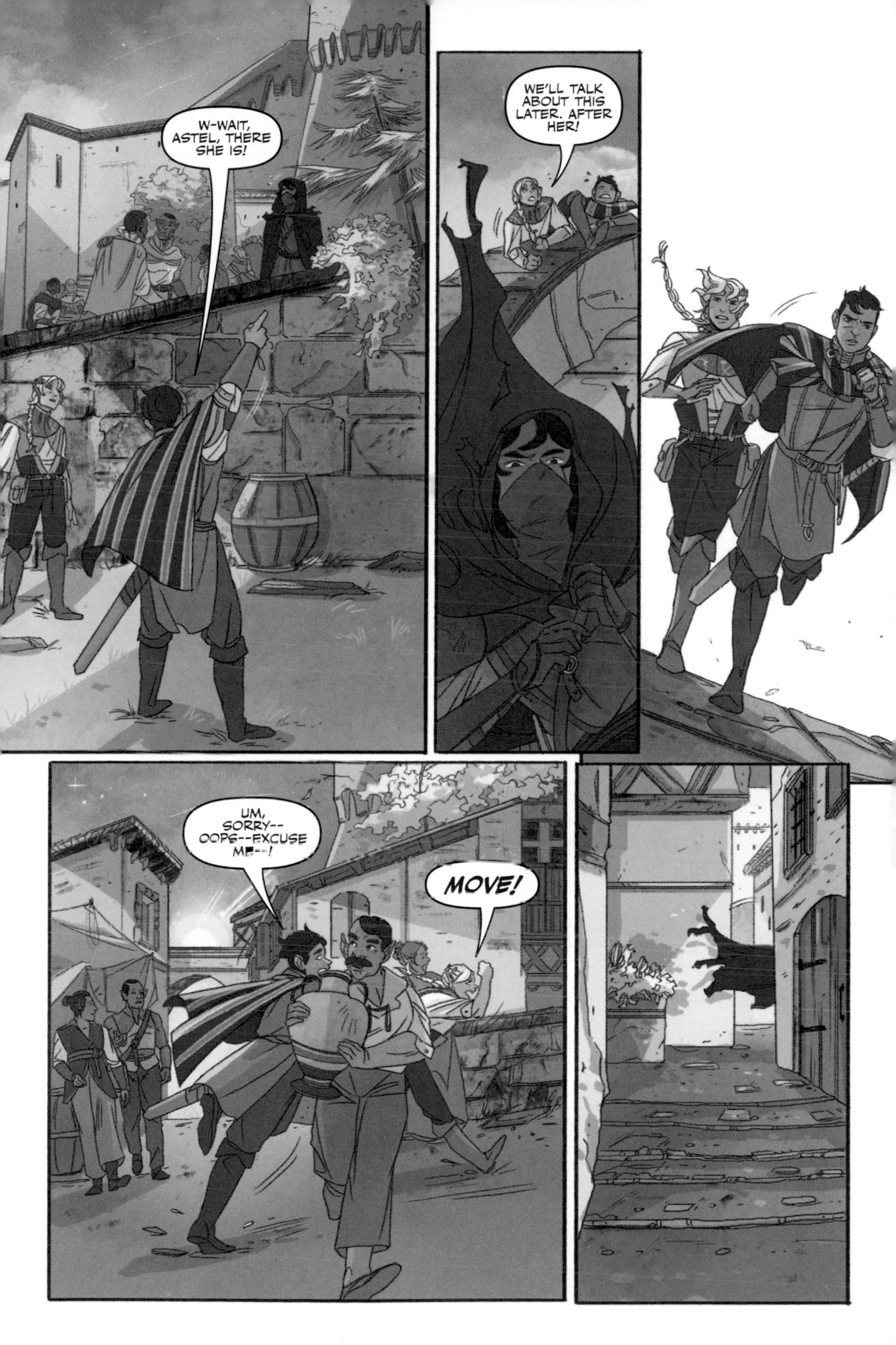
W-WAIT, ASTEL, THERE SHE IS!
WE'LL TALK ABOUT THIS LATER. AFTER HER!
UM, SORRY--OOPS--EXCUSE ME--!
MOVE!

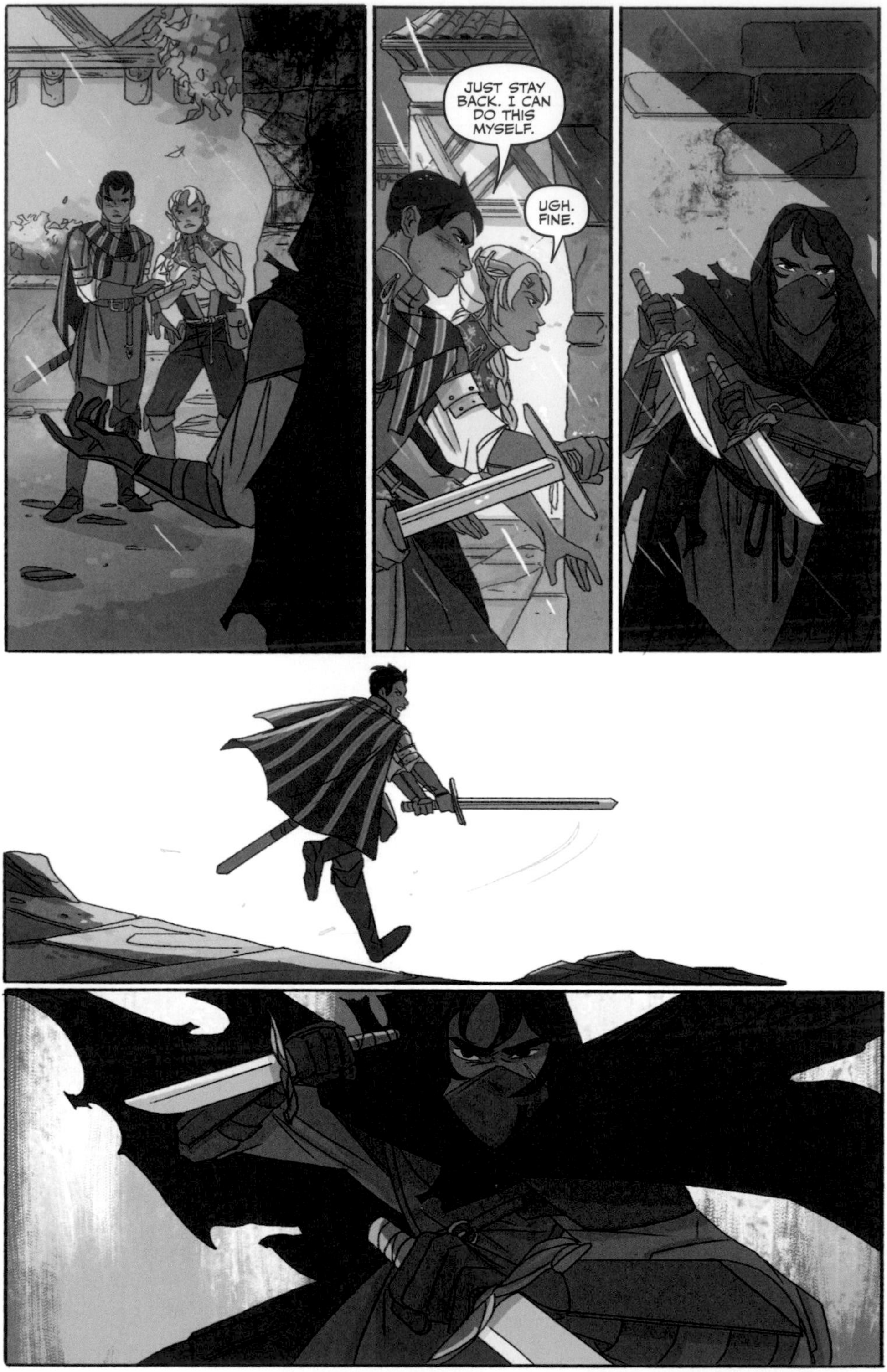
JUST STAY BACK. I CAN DO THIS MYSELF.
UGH. FINE.

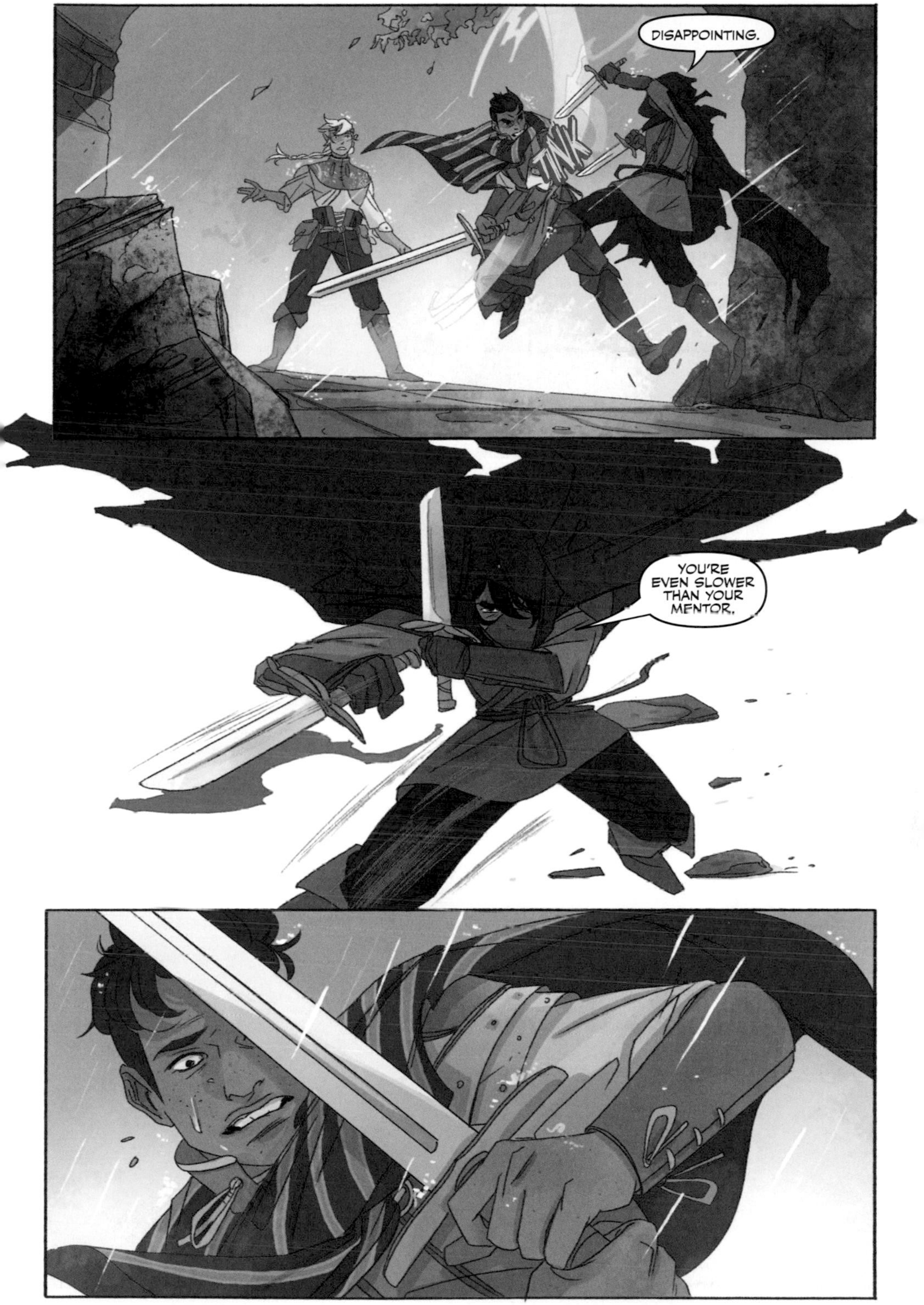
DISAPPOINTING.
TINK
YOU'RE EVEN SLOWER THAN YOUR MENTOR.

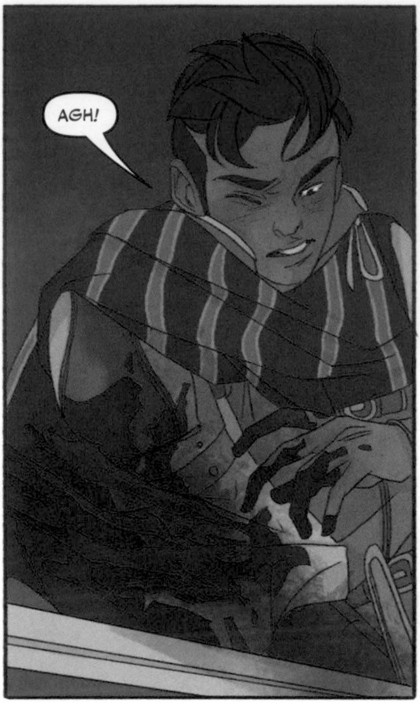
AGH!

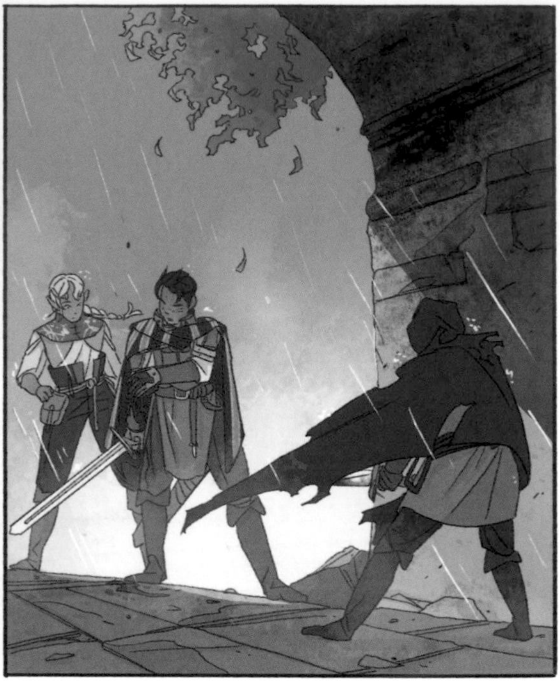

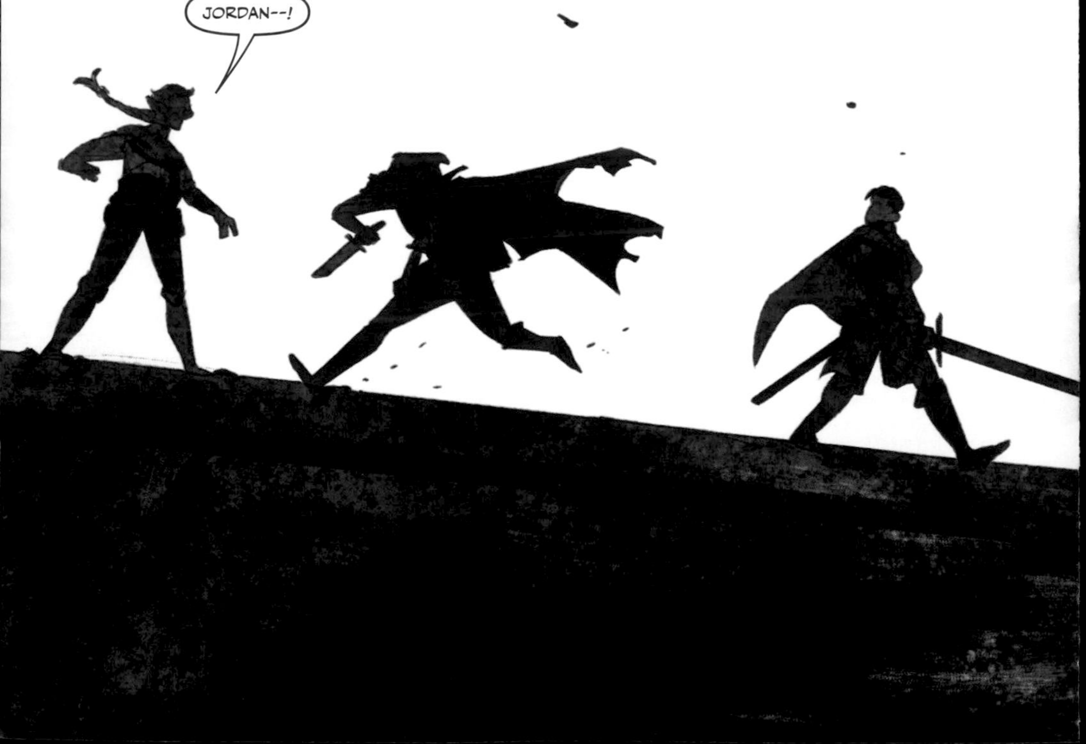
JORDAN--!

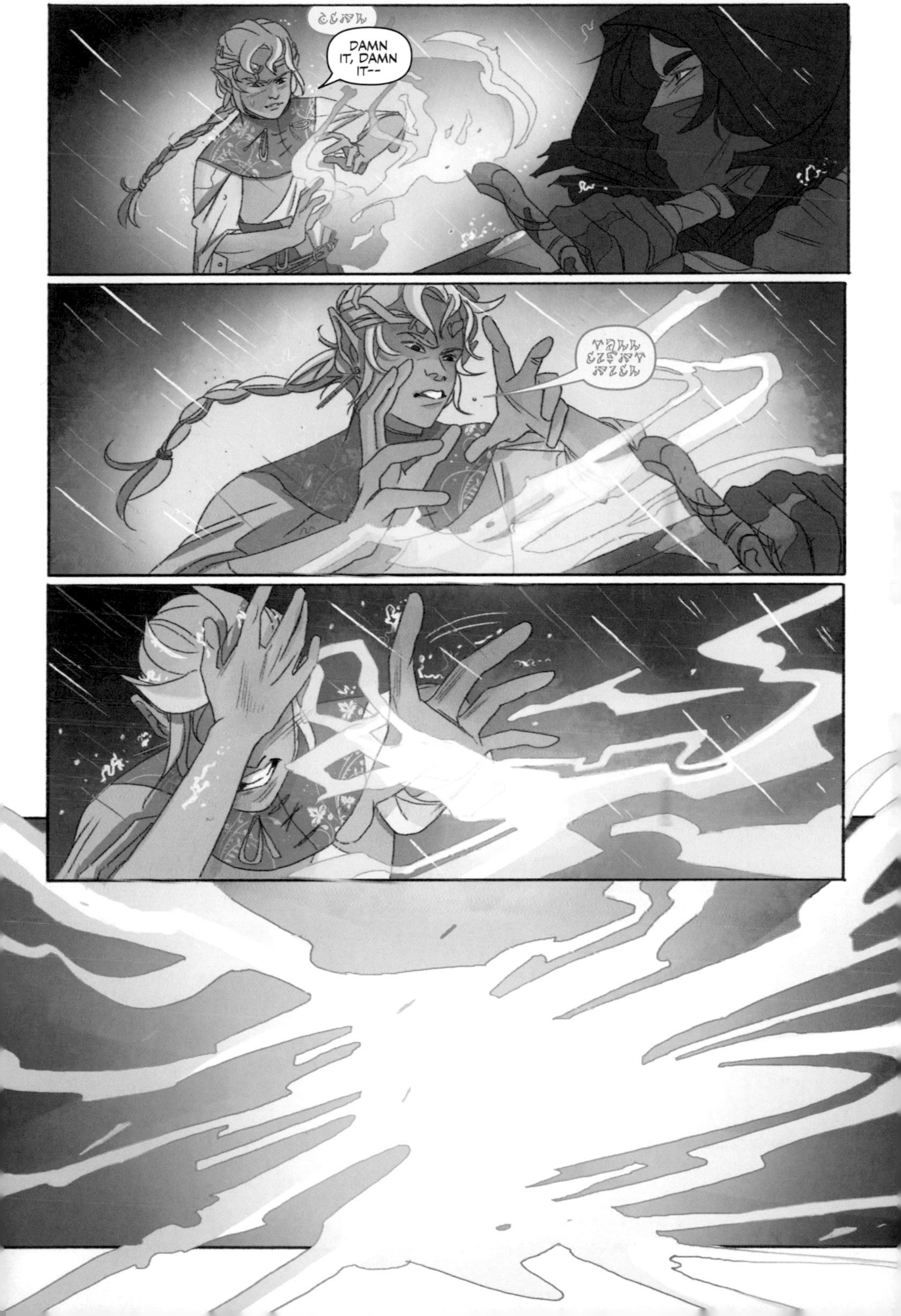
DAMN IT, DAMN IT--

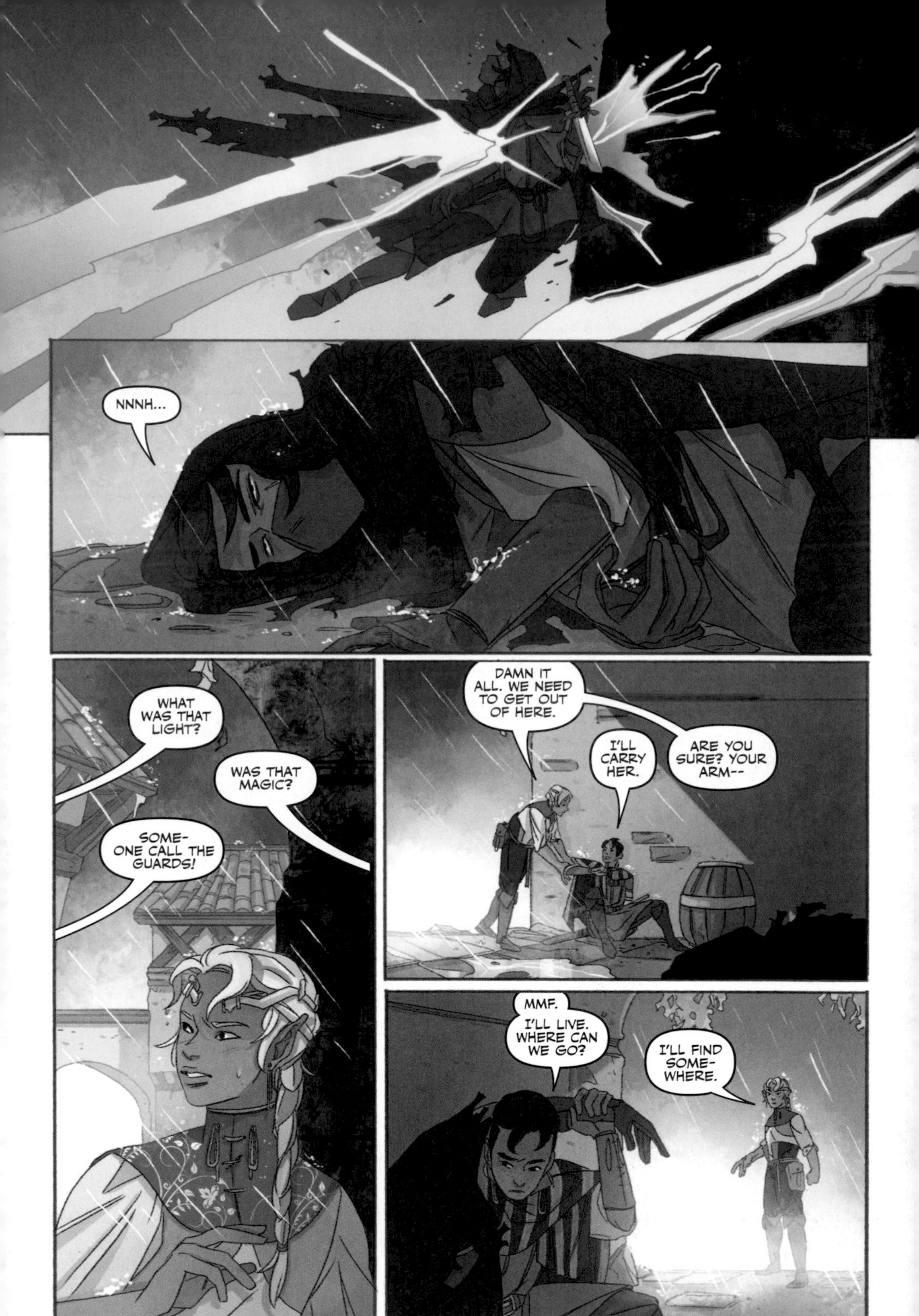
NNNH...
WHAT WAS THAT LIGHT?
WAS THAT MAGIC?
SOME-ONE CALL THE GUARDS!
DAMN IT ALL. WE NEED TO GET OUT OF HERE.
I'LL CARRY HER.
ARE YOU SURE? YOUR ARM--
MMF.
I'LL LIVE. WHERE CAN WE GO?
I'LL FIND SOME-WHERE.

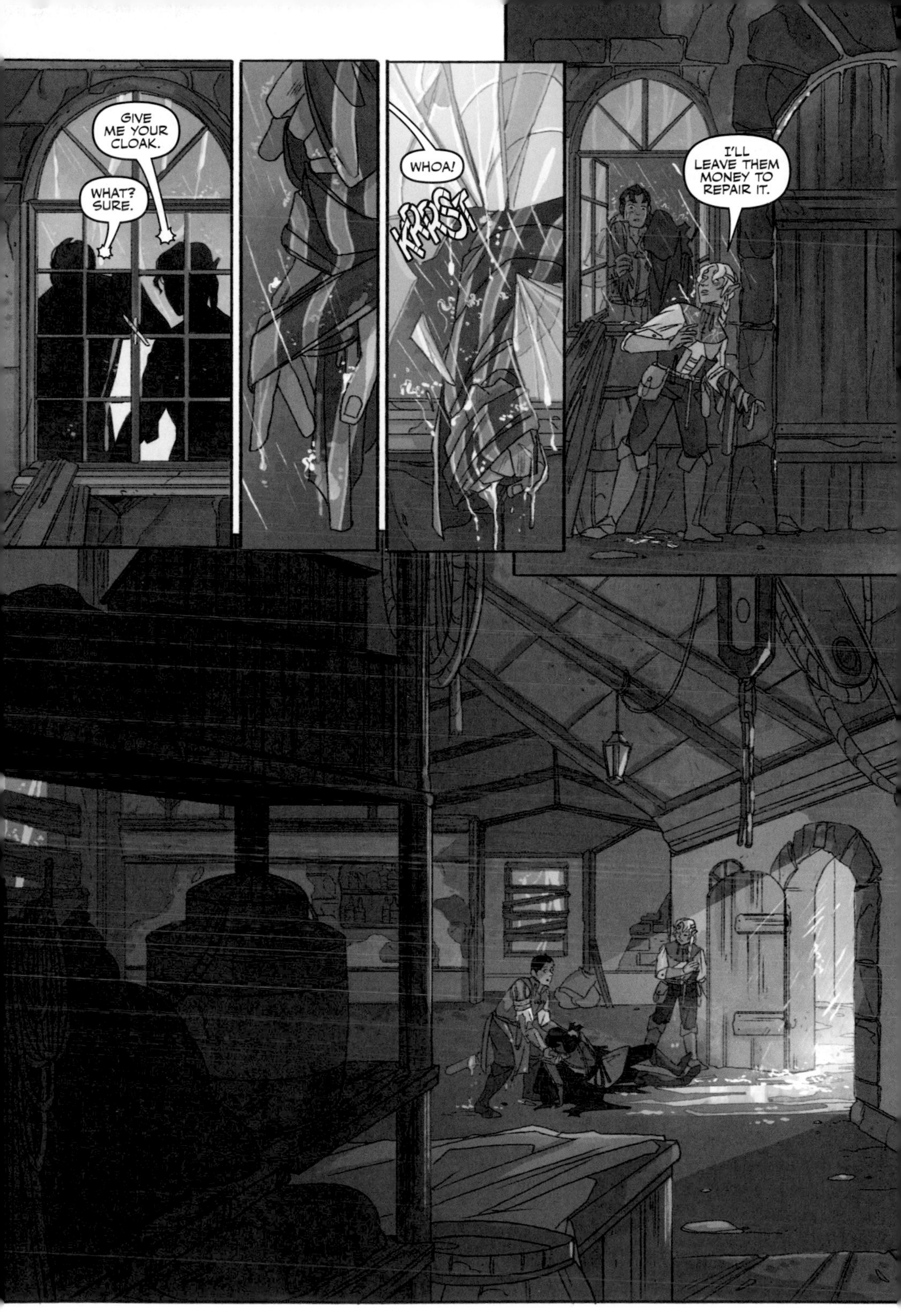
GIVE ME YOUR CLOAK.
WHAT? SURE.
WHOA!
KRRST
I'LL LEAVE THEM MONEY TO REPAIR IT.

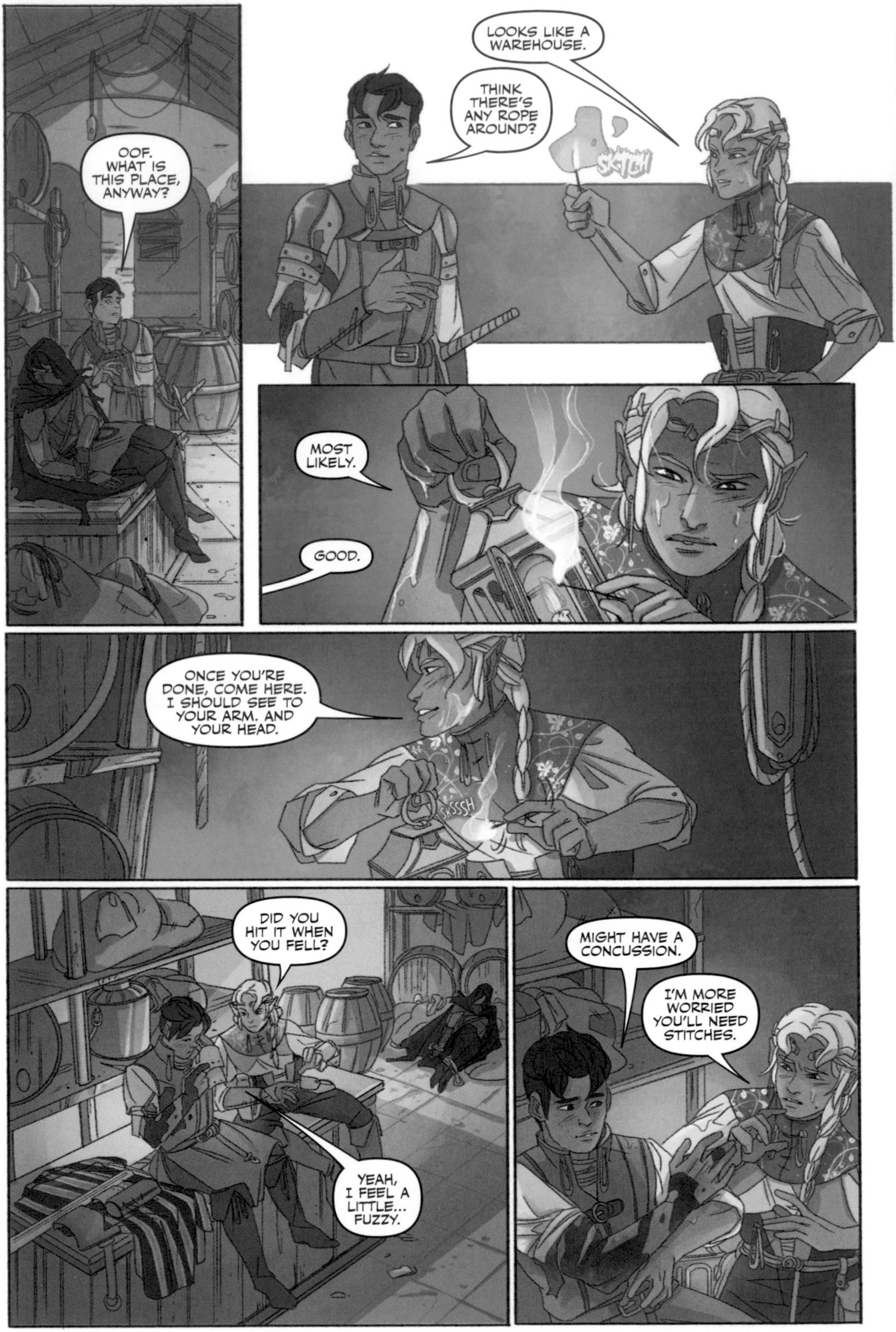
OOF. WHAT IS THIS PLACE, ANYWAY?
THINK THERE'S ANY ROPE AROUND?
LOOKS LIKE A WAREHOUSE.
SKTCH
MOST LIKELY.
GOOD.
ONCE YOU'RE DONE, COME HERE. I SHOULD SEE TO YOUR ARM. AND YOUR HEAD.
SKSSSH
DID YOU HIT IT WHEN YOU FELL?
YEAH, I FEEL A LITTLE... FUZZY.
MIGHT HAVE A CONCUSSION.
I'M MORE WORRIED YOU'LL NEED STITCHES.

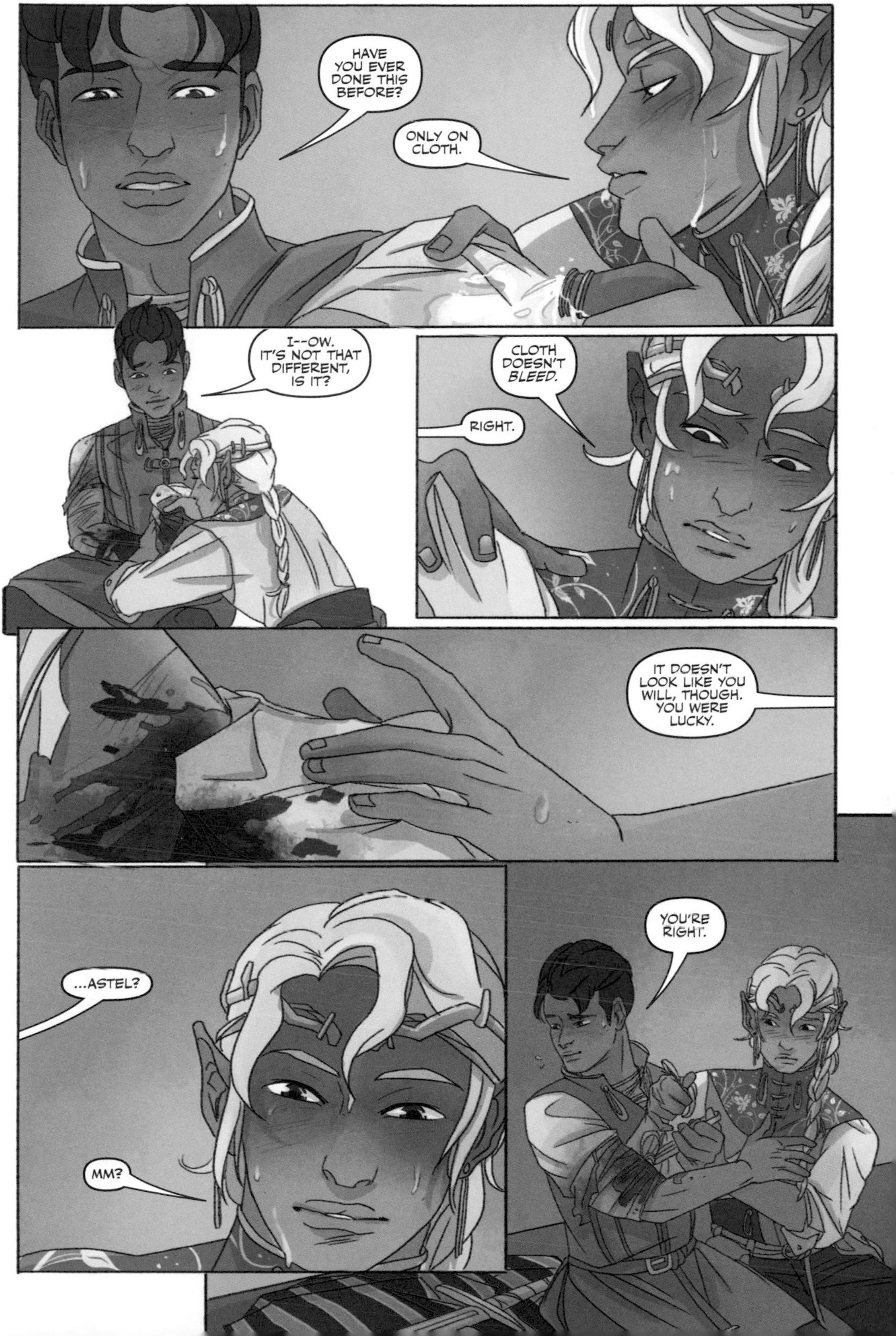
HAVE YOU EVER DONE THIS BEFORE?
ONLY ON CLOTH.
I--OW. IT'S NOT THAT DIFFERENT, IS IT?
CLOTH DOESN'T *BLEED.*
RIGHT.
IT DOESN'T LOOK LIKE YOU WILL, THOUGH. YOU WERE LUCKY.
...ASTEL?
MM?
YOU'RE RIGHT.

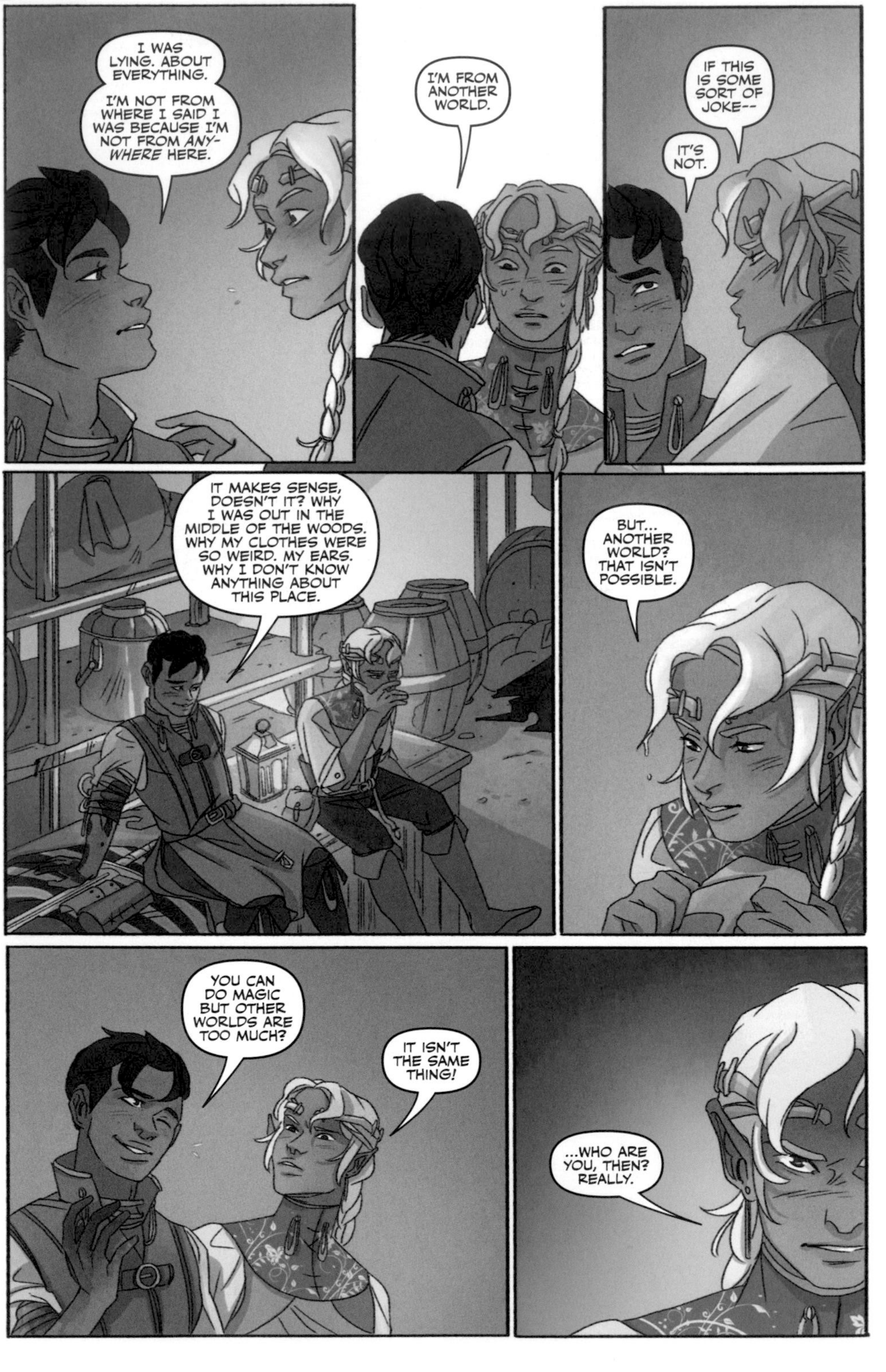
I WAS LYING. ABOUT EVERYTHING.
I'M NOT FROM WHERE I SAID I WAS BECAUSE I'M NOT FROM *ANY-WHERE* HERE.
I'M FROM ANOTHER WORLD.
IF THIS IS SOME SORT OF JOKE--
IT'S NOT.
IT MAKES SENSE, DOESN'T IT? WHY I WAS OUT IN THE MIDDLE OF THE WOODS. WHY MY CLOTHES WERE SO WEIRD. MY EARS. WHY I DON'T KNOW ANYTHING ABOUT THIS PLACE.
BUT... ANOTHER WORLD? THAT ISN'T POSSIBLE.
YOU CAN DO MAGIC BUT OTHER WORLDS ARE TOO MUCH?
IT ISN'T THE SAME THING!
...WHO ARE YOU, THEN? REALLY.

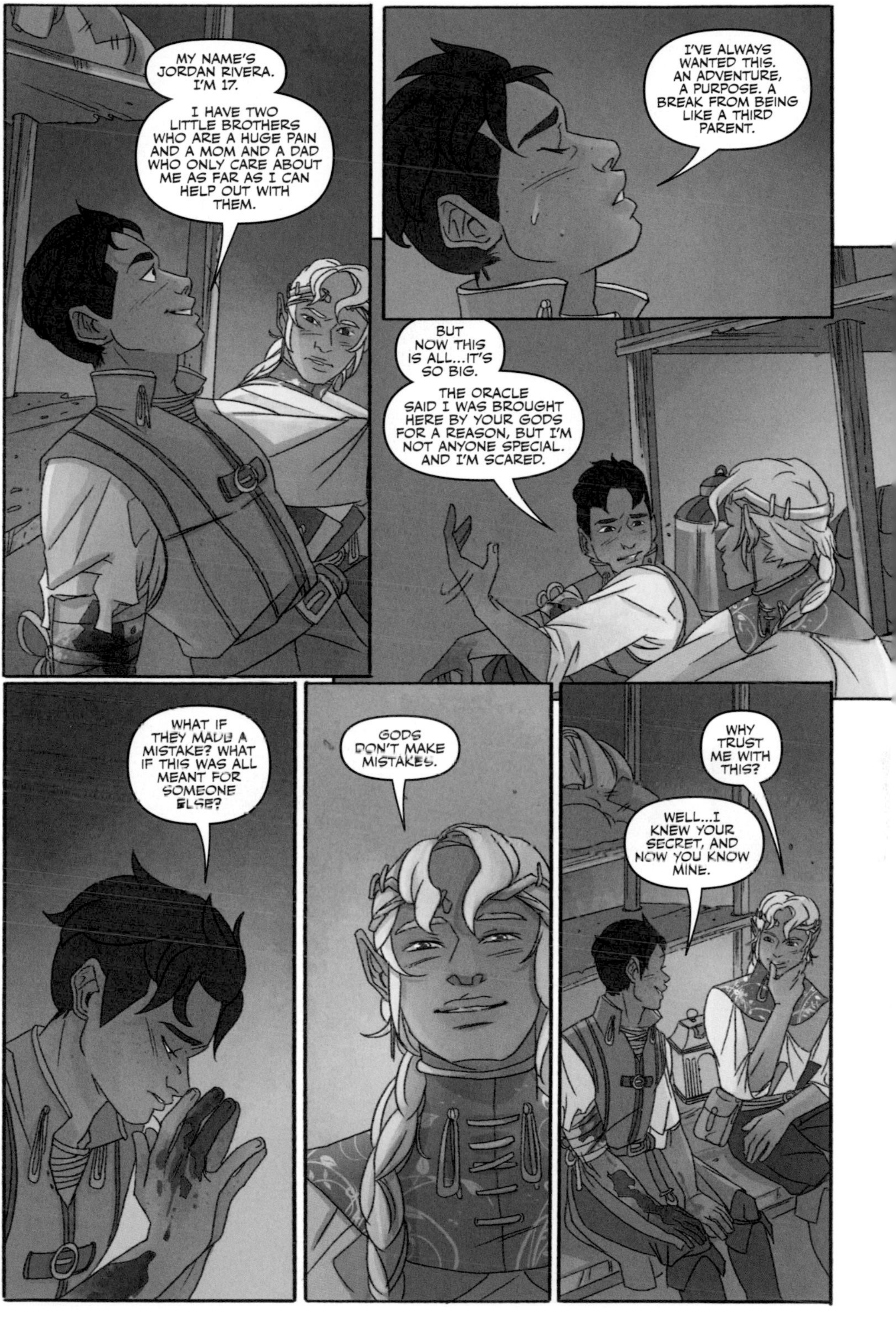
MY NAME'S JORDAN RIVERA. I'M 17.
I HAVE TWO LITTLE BROTHERS WHO ARE A HUGE PAIN AND A MOM AND A DAD WHO ONLY CARE ABOUT ME AS FAR AS I CAN HELP OUT WITH THEM.
I'VE ALWAYS WANTED THIS. AN ADVENTURE, A PURPOSE. A BREAK FROM BEING LIKE A THIRD PARENT.
BUT NOW THIS IS ALL...IT'S SO BIG.
THE ORACLE SAID I WAS BROUGHT HERE BY YOUR GODS FOR A REASON, BUT I'M NOT ANYONE SPECIAL. AND I'M SCARED.
WHAT IF THEY MADE A MISTAKE? WHAT IF THIS WAS ALL MEANT FOR SOMEONE ELSE?
GODS DON'T MAKE MISTAKES.
WHY TRUST ME WITH THIS?
WELL...I KNEW YOUR SECRET, AND NOW YOU KNOW MINE.

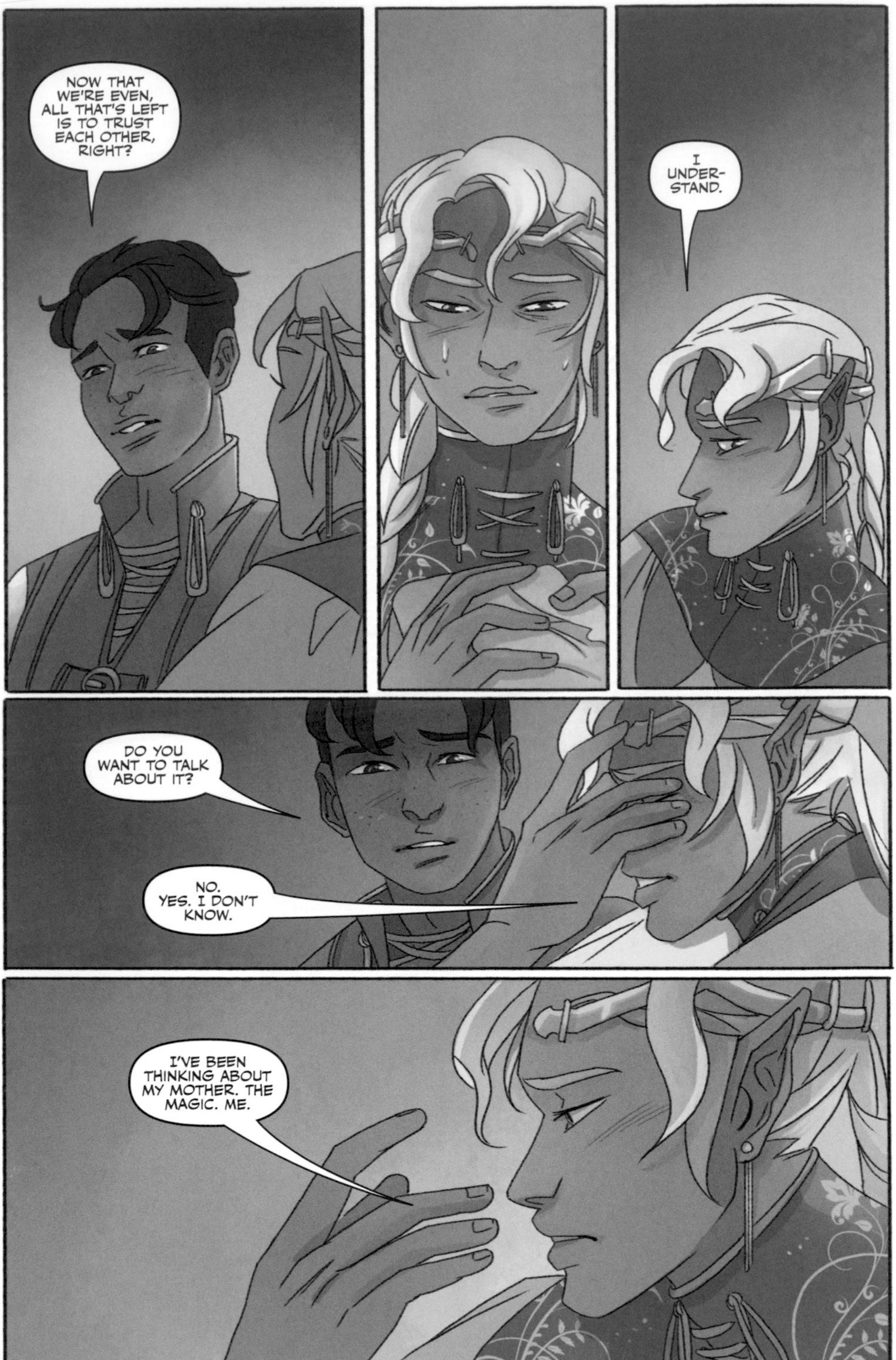
NOW THAT WE'RE EVEN, ALL THAT'S LEFT IS TO TRUST EACH OTHER, RIGHT?
I UNDER-STAND.
DO YOU WANT TO TALK ABOUT IT?
NO. YES. I DON'T KNOW.
I'VE BEEN THINKING ABOUT MY MOTHER. THE MAGIC. ME.

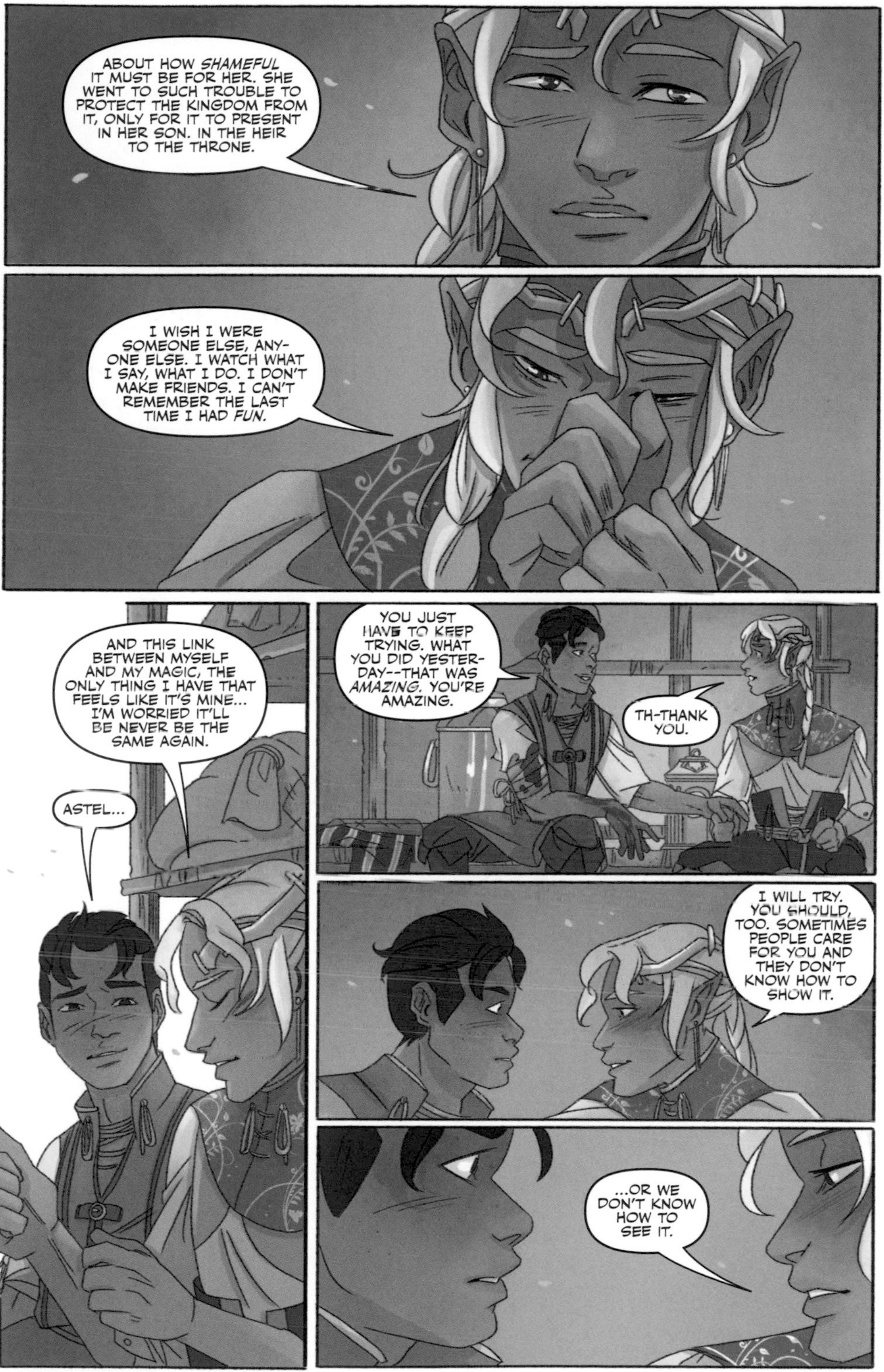
ABOUT HOW *SHAMEFUL* IT MUST BE FOR HER. SHE WENT TO SUCH TROUBLE TO PROTECT THE KINGDOM FROM IT, ONLY FOR IT TO PRESENT IN HER SON. IN THE HEIR TO THE THRONE.
I WISH I WERE SOMEONE ELSE, ANY-ONE ELSE. I WATCH WHAT I SAY, WHAT I DO. I DON'T MAKE FRIENDS. I CAN'T REMEMBER THE LAST TIME I HAD *FUN.*
AND THIS LINK BETWEEN MYSELF AND MY MAGIC, THE ONLY THING I HAVE THAT FEELS LIKE IT'S MINE... I'M WORRIED IT'LL BE NEVER BE THE SAME AGAIN.
ASTEL...
YOU JUST HAVE TO KEEP TRYING. WHAT YOU DID YESTER-DAY--THAT WAS *AMAZING.* YOU'RE AMAZING.
TH-THANK YOU.
I WILL TRY. YOU SHOULD, TOO. SOMETIMES PEOPLE CARE FOR YOU AND THEY DON'T KNOW HOW TO SHOW IT.
...OR WE DON'T KNOW HOW TO SEE IT.

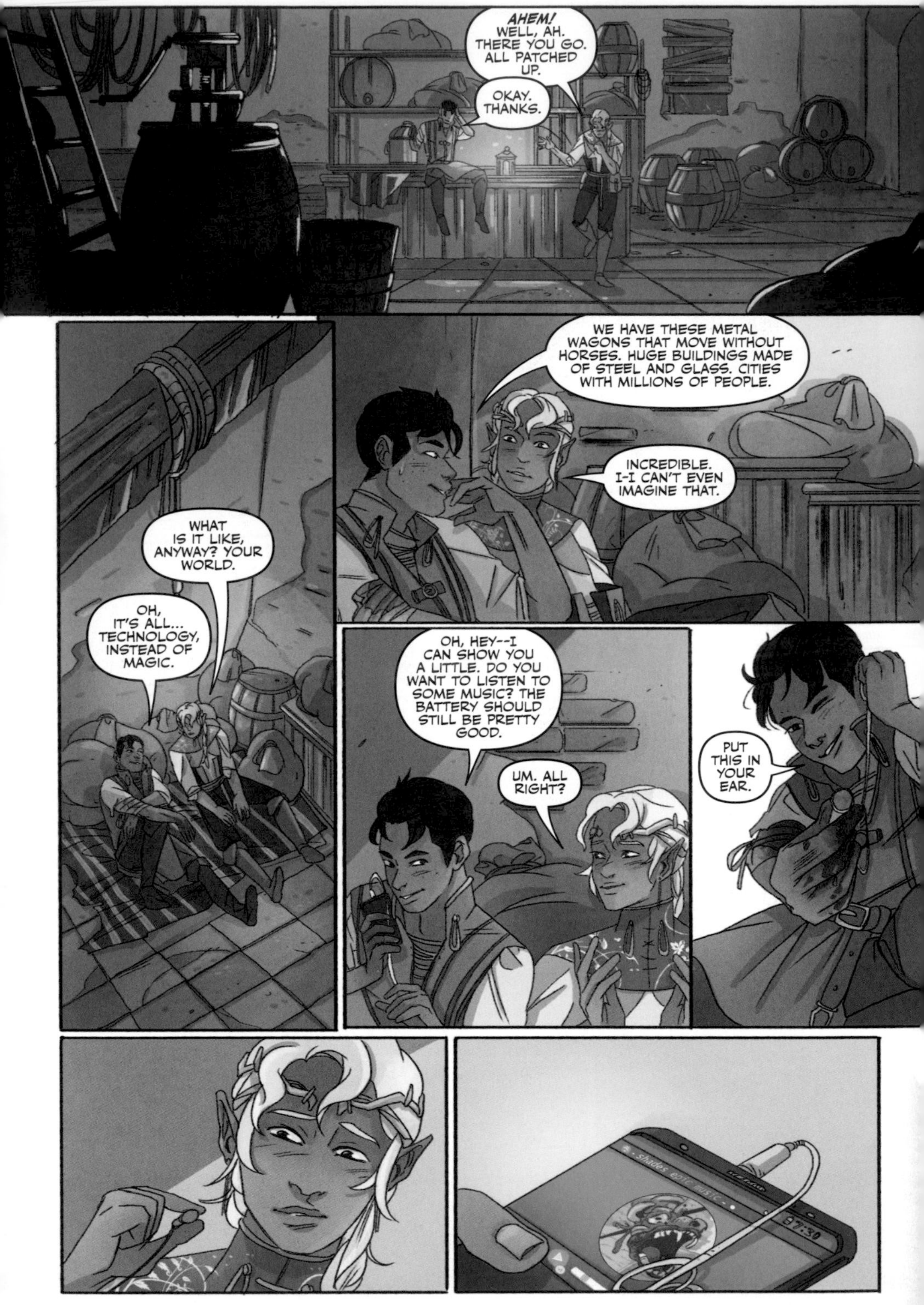
AHEM! WELL, AH. THERE YOU GO. ALL PATCHED UP.
OKAY. THANKS.
WHAT IS IT LIKE, ANYWAY? YOUR WORLD.
OH, IT'S ALL... TECHNOLOGY, INSTEAD OF MAGIC.
WE HAVE THESE METAL WAGONS THAT MOVE WITHOUT HORSES. HUGE BUILDINGS MADE OF STEEL AND GLASS. CITIES WITH MILLIONS OF PEOPLE.
INCREDIBLE. I-I CAN'T EVEN IMAGINE THAT.
OH, HEY--I CAN SHOW YOU A LITTLE. DO YOU WANT TO LISTEN TO SOME MUSIC? THE BATTERY SHOULD STILL BE PRETTY GOOD.
UM. ALL RIGHT?
PUT THIS IN YOUR EAR.

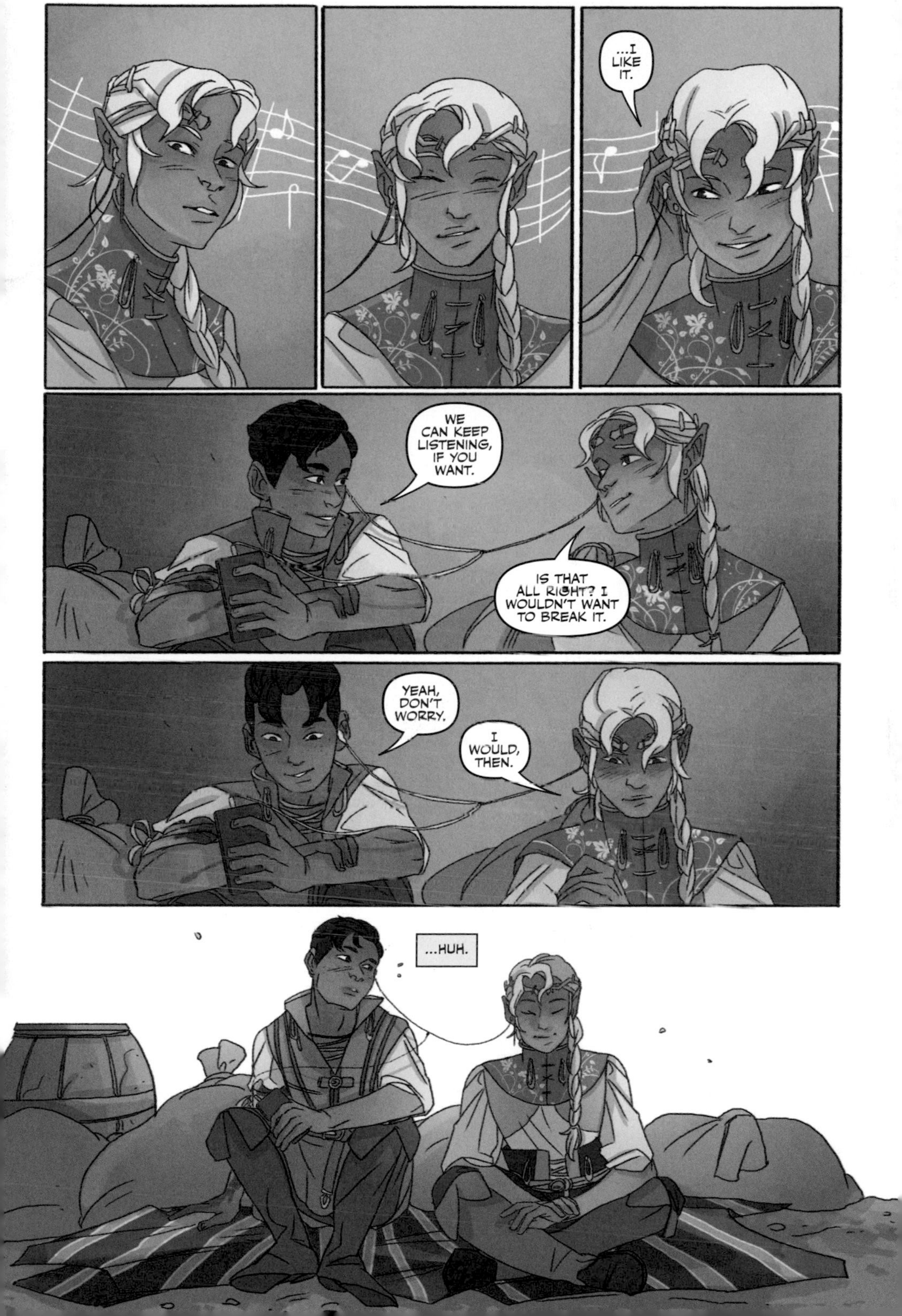
...I LIKE IT.
WE CAN KEEP LISTENING, IF YOU WANT.
IS THAT ALL RIGHT? I WOULDN'T WANT TO BREAK IT.
YEAH, DON'T WORRY.
I WOULD, THEN.
...HUH.

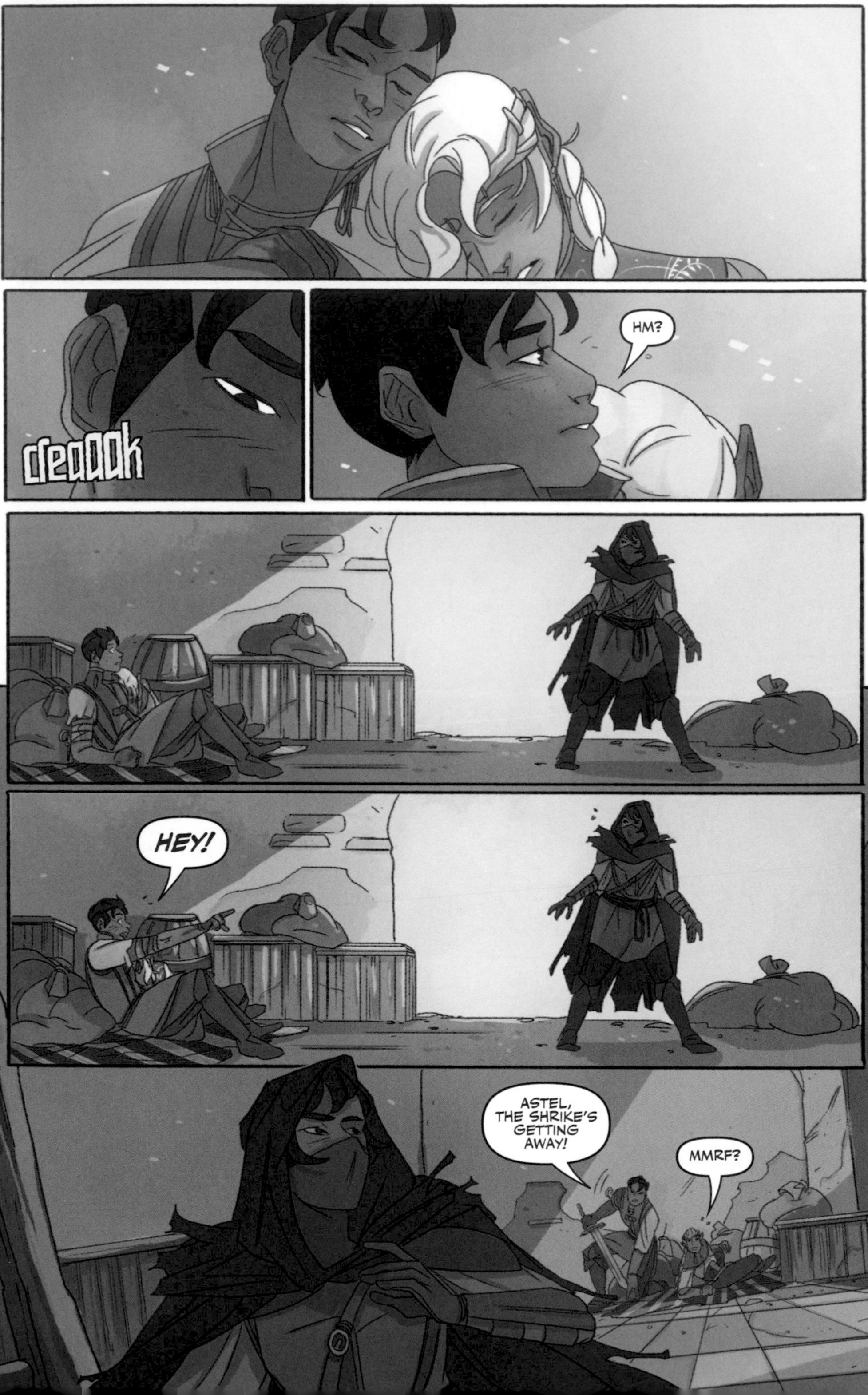
creaaak
HM?
HEY!
ASTEL, THE SHRIKE'S GETTING AWAY!
MMRF?

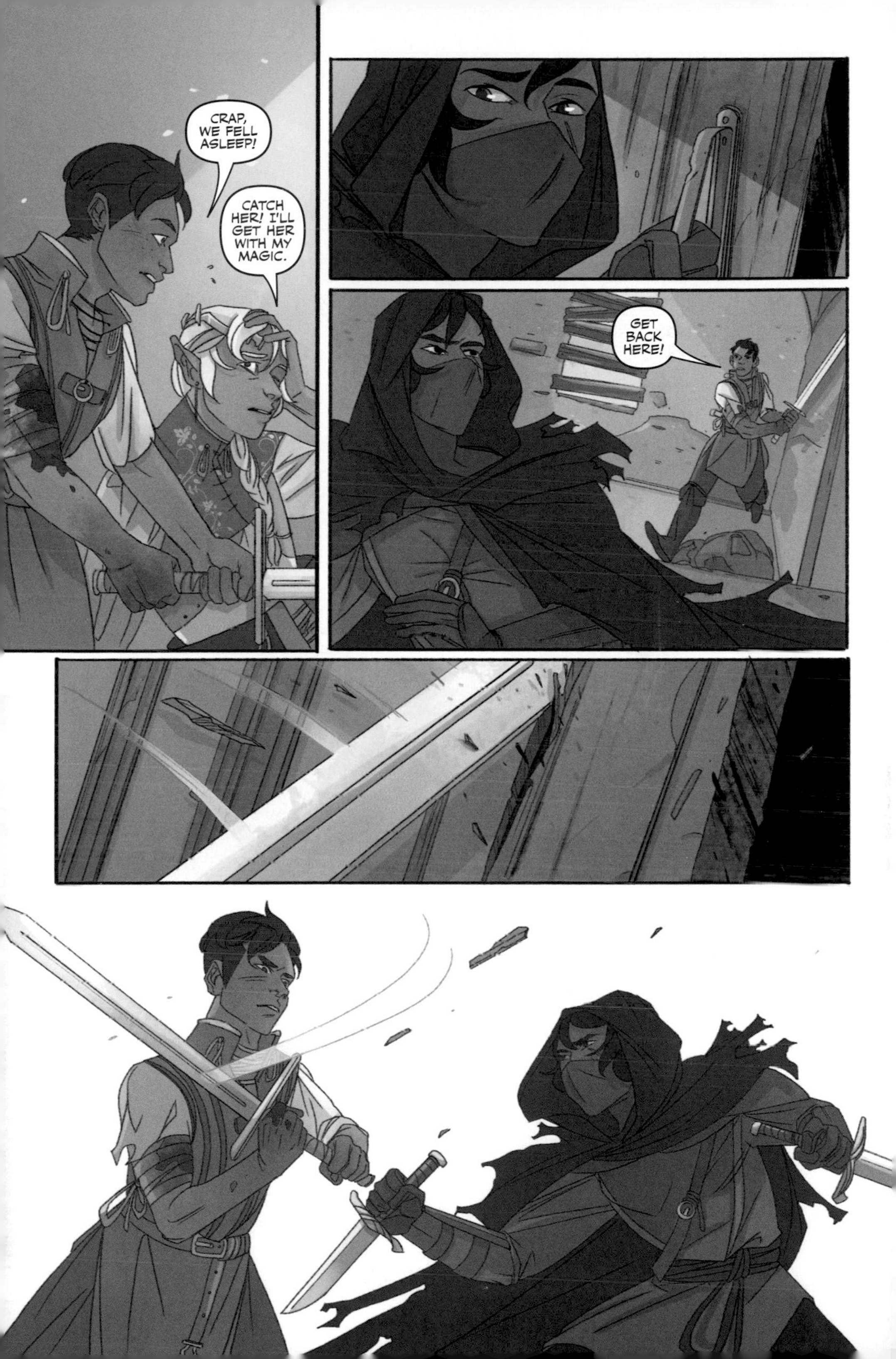
CRAP, WE FELL ASLEEP!
CATCH HER! I'LL GET HER WITH MY MAGIC.
GET BACK HERE!

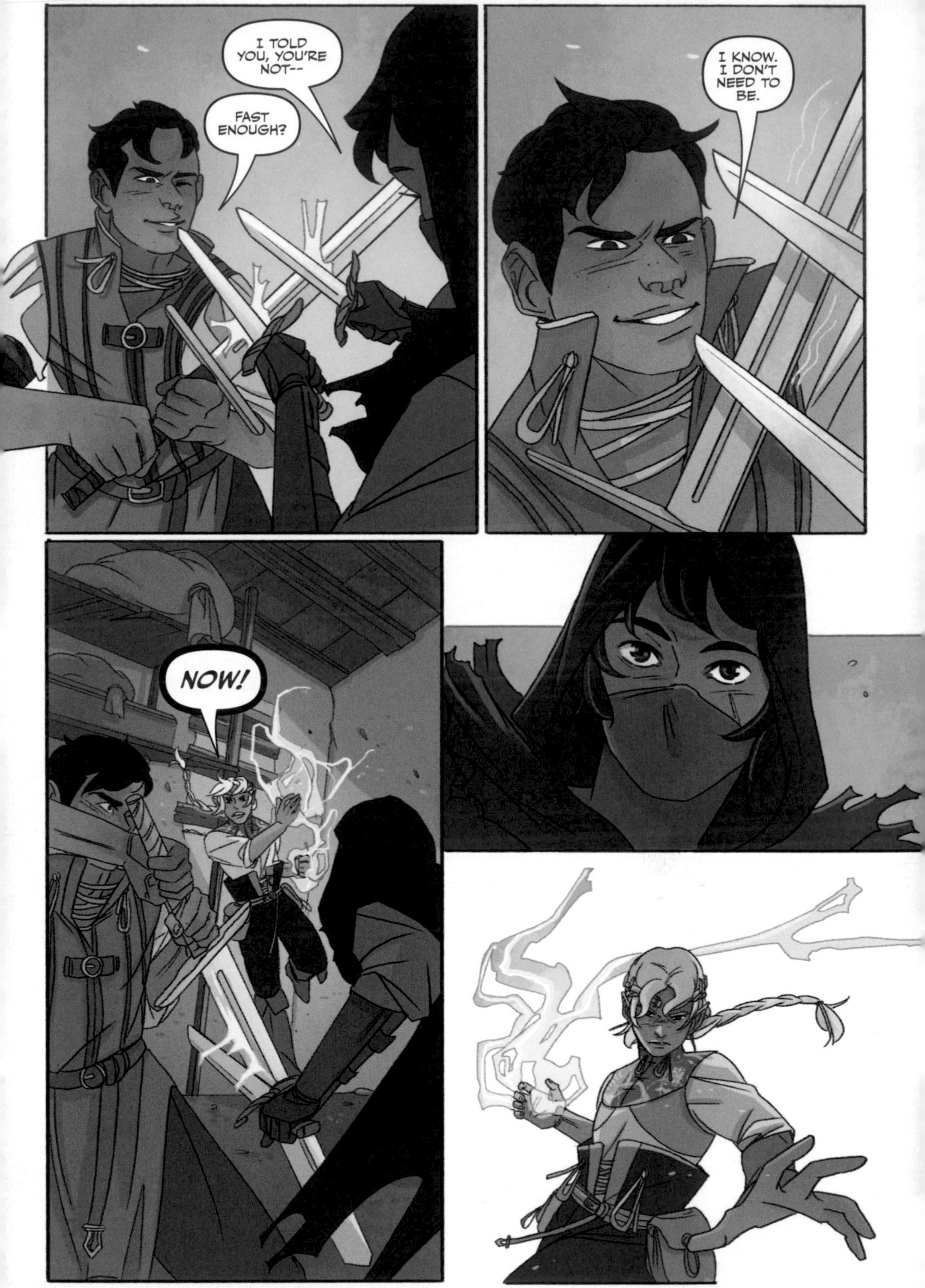
I TOLD YOU, YOU'RE NOT--
FAST ENOUGH?
I KNOW. I DON'T NEED TO BE.
NOW!

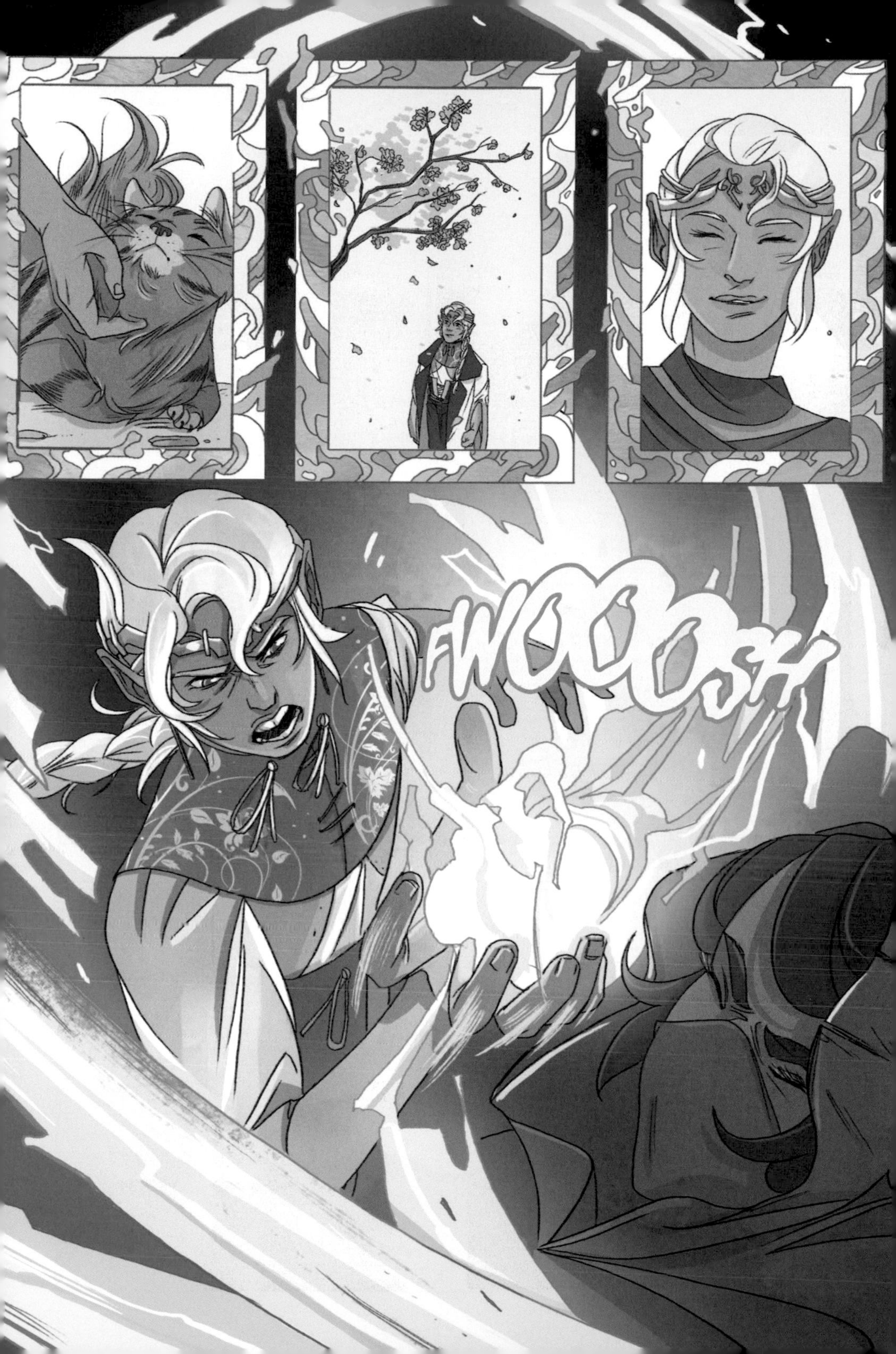
FWOOOSH

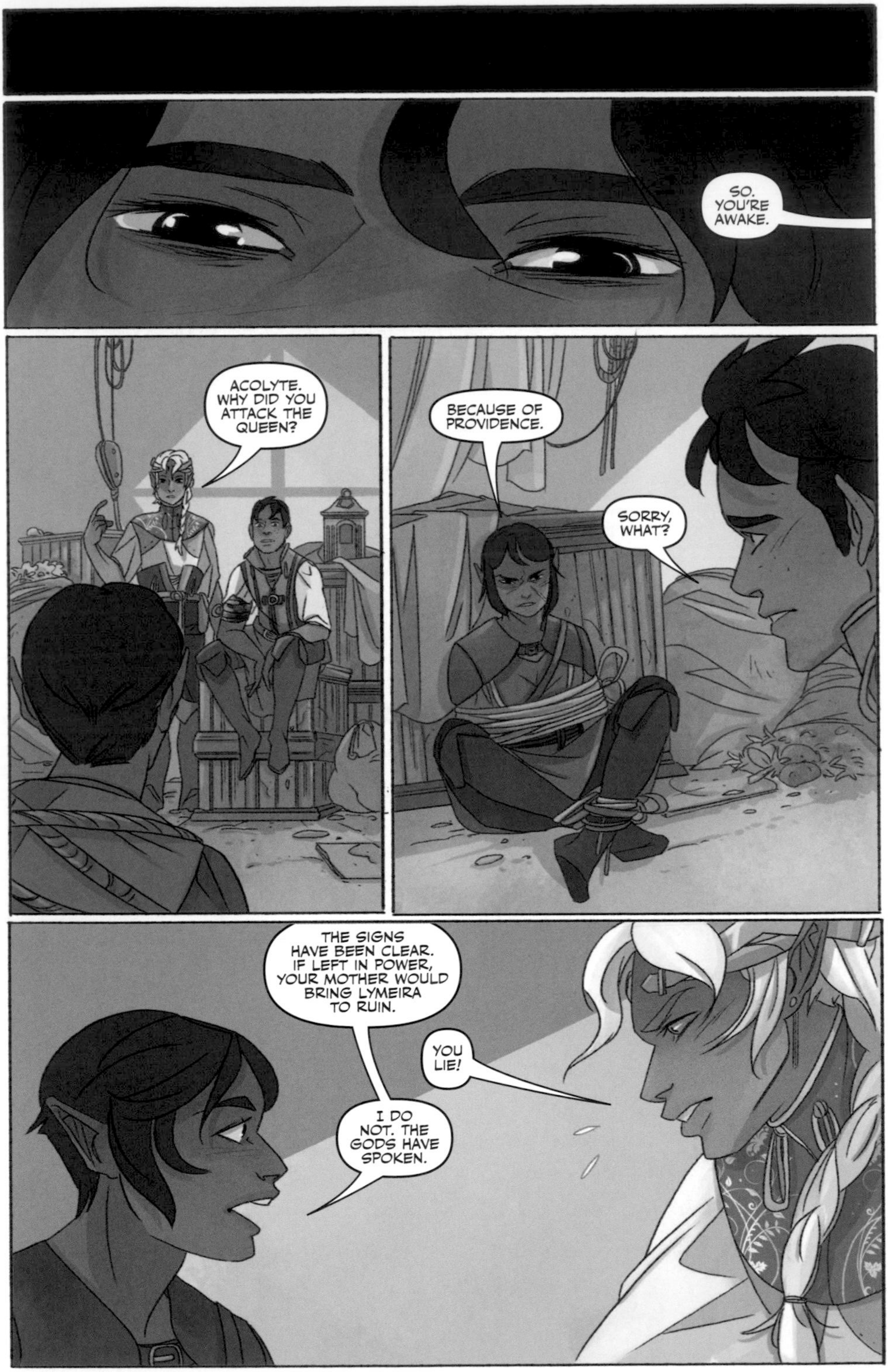
SO. YOU'RE AWAKE.
ACOLYTE. WHY DID YOU ATTACK THE QUEEN?
BECAUSE OF PROVIDENCE.
SORRY, WHAT?
THE SIGNS HAVE BEEN CLEAR. IF LEFT IN POWER, YOUR MOTHER WOULD BRING LYMEIRA TO RUIN.
YOU LIE!
I DO NOT. THE GODS HAVE SPOKEN.

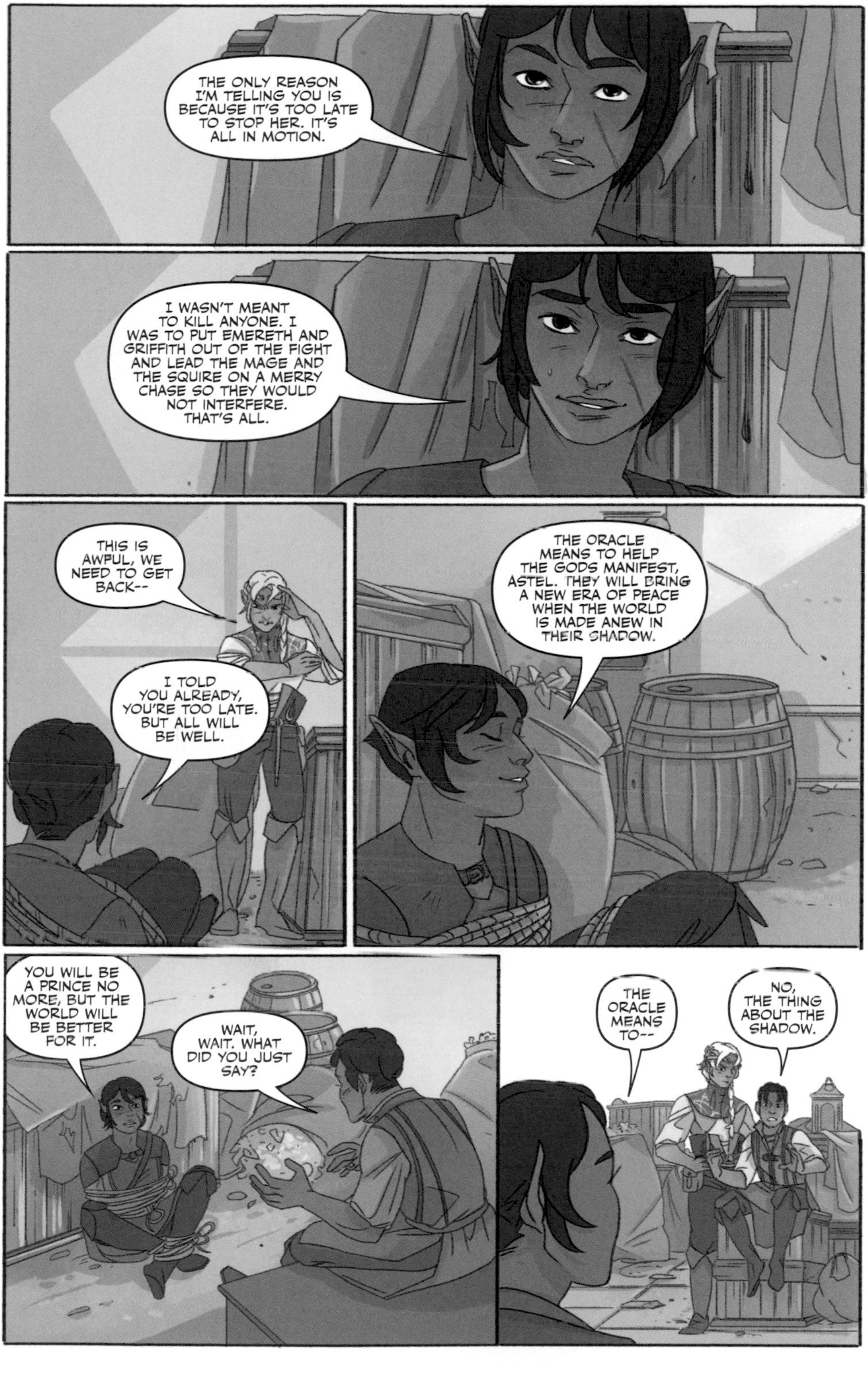
THE ONLY REASON I'M TELLING YOU IS BECAUSE IT'S TOO LATE TO STOP HER. IT'S ALL IN MOTION.
I WASN'T MEANT TO KILL ANYONE. I WAS TO PUT EMERETH AND GRIFFITH OUT OF THE FIGHT AND LEAD THE MAGE AND THE SQUIRE ON A MERRY CHASE SO THEY WOULD NOT INTERFERE. THAT'S ALL.
THIS IS AWFUL, WE NEED TO GET BACK--
I TOLD YOU ALREADY, YOU'RE TOO LATE. BUT ALL WILL BE WELL.
THE ORACLE MEANS TO HELP THE GODS MANIFEST, ASTEL. THEY WILL BRING A NEW ERA OF PEACE WHEN THE WORLD IS MADE ANEW IN THEIR SHADOW.
YOU WILL BE A PRINCE NO MORE, BUT THE WORLD WILL BE BETTER FOR IT.
WAIT, WAIT. WHAT DID YOU JUST SAY?
THE ORACLE MEANS TO--
NO, THE THING ABOUT THE SHADOW.

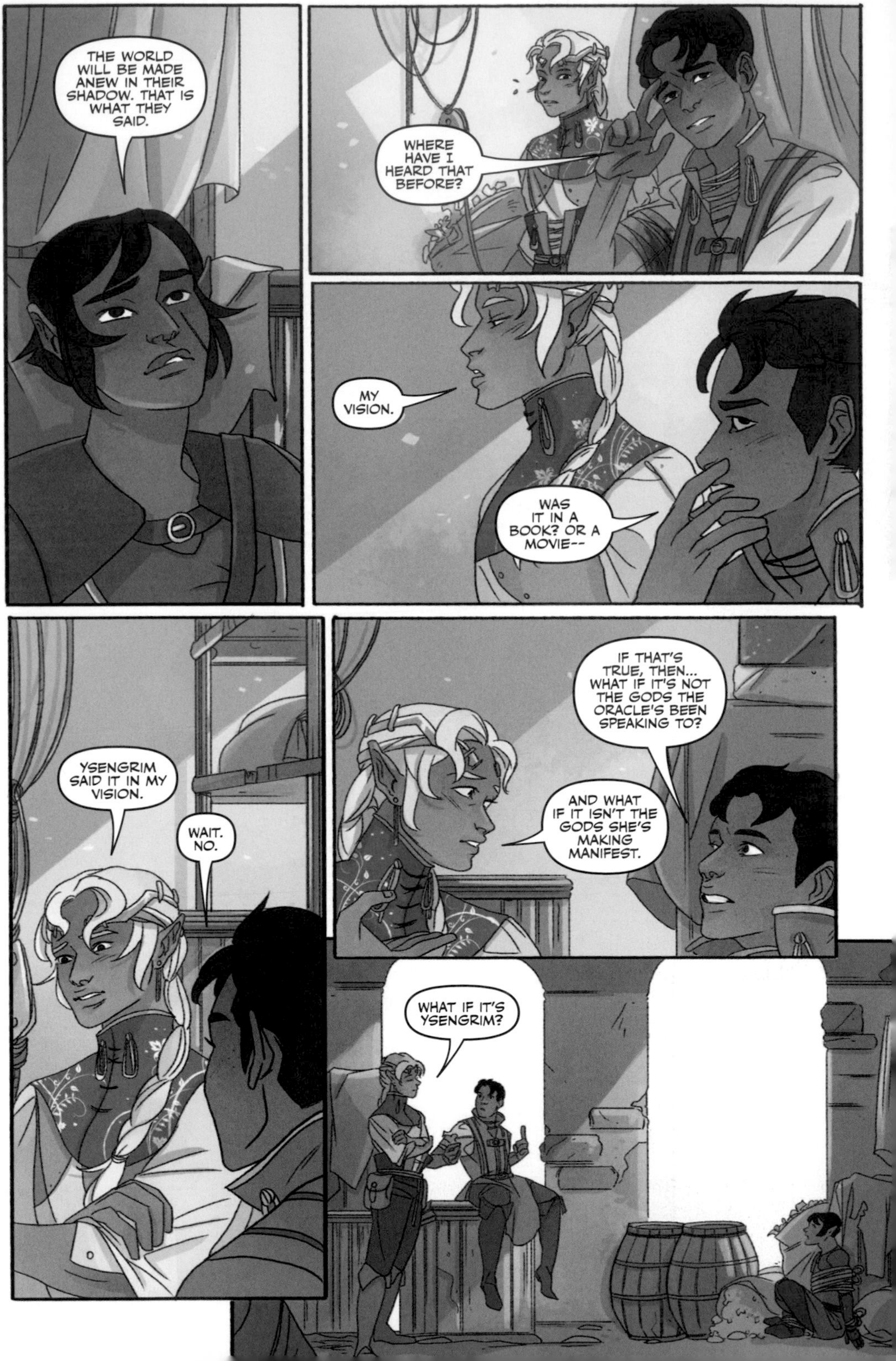
THE WORLD WILL BE MADE ANEW IN THEIR SHADOW. THAT IS WHAT THEY SAID.
WHERE HAVE I HEARD THAT BEFORE?
MY VISION.
WAS IT IN A BOOK? OR A MOVIE--
YSENGRIM SAID IT IN MY VISION.
WAIT. NO.
IF THAT'S TRUE, THEN... WHAT IF IT'S NOT THE GODS THE ORACLE'S BEEN SPEAKING TO?
AND WHAT IF IT ISN'T THE GODS SHE'S MAKING MANIFEST.
WHAT IF IT'S YSENGRIM?

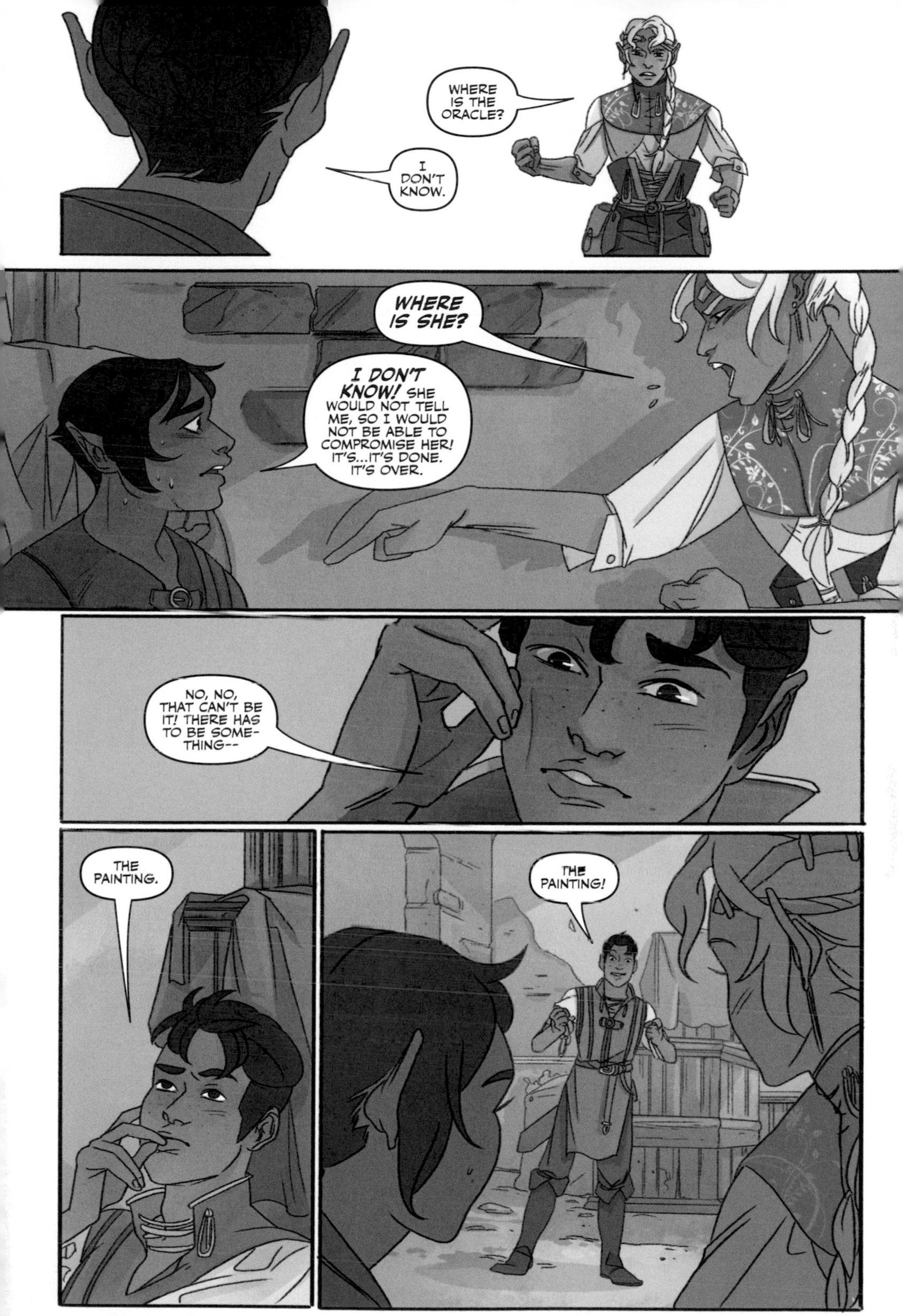
WHERE IS THE ORACLE?
I DON'T KNOW.
WHERE IS SHE?
I DON'T KNOW! SHE WOULD NOT TELL ME, SO I WOULD NOT BE ABLE TO COMPROMISE HER! IT'S...IT'S DONE. IT'S OVER.
NO, NO, THAT CAN'T BE IT! THERE HAS TO BE SOME-THING--
THE PAINTING.
THE PAINTING!

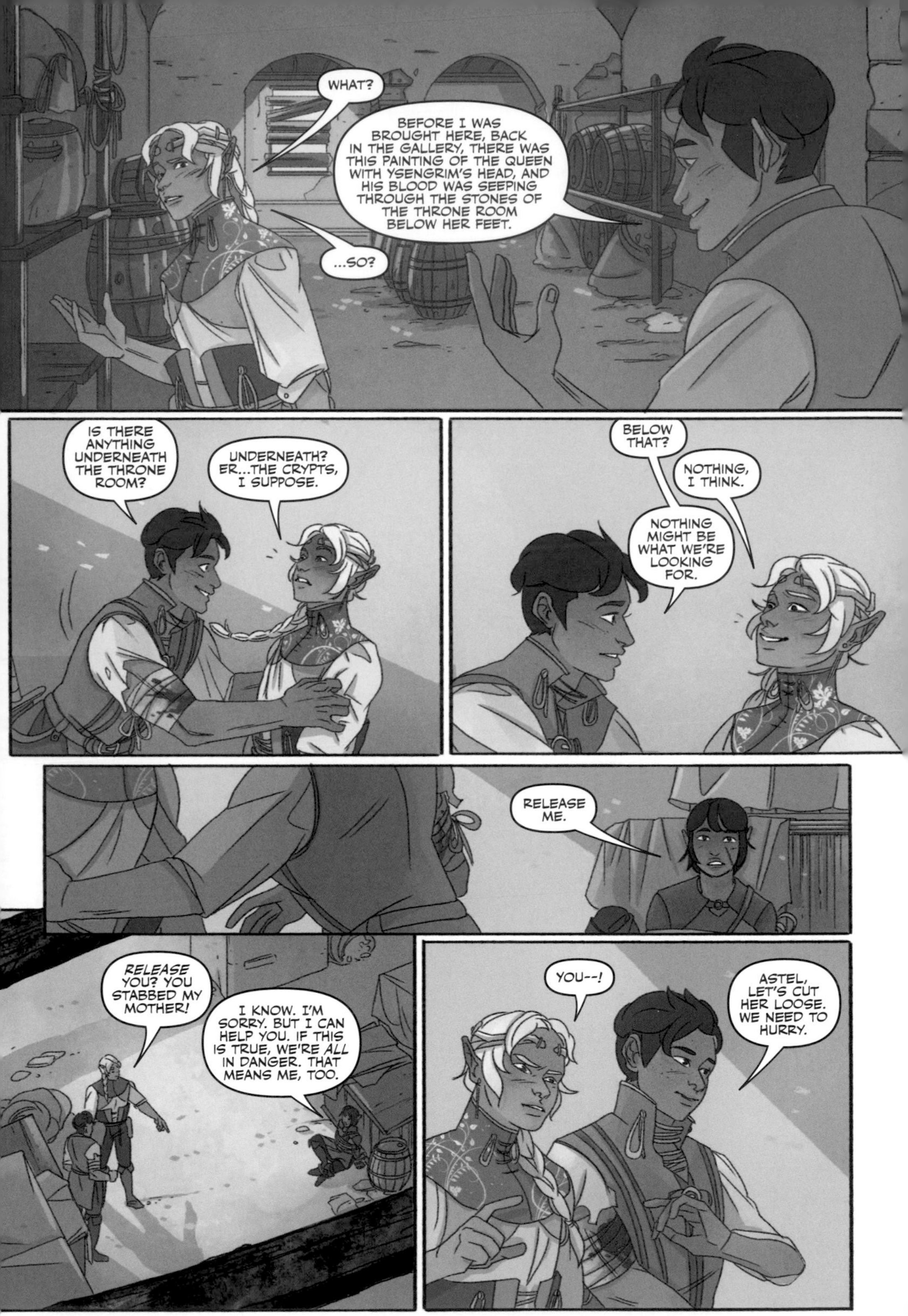
WHAT?
BEFORE I WAS BROUGHT HERE, BACK IN THE GALLERY, THERE WAS THIS PAINTING OF THE QUEEN WITH YSENGRIM'S HEAD, AND HIS BLOOD WAS SEEPING THROUGH THE STONES OF THE THRONE ROOM BELOW HER FEET.
...SO?
IS THERE ANYTHING UNDERNEATH THE THRONE ROOM?
UNDERNEATH? ER...THE CRYPTS, I SUPPOSE.
BELOW THAT?
NOTHING, I THINK.
NOTHING MIGHT BE WHAT WE'RE LOOKING FOR.
RELEASE ME.
*RELEASE* YOU? YOU STABBED MY MOTHER!
I KNOW. I'M SORRY. BUT I CAN HELP YOU. IF THIS IS TRUE, WE'RE *ALL* IN DANGER. THAT MEANS ME, TOO.
YOU--!
ASTEL, LET'S CUT HER LOOSE. WE NEED TO HURRY.

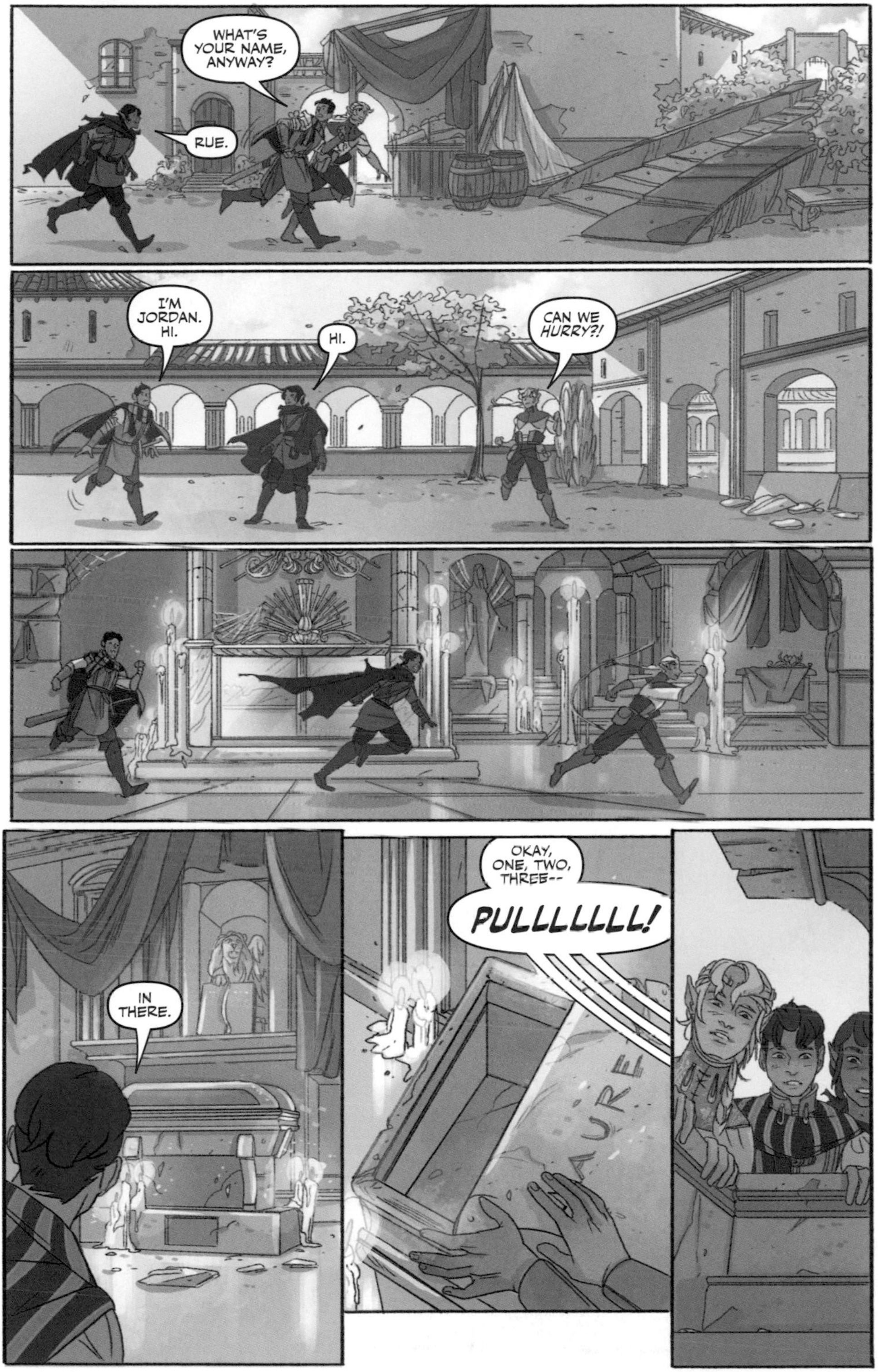
WHAT'S YOUR NAME, ANYWAY?
RUE.
I'M JORDAN. HI.
HI.
CAN WE *HURRY?!*
IN THERE.
OKAY, ONE, TWO, THREE--
PULLLLLLL!
AURE

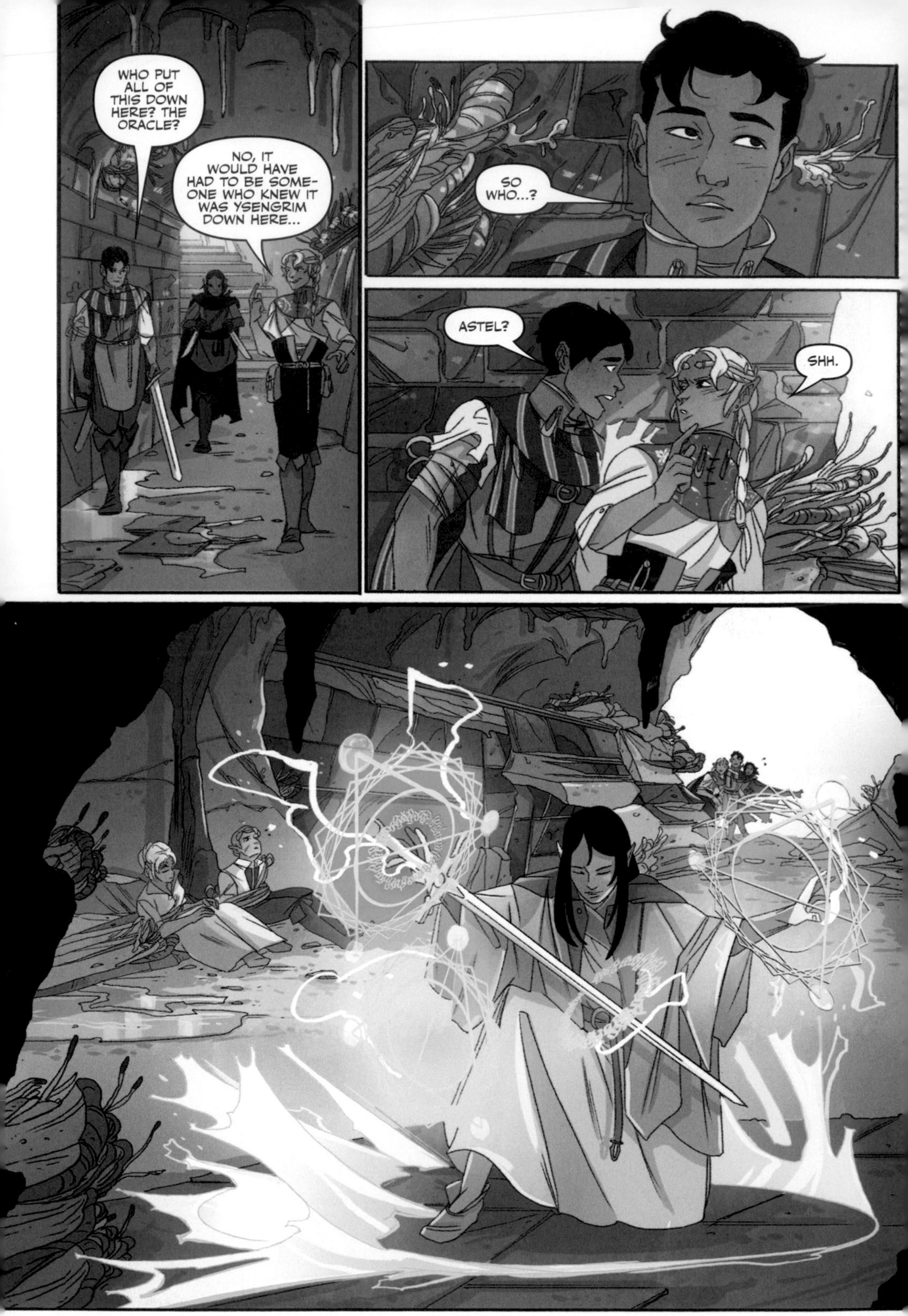
WHO PUT ALL OF THIS DOWN HERE? THE ORACLE?
NO, IT WOULD HAVE HAD TO BE SOME-ONE WHO KNEW IT WAS YSENGRIM DOWN HERE...
SO WHO...?
ASTEL?
SHH.

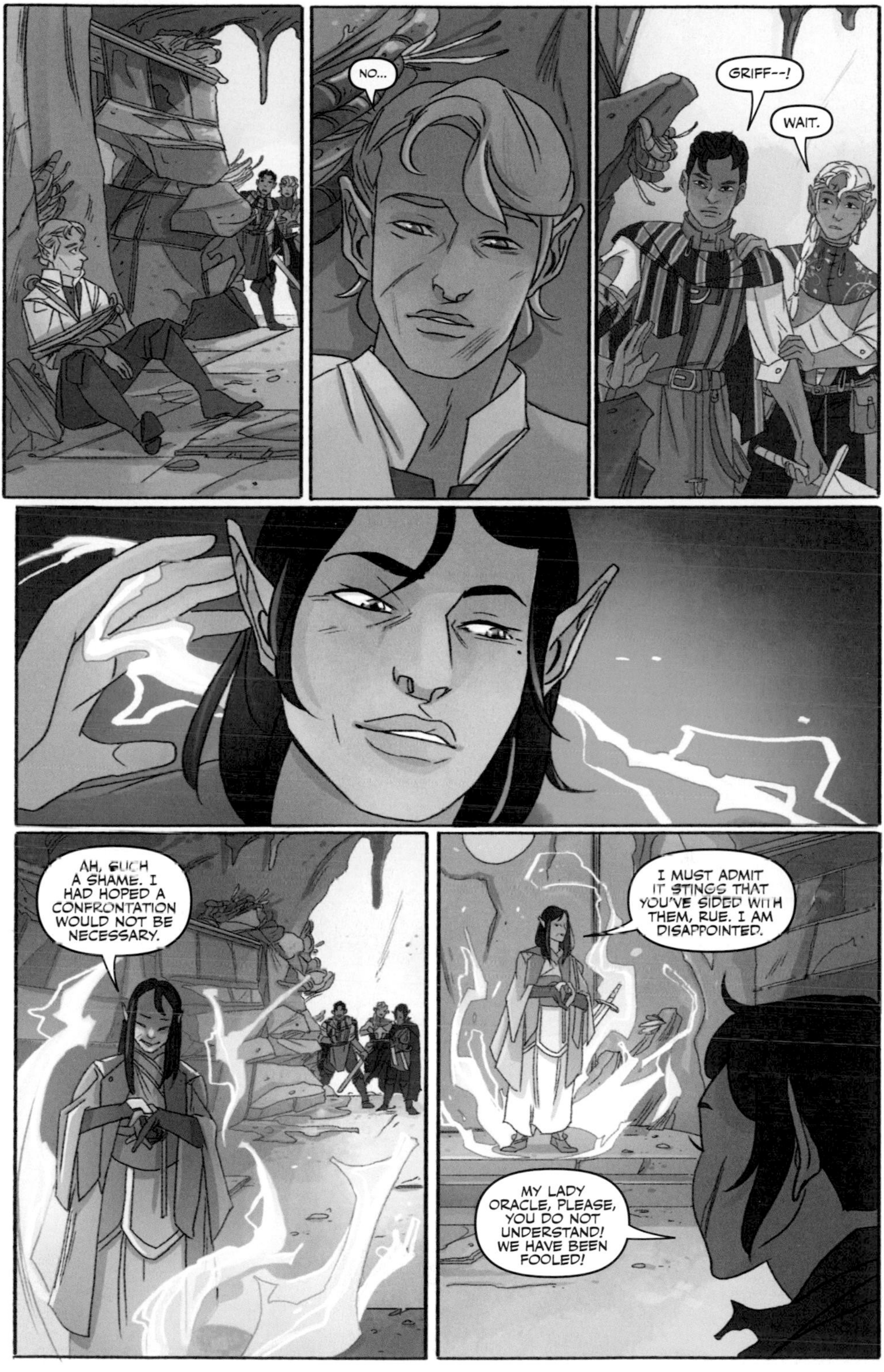
NO...
GRIFF--!
WAIT.
AH, SUCH A SHAME. I HAD HOPED A CONFRONTATION WOULD NOT BE NECESSARY.
I MUST ADMIT IT STINGS THAT YOU'VE SIDED WITH THEM, RUE. I AM DISAPPOINTED.
MY LADY ORACLE, PLEASE, YOU DO NOT UNDERSTAND! WE HAVE BEEN FOOLED!

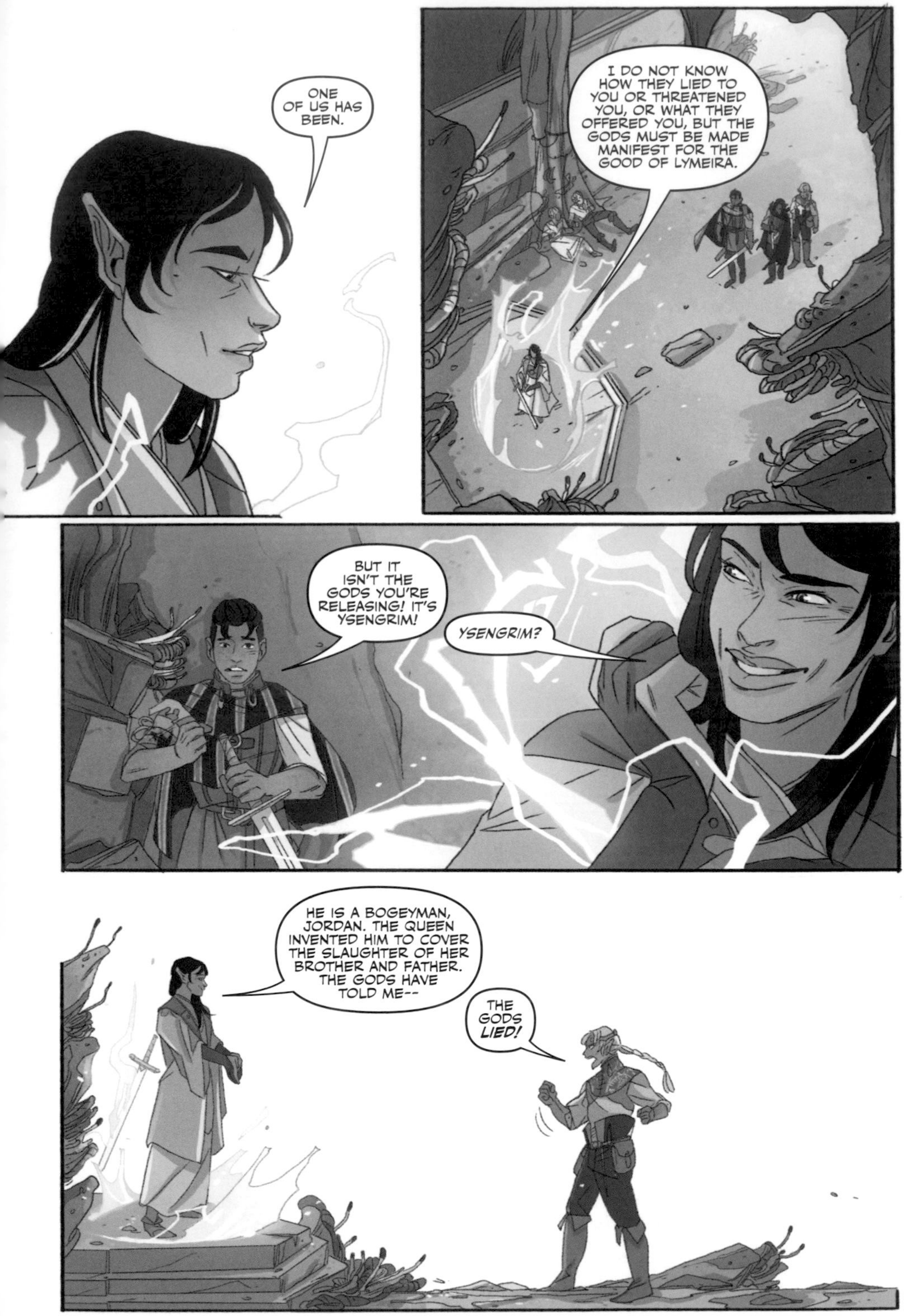
ONE OF US HAS BEEN.
I DO NOT KNOW HOW THEY LIED TO YOU OR THREATENED YOU, OR WHAT THEY OFFERED YOU, BUT THE GODS MUST BE MADE MANIFEST FOR THE GOOD OF LYMEIRA.
BUT IT ISN'T THE GODS YOU'RE RELEASING! IT'S YSENGRIM!
YSENGRIM?
HE IS A BOGEYMAN, JORDAN. THE QUEEN INVENTED HIM TO COVER THE SLAUGHTER OF HER BROTHER AND FATHER. THE GODS HAVE TOLD ME--
THE GODS *LIED!*

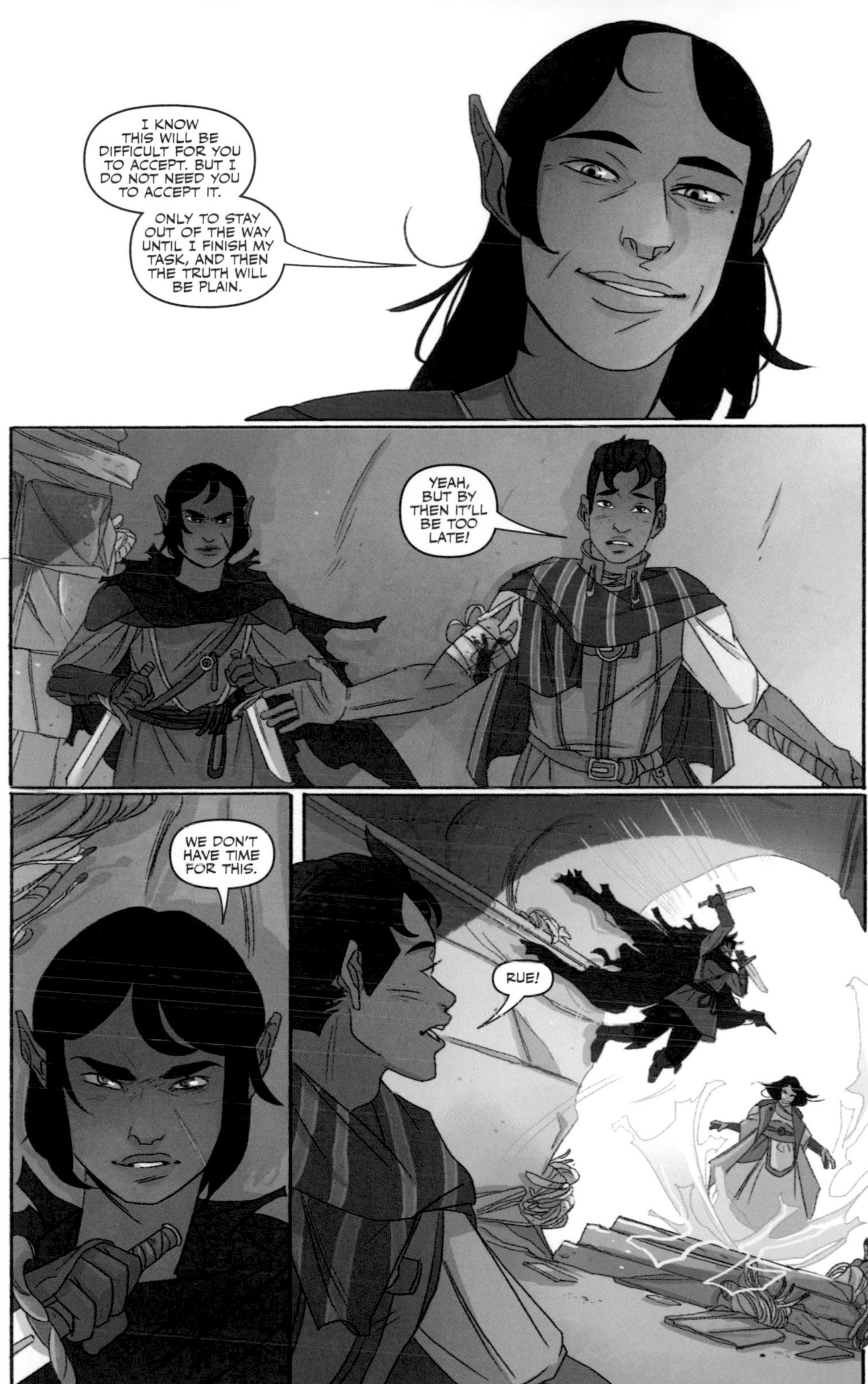
I KNOW THIS WILL BE DIFFICULT FOR YOU TO ACCEPT. BUT I DO NOT NEED YOU TO ACCEPT IT.
ONLY TO STAY OUT OF THE WAY UNTIL I FINISH MY TASK, AND THEN THE TRUTH WILL BE PLAIN.
YEAH, BUT BY THEN IT'LL BE TOO LATE!
WE DON'T HAVE TIME FOR THIS.
RUE!

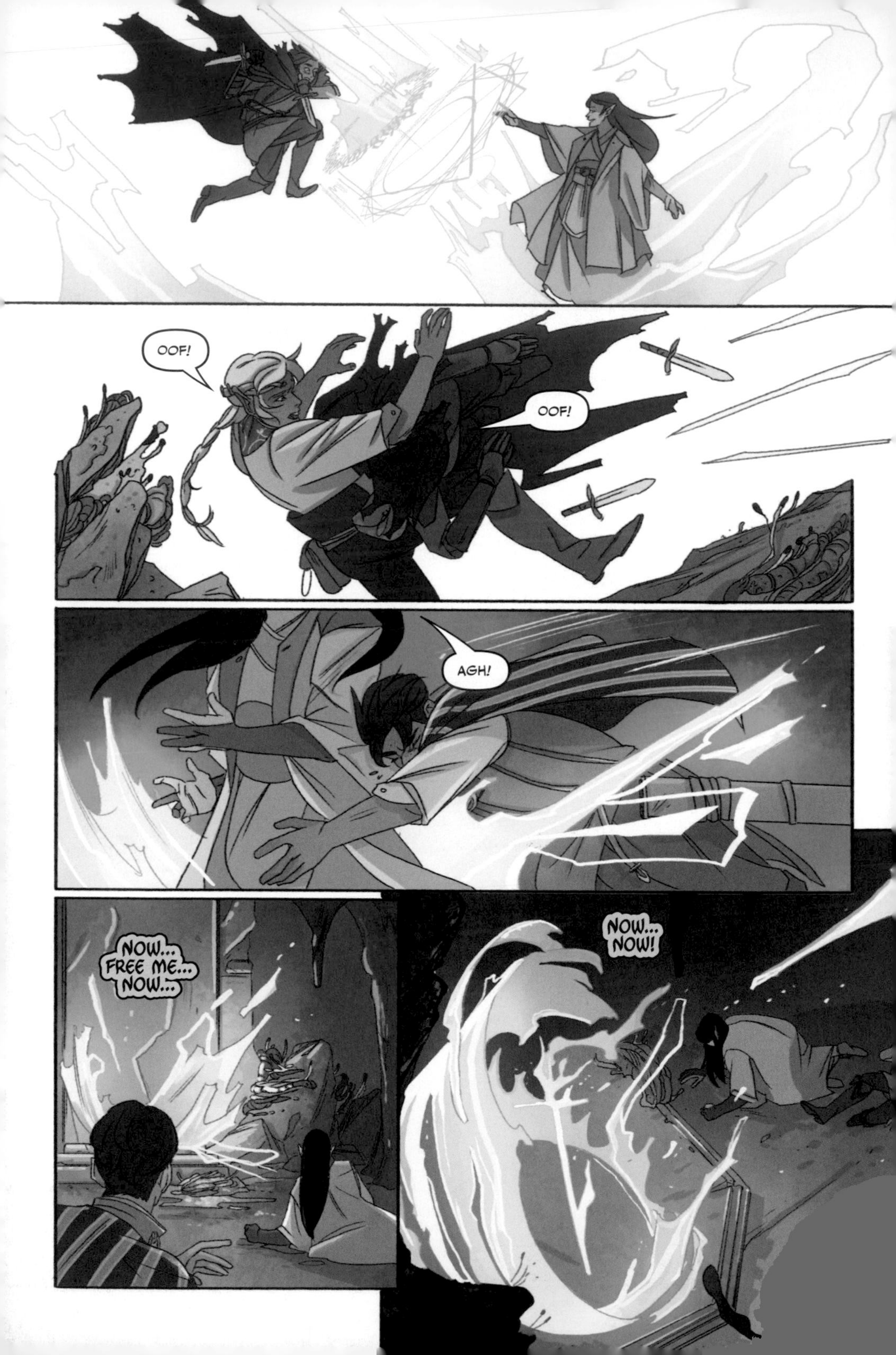
OOF!
OOF!
AGH!
NOW... FREE ME... NOW...
NOW... NOW!

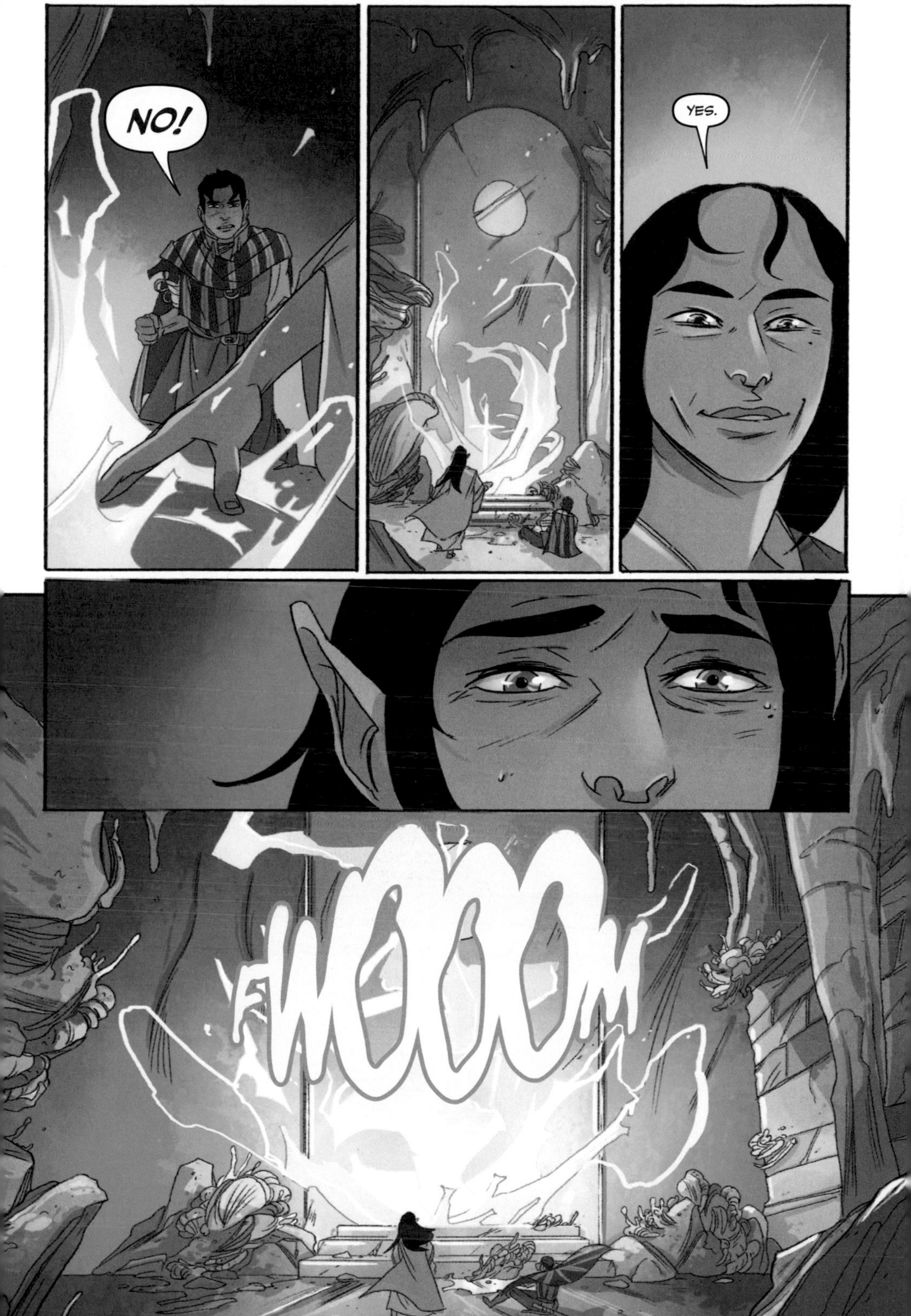
NO!
YES.
FWOOOM

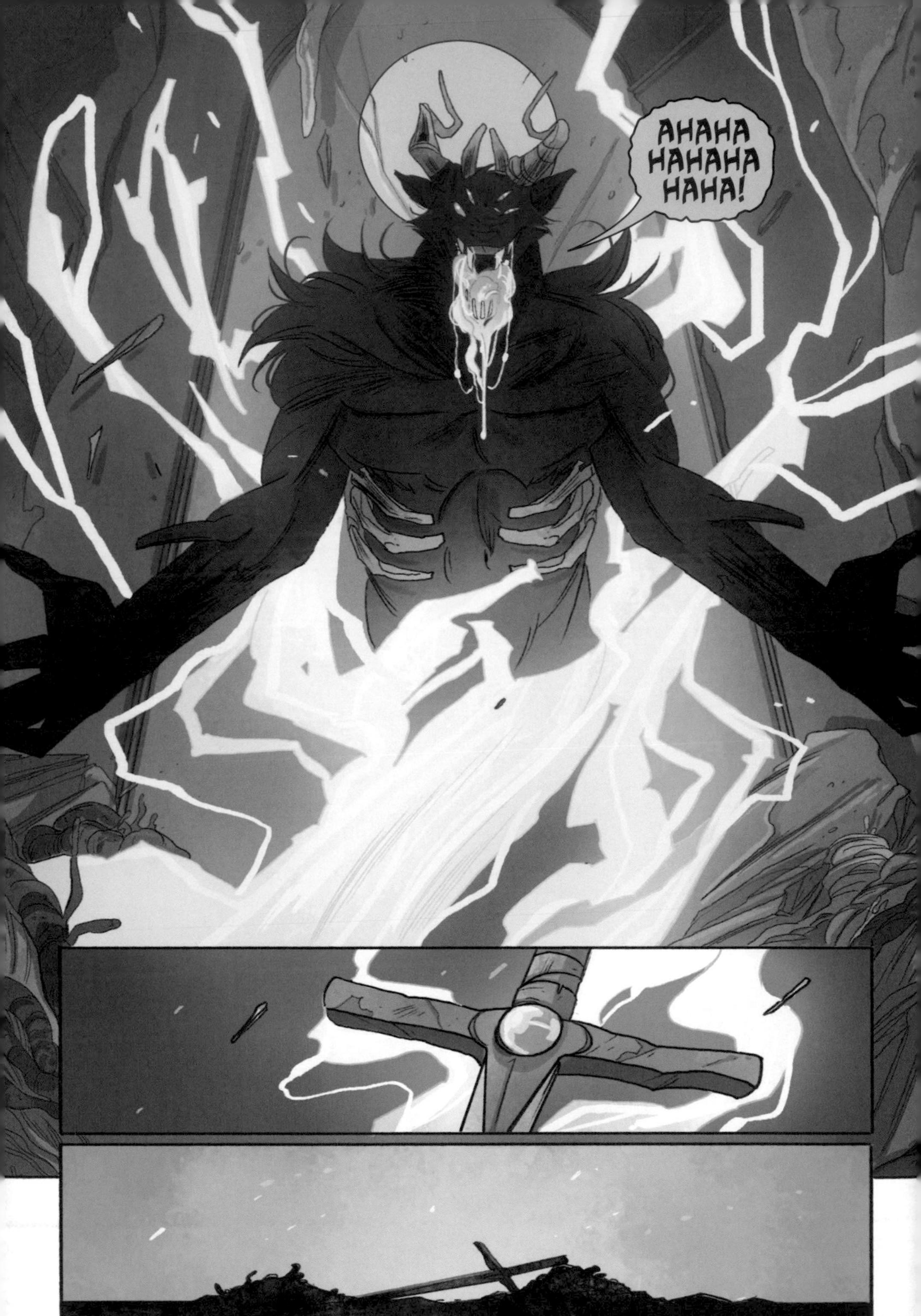
AHAHA
HAHAHA
HAHA!

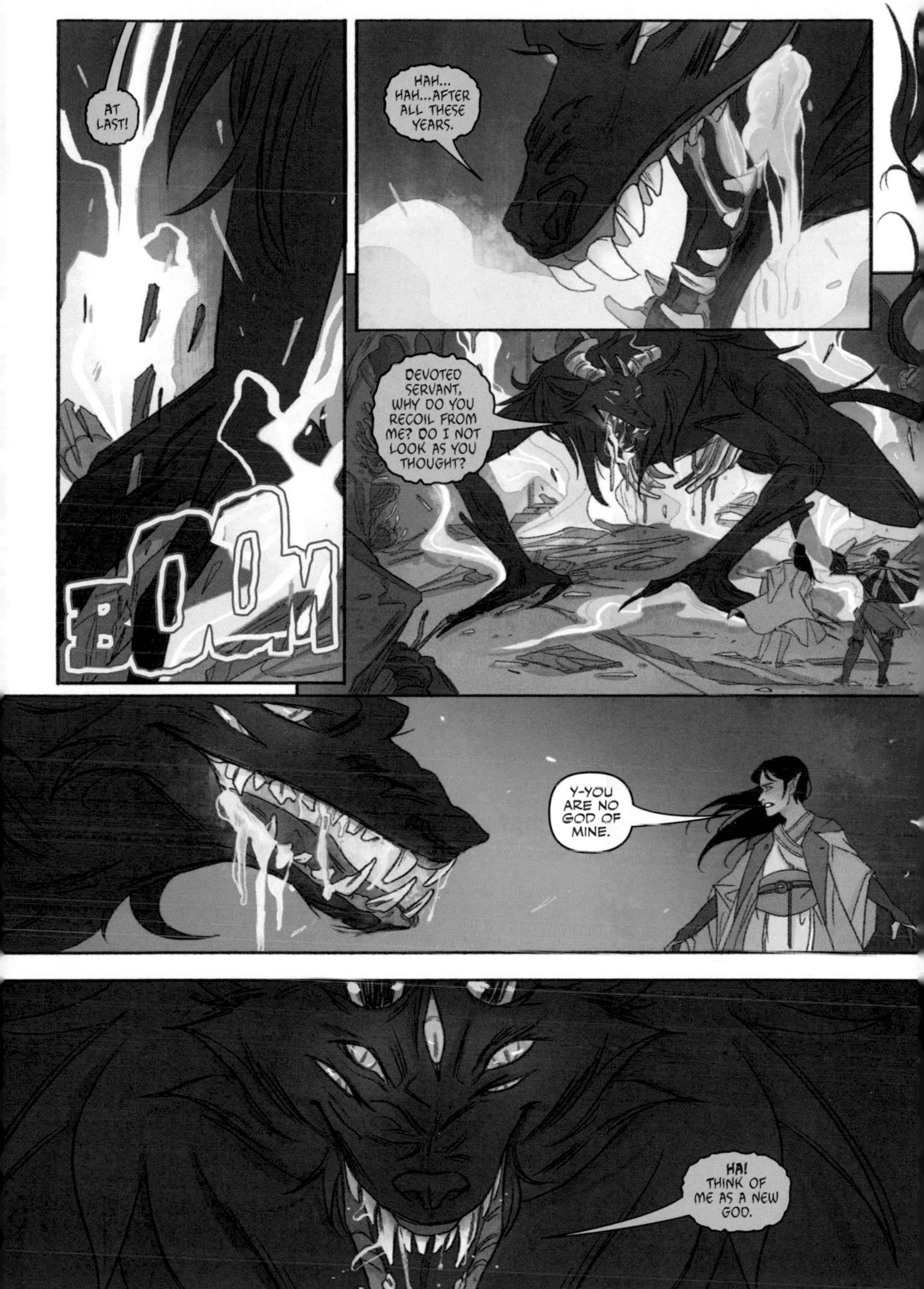
AT LAST!
BOOM
HAH... HAH...AFTER ALL THESE YEARS.
DEVOTED SERVANT, WHY DO YOU RECOIL FROM ME? DO I NOT LOOK AS YOU THOUGHT?
Y-YOU ARE NO GOD OF MINE.
HA! THINK OF ME AS A NEW GOD.

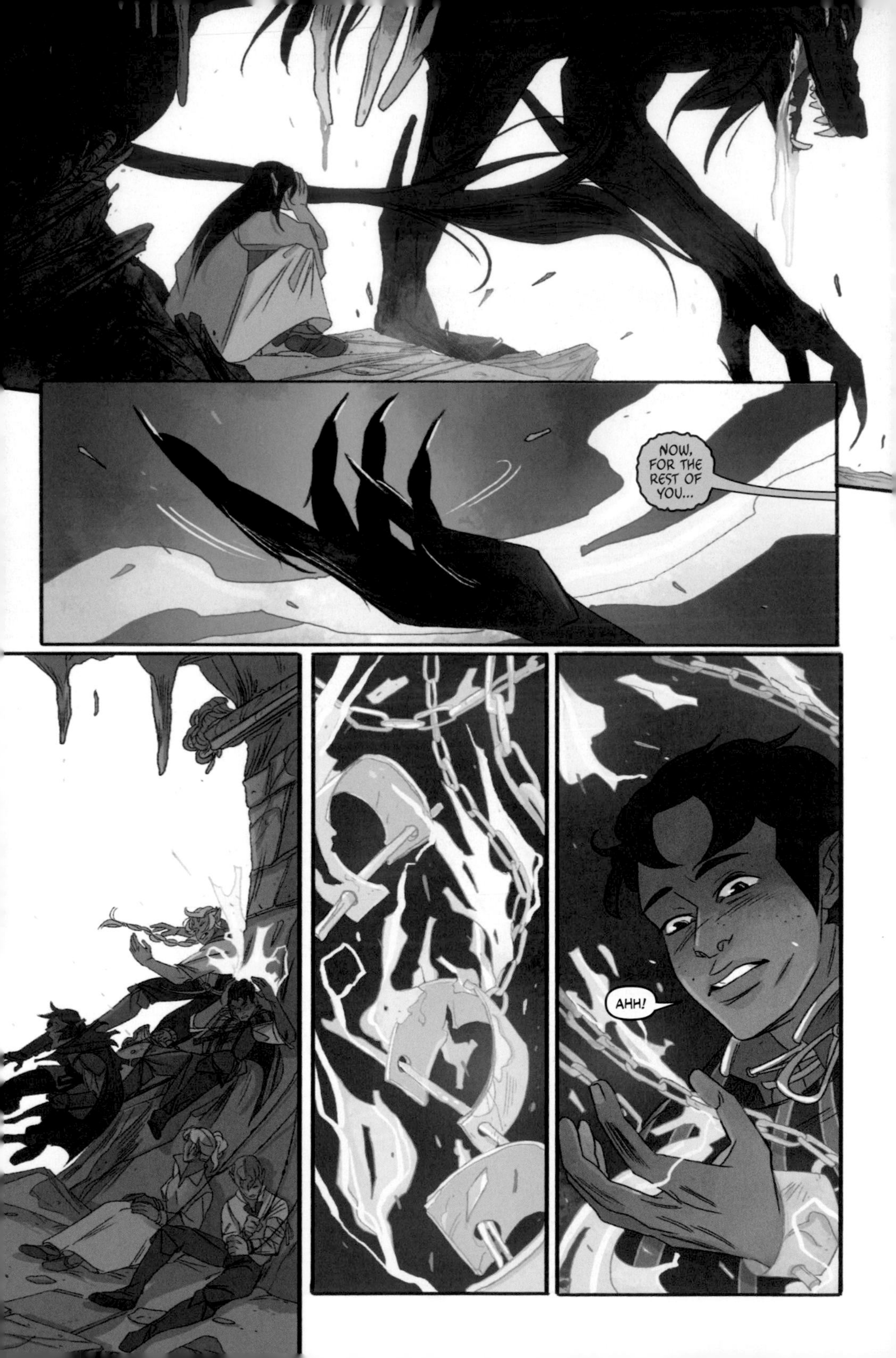
NOW, FOR THE REST OF YOU...
AHH!

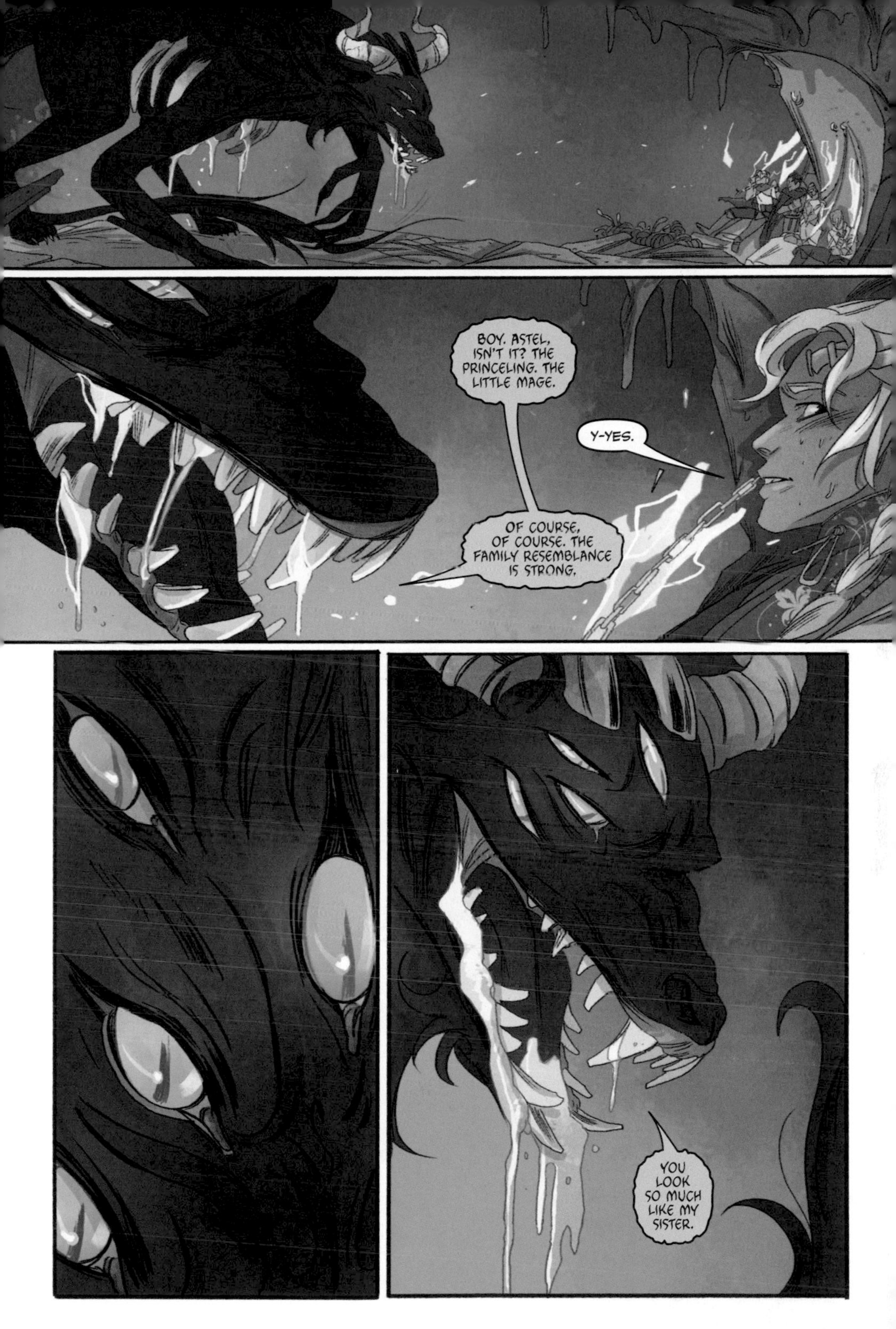
BOY. ASTEL, ISN'T IT? THE PRINCELING. THE LITTLE MAGE.
Y-YES.
OF COURSE, OF COURSE. THE FAMILY RESEMBLANCE IS STRONG.
YOU LOOK SO MUCH LIKE MY SISTER.

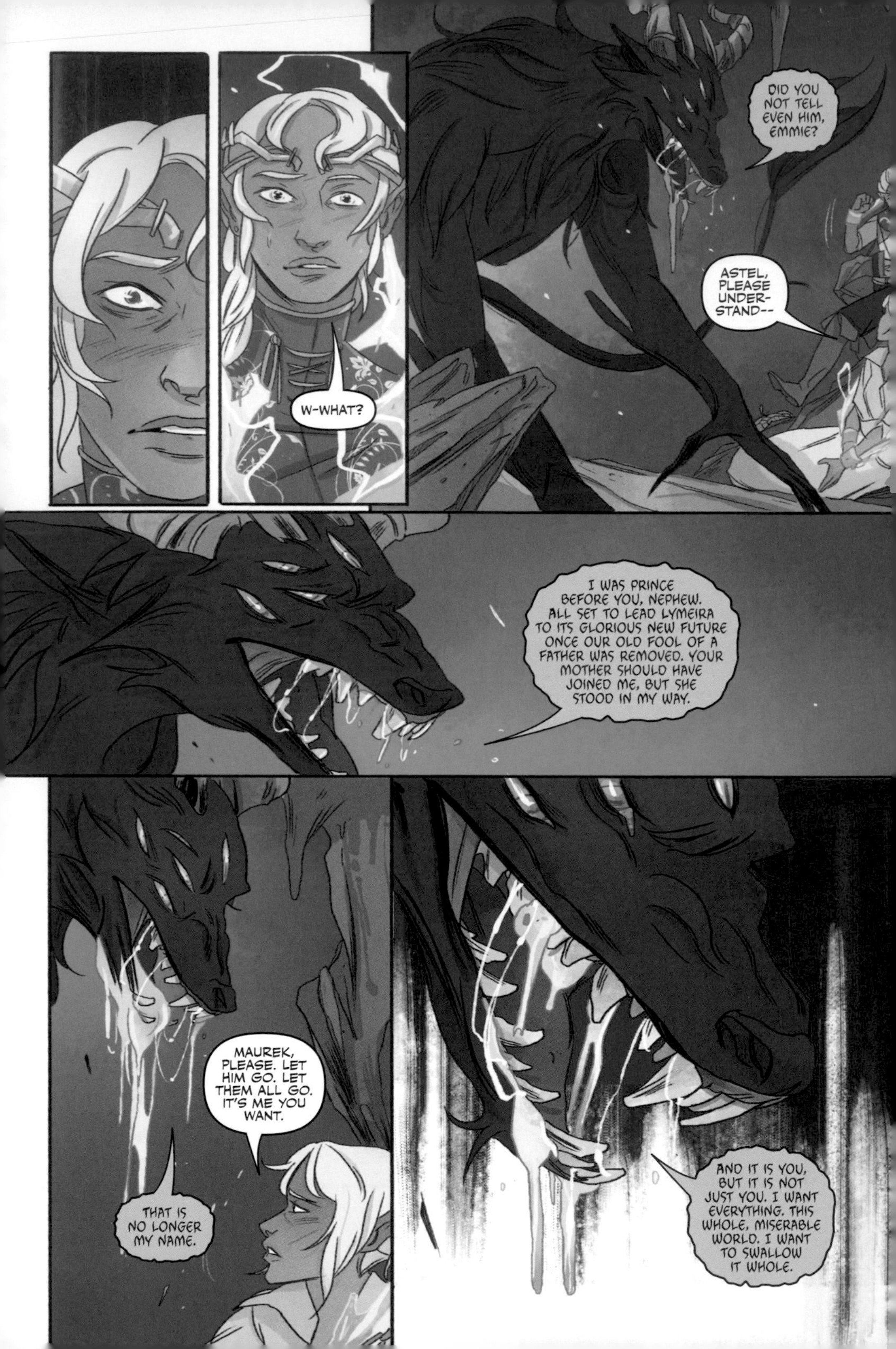
DID YOU NOT TELL EVEN HIM, EMMIE?
ASTEL, PLEASE UNDER-STAND--
W-WHAT?
I WAS PRINCE BEFORE YOU, NEPHEW. ALL SET TO LEAD LYMEIRA TO ITS GLORIOUS NEW FUTURE ONCE OUR OLD FOOL OF A FATHER WAS REMOVED. YOUR MOTHER SHOULD HAVE JOINED ME, BUT SHE STOOD IN MY WAY.
MAUREK, PLEASE. LET HIM GO. LET THEM ALL GO. IT'S ME YOU WANT.
THAT IS NO LONGER MY NAME.
AND IT IS YOU, BUT IT IS NOT JUST YOU. I WANT EVERYTHING. THIS WHOLE, MISERABLE WORLD. I WANT TO SWALLOW IT WHOLE.

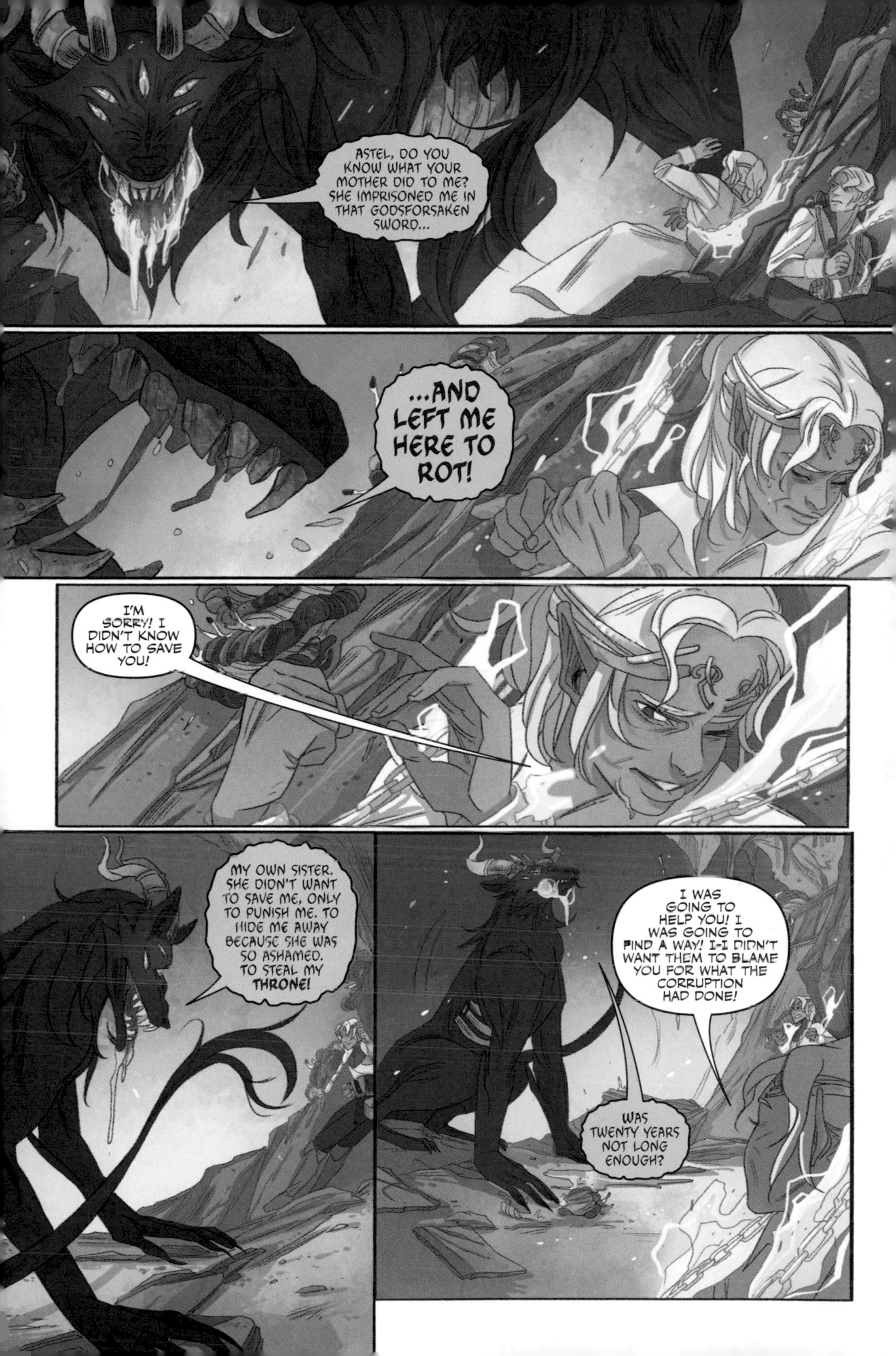
ASTEL, DO YOU KNOW WHAT YOUR MOTHER DID TO ME? SHE IMPRISONED ME IN THAT GODSFORSAKEN SWORD...
...AND LEFT ME HERE TO ROT!
I'M SORRY! I DIDN'T KNOW HOW TO SAVE YOU!
MY OWN SISTER. SHE DIDN'T WANT TO SAVE ME, ONLY TO PUNISH ME. TO HIDE ME AWAY BECAUSE SHE WAS SO ASHAMED. TO STEAL MY **THRONE!**
I WAS GOING TO HELP YOU! I WAS GOING TO FIND A WAY! I-I DIDN'T WANT THEM TO BLAME YOU FOR WHAT THE CORRUPTION HAD DONE!
WAS TWENTY YEARS NOT LONG ENOUGH?

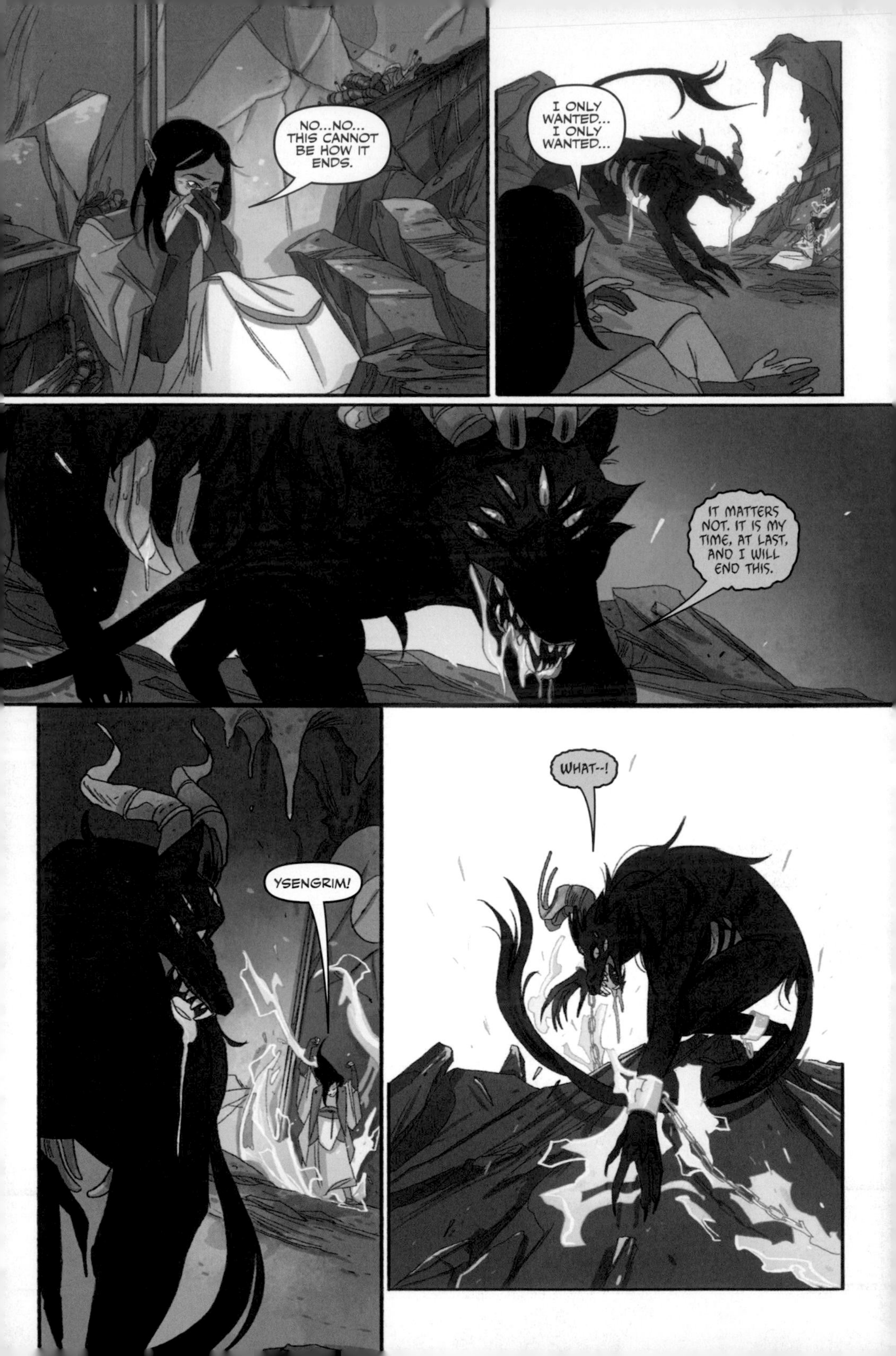
NO...NO... THIS CANNOT BE HOW IT ENDS.
I ONLY WANTED... I ONLY WANTED...
IT MATTERS NOT. IT IS MY TIME, AT LAST, AND I WILL END THIS.
YSENGRIM!
WHAT--!

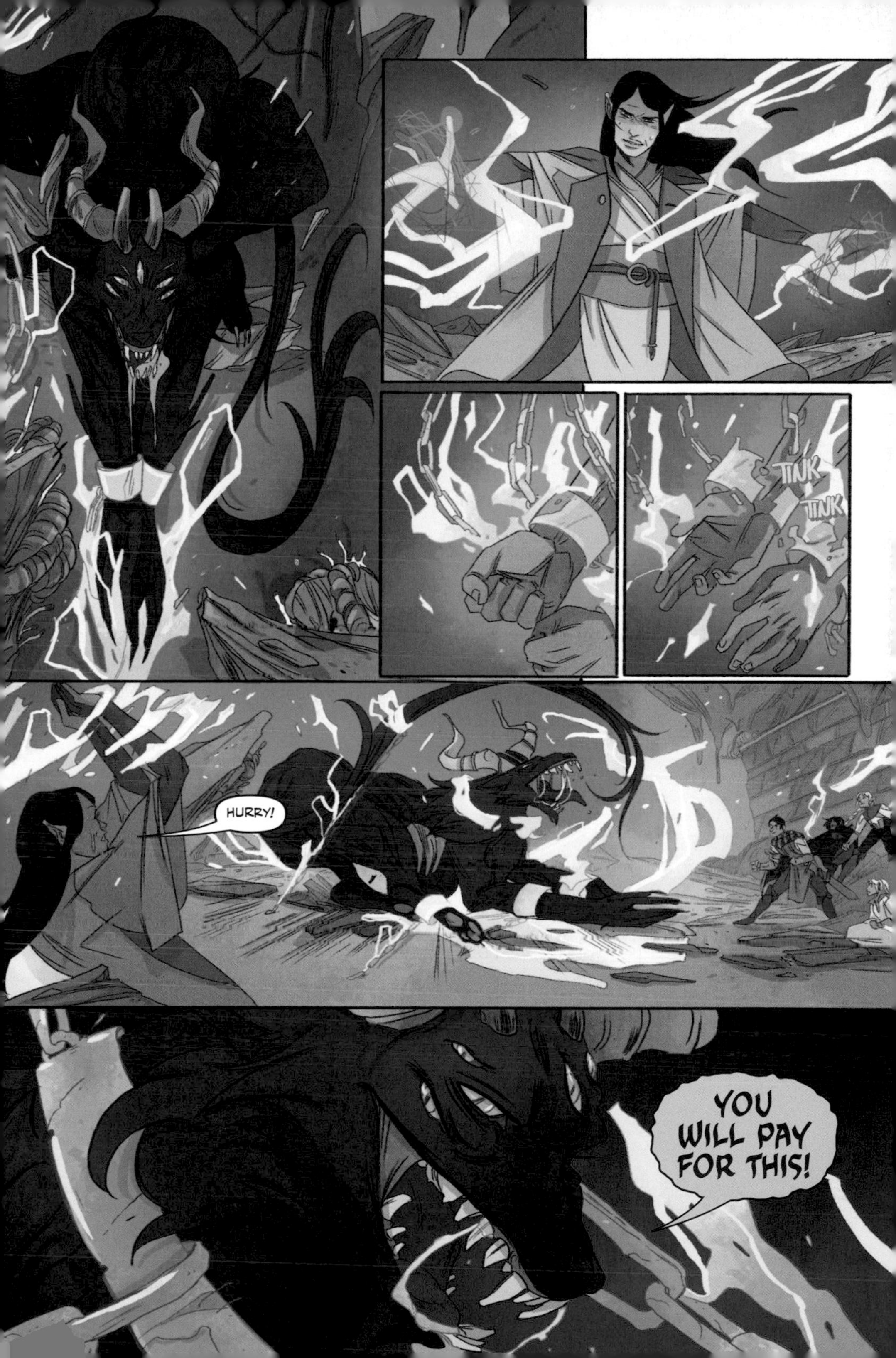
TINK
TINK
HURRY!
YOU WILL PAY FOR THIS!

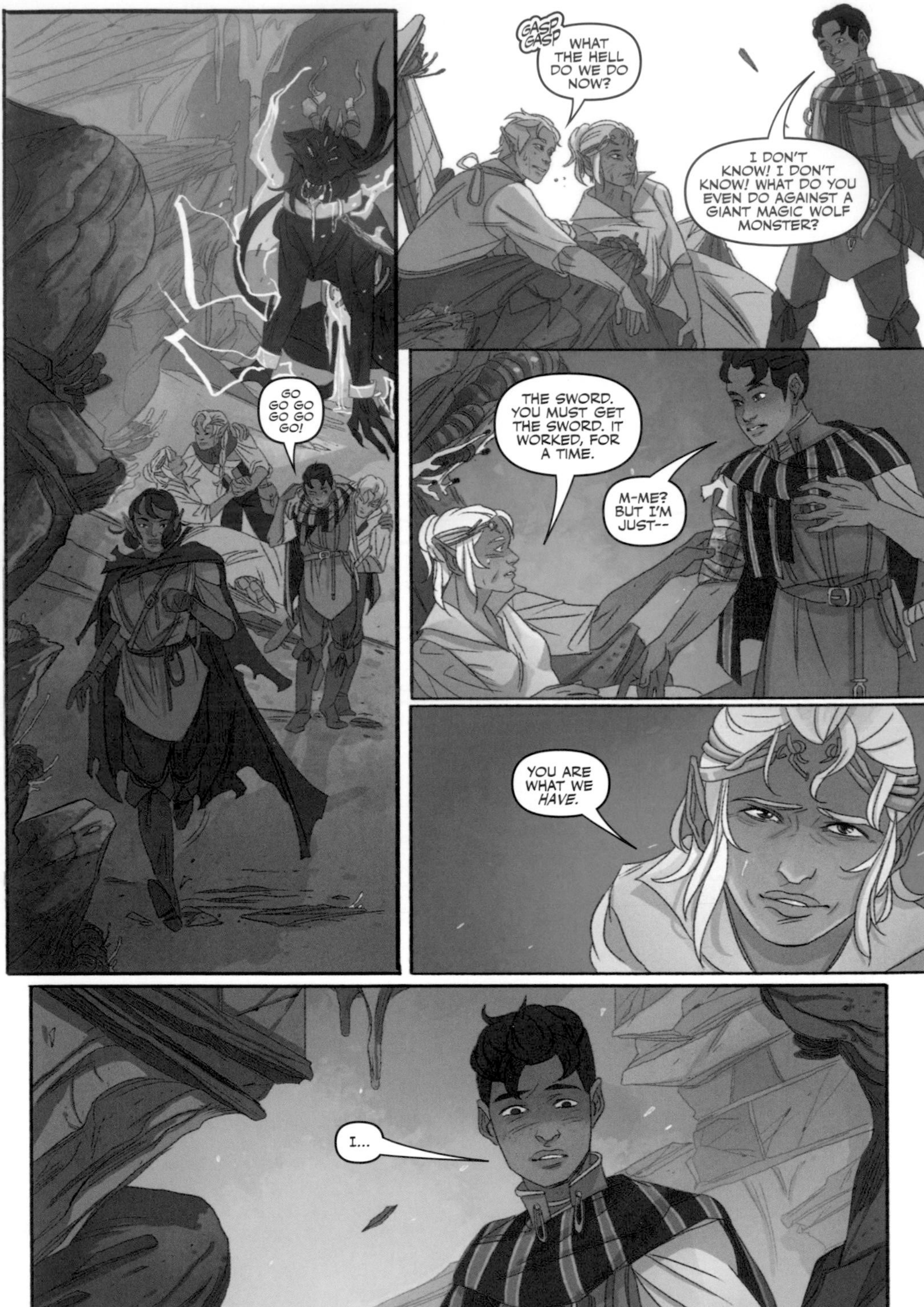
GO GO GO GO GO GO!
GASP GASP
WHAT THE HELL DO WE DO NOW?
I DON'T KNOW! I DON'T KNOW! WHAT DO YOU EVEN DO AGAINST A GIANT MAGIC WOLF MONSTER?
THE SWORD. YOU MUST GET THE SWORD. IT WORKED, FOR A TIME.
M-ME? BUT I'M JUST--
YOU ARE WHAT WE HAVE.
I...

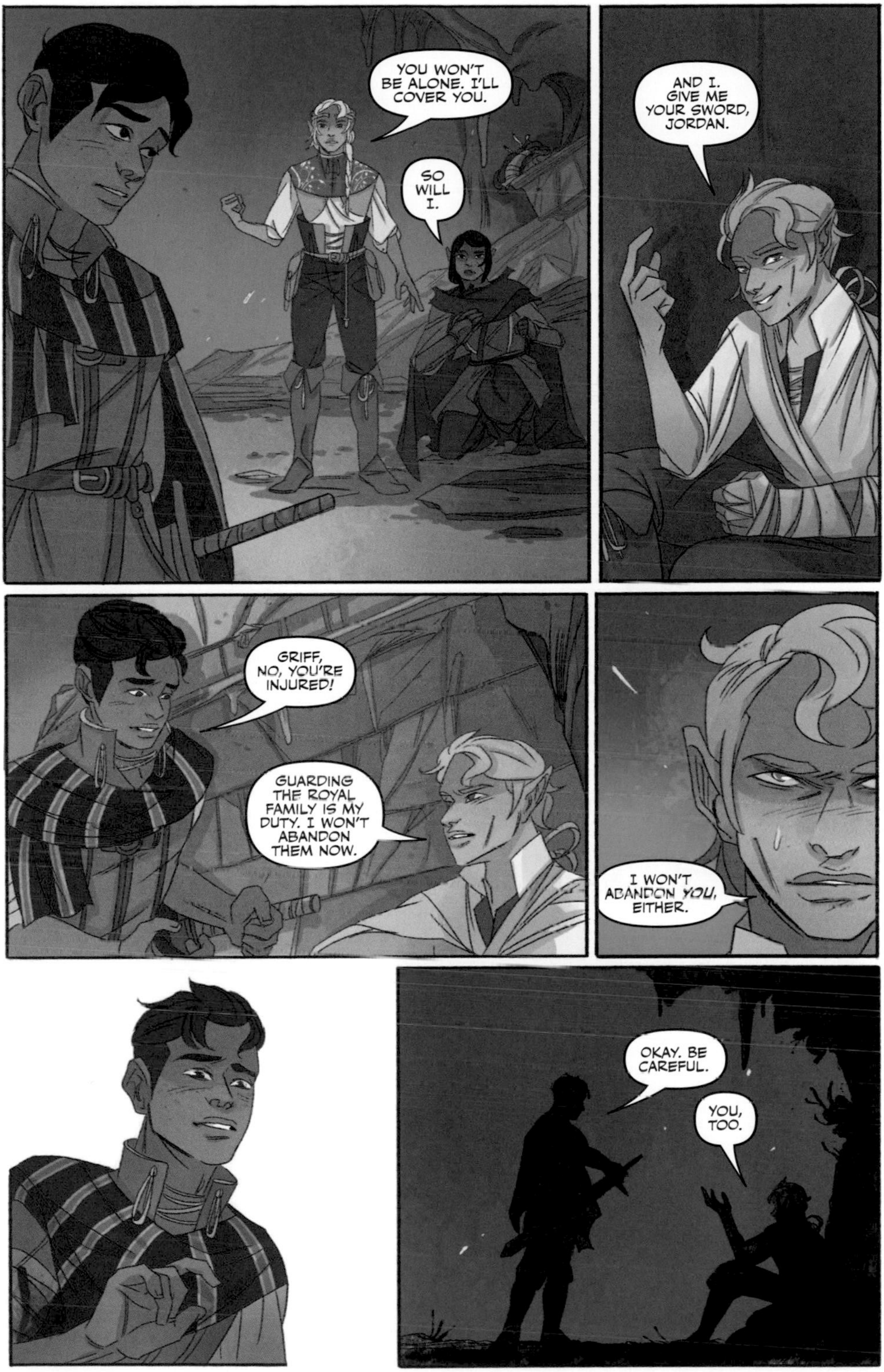
YOU WON'T BE ALONE. I'LL COVER YOU.
SO WILL I.
AND I. GIVE ME YOUR SWORD, JORDAN.
GRIFF, NO, YOU'RE INJURED!
GUARDING THE ROYAL FAMILY IS MY DUTY. I WON'T ABANDON THEM NOW.
I WON'T ABANDON YOU, EITHER.
OKAY. BE CAREFUL.
YOU, TOO.

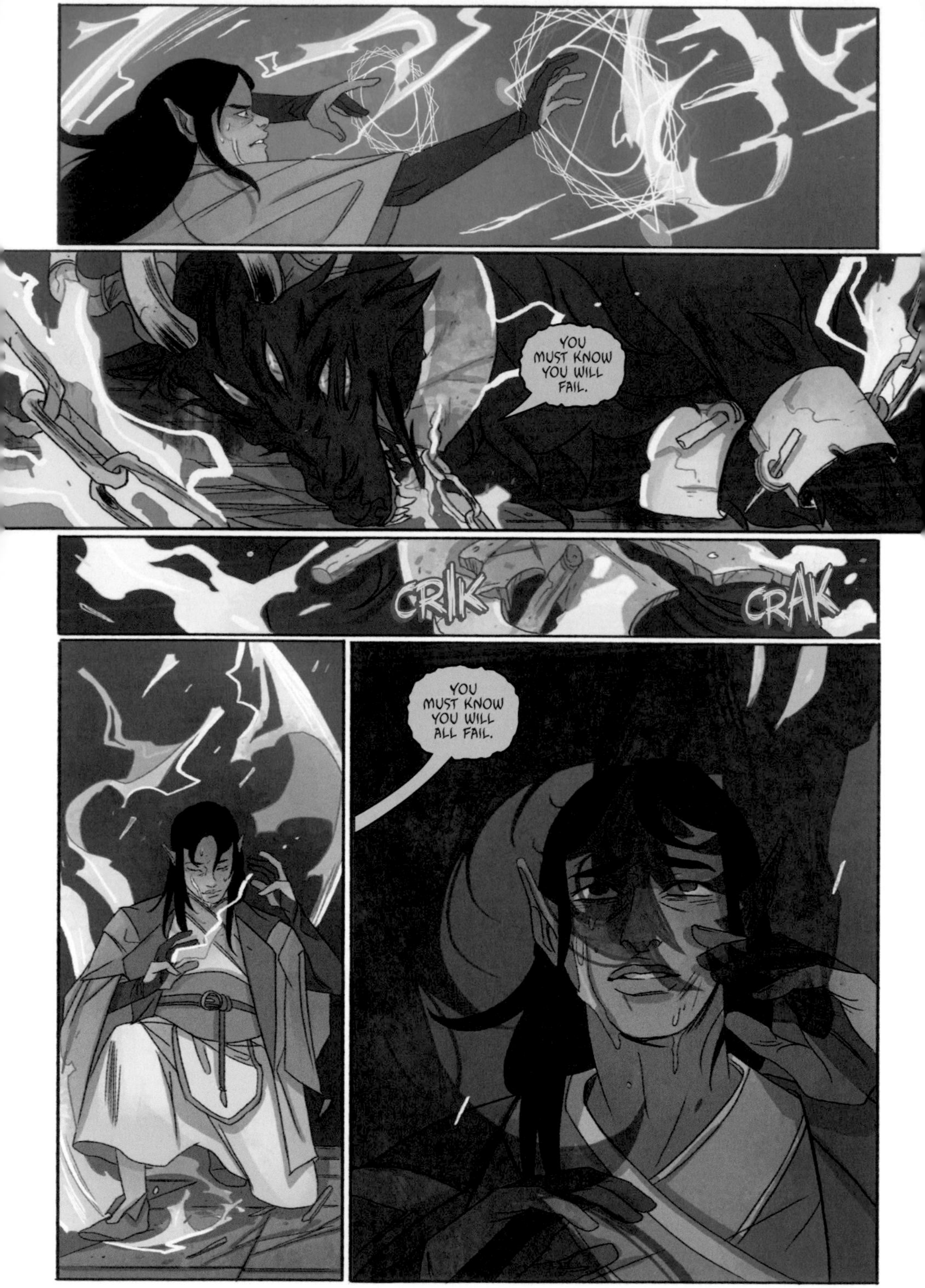
YOU MUST KNOW YOU WILL FAIL.
CRIK
CRAK
YOU MUST KNOW YOU WILL ALL FAIL.

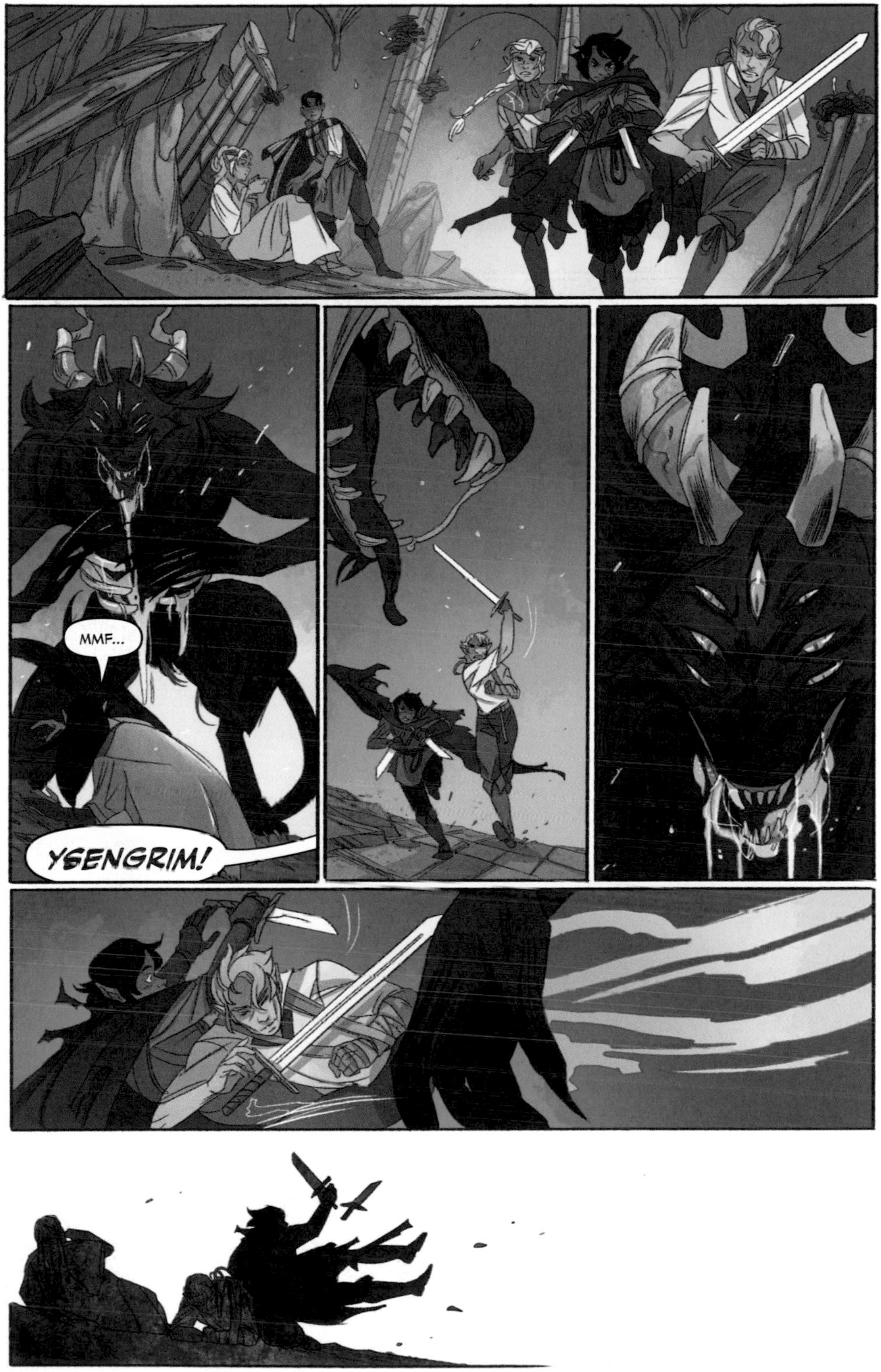
MMF...
YSENGRIM!

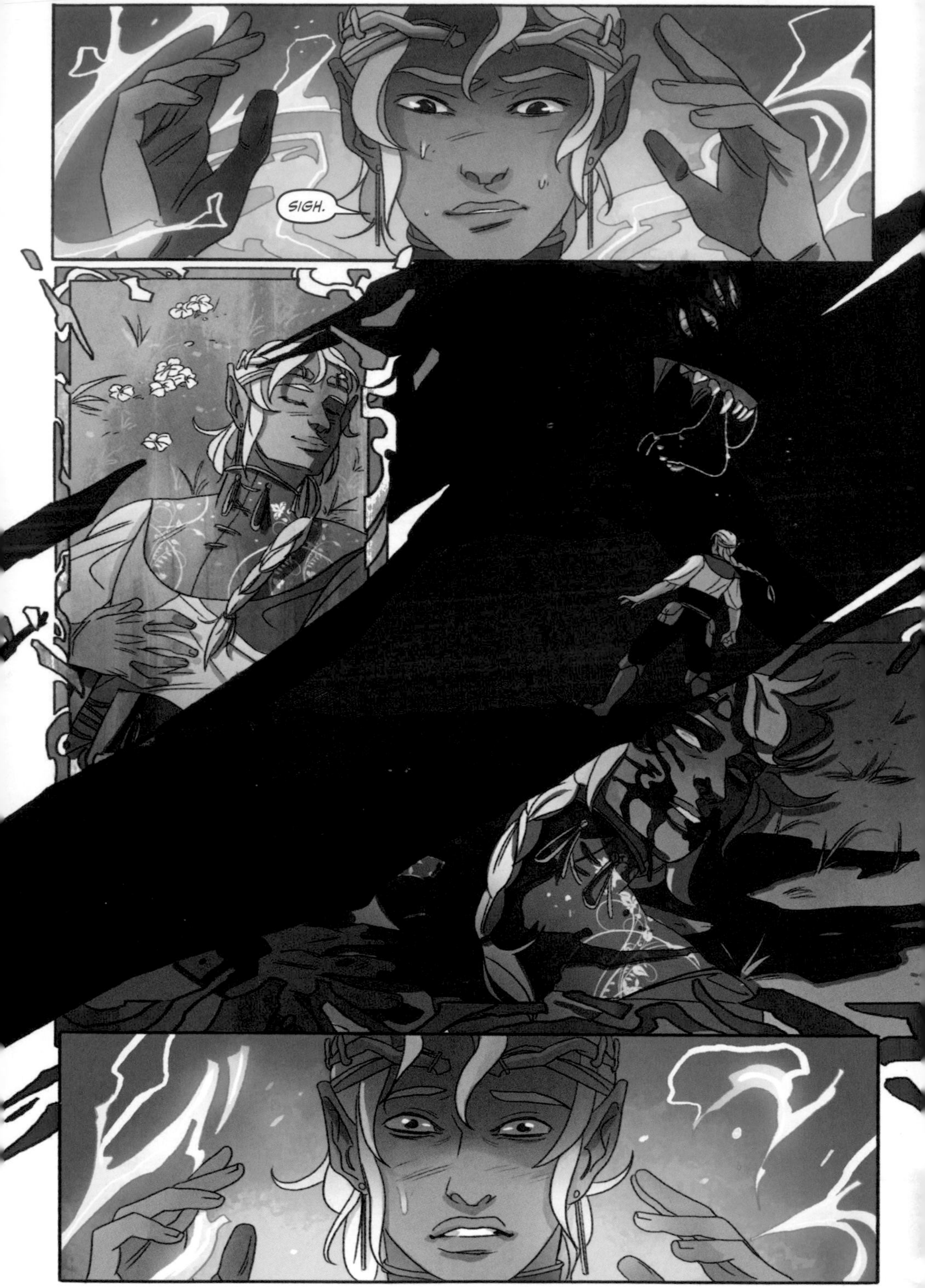
SIGH.

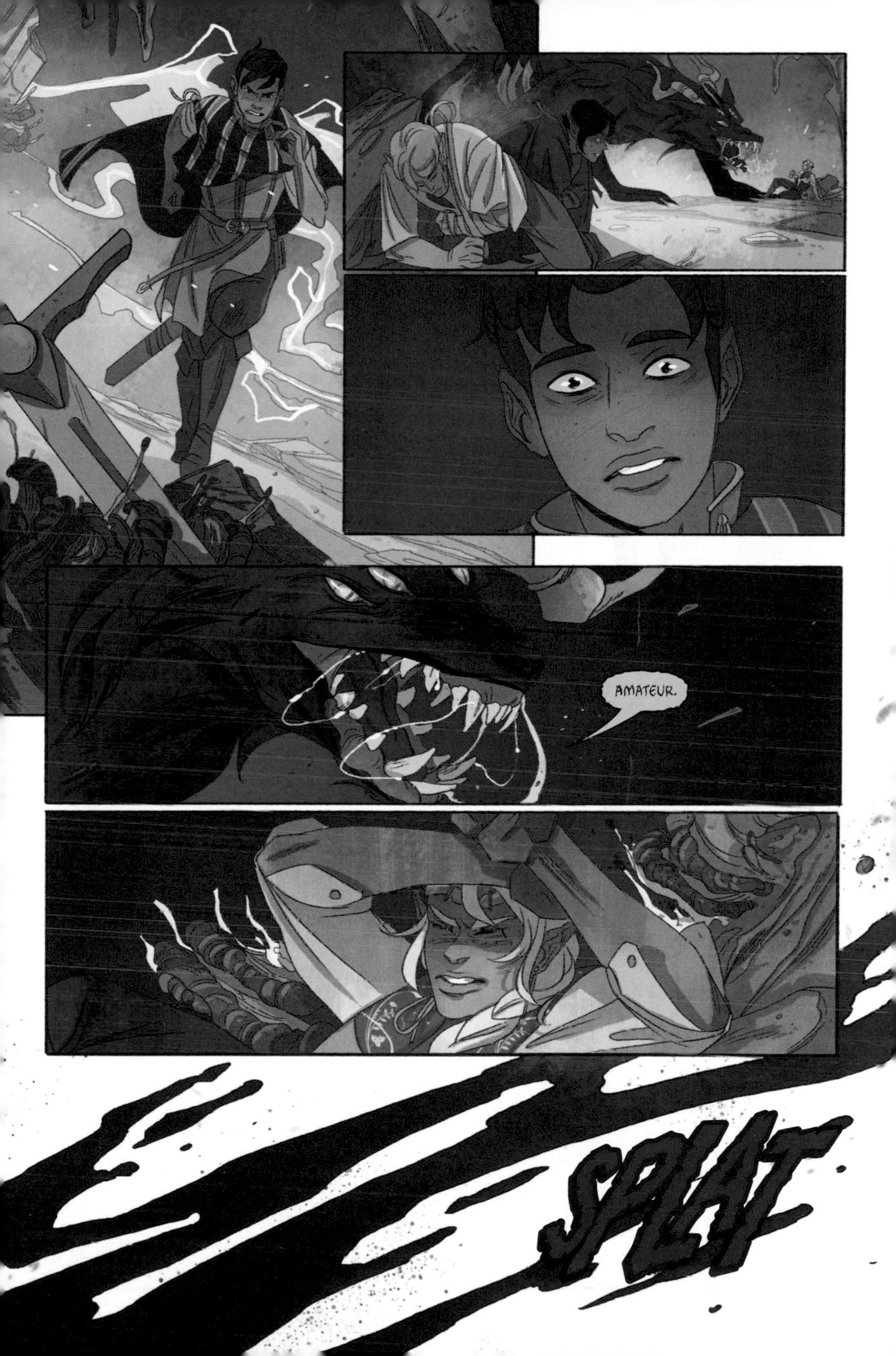
AMATEUR.
SPLAT

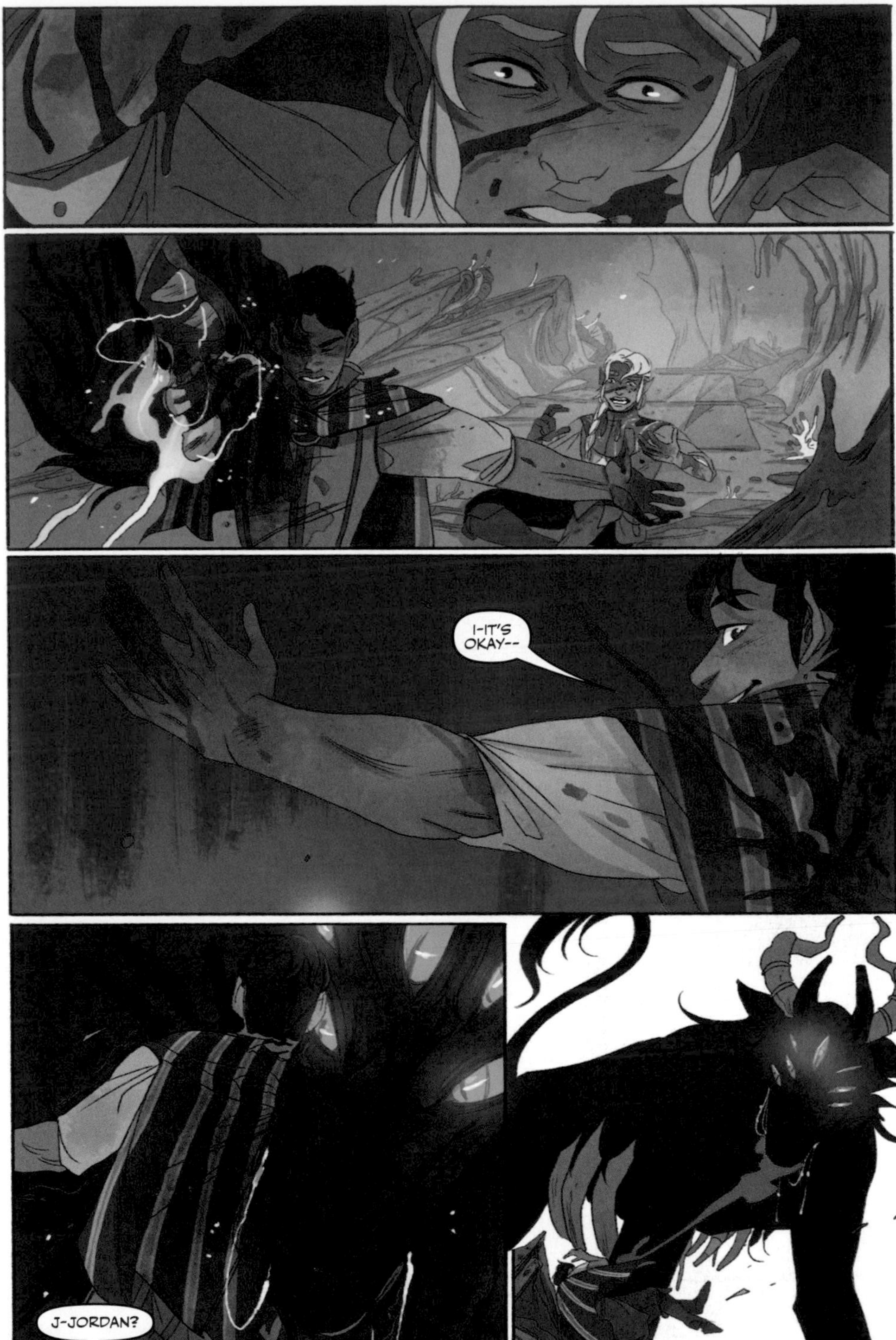
I-IT'S OKAY--
J-JORDAN?

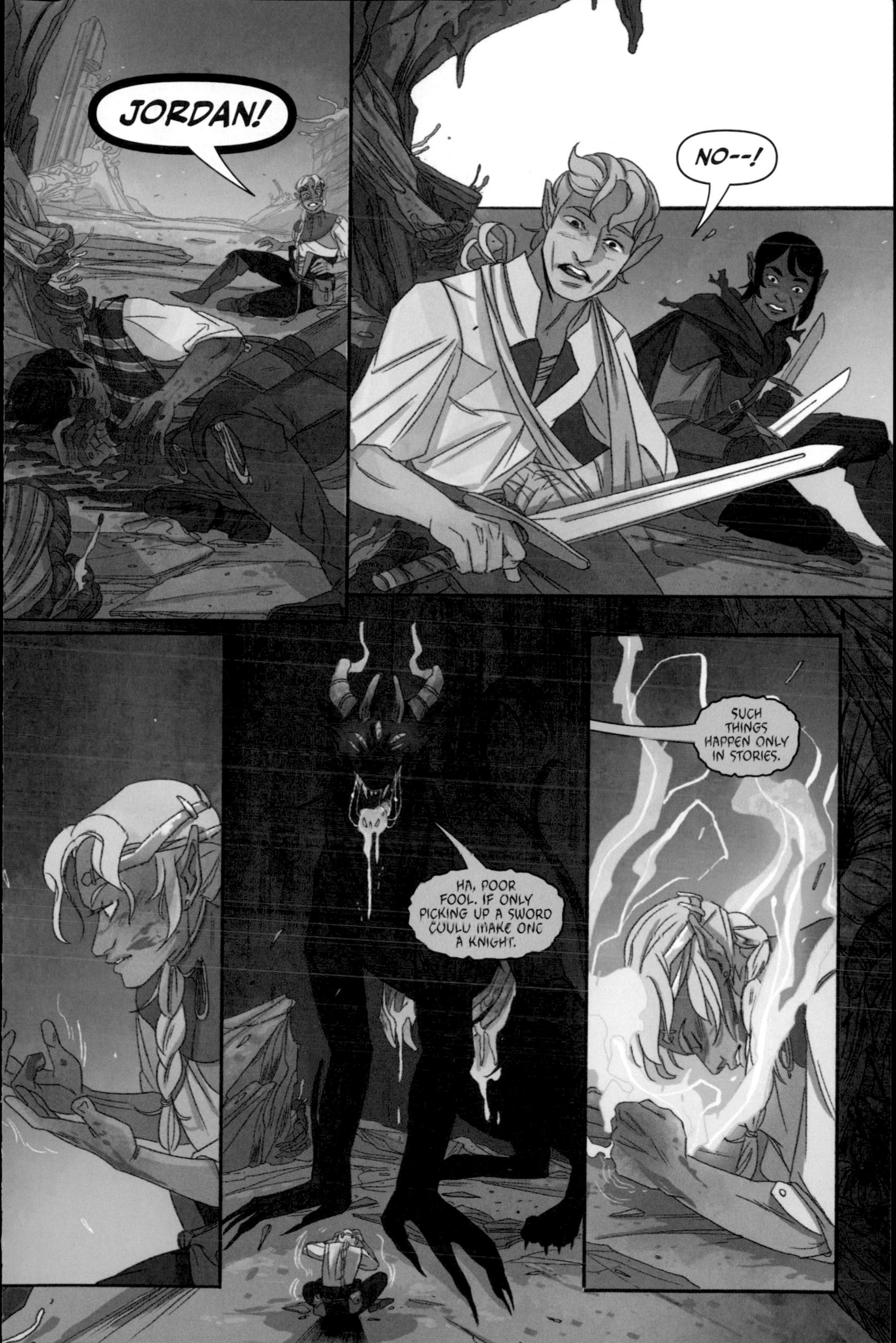
JORDAN!
NO--!
HA, POOR FOOL. IF ONLY PICKING UP A SWORD COULD MAKE ONE A KNIGHT.
SUCH THINGS HAPPEN ONLY IN STORIES.

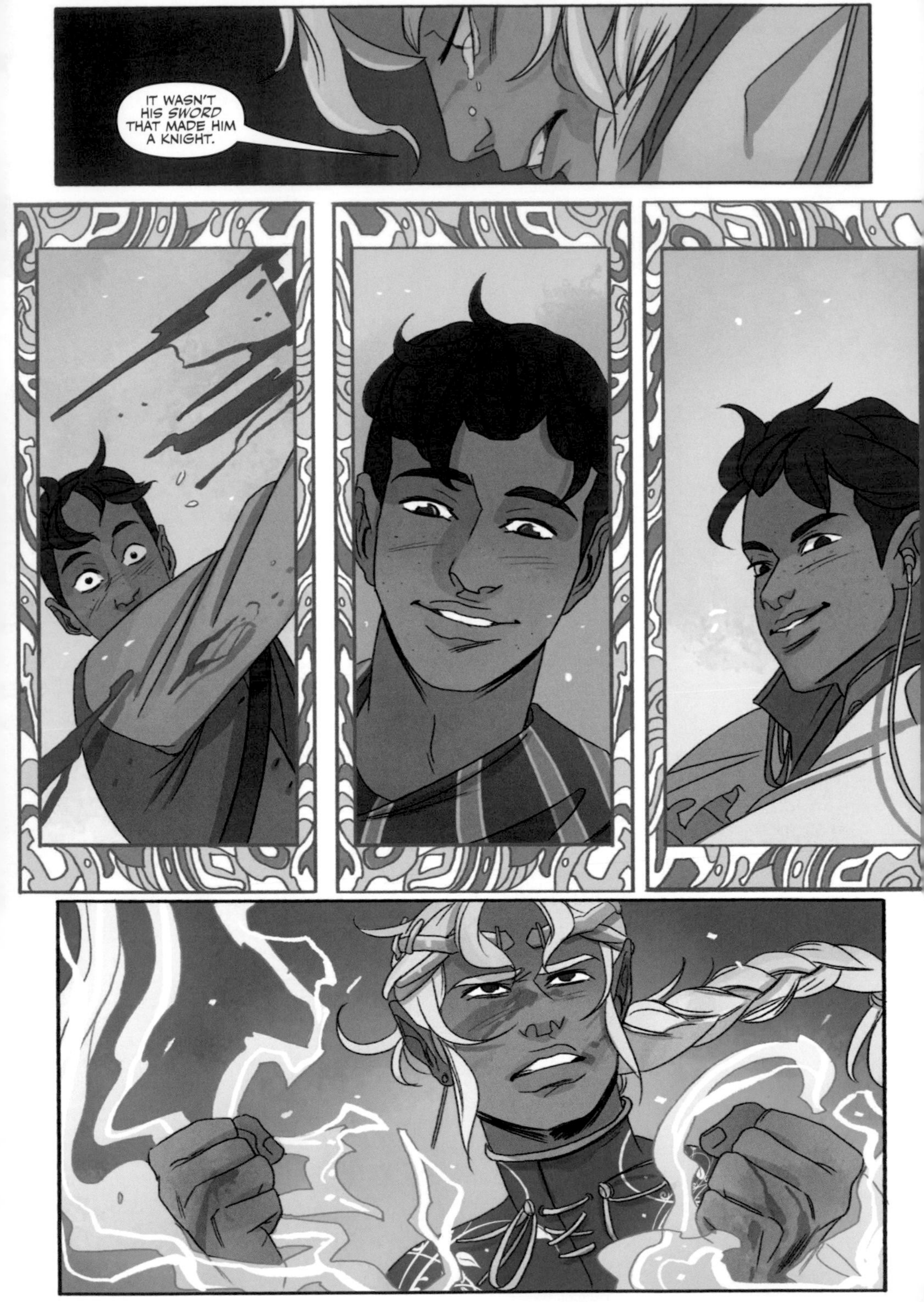
IT WASN'T HIS *SWORD* THAT MADE HIM A KNIGHT.

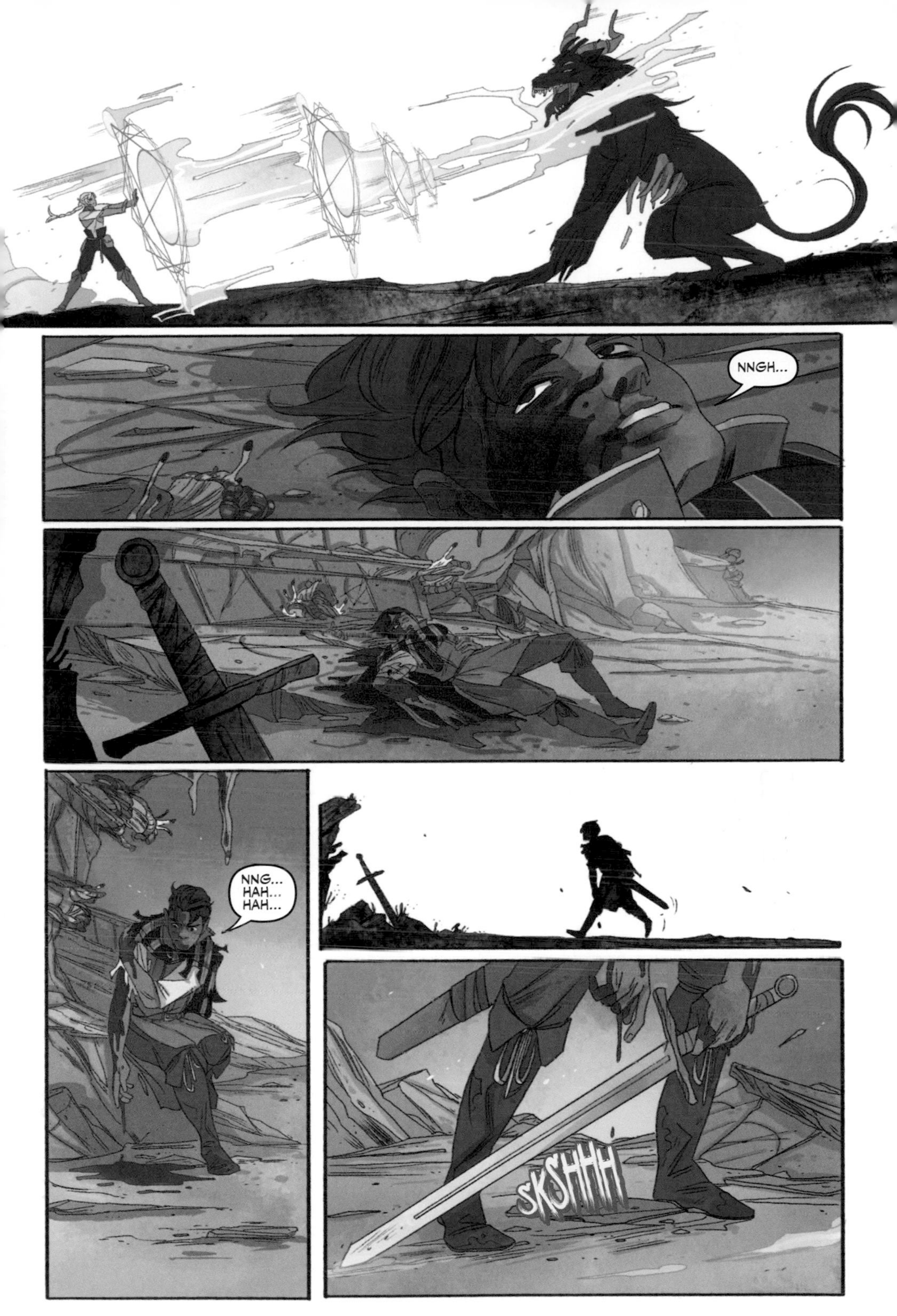
NNGH...
NNG... HAH... HAH...
SKSHHH

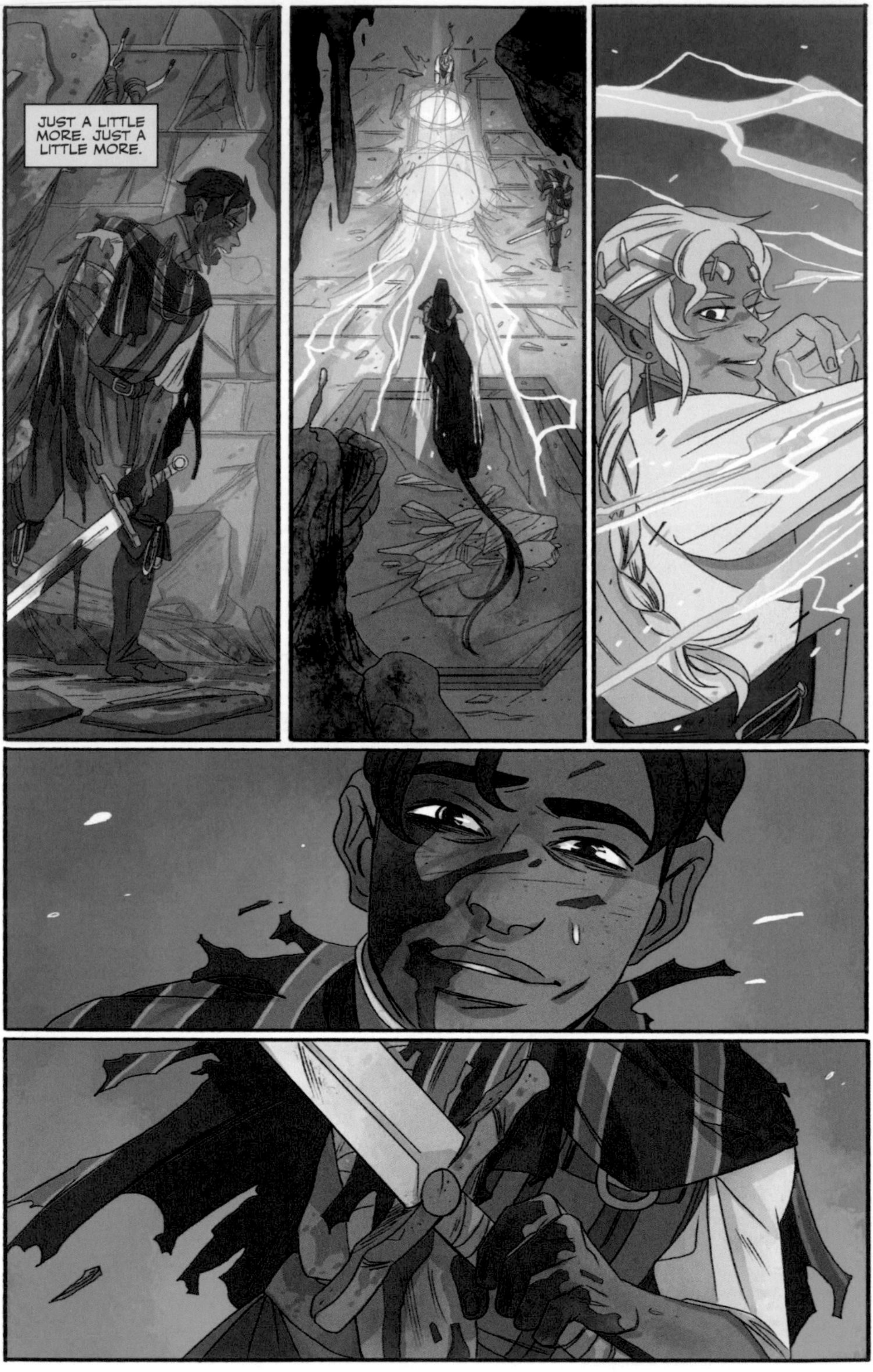
JUST A LITTLE MORE. JUST A LITTLE MORE.

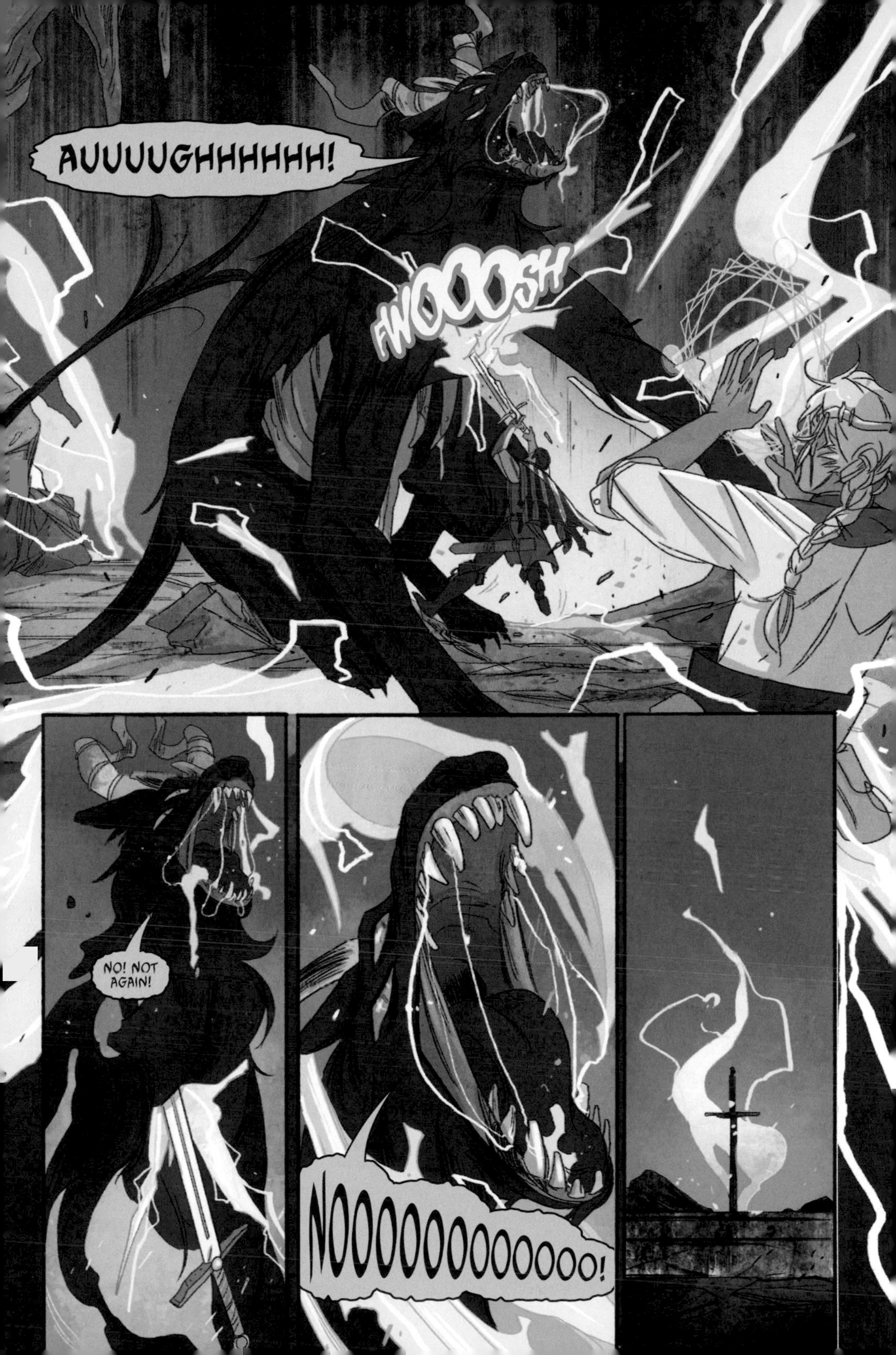
AUUUUGHHHHHH!
FWOOOSH
NO! NOT AGAIN!
NOOOOOOOOOOOO!

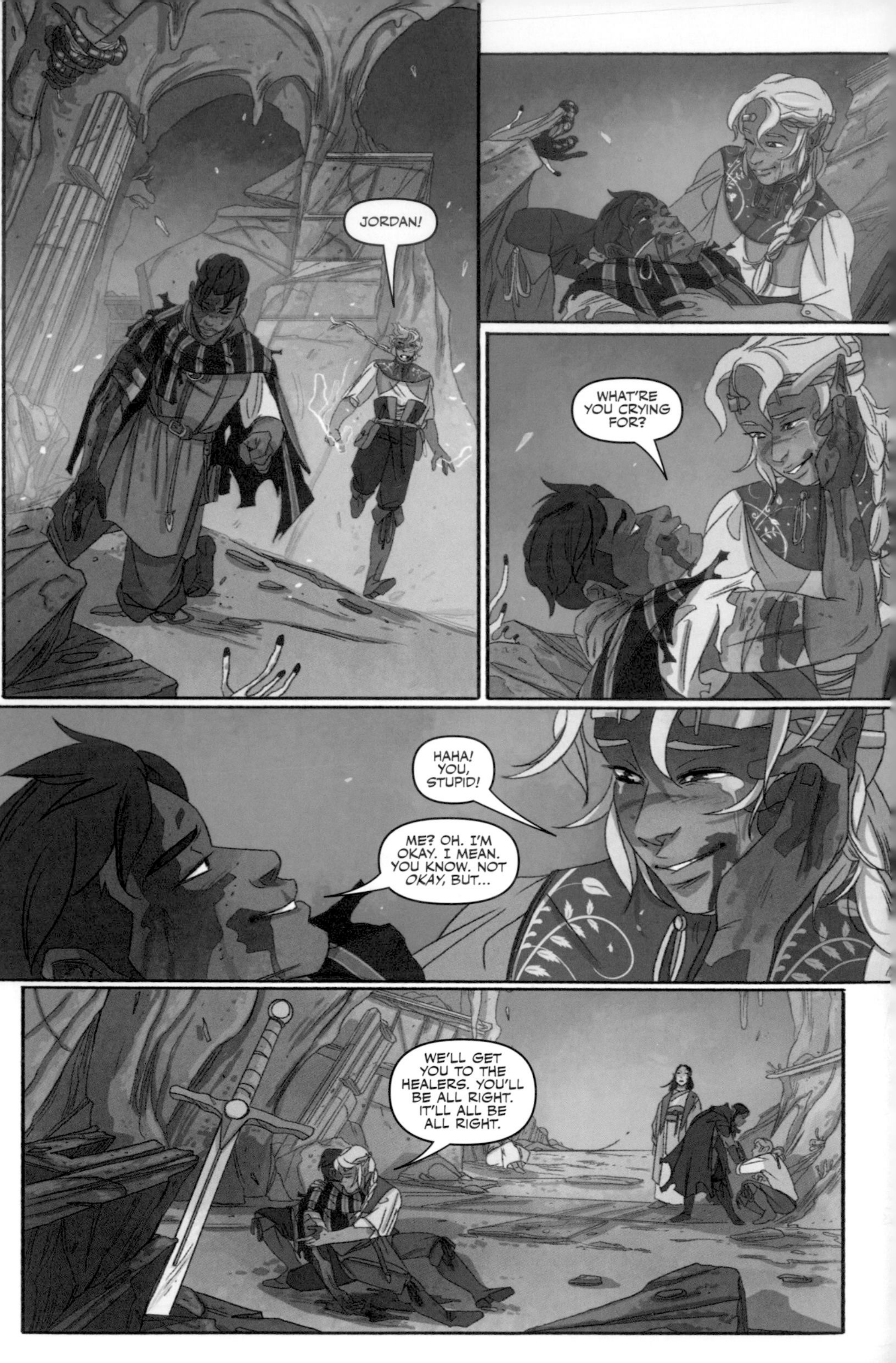
JORDAN!
WHAT'RE YOU CRYING FOR?
HAHA! YOU, STUPID!
ME? OH. I'M OKAY. I MEAN. YOU KNOW. NOT *OKAY*, BUT...
WE'LL GET YOU TO THE HEALERS. YOU'LL BE ALL RIGHT. IT'LL ALL BE ALL RIGHT.

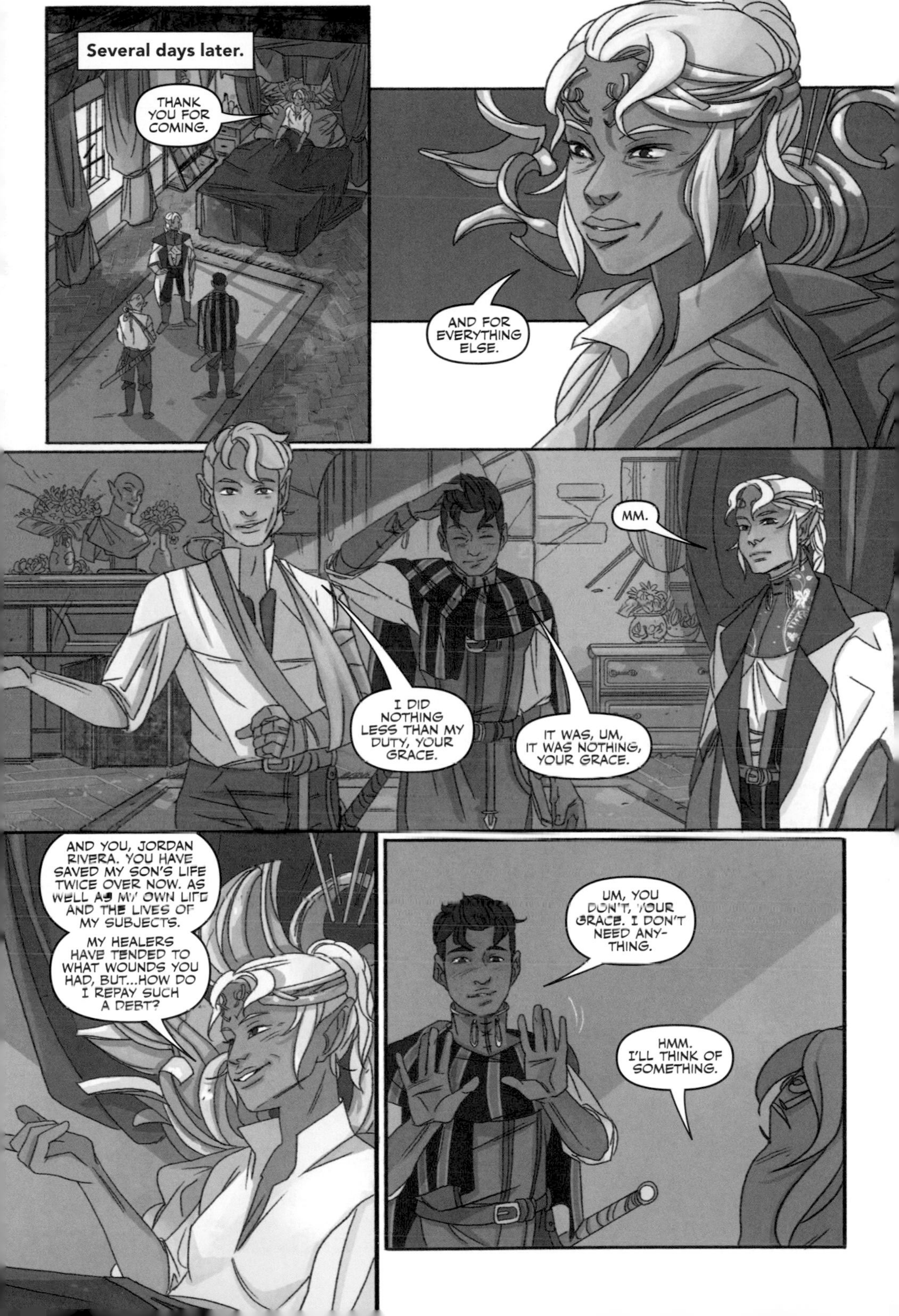
Several days later.
THANK YOU FOR COMING.
AND FOR EVERYTHING ELSE.
MM.
I DID NOTHING LESS THAN MY DUTY, YOUR GRACE.
IT WAS, UM, IT WAS NOTHING, YOUR GRACE.
AND YOU, JORDAN RIVERA. YOU HAVE SAVED MY SON'S LIFE TWICE OVER NOW. AS WELL AS MY OWN LIFE AND THE LIVES OF MY SUBJECTS.
MY HEALERS HAVE TENDED TO WHAT WOUNDS YOU HAD, BUT...HOW DO I REPAY SUCH A DEBT?
UM, YOU DON'T, YOUR GRACE. I DON'T NEED ANYTHING.
HMM. I'LL THINK OF SOMETHING.

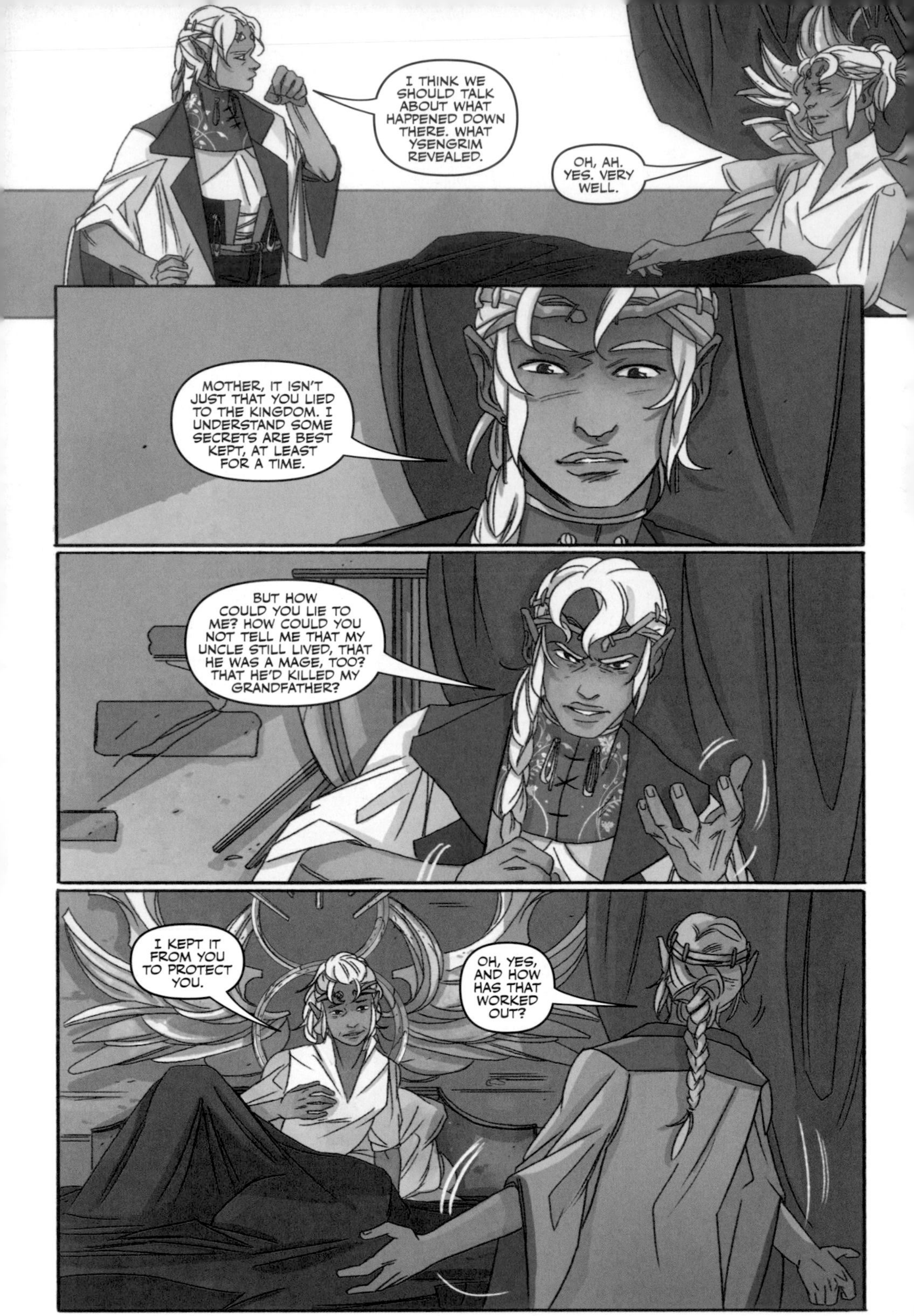
I THINK WE SHOULD TALK ABOUT WHAT HAPPENED DOWN THERE. WHAT YSENGRIM REVEALED.
OH, AH. YES. VERY WELL.
MOTHER, IT ISN'T JUST THAT YOU LIED TO THE KINGDOM. I UNDERSTAND SOME SECRETS ARE BEST KEPT, AT LEAST FOR A TIME.
BUT HOW COULD YOU LIE TO ME? HOW COULD YOU NOT TELL ME THAT MY UNCLE STILL LIVED, THAT HE WAS A MAGE, TOO? THAT HE'D KILLED MY GRANDFATHER?
I KEPT IT FROM YOU TO PROTECT YOU.
OH, YES, AND HOW HAS THAT WORKED OUT?

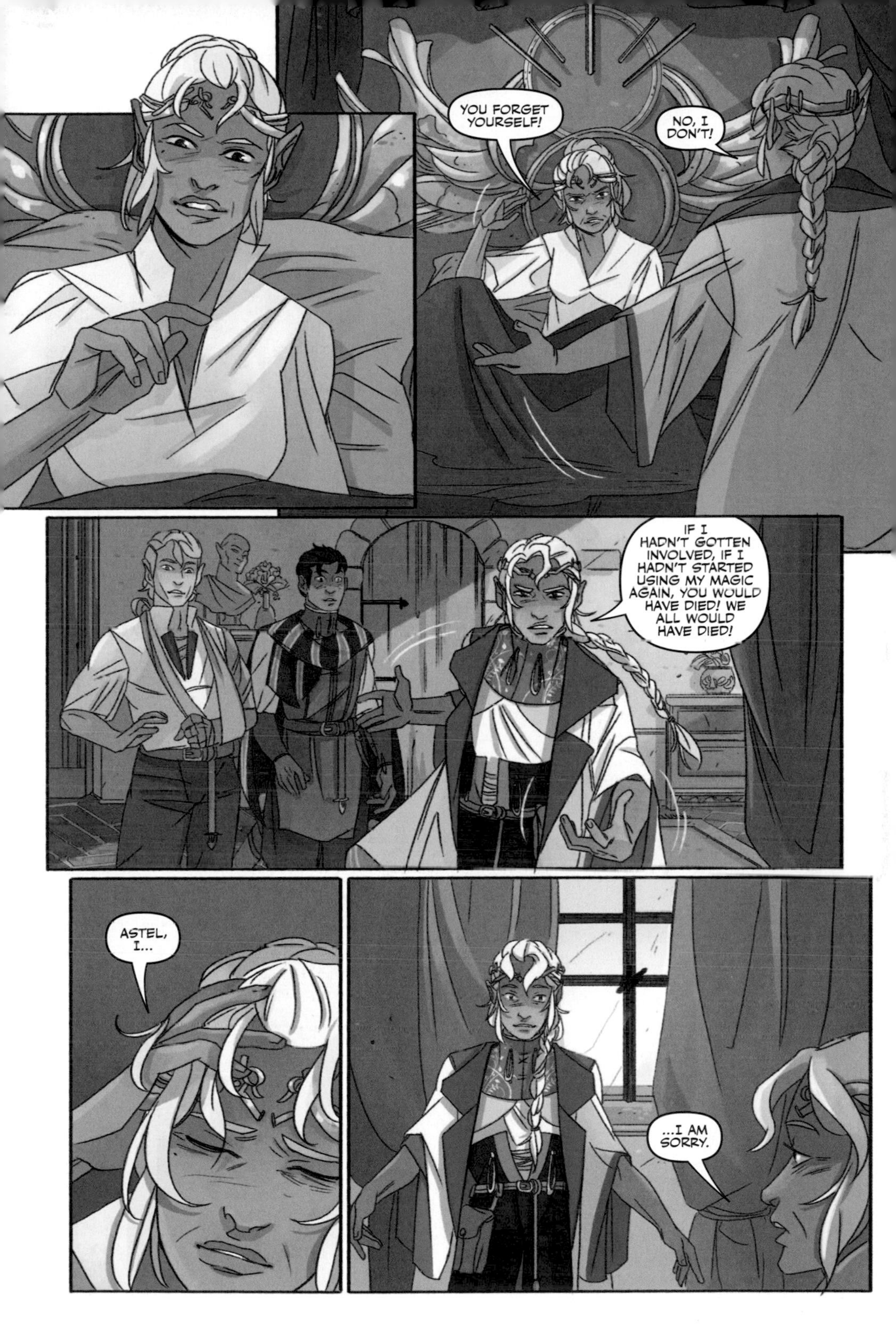
YOU FORGET YOURSELF!
NO, I DON'T!
IF I HADN'T GOTTEN INVOLVED, IF I HADN'T STARTED USING MY MAGIC AGAIN, YOU WOULD HAVE DIED! WE ALL WOULD HAVE DIED!
ASTEL, I...
...I AM SORRY.

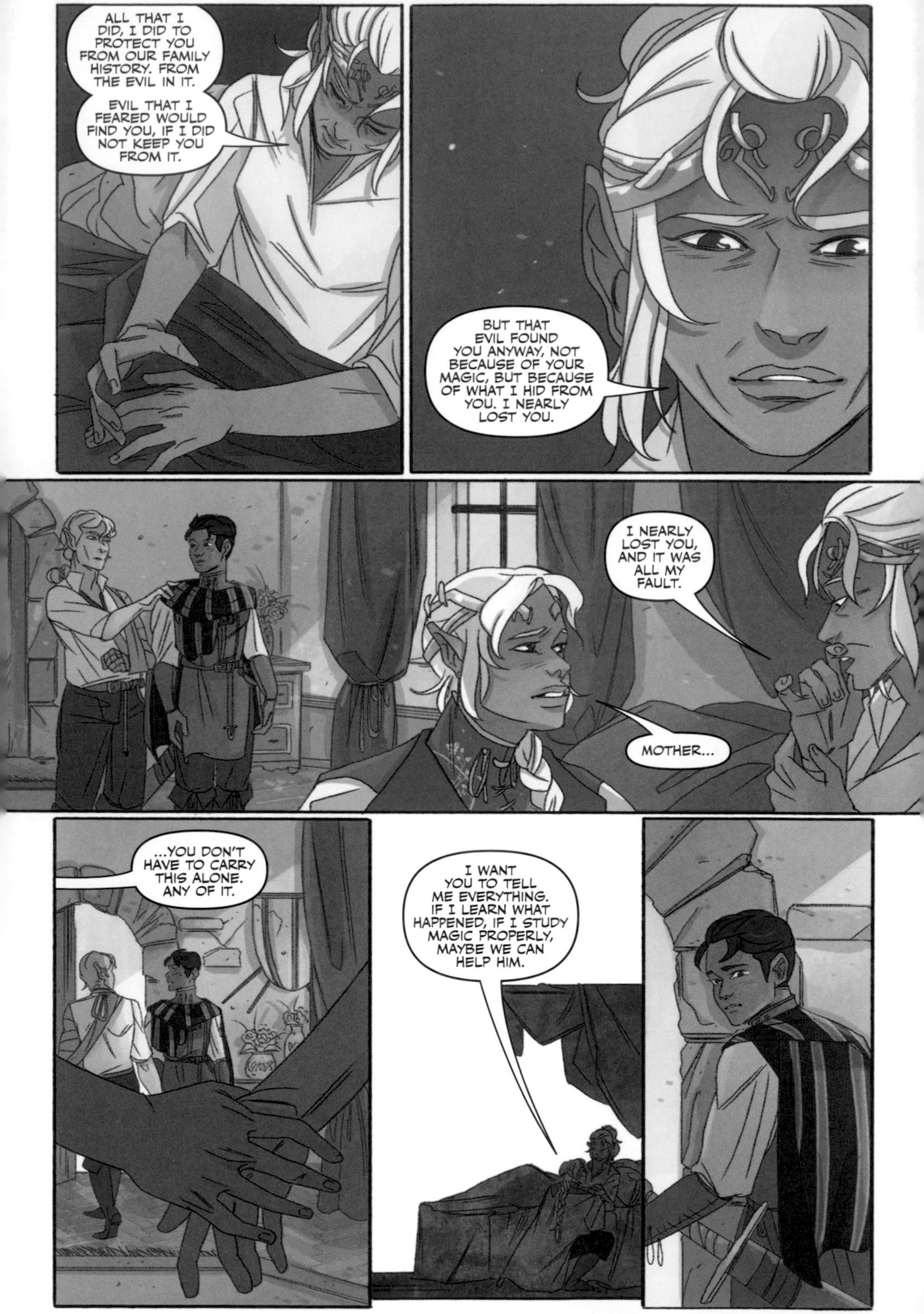
ALL THAT I DID, I DID TO PROTECT YOU FROM OUR FAMILY HISTORY. FROM THE EVIL IN IT.
EVIL THAT I FEARED WOULD FIND YOU, IF I DID NOT KEEP YOU FROM IT.
BUT THAT EVIL FOUND YOU ANYWAY, NOT BECAUSE OF YOUR MAGIC, BUT BECAUSE OF WHAT I HID FROM YOU. I NEARLY LOST YOU.
I NEARLY LOST YOU, AND IT WAS ALL MY FAULT.
MOTHER...
...YOU DON'T HAVE TO CARRY THIS ALONE. ANY OF IT.
I WANT YOU TO TELL ME EVERYTHING. IF I LEARN WHAT HAPPENED, IF I STUDY MAGIC PROPERLY, MAYBE WE CAN HELP HIM.

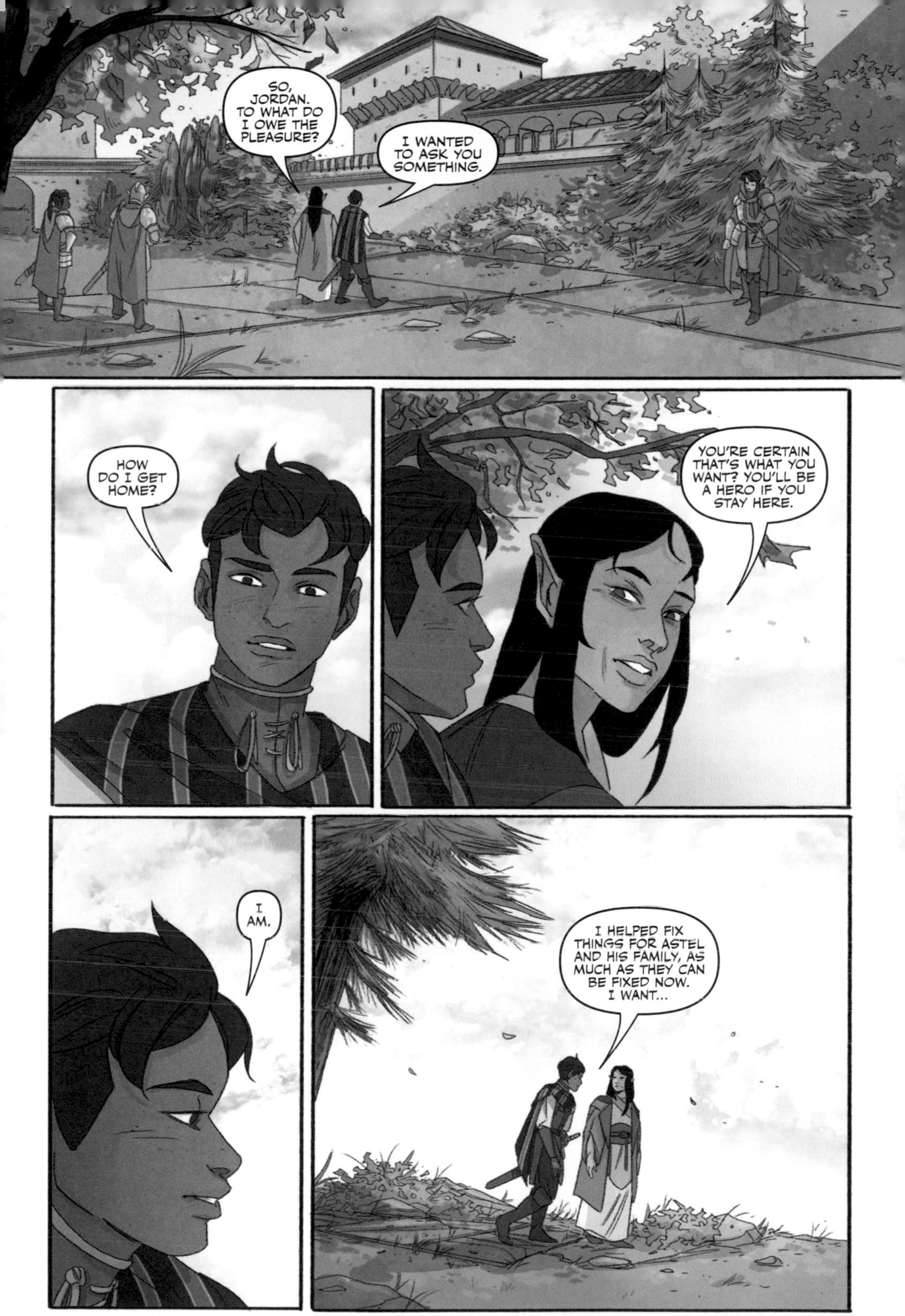
SO, JORDAN. TO WHAT DO I OWE THE PLEASURE?
I WANTED TO ASK YOU SOMETHING.
HOW DO I GET HOME?
YOU'RE CERTAIN THAT'S WHAT YOU WANT? YOU'LL BE A HERO IF YOU STAY HERE.
I AM.
I HELPED FIX THINGS FOR ASTEL AND HIS FAMILY, AS MUCH AS THEY CAN BE FIXED NOW. I WANT...

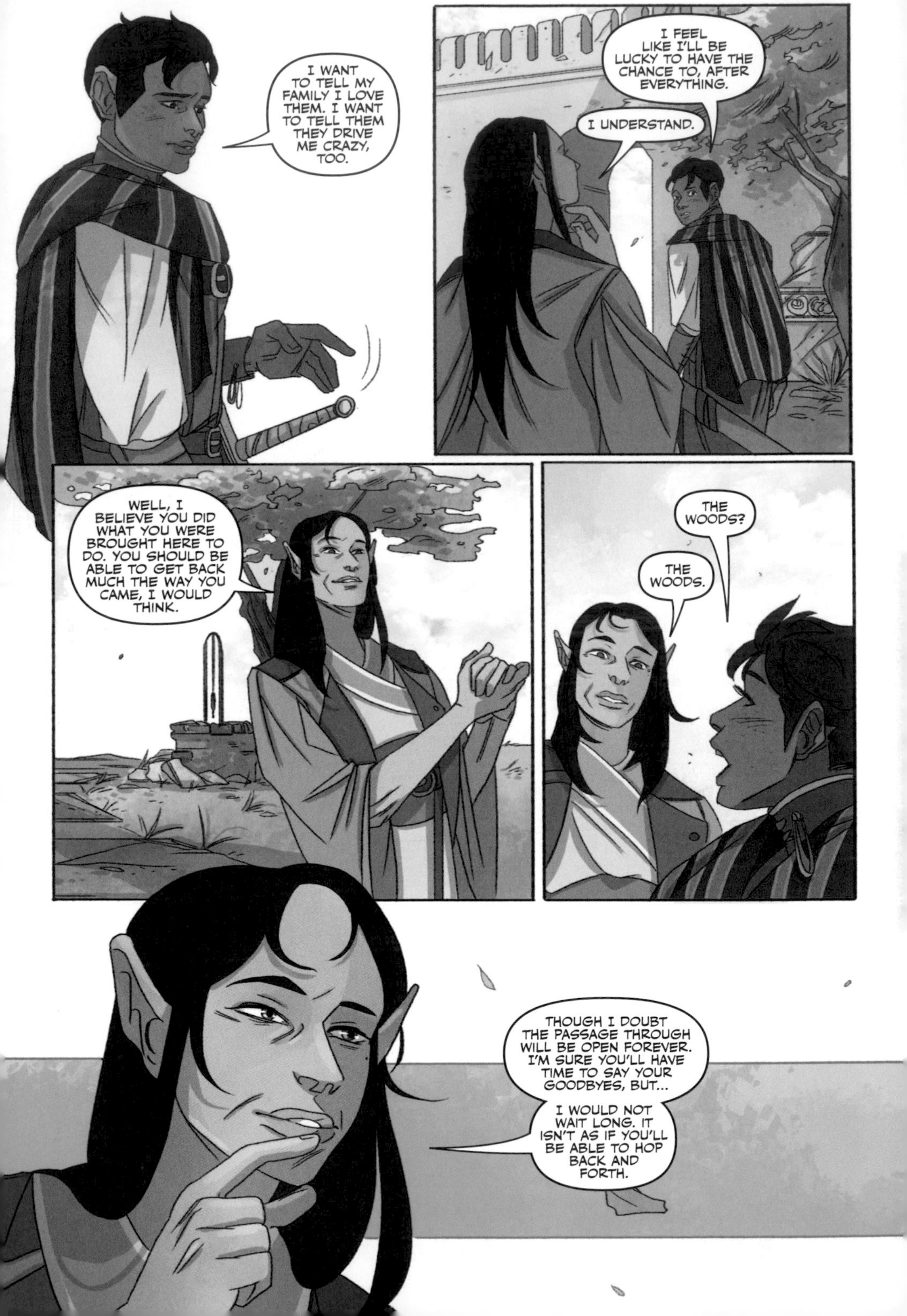
I WANT TO TELL MY FAMILY I LOVE THEM. I WANT TO TELL THEM THEY DRIVE ME CRAZY, TOO.
I FEEL LIKE I'LL BE LUCKY TO HAVE THE CHANCE TO, AFTER EVERYTHING.
I UNDERSTAND.
WELL, I BELIEVE YOU DID WHAT YOU WERE BROUGHT HERE TO DO. YOU SHOULD BE ABLE TO GET BACK MUCH THE WAY YOU CAME, I WOULD THINK.
THE WOODS?
THE WOODS.
THOUGH I DOUBT THE PASSAGE THROUGH WILL BE OPEN FOREVER. I'M SURE YOU'LL HAVE TIME TO SAY YOUR GOODBYES, BUT...
I WOULD NOT WAIT LONG. IT ISN'T AS IF YOU'LL BE ABLE TO HOP BACK AND FORTH.

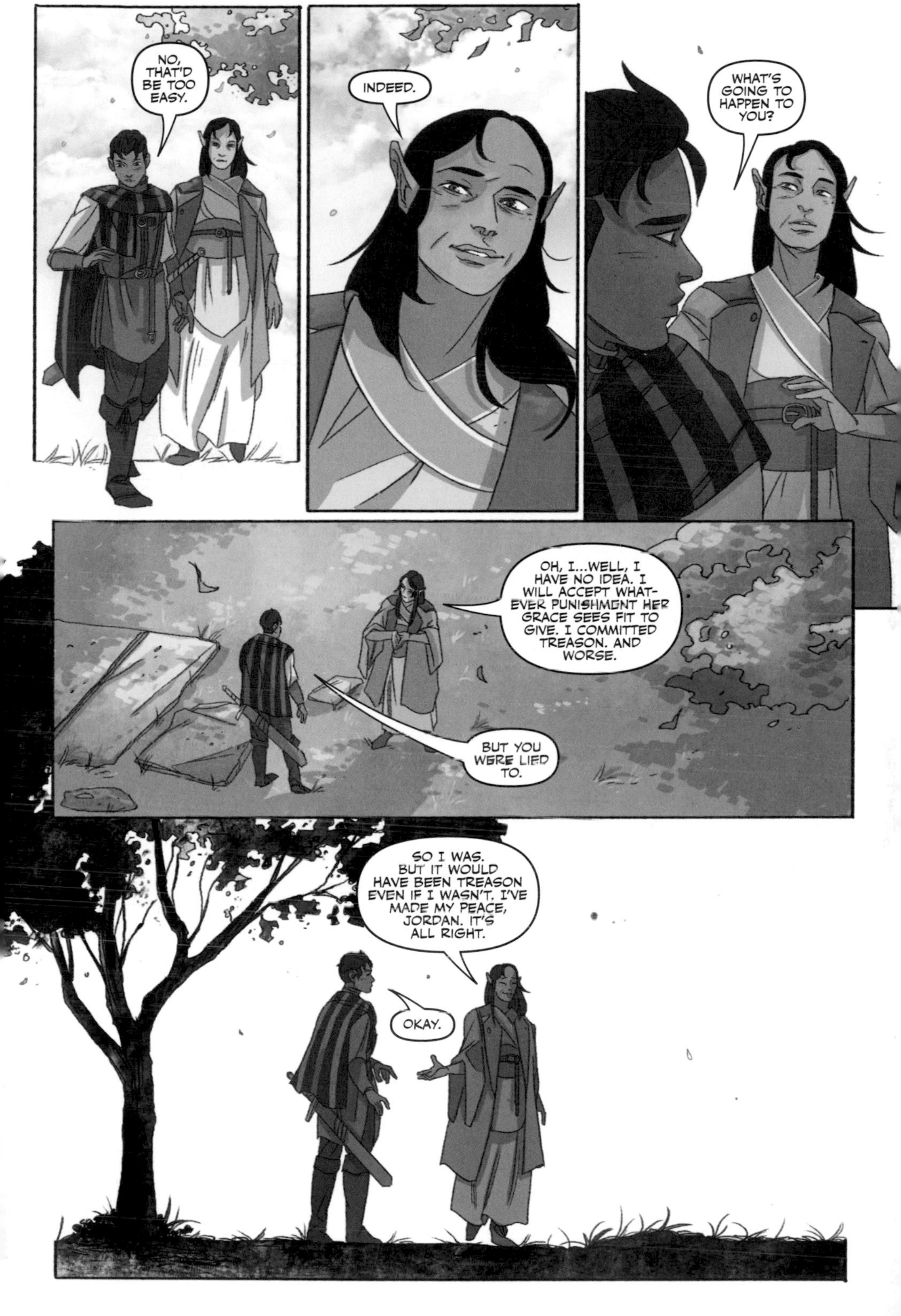
NO, THAT'D BE TOO EASY.
INDEED.
WHAT'S GOING TO HAPPEN TO YOU?
OH, I...WELL, I HAVE NO IDEA. I WILL ACCEPT WHAT-EVER PUNISHMENT HER GRACE SEES FIT TO GIVE. I COMMITTED TREASON. AND WORSE.
BUT YOU WERE LIED TO.
SO I WAS. BUT IT WOULD HAVE BEEN TREASON EVEN IF I WASN'T. I'VE MADE MY PEACE, JORDAN. IT'S ALL RIGHT.
OKAY.

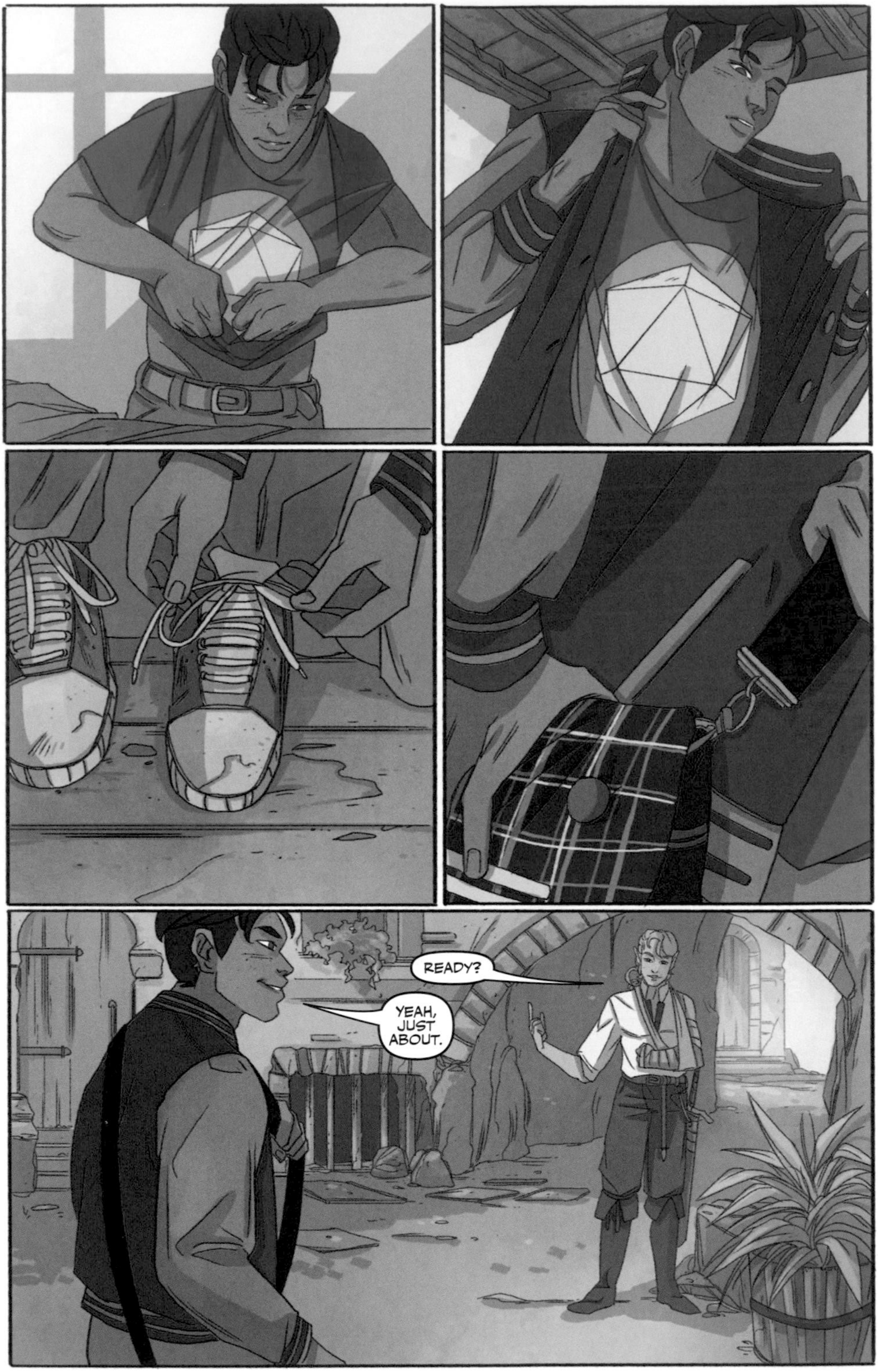
READY?
YEAH, JUST ABOUT.

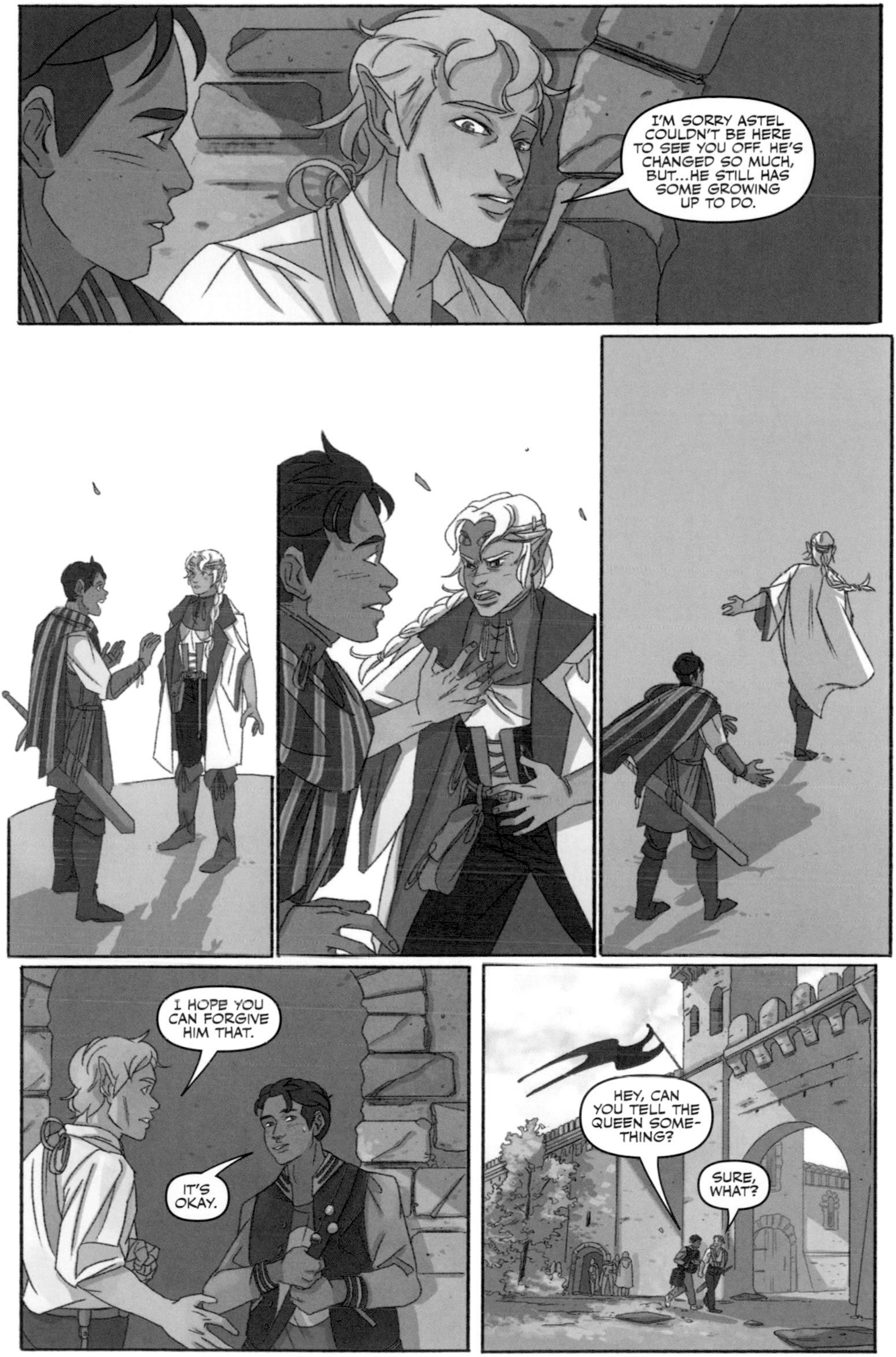
I'M SORRY ASTEL COULDN'T BE HERE TO SEE YOU OFF. HE'S CHANGED SO MUCH, BUT...HE STILL HAS SOME GROWING UP TO DO.
I HOPE YOU CAN FORGIVE HIM THAT.
IT'S OKAY.
HEY, CAN YOU TELL THE QUEEN SOME-THING?
SURE, WHAT?

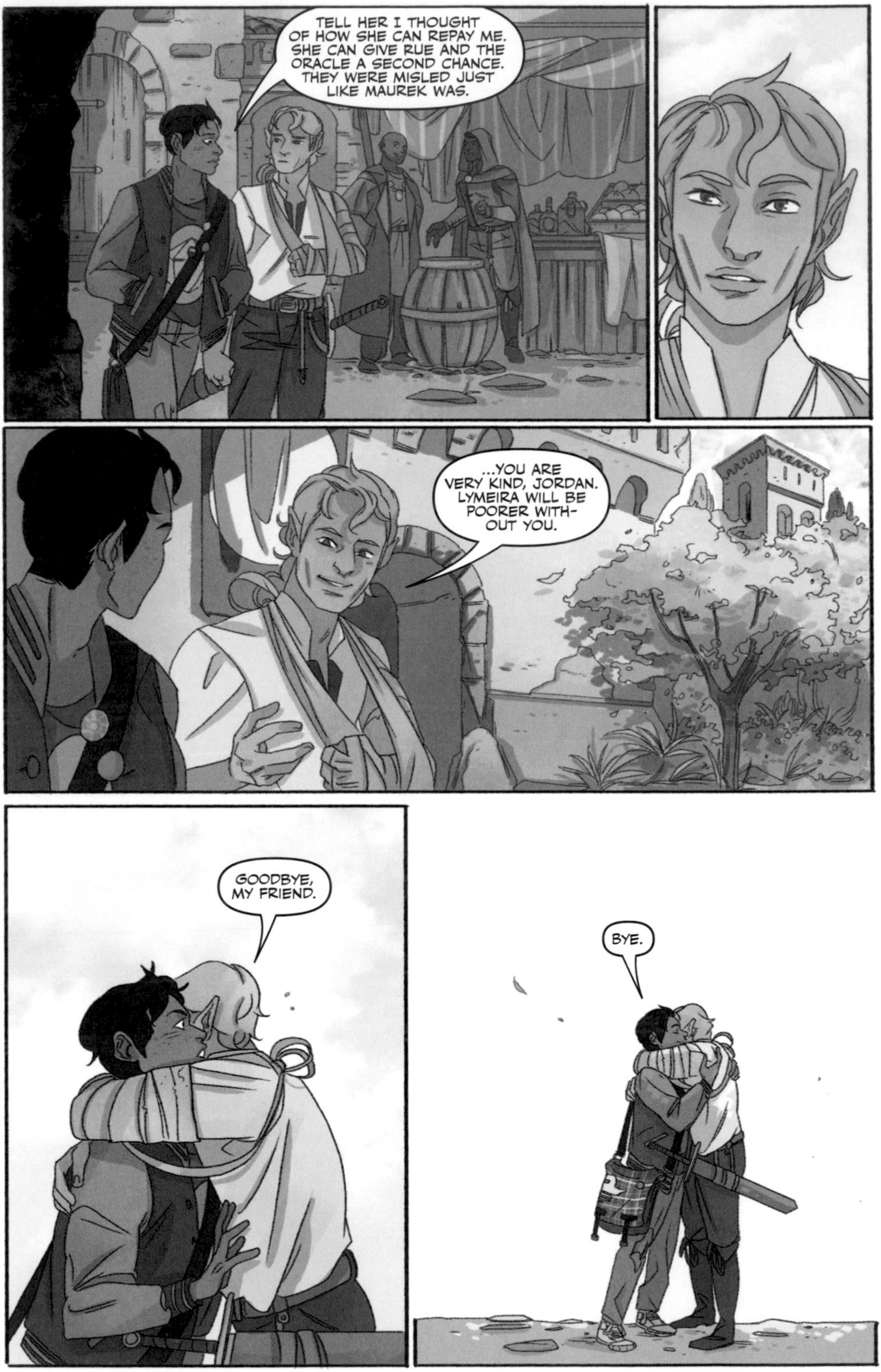
TELL HER I THOUGHT OF HOW SHE CAN REPAY ME. SHE CAN GIVE RUE AND THE ORACLE A SECOND CHANCE. THEY WERE MISLED JUST LIKE MAUREK WAS.
...YOU ARE VERY KIND, JORDAN. LYMEIRA WILL BE POORER WITH-OUT YOU.
GOODBYE, MY FRIEND.
BYE.

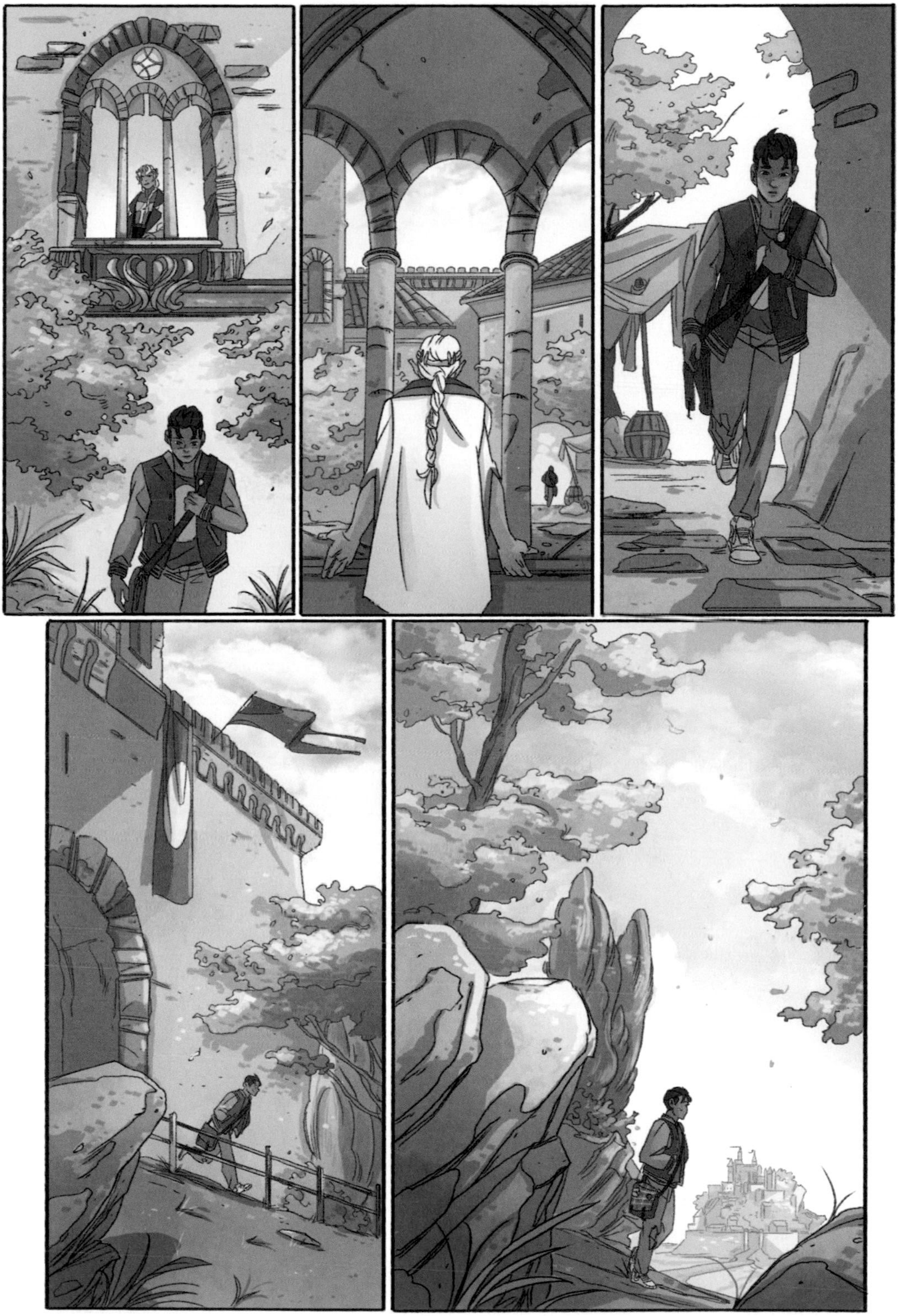

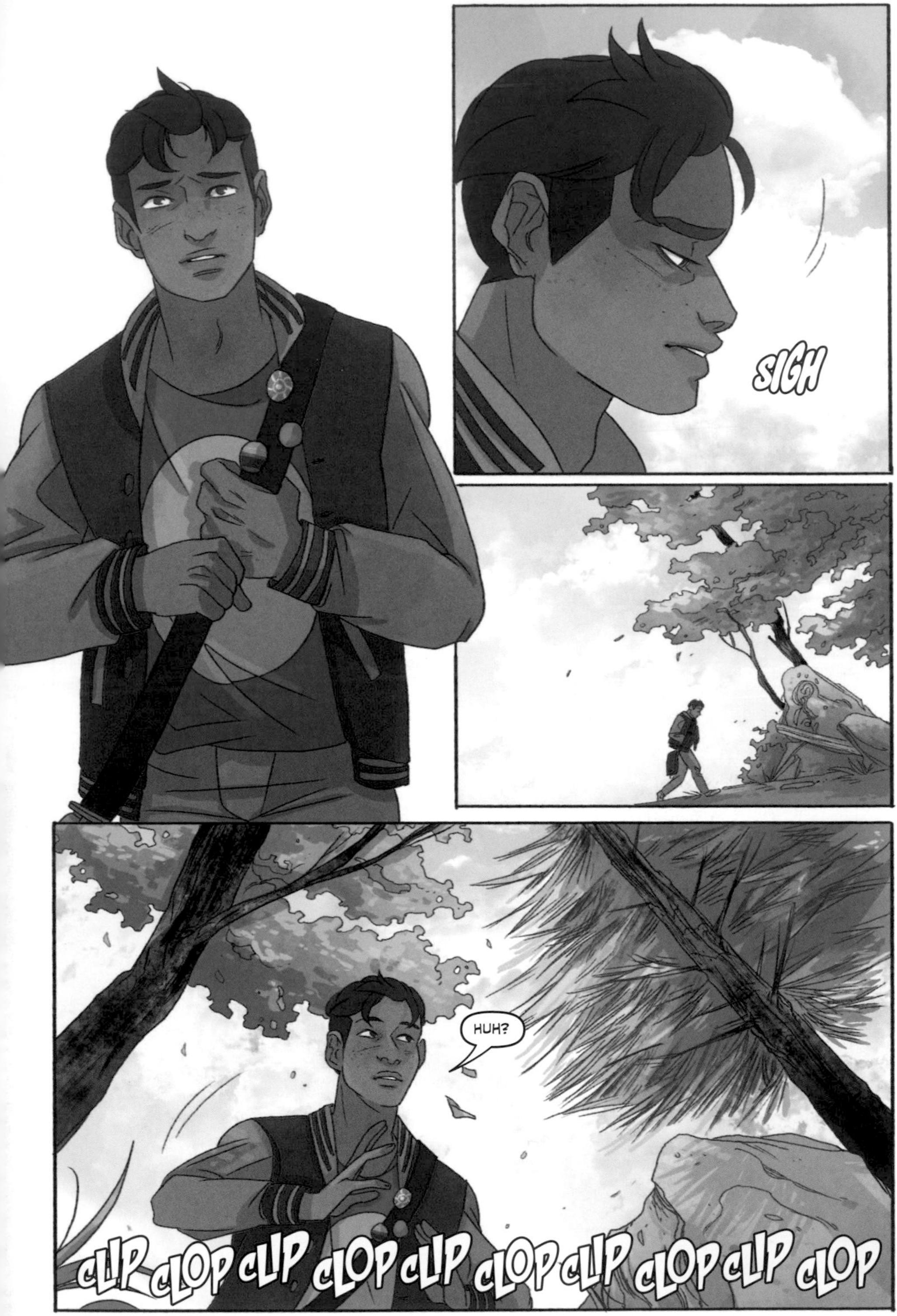
SIGH
HUH?
CLIP CLOP CLIP CLOP CLIP CLOP CLIP CLOP CLIP CLOP

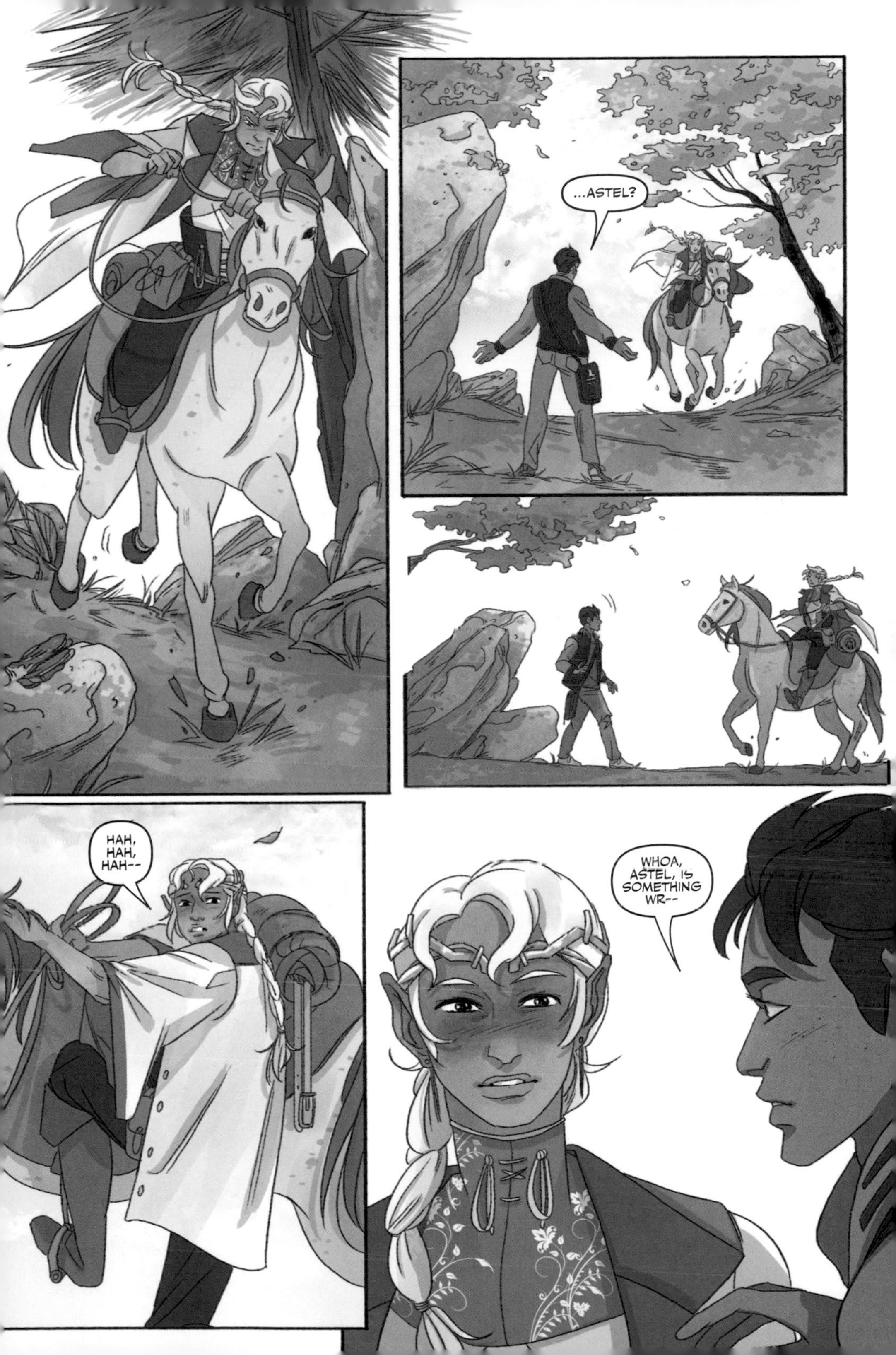
...ASTEL?
HAH, HAH, HAH--
WHOA, ASTEL, IS SOMETHING WR--

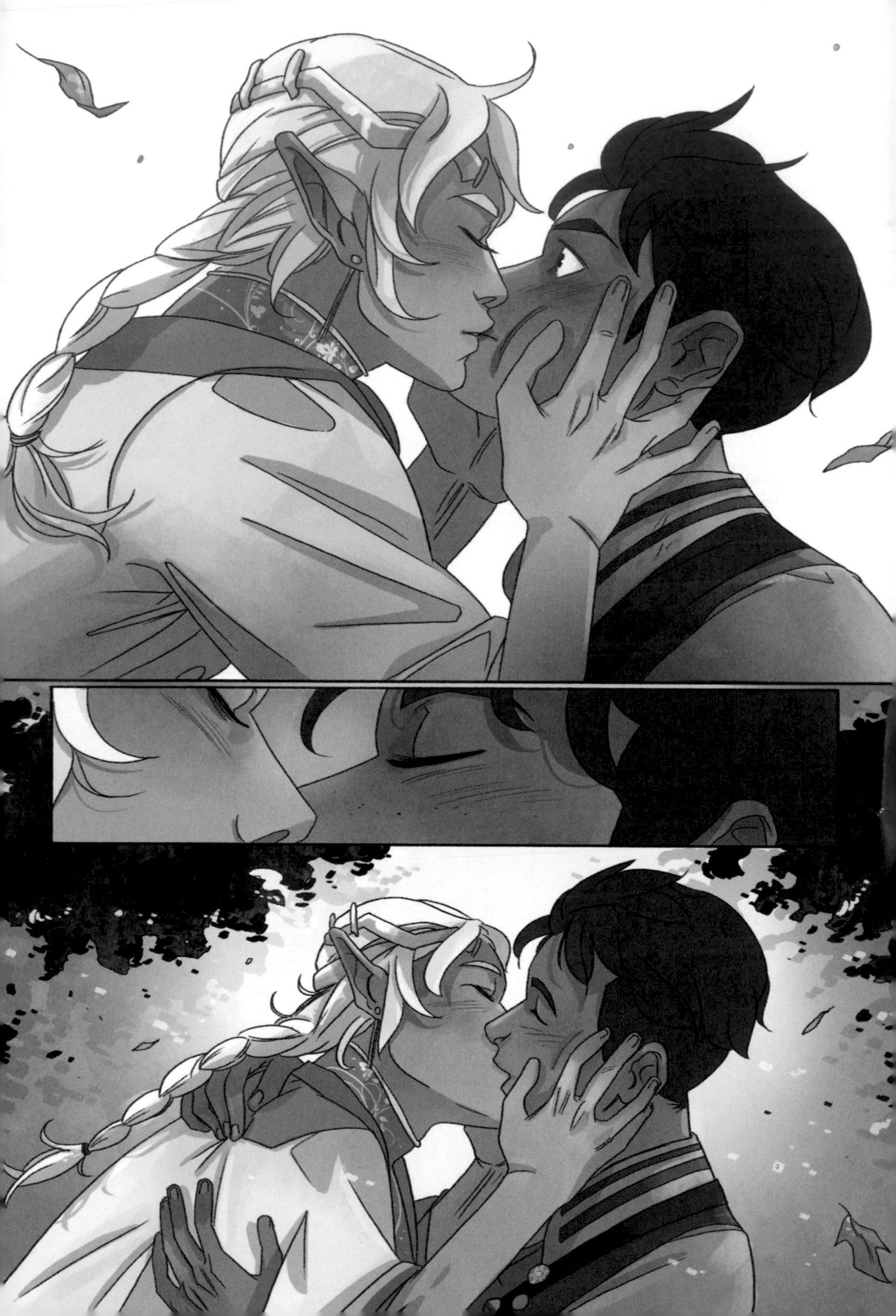

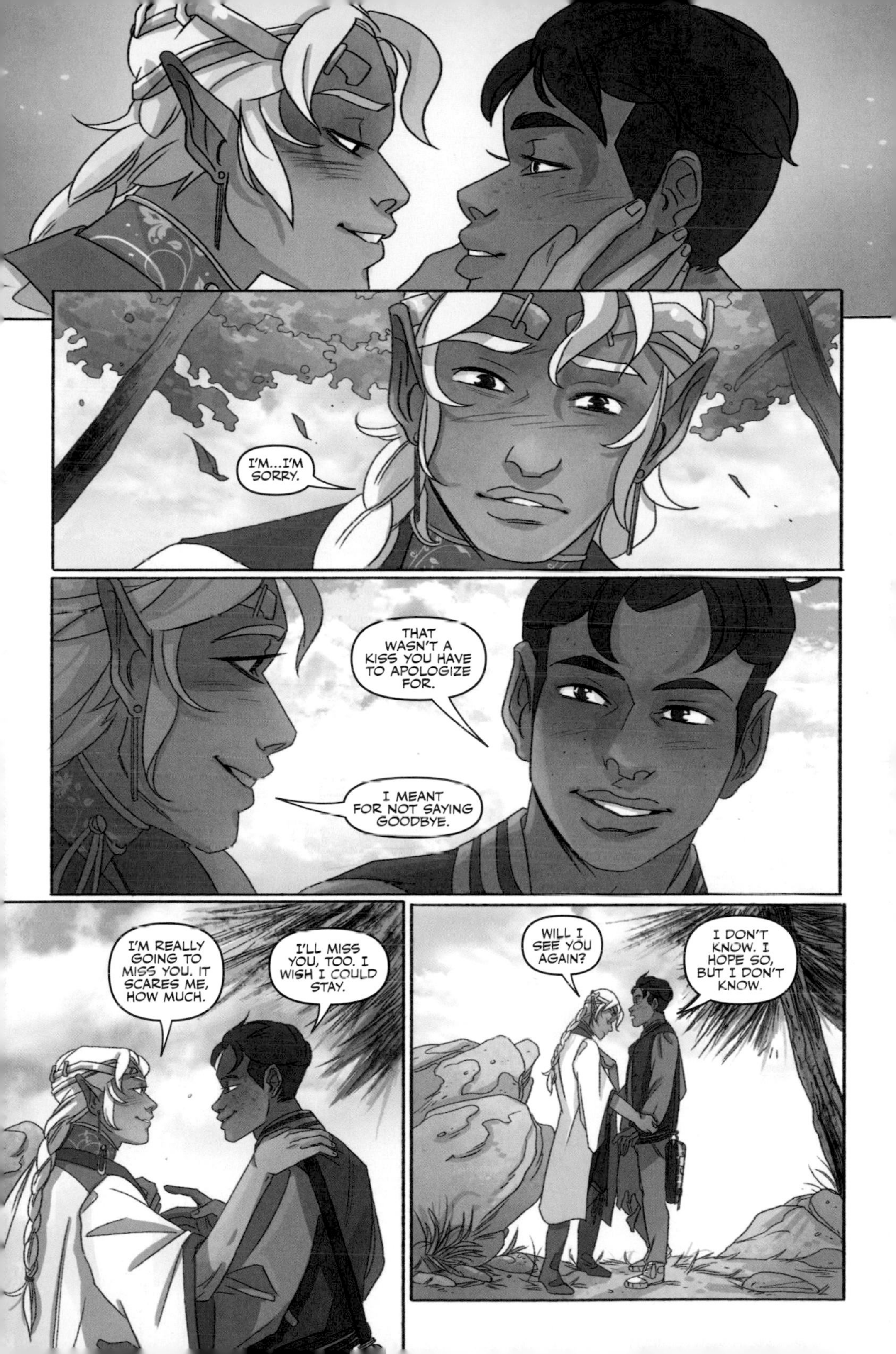
I'M...I'M SORRY.
THAT WASN'T A KISS YOU HAVE TO APOLOGIZE FOR.
I MEANT FOR NOT SAYING GOODBYE.
I'M REALLY GOING TO MISS YOU. IT SCARES ME, HOW MUCH.
I'LL MISS YOU, TOO. I WISH I COULD STAY.
WILL I SEE YOU AGAIN?
I DON'T KNOW. I HOPE SO, BUT I DON'T KNOW.

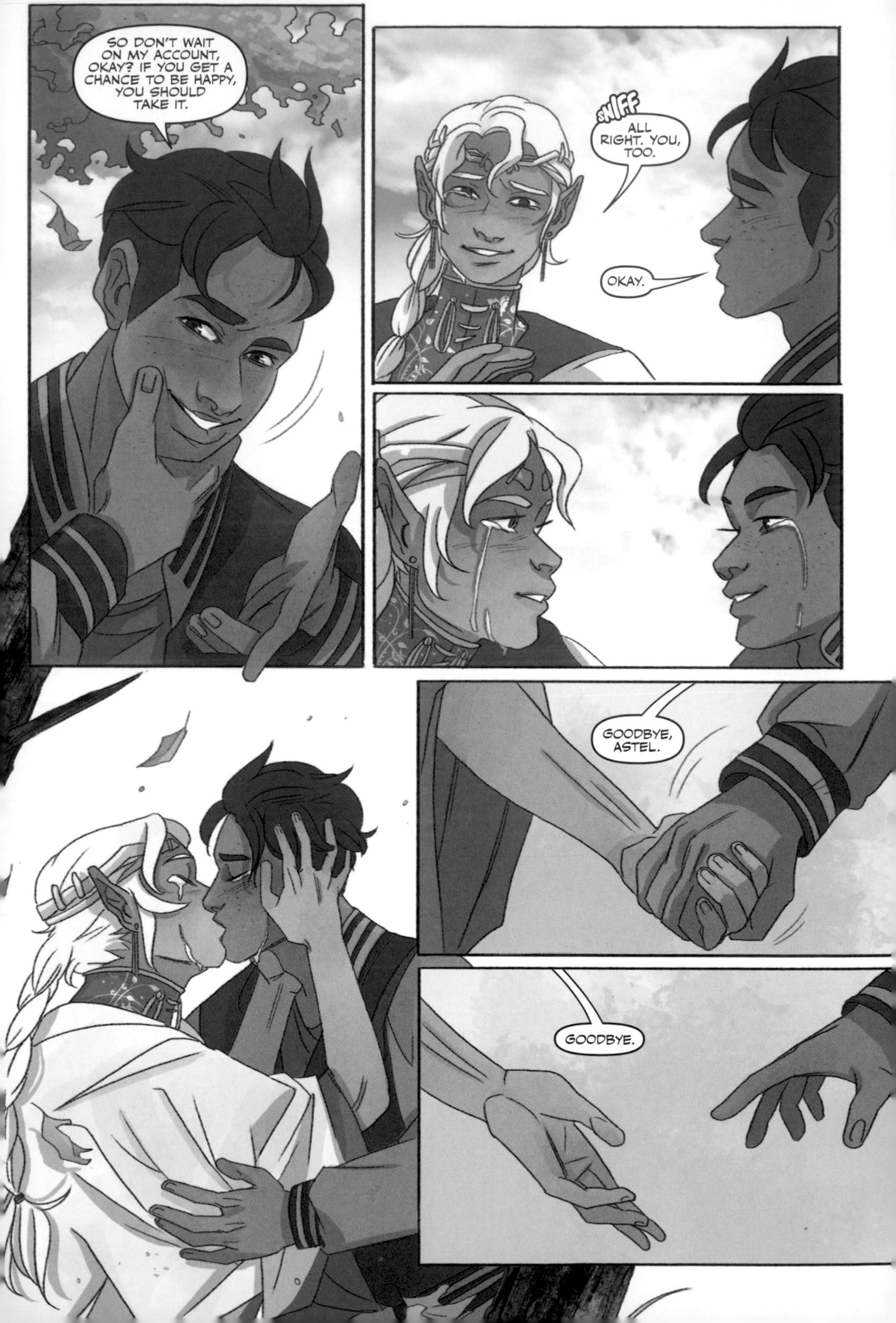
SO DON'T WAIT ON MY ACCOUNT, OKAY? IF YOU GET A CHANCE TO BE HAPPY, YOU SHOULD TAKE IT.
SNIFF
ALL RIGHT. YOU, TOO.
OKAY.
GOODBYE, ASTEL.
GOODBYE.

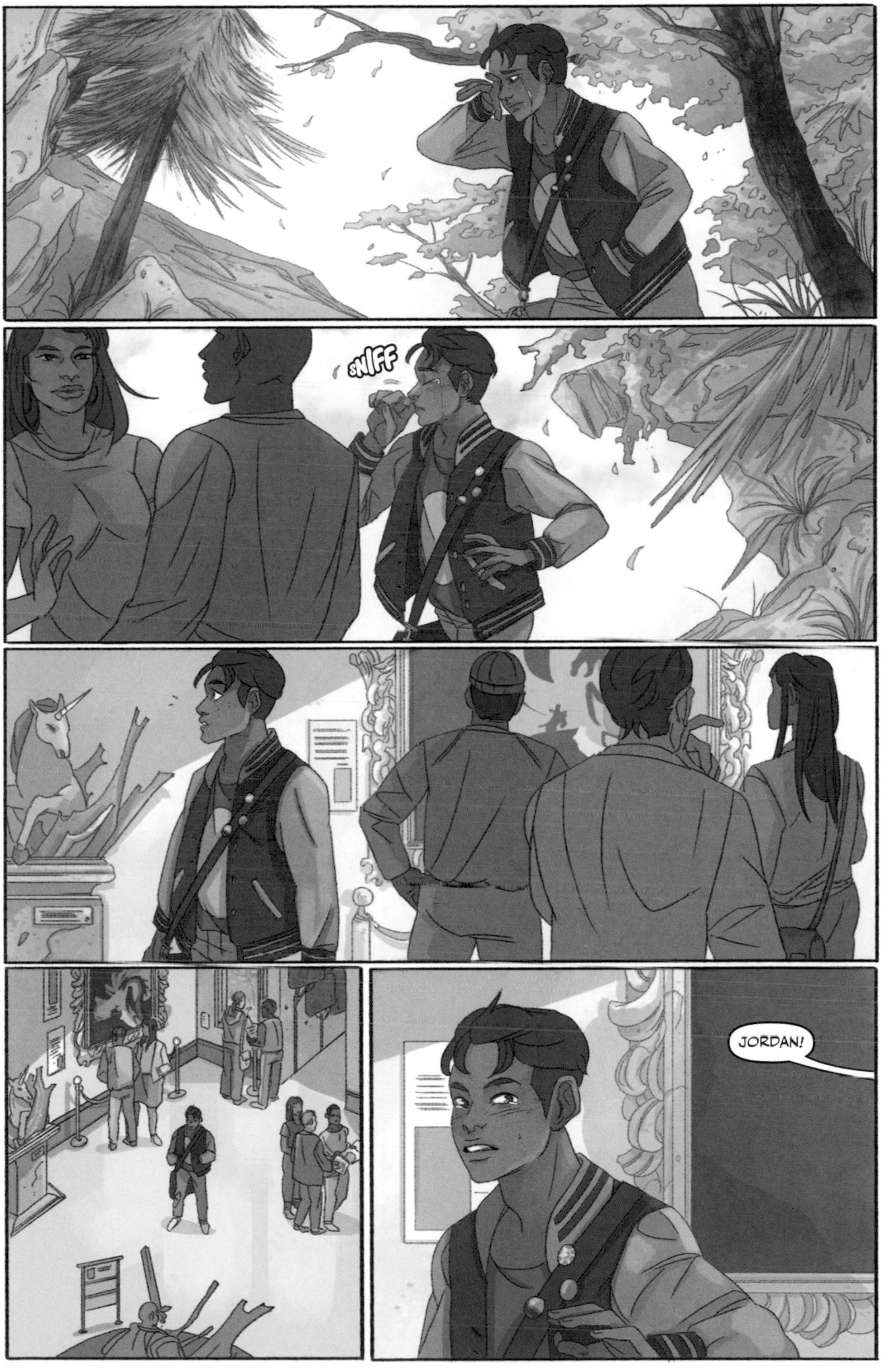
SNIFF
JORDAN!

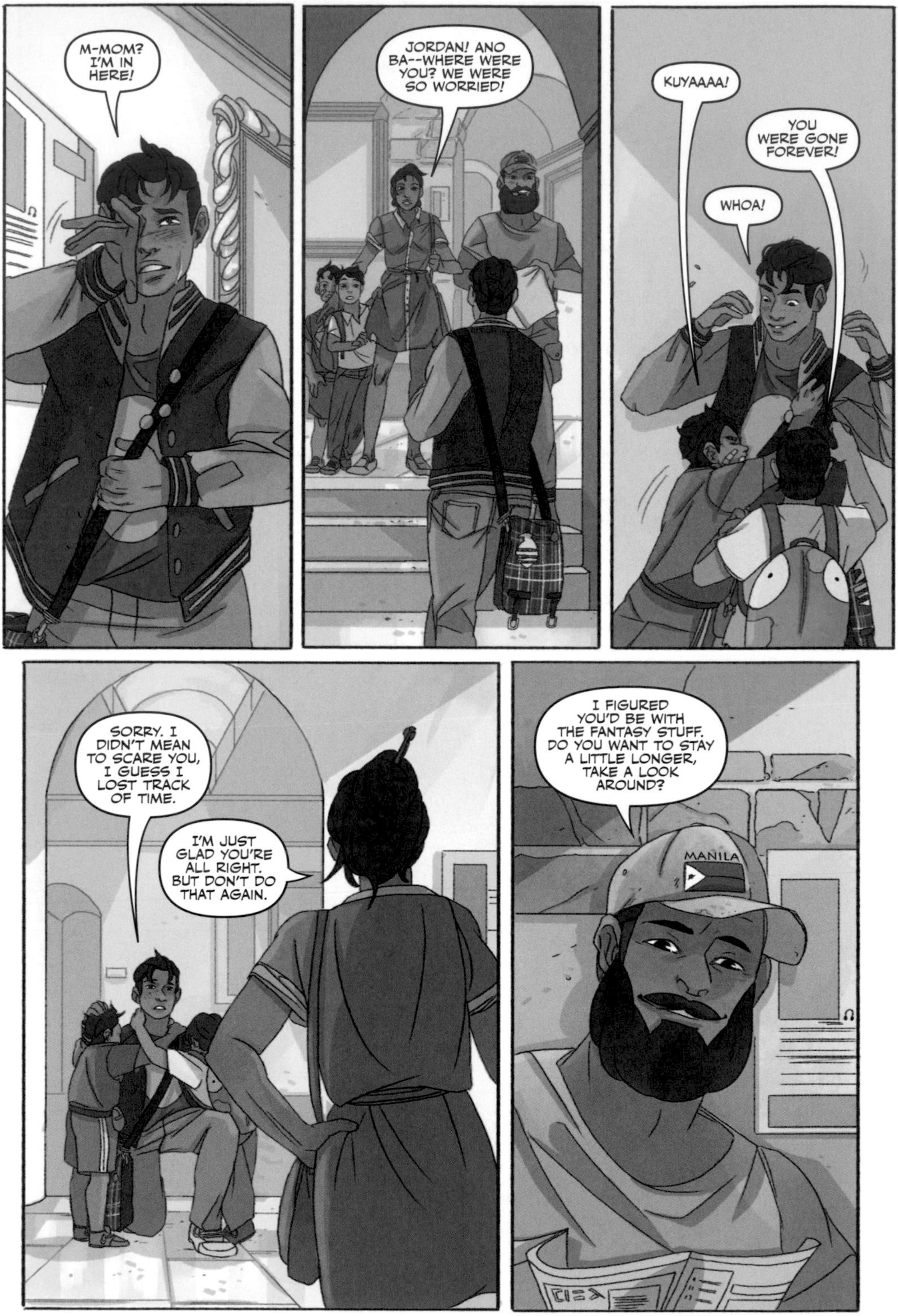
M-MOM? I'M IN HERE!
JORDAN! ANO BA--WHERE WERE YOU? WE WERE SO WORRIED!
KUYAAAA!
YOU WERE GONE FOREVER!
WHOA!
SORRY. I DIDN'T MEAN TO SCARE YOU, I GUESS I LOST TRACK OF TIME.
I'M JUST GLAD YOU'RE ALL RIGHT. BUT DON'T DO THAT AGAIN.
I FIGURED YOU'D BE WITH THE FANTASY STUFF. DO YOU WANT TO STAY A LITTLE LONGER, TAKE A LOOK AROUND?
MANILA

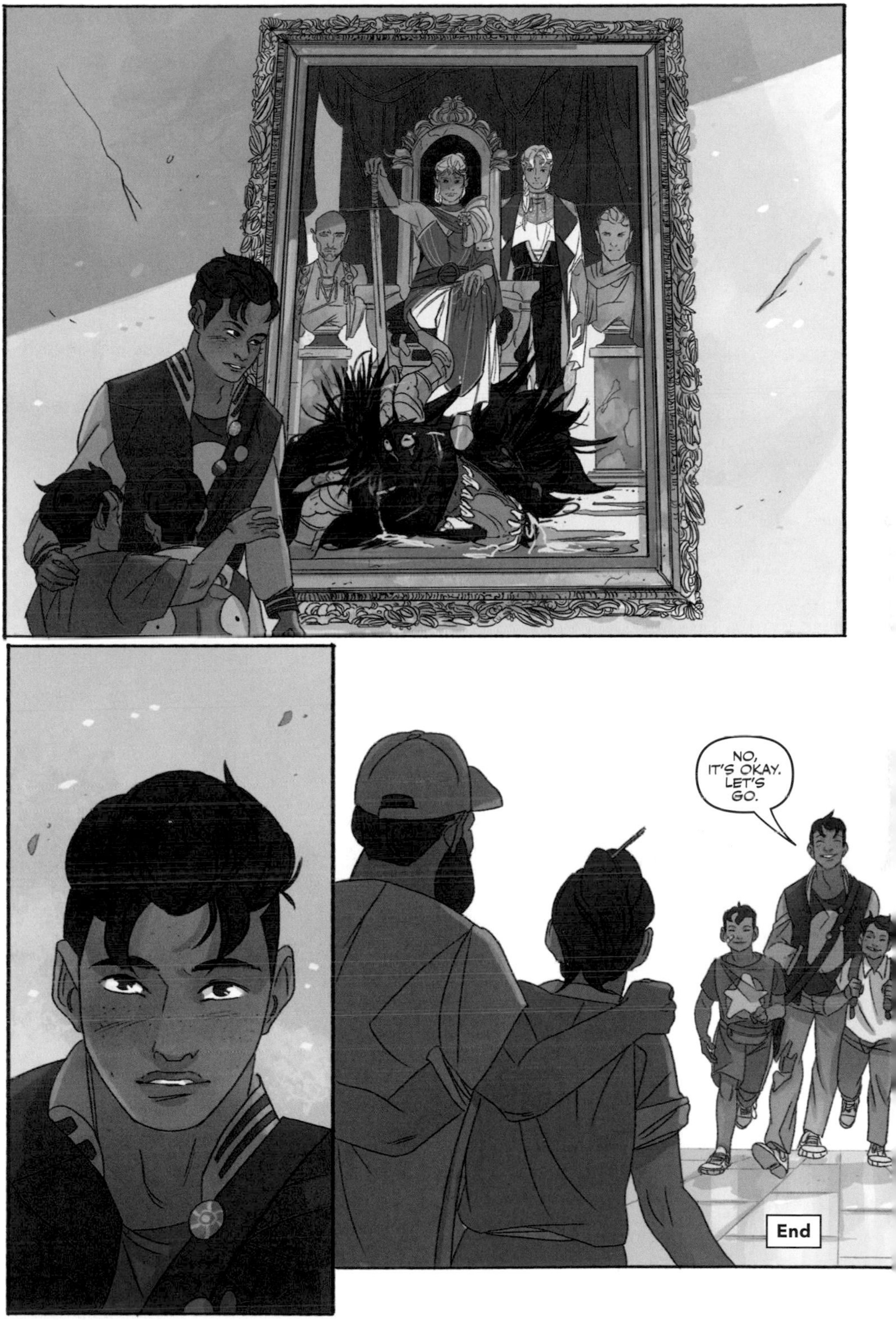
NO, IT'S OKAY. LET'S GO.
End

IN THE
SHADOW
OF THE
THRONE

**Kate Sheridan** is a nonbinary cartoonist and illustrator from Philadelphia who loves monsters, ornithology, and the sea. Other published works include the short "GHOSTBOT" in the Eisner-nominated anthology Flash Forward: An Illustrated Guide to Possible (and Not So Possible) Tomorrows, Fionna & Cake: Party Bash Blues, and the self-published short Fallow Time.

*"THE HUGEST OF THANK-YOUS TO GAIA, MIKE, MICAH, CAT, AND THE MAD CAVE TEAM FOR HELPING TO MAKE THIS BOOK A REALITY. THANK YOU FOR BRINGING JORDAN AND ASTEL'S WORLD TO LIFE IN SUCH A LUSH AND REALIZED WAY. I'M BLOWN AWAY AT HOW LUCKY I AM TO HAVE SUCH A SKILLED SLATE OF CO-CREATORS. TO CAT, MY BEST FRIEND, WHOSE KNOWLEDGE AND SKILL AND SENSE OF HUMOR AS A WRITER/SENSITIVITY READER HELPED THIS BOOK BE WHAT IT COULD BE. AND THANK YOU TO MY PARENTS, MY FIRST AND LONGEST-RUNNING CHEERLEADERS, WHO ARE ALWAYS FIRST IN LINE TO SUPPORT ME AND MY WORK."*

**Gaia Cardinali** is an Italian comic artist. She took a master's degree in comics and illustration at the Bologna fine arts academy in 2015. After an early career as a grapes harvester, Gaia decided to put her hands to better use. With a long-time interest in medieval and fantasy stories, she created, wrote, and drew Viktoria, her first graphic novel, which was published by the Italian publisher Tunuè in 2017. In 2020, she was a colorist on the Disney/Dark Horse release of Mulan. A year later, she drew La Leonessa di Dordona, which Tunué also published. Like a hedge knight on her quest, she always looks for her next story.

*"A BIG THANK YOU TO ENRICO AND ELSA FOR BEING THE BEST POSSIBLE FAMILY. THANK YOU TO FRA, MARCO, ARI, GABRI, GINMY, AND SILVIA FOR MAKING EVERY DAY CRAZIER THAN IT SHOULD BE. THANK YOU TO GIUSY AND RICCARDO, WHO HELPED ME FLAT THIS GRAPHIC NOVEL. YOU GUYS ARE PRECIOUS. THANK YOU TO THE AMAZING TEAM AT MADCAVE FOR MAKING THIS GRAPHIC NOVEL A REALITY."*

**Micah Myers** is a Ringo nominated comic book letterer who has worked for DC, Image, Dark Horse, IDW, Mad Cave, Heavy Metal, Webtoon, Comixology, and many others. He also occasionally writes and has his own series about a team of D-List villains, The Disasters.

*"THANK YOU TO TIFF, JAKE, AND CHARI. LOVE YOU ALL."*

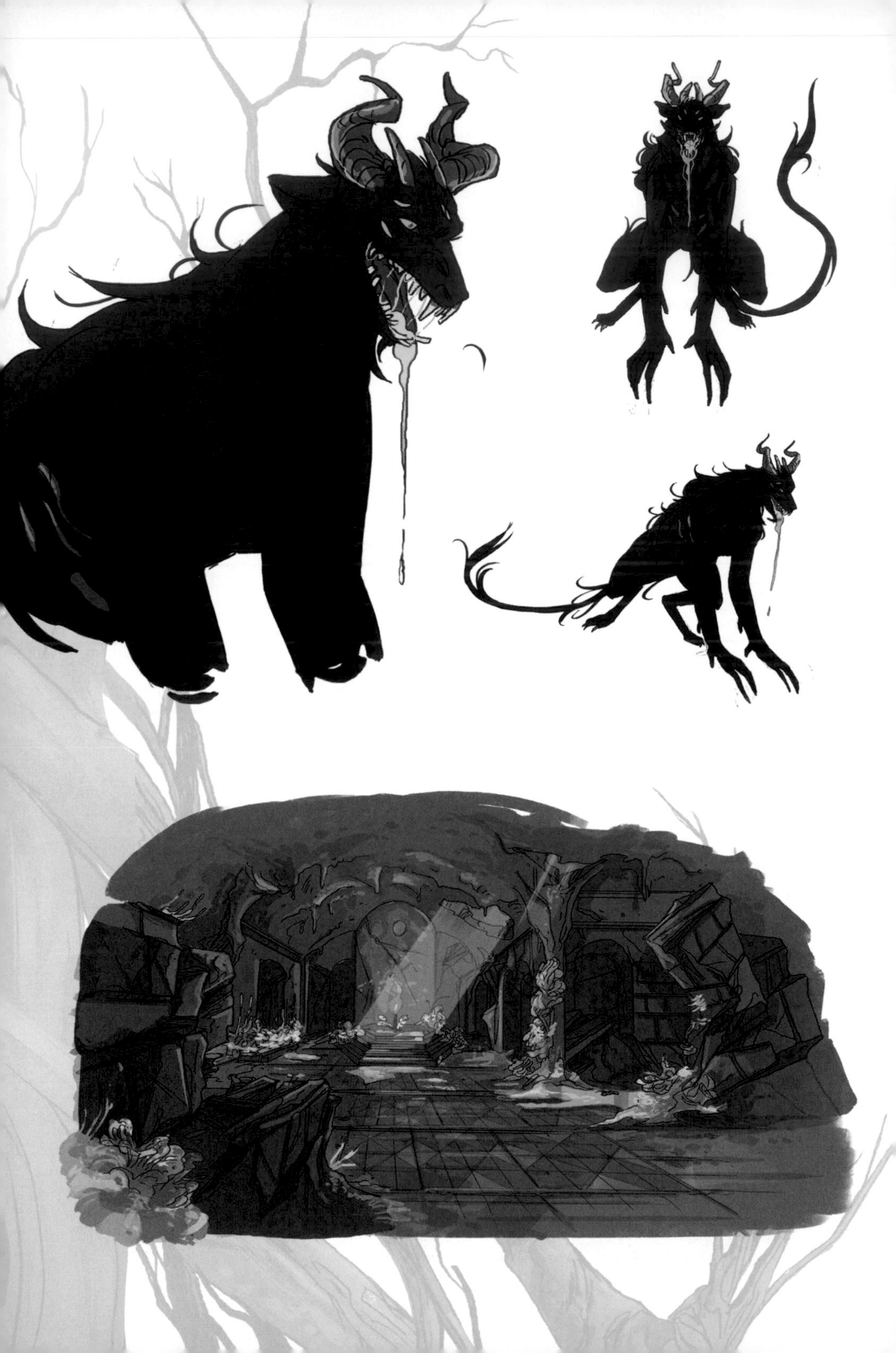

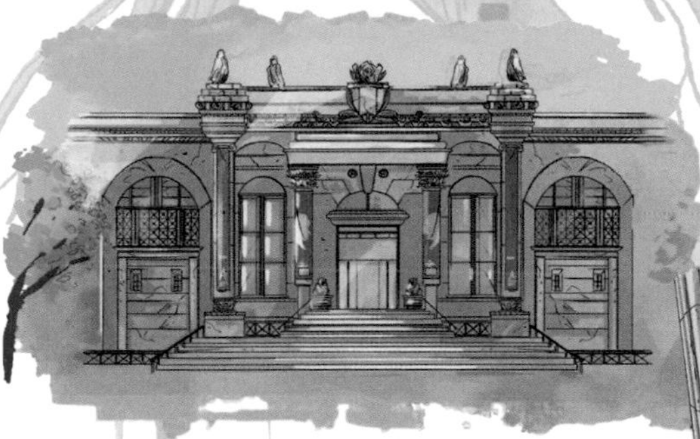
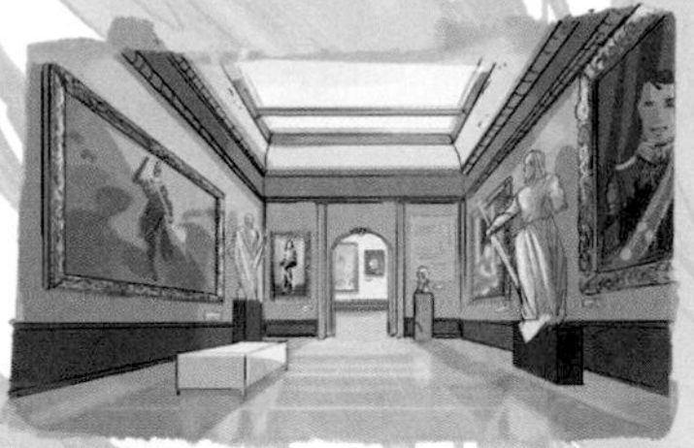
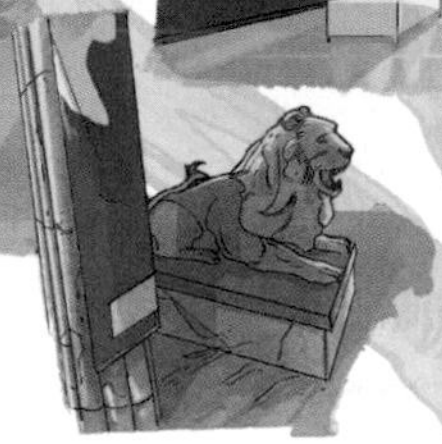
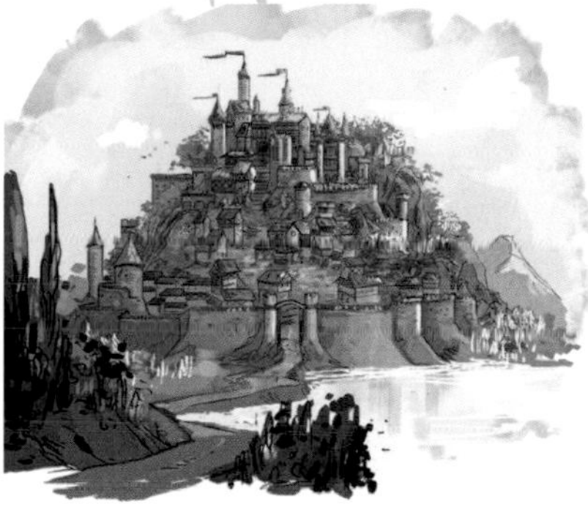
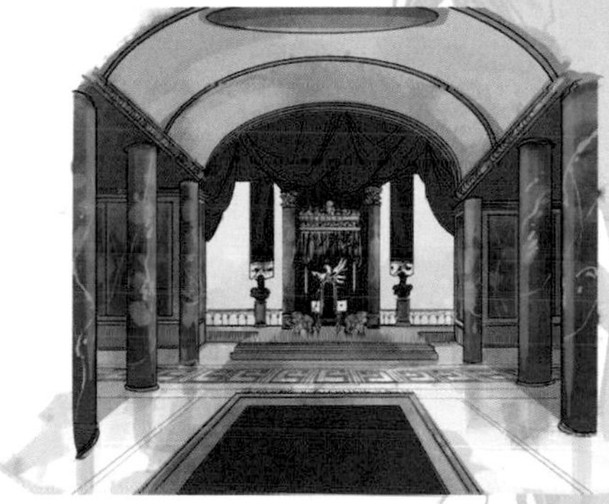
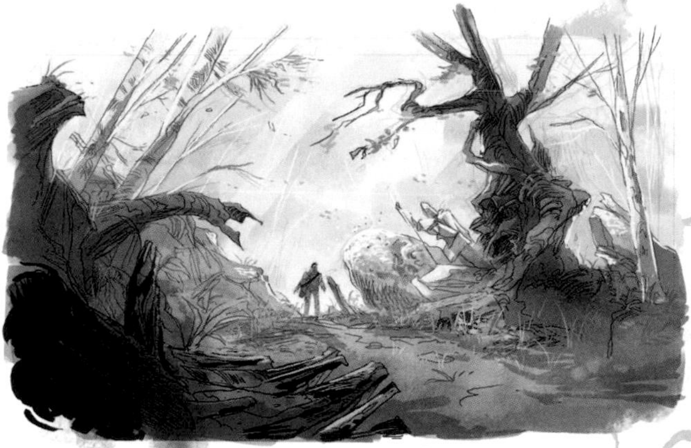
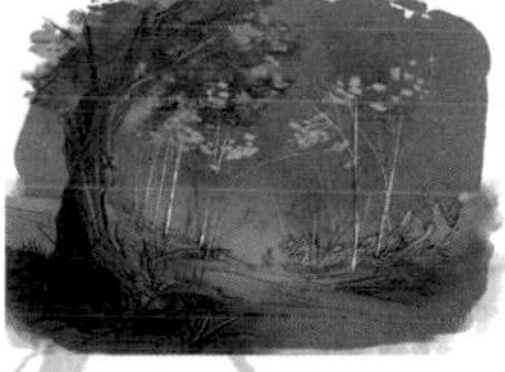
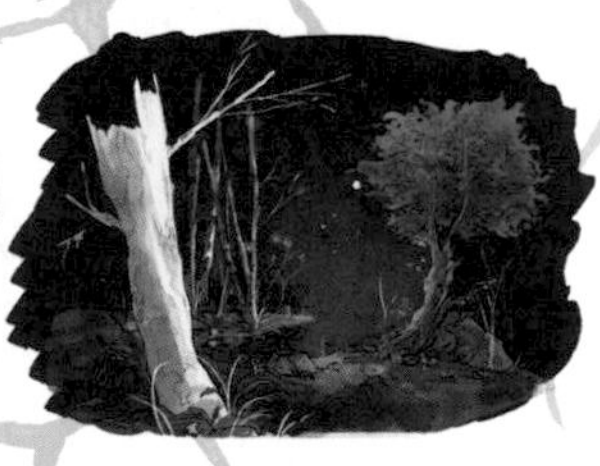

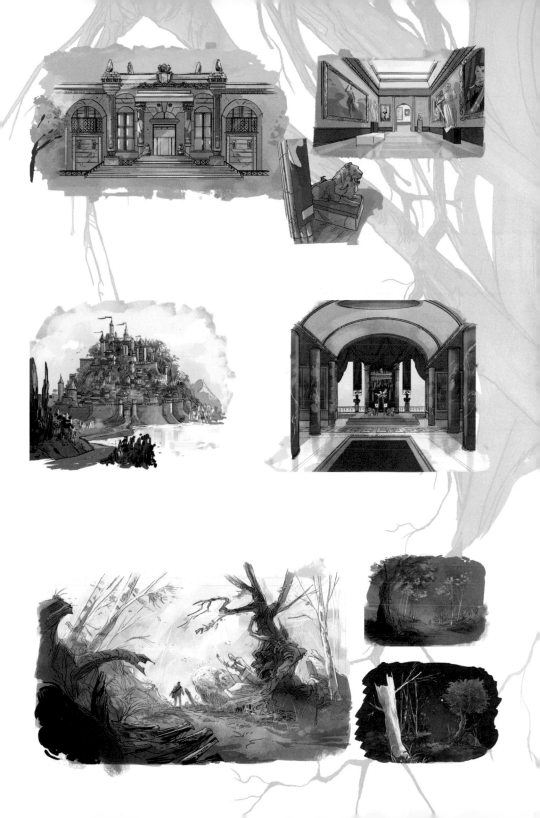

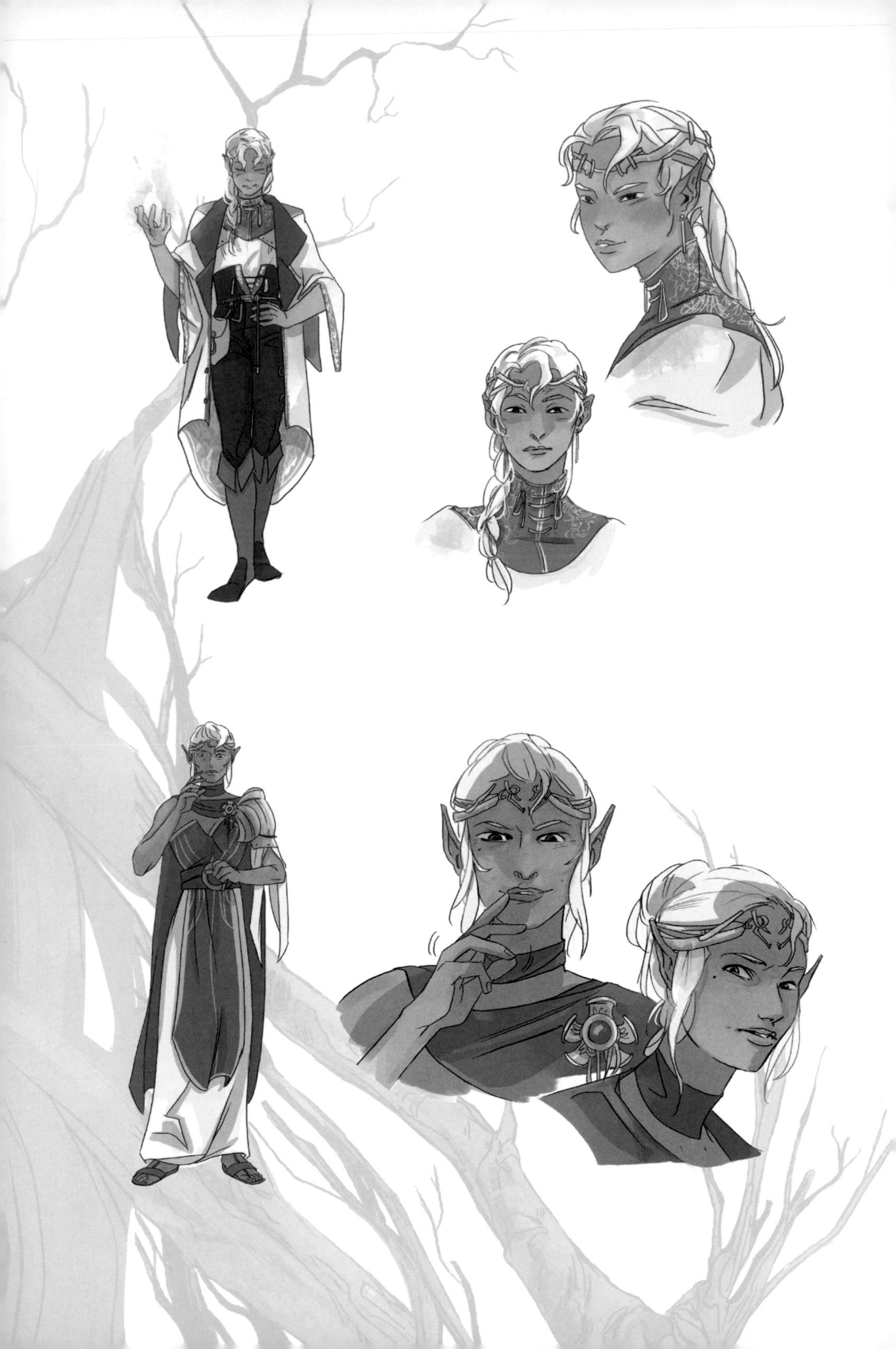

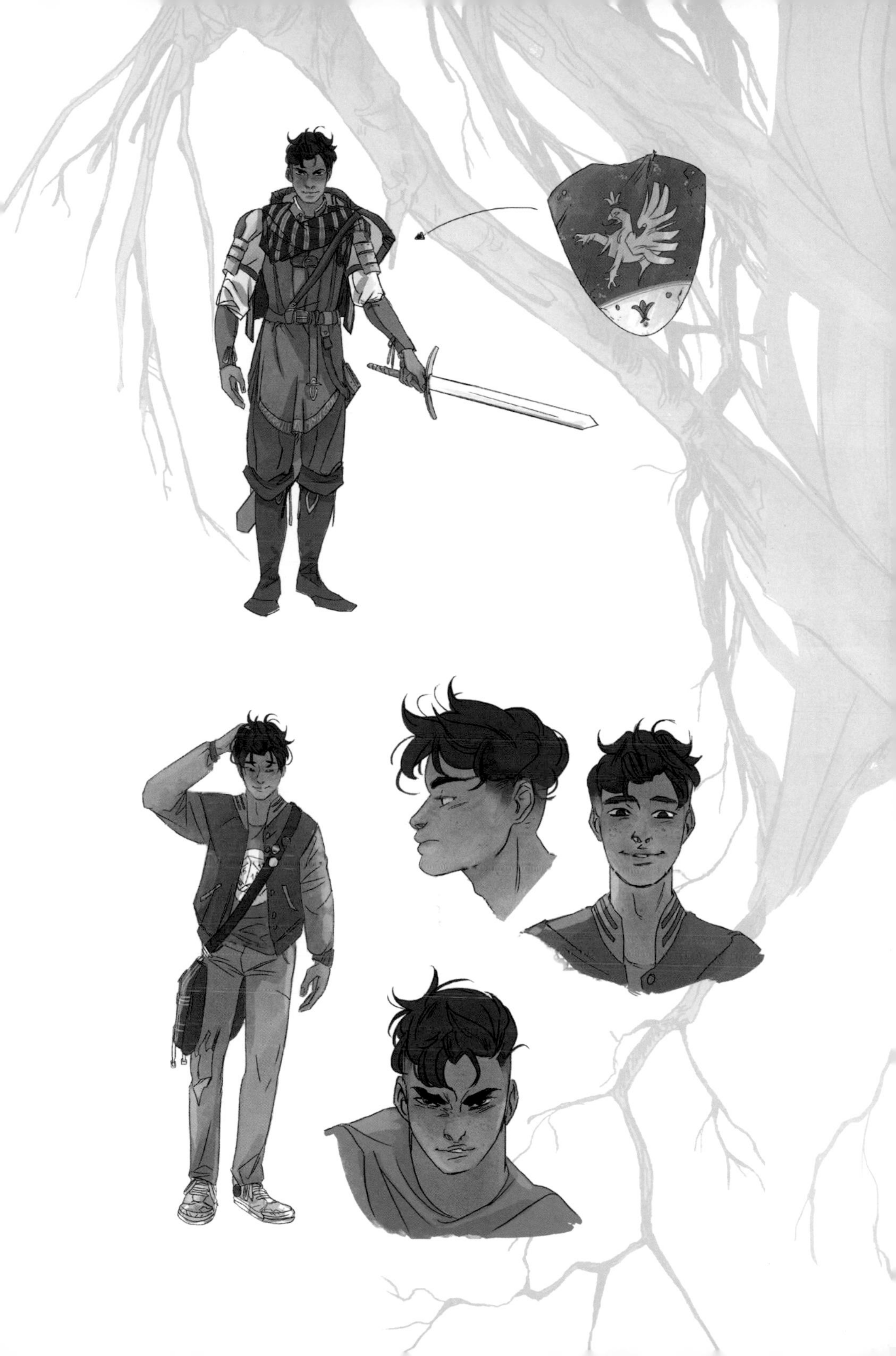

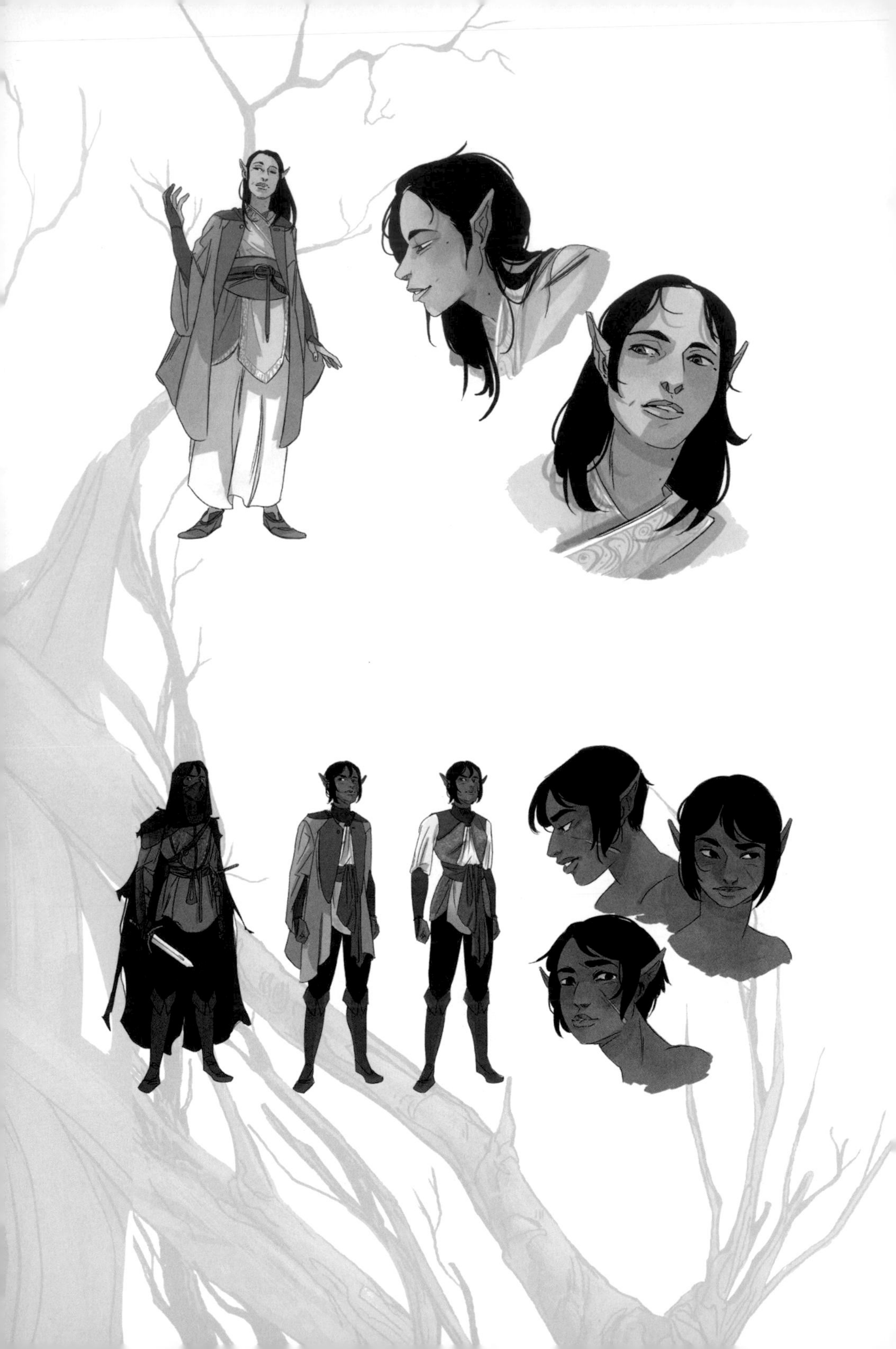